# STORM OF FURY, WINDS OF LEGEND

## ANDREW WOOD

Published by Inkshares, Inc., Oakland, California
www.inkshares.com

Edited by Story Perfect Editing Services

Cover Design by Dreamscape Cover Designs
Interior Design by Kevin G. Summers

ISBN: 9781947848115
e-ISBN: 9781947848122
LCCN: 2017956964

First edition

Printed in the United States of America

This book is dedicated to my father, Jonathan Wood. If not for him I wouldn't have written a single word of this book. Thank you for always supporting me and my projects.

*Storm of Fury* is also dedicated to every other person who picked up this book. Let it be as exciting a journey for you as it was for me.

# BOOK ONE

## Winds of Legend

# ONE

*"None can stand before the storm. Na'lek's rage is eternal and his might is absolute. Tremble before his Fury and beg for forgiveness. Only then will he guide you away from the darkness of your sin. Only then will you be saved from his wrath."*

—From the Tomes of Regret, Verse 12 of Repentance

THE WIND WAS singing today—that was never a good sign. Surging outward from the storm, the roiling wind churned as it sped over the shattered rocks of the wasteland. Its song was the herald of coming destruction, and it carried with it the scent of rot and decay.

This wind continued its journey until it came upon a lonely watchtower, which it scaled to playfully rustle the cloak of the young man who stood atop it. Kaven grimaced at the wind's cold bite and attempted to pull his cloak away from its grasp. But as he did, the wind instead took his bow, sending it skidding across the tower. With a cry of dismay, Kaven scurried after it, managing to retrieve his weapon before it flew over the tower's side. He returned to his position at the edge of the roof and frowned in worry. When the wind rose like this, it meant a storm band was coming. Or worse.

"Any sign of movement?" The watchkeeper opened the trapdoor and stepped up onto the roof, startling Kaven so that he almost toppled over the side of the tower.

Managing to catch himself before taking a fatal dive, he hastily turned to greet his commander. Kaven unconsciously brushed curls of brown hair out of his eyes and then suddenly realized that he had forgotten to salute. He remedied that quickly, flushing with embarrassment.

"Nothing but the wind, sir," Kaven informed his commander, having to shout over the constant gusts roaring past him. His hair continued to whip about his face, striking his eyes with unnerving accuracy. "Though, from the look of things, something's on the way."

Kaven winced as the watchkeeper clasped his shoulder with a gauntleted hand. "Something's always on the way, lad," he said. "Keep up the good work." The man stared out at the horizon, frowning, and then turned and descended back into the safety of the tower, leaving Kaven alone with the wind once more.

Kaven looked upward, staring at the violet and black clouds high above, which twisted and writhed ominously in the wind. He shuddered as a clap of thunder rang out in the distance. Here, on the decimated landscape beneath the tortured sky, thunder often meant death. Even on the outskirts of the storm, where it was weakest, thunder was the herald of destruction. He had nothing to fear from the thunder itself, of course, but rather the black lightning that, contrary to how storms were supposed to behave, followed in its wake. If Kaven looked out to the horizon, far from the tower, he could see the source of this threat: a storm so terrible and mighty that even thousands of years of bloodshed had done nothing to dampen its ferocity.

This storm was the reason Kaven stood on a tower in a ruined wasteland. This storm was the cause of his fears. This storm . . . was the Fury. Encompassing the center of the continent of Stormvault, the Fury was the curse of his people's god, Na'lek. Composed of terrible winds, violet clouds, and lethal lightning, the Fury was the manifestation of Na'lek's eternal wrath, placed upon Lantrelia ages ago, set to punish humanity by sending forth legions of monsters to slaughter them.

The Zealots, the leaders of the Church of Na'lek, had long ago been gifted with the key to humanity's survival: the Tomes of Regret. In the Tomes, one instruction was explicitly clear: fight the Fury's monsters to pacify Na'lek's rage. As his father had fought the Fury, so now did Kaven. Just as Na'lek had commanded.

Kaven found himself entranced by the swirling black and violet storm, where thousands of men had given their lives so they might live with Na'lek in his city, Shilanti. The Fury was the ultimate symbol of humanity's failure. Lantrelia, the world on which mankind lived, had not been created to be fouled by sin.

And so, Kaven stood on a watchtower situated far out on the Fields of Glory, the ancient battlefield where the Fury had clashed with mankind countless times. Kaven was not fond of the name, he saw little glory in the deaths of his fellow soldiers. Leave it to the people of Stormgarde—the kingdom that bordered Regelia to the west—to give a place such a name. He wondered why the name had stuck throughout the centuries. Perhaps the Fields of Wrath would be better? Or maybe . . .

Thunder slammed across the landscape, and the broken stones beneath the tower shook with its power. A storm band was upon them. "Lightning!" he screamed, panicked as he sensed his own death approaching. He dashed toward the trapdoor.

The lightning came almost immediately. A bolt of black light arced downward from the Fury, lancing into the ground beside the watchtower. Kaven's vision went dark, as if someone had covered his eyes. He stumbled, falling beside the trapdoor, hands over his head in a futile attempt to avert the Fury's attack.

Kaven's vision cleared—the Fury's darkness didn't last long—and he peered over the side to see where the strike had landed. Where the black lightning had struck, a round hole, big enough for Kaven to sit in, had been carved from the ground. The Fury's lightning disintegrated what it touched, obliterating it from Lantrelia like a candle being snuffed out. There was one mercy Na'lek had given his people in that the thunder came before the lightning, giving brief warning to the coming strike. After centuries of being assaulted by the Fury, thousands of these lightning pits covered the Fields of Glory.

Another clap of thunder echoed across the wasteland, and Kaven leapt to his feet, wrenching open the trapdoor and throwing himself down the hole just as the sky grew black again. The trapdoor slammed shut, and the lightning hit the tower's stone wall.

Kaven crashed into the wooden floor of the tower's second level with a rather undignified thud. He groaned but managed to look up at the stone roof above him. Much to Kaven's relief, the lightning strike had not penetrated the tower. The watchtowers were all built thick to withstand multiple strikes. Once a week, a sorcerer would come to repair the damage, lest the tower crumble.

He stood, dusting himself off. Six soldiers looked up from where they were seated around the edges of the tower. Like himself, they were here to give warning to the kingdoms if the Fury was preparing an assault. "There's lightning," he mumbled softly, grimacing. Of course, the soldier would already be aware of the storm band.

While on the watchman's shift, it was Kaven's job to stand atop the tower and watch for the Fury's attacks, which he couldn't do if there was a storm band active. There was, thank Na'lek, a second, albeit less effective, way to observe the wasteland.

Kaven made his way to the center of the circular room and lifted a second trapdoor. He descended into the base of the tower, using the ladder this time. That was always smarter.

As Kaven stepped down onto the floor, the watchkeeper nodded toward him. "Glad to see you survived."

"Thanks," Kaven grumbled. He knew the watchkeeper was jesting, but he was unable to keep a hint of spite out of his voice. He detested being put on the rooftop while the other soldiers lounged inside. Everyone hated that lonely position, as it left a person more exposed to the Fury. However, each soldier had to work the shift at one point, so Kaven was not alone in that torment.

Inside this room were four square holes where stonework had been strategically removed. A soldier could look through the stone to see the Fields beyond. This view was drastically limited compared to the rooftop, but it would serve while they waited out the storm band. Three of the soldiers from above had already come down to stand watch at the holes, and Kaven positioned himself before the remaining opening.

They all looked up instinctively as another roll of thunder sounded. "It's been three days since our section was attacked," the watchkeeper said. "Stay watchful."

"Yes, sir," Kaven chorused with the other soldiers. He dutifully watched the Fields of Glory but saw nothing but the distant violet clouds on the horizon, blowing in the wind. During the next hour, thunder rumbled occasionally, but the storm band soon passed, strong winds blowing it out of the vicinity with great speed.

There was something to be said for peace, but Kaven found himself dreadfully bored. As the hours crept by, he couldn't help but wonder if death would be preferable to the agonizing wait. At least then his soul would be in Shilanti, feasting for an eternity.

As he watched the broken, crumbling Fields, Kaven blinked in surprise when he saw something move. He tried to peer closer. Yes, there was something there. It was a dark shape of some kind, darting between the pits and drawing closer.

"Sir," he called back, feeling a wave of fear. "Sir, there's a Silent One!"

The watchkeeper ordered Kaven aside and peered through the gap. He cursed sharply. "By the Fury, there's two, no, three of them out there!" He rounded on his command. "Gather your weapons and report to the roof! Pray to Na'lek there's only three."

Silent Ones! Kaven had seen these monsters before, but he had never been unfortunate enough to fight one. The Silent Ones were far more terrible than Bouncers or Spinereavers. If this was an invasion, then the kingdom was in danger. Quickly, he unslung his bow and climbed upward with his fellow soldiers as the warning was relayed to the men above.

Kaven, joined by the ten other men, quickly rushed to the top of the tower and positioned himself behind the protection of the battlements, where he readied an arrow across his bowstring. Kaven pulled his string taut with sweaty fingers, heart hammering as he aimed at one of the three dark shapes moving silently toward the watchtower.

The wind howled, beating against them, as if purposefully trying to throw off their aim. In Kaven's case, his own hair was trying to blind him. Though he couldn't do much about his unkempt hair, he didn't have to worry about the wind affecting the flight of his arrow. The watchtowers were all issued Spinereaver arrows, which moved so fast they defied even the Fury's mighty winds.

"Find your marks," the watchkeeper commanded, his own bow drawn and ready.

Kaven closed one eye, holding his bow steady despite his trembling fingers. The Silent Ones moved closer, living embodiments of Na'lek's rage. They had come to kill. Kaven breathed in deeply. This is what he had trained for.

"Loose!"

Kaven released, his arrow joining the other ten as they snapped from bowstrings and surged downward with incredible speed. He followed his arrow and watched it ricochet harmlessly off a rock, a good ten feet from his intended target. *Titans take me!* His fear was momentarily trumped by his disappointment. Kaven's hair had better accuracy striking his eyes than his bow with Fury-spawn.

Even so, the Silent Ones did not escape. The closest one died first, but barely, dropping with a shaft in his throat. The second Silent One toppled into a pit, struck through the heart, while the last one fell backward, pierced by two arrows.

The watchkeeper nodded in satisfaction. "Well done, lads." He squinted toward the horizon. "But I think I see more. Many more. Kaven, I want you to move out! We're taking shelter in the tower, but you must bring warning to Regelia."

Kaven hesitated, beginning to protest. What if they caught him? But the watchkeeper shouted over him. "Go Titans take you!"

Despite being cursed at, Kaven saluted hastily and descended back into the tower ahead of the other men. He sighed as he went, putting his bow back over his shoulder. Why couldn't he aim? He had trained with his bow for years! Ever since he had failed out of the university, he had devoted himself to learning the art of the sword and bow. He kicked the hardwood door as he exited the tower, but he immediately regretted it as pain lanced up his foot. He heard the door's bolt click as the watchkeeper locked him out, preparing to endure the coming onslaught.

Kaven immediately took off running, praying silently to Na'lek that he could bring warning in time. His home, the proud kingdom of Regelia, was strong. Yet the Silent Ones were unpredictable, and the Fury recently seemed to be spawning them in greater numbers.

He sprinted across the barren wasteland, dodging around the pits left behind by the lightning. They weren't terribly deep, but his ankles certainly wouldn't thank him if he tripped into one. Another clap of thunder resounded across the Fields, and Kaven glanced back at the twisting clouds. On the horizon, he could see faint flashes of black lightning. With a shiver, he realized that he was racing Na'lek himself.

The race didn't last long, however, as the Portal-Tower was close by. Standing alone on the ruined Fields of Glory, the tower was a forlorn sight. It was a crude wooden structure, nearly thirty feet high, with a wooden ramp that spiraled up and around the tower.

Atop it was a portal, held open by four sorcerers at all times. The Four Kingdoms all had a dozen or more Portal-Towers, creating passages into other lands and spanning thousands of miles. The Church of Na'lek maintained and operated them.

Maintaining a tower was one of the most dangerous jobs in Lantrelia. Portals were the most unstable of all magical constructs and could detonate if not handled with extreme care. The elevation of the Portal-Tower would help to limit the earthquakes that would follow in the wake of a portal's explosion. This was why the tower was so crudely built, so that it could easily be replaced if destroyed. Crossing through a portal was a harrowing experience, due to the extreme danger of the unstable magic. Yet, with four sorcerers maintaining it, the portal was relatively safe. Besides, there was no room for cowardice; Kaven had a warning to bring.

As Kaven approached the Portal-Tower, he couldn't help but worry that the portal might snap shut at any second, severing him in two, or simply detonate and vaporize him altogether. However, crossing through was necessary to bring a timely warning. This portal would jump over ten miles of the wasteland, giving them a considerable lead on the advancing monsters.

Kaven ascended the Portal-Tower quickly, glancing backward to look for the Silent Ones. He didn't see them. *Thank Na'lek those things are slow,* he thought nervously. The fear of death spurred him to greater speeds.

He swiftly reached the top, where the four sorcerers stood in a box formation around the ovular gap in reality. The portal looked like a round, glassless window, framed by a swirling vortex of blue and black energy.

Kaven peered through it, and beyond he saw the Barrier Wall. The Wall was a behemoth of gray and white stone standing three hundred feet high, and wide enough to allow ten horses to ride abreast. It stretched through all Four Kingdoms, encircling the Fury entirely. The Wall had stood for thousands of years, shielding Lantrelia from Na'lek's wrath.

The sorcerers, three men and one woman, turned to regard him. They wore crimson robes and had swords strapped to their waists. "What ails the tower?" the woman asked. They stood with their hands raised, even as the woman spoke, keeping careful control over their spellwork.

Kaven fidgeted, uncomfortable being so close to the portal. He couldn't help but imagine that it might explode at any moment. Such a catastrophe wasn't likely, but it also wasn't unheard of. "We have Silent Ones on the way," he said. *Na'lek preserve us,* he thought, glancing at the portal.

The sorceress nodded. "Right then. Cross through, young one, and we'll shut down the portal before those Fury-spawn get through."

Kaven nodded, but he hesitated before the tear in the fabric of Lantrelia. It hung before him, its edges rippling and frothing like watery rapids. *One step,* he told himself, his body swaying with indecision. *One step and it's over.* With a deep breath, Kaven steeled his nerves and moved forward.

As he passed through the gap, his foot stepping from this Portal-Tower to the one on the other side, Kaven dared not look up. It was said that you could see in-between realities when you looked up at that thin line of the portal in between the towers. Some claimed that you could see stars that did not exist in the sky and swirling colors that had no name. Some said that they had glimpsed the heart of Lantrelia itself, beating like a living thing as it pumped magic into the world. One man had reported looking up to see himself looking back down. Not one soul could claim to understand the workings of a portal.

Kaven kept his gaze averted, remembering tales of travelers who peered upward and vanished without a trace. He refused to join those hapless fools. He didn't want to see what lurked outside of existence itself. What else could it be but the domain of Na'lek? Such a thing was not meant for mortal eyes. Besides, he was so scared that he jumped through the portal, leaving little time for such observations.

Miraculously, the portal did not snap shut and cut him in half. It didn't explode and tear the flesh from his bones. He wasn't pulled into the unfathomable of the in-between. Instead, he emerged safely onto another Portal-Tower, perhaps five hundred feet from the Barrier Wall that protected the kingdom of Regelia.

*Thank you,* Kaven prayed, his legs shaking with fright. *Thank you, Na'lek.* He began to move toward the ramp and descended back toward the Fields of Glory as the sorceress and one of the men crossed through the portal backward. All four would have to come over to this side before closing the portal, otherwise they could never escape the Silent Ones in time. It was an especially dangerous task, but there was no alternative. It was at times like this that Kaven was grateful he had no talent in magic.

He stepped down onto the rocky landscape and began moving toward the Wall. Its gates, twin shields of pure iron—each depicting the carved image of a man raising a sword in triumph—were still open, waiting for him. Glancing back, Kaven looked for signs of the Silent Ones as he moved toward the safety of the Wall, but he saw—

*CRACK!*

Kaven was suddenly thrown flat on his face as a wave of force slammed into him. The portal exploded in a brilliant purple fireball that shot high into the air with a loud roar. The wooden Portal-Tower was torn to pieces, which froze in midair, only to fade away like melting ice. All this happened in the space of a second and was followed then by a stream of crimson rain that spattered to the ground with sickening wet *thwack*s, barely missing Kaven.

Horrified, Kaven rose to his feet as the fire dissipated. The Fury rumbled above him, sounding like Na'lek's pleased laughter. Kaven stood frozen, shocked beyond thought or motion. A soldier shouted something from atop the Wall. They wouldn't come out to search for survivors; no one survived through that kind of power.

Kaven felt sick, weak, and his legs knocked together as he forced himself to stumble toward safety. He'd seen men die before, but . . . but not like that. Kaven fell to his knees and vomited on the ground, tears starting to fall. *Coward,* he berated himself.

Three soldiers rushed out toward him. They wore bronze armor and closed-faced helmets. Swords were sheathed at their waists, and shields hung on their backs. Crimson tabards were worn over their breastplates, depicting an upraised sword. A bolt of black lightning wrapped around the blade like a twisting snake. The crest of Regelia.

"Are you all right, boy?" one man asked.

Kaven only nodded as the two hauled him to his feet.

"What's coming?" asked the second.

"S-Silent Ones," Kaven muttered, letting himself be led through the the gates. The great iron barriers began to close behind them. "I don't know h-how many."

The soldiers repeated Kaven's warning, shouting it out to the soldiers above. They led him up the stone steps, toward the top of the Wall. "I'm f-feeling better," Kaven said when they reached the top, seperating himself from the support of the soldiers. "Really."

"Report to Captain Mayn," one instructed, and the two hurried off to join the ranks of soldiers assembling along the edges of the Wall. The Fury's winds howled, sending purple and black clouds spinning closer and closer toward them with each passing moment.

Kaven hurried away, driven by a mixture of panic and adrenaline. He didn't feel like vomiting anymore, but the image of red rain was still burned into his mind. *I'm strong,* he told himself. *I survived, and I will fight the Fury.*

By the time he reached the command post, Captain Mayn was already having attendants strap on her armor. Tying her brown hair up into a bun, she slid a domed helmet onto her head. The front of the helm was cutaway, leaving her face exposed. Mayn was a young woman, tall, slender, and strong, with sharp brown eyes. Kaven had served under her for the entirety of his short military career.

Mayn glanced down at him, concern in her eyes. "Are you a'right, lad?"

"Yes, ma'am," he replied with a quick salute. But he saw the portal exploding in his mind, catching a glimpse of the burning tower from his flattened position. *That could have been me.* Shaking his head, he hurried to give his report. "We killed three Silent Ones at the tower. More are coming. Many more."

Captain Mayn walked across the Wall, surveying the battalions of soldiers, all standing in formation. Their eyes were focused straight out at the Fury, keeping watch on the horizon. Kaven hurried to keep up with her.

"How long ago?" the Wall-Captain asked, her eyes darting up toward the twisting violet clouds.

"It's only been five minutes, Captain." Kaven tried to remember exactly how long it had taken him to reach the tower, but he couldn't quite recall. *Idiot,* he thought. *This is exactly why you were expelled.*

"Five minutes," the captain mused, putting a hand on the hilt of the sword strapped at her waist. "They'll be here soon; the Fury hungers today. I smell a storm band. What say you, Kaven?"

Kaven shook his head. "We had a small one right before the attack, but it was quickly dispersed. We're not going to get any lightning today, ma'am." Thunder rumbled in the distance, a flash of black streaking through the distant storm. Kaven winced at the sound. "Not yet, that is," he added, feeling embarrassed.

Captain Mayn smiled. "Not to worry, lad. Lightning we can handle easily enough."

A lookout on a raised platform began to shout. "Captain Mayn, they're here."

Narrowing her eyes, Captain Mayn stared out across the scarred land. Kaven joined her, and saw them. Dozens of Silent

Ones were sprinting across the Fields of Glory, effortlessly navigating around the many pits as they approached.

"Take up your positions," Mayn ordered. "Make ready for battle. The Fury will not have us this day!"

A robust gust of wind surged from the Fury, and with it came debris from the Fields. Kaven dropped to the ground instinctively, as did the other soldiers. Debris wasn't often blown back into the Four Kingdoms, but when it was, even small pebbles could become lethal projectiles.

For a moment, he worried that he'd see fragments of his own watchtower. But the towers were built to withstand the Fury, and his fellow guards would be tucked away inside, weathering the assault. Besides, it became swiftly apparent that the debris was not of Lantrelia.

Fragments of plants smashed into the Wall; some were branches from ordinary trees or bushes, while others were things Kaven had never seen before. Bulging purple leaves, swollen with liquid, bounced against the erect shields of the guardsmen. Kaven leapt out of the way as a large black shape missed him by a few feet. The thing—Kaven supposed it was a rock of some sort—sank into the Wall like a stone thrown into a pond.

Kaven screamed, ducking too late as a gigantic emerald stone slammed into his head . . . only to pass right through. Confused, Kaven straightened, his heart beating against the back of his rib cage. Had that rock been made of mist?

He retreated to the back of the Wall, fearful of more debris. Fortunately, the wind began to calm once more, and the soldiers rallied to face the approaching swarm of Fury-spawn. Dark shapes swooped up into the air, and Kaven recoiled, expecting more projectiles, yet a single glance showed his mistake. Framed against the Eternal Storm of the Fury, the Silent Ones hung in the air like dark stars, ready to strike.

# TWO

*"Most terrible of Na'lek's pawns are the Titans. Where they walk, devastation follows. Pray to the Zealots, that they may show you mercy."*

—From the Tomes of Regret, Verse 27 of Power

KAVEN STARED AT the Silent Ones, frozen in place by the fearful sight. High above the Barrier Wall, the creatures hovered before the soldiers of Regelia. The monsters looked to Kaven like gigantic bipedal insects. Encased in stony carapace, the Silent Ones had a natural armor that rivaled the best Stormgardian steel. They had no faces, only green and white chitin where eyes and mouth should have been. The Silent Ones held a magic foreign to Lantrelia, and though they seemed to be flying, they instead stood on the air as if it were stone.

In unison with the other soldiers, Kaven raised his bow toward the Silent Ones, arrows pointed toward the narrow chests of their enemies. Kaven seldom saw a monster so close, and he found the sight to be harrowing. Each Silent One was a fragment of Na'lek's rage, made incarnate by the god's infinite power, created for the sole purpose of killing men. To gain redemption, Kaven was to kill the creatures of the Fury and prove his worth. Otherwise, he would not ascend to Shilanti and live with Na'lek in paradise, but instead his soul would be forever destroyed.

Time seemed to stretch into eternity as they waited, the soldiers of Regelia facing the Fury-spawn, as the Eternal Storm raged in the distance. Kaven dared not make a sound, and his fellow soldiers echoed his silence. No war cries were uttered, no one called out in challenge. Save for the singing wind, there was no sound at all. This was how the Silent Ones came.

Mayn did not give the call to attack, and Kaven found that he had no desire to do so regardless. He found himself admiring the Silent Ones, even as they began to slowly descend toward the Wall.

Feeling as if his mind was in a fog, Kaven blinked slowly, his bow slackening as he tried to focus. One thing was clear to him: he did not want to fight the Silent Ones. *Let them come,* his mind told him dully. *This must be.*

The Silent Ones brought their four arms down as one, extending sharpened claws. They came slowly, unhurried as they drifted closer and closer to the Wall. Through the cloud of his mind, Kaven tried to remember something. It tugged at his thoughts, a string that led out of the dense fog. There was something about the Silent Ones. What magic did they possess? It was so hard to think . . .

"Find your faith, soldiers of Regelia!" A loud, clear voice penetrated Kaven's confusion. "The Curse of Silence will not hold you! Fight against the Fury, and be not entranced by its shadow!"

The spell was broken. With a start, Kaven became aware of his surroundings. He gasped, realizing what had happened to him. The Curse of Silence deadened the minds of men, leaving them powerless in the grasp of the Silent Ones. He turned to see his savior, the one who had broken the spell.

Garbed in a violet tunic, a priest of Na'lek stood with them on the Wall, hands raised toward the tortured sky as he sang praises to Na'lek and prayers for forgiveness. Even as the priest sang, the wind died to nothing more than a slight breeze. Turning back to the enemy, Kaven quickly raised his bow toward the descending monsters, his fears redoubled and his heart pounding as adrenaline surged through him. The Silent Ones did not increase their pace. Perhaps they were unaware that their curse had been broken, or perhaps they simply did not care.

Mayn finally gave the command. "Wall-Guard, give them a proper Regelian welcome!"

Kaven released, and his arrow cut through the air to strike a Silent One through the chest. A dozen more Fury-spawn fell, struck down from below. Kaven cheered, jumping into the air victoriously as the Silent One he had hit smashed into the Wall's edge and toppled to the field below. *I got one!* Dozens still managed to land on the Wall. The Curse of Silence filled the air again, and Kaven sluggishly drew another arrow, shaking his head to clear his thoughts.

*So easy to die,* he told himself, looking longingly at the bladelike claws of a Silent One. *Just let it happen. One powerful slice, and it's all over.* Yet the priest sang on, and Kaven managed to fight his way out of the monster's grasp.

Mayn directed her forces back across the Wall as the Silent Ones stepped forward, and Kaven retreated backward, bow still raised toward the oncoming foe.

A scraping noise began to fill the air, coming from beneath the Wall as a groan of metal on metal. Blocks of the Wall, at the opposite edge from where Kaven was standing, were lifting and sliding aside as iron bars, six feet tall, began to rise out of the Wall. There were ten of them, five set on the edge of the Wall with a space of six feet between, and the remaining set parallel to the others, at ten feet. An iron spring wound its way up each pole, coiling like a serpent, and atop that sat an iron sphere as large as Kaven's fist.

Kaven couldn't help but smile at the sight of them. The Firerods were Regelia's deadliest weapon. They began to vibrate, emanating a low, buzzing hum.

The Silent Ones approached in perfect unison, with the deathly calm and interminable speed of a thunderstorm. But, like lightning, they could strike with terrible speed at any moment. The Silent Ones were blind, relying on hearing for movement. They regarded the hum of the Firerods with tilted heads but continued their advance.

"Steady," Captain Mayn commanded, watching the Silent Ones carefully. Kaven tried to do as instructed, but even with the Firerods activating, he was still apprehensive.

The humming of the Firerods grew louder as the Silent Ones passed between them, still weaving their sickening curse. Mayn held her bow steady, arrow pointed straight toward a monster's heart.

"Hold," she ordered.

Kaven began to sweat, his body shaking as he forced himself to remain where he was. It would be so easy to approach them. The Silent Ones would be gentle; a swift, careful cut to his throat and he would never worry again. It would be so easy. *So easy.*

"Down!" Mayn issued the command, and with effort Kaven forced himself to duck, dropping to the ground in unison with the other troops. As one, the Firerods were unleashed upon the attackers. Bolts of blue lightning burst from one pole to the next, passing through startled Silent Ones as it danced from each Firerod, catching anything in its path. Without making a sound, the monsters collapsed together, large holes burned through their rigid carapaces. The spell was broken once more.

The smell of scorched flesh filled the air, rising from the twitching Silent Ones as green ichor oozed from their charred corpses. The Firerods ceased vibrating and began to retract back into the Wall.

Kaven rushed forward with the other soldiers but stood back as they drew swords and drove their blades into the heads of the Silent Ones. With these monsters, it was hard to tell whether they were dead or not. Best to be careful. Kaven put up his bow, breathing deeply in relief. Fear was slow to leave, and the image of the dead sorcerers resurfaced in his mind. He turned away from the corpses, lest he vomit.

He felt calmer when he looked to the Firerods. Kaven couldn't help but marvel at their technological ingenuity. Invented by a close friend of Kaven's parents, the Firerods harnessed the raw magic of the Fury and siphoned it into deadly bursts. In most battles, they were used to blast monsters on the ground, but if attackers reached the top of the Wall, the Firerods could bounce the lightning-like energy between themselves, catching invaders in a deadly matrix.

"Well done," said Captain Mayn. "The Fury has been denied access into Regelia once more, and we advance further down the path to redemption. Bury the corpses in the Fields so that Na'lek might reclaim their souls. Alert the watchtowers that the danger has passed. Na'lek send that's the only attack today."

The soldiers went about their assigned chores, rolling the Silent Ones over the side of the Wall as the gates were open. Servants, clad in gray tunics, set about the burial of the dead within the Wall's shadow, dumping the Silent Ones unceremoniously into a single grave.

Kaven noticed a small glowing stone that had been dropped by one of the monsters. Frowning, he picked it up and looked it over, rolling it in his palm with one finger. Intrigued by its crimson glow, he pocketed the stone for future examination.

A startled cry suddenly rang across the Wall. "Captain Mayn! Captain Mayn!" A lookout was dancing in place, eyes wide with terror and shaking visibly. "It's a . . . it's a . . ." Unable to speak, the man simply pointed out into the Fury.

Kaven followed his gaze and felt his heat plummet into the depths of his being. Mayn saw it too and turned pale as a corpse. Standing on the horizon was a small figure, appearing no larger than a man at this distance. Yet, even so, it was unmistakably a Titan.

Kaven fell to his knees, crying out to Na'lek in terror. And he wasn't the only one. Strong and proud men collapsed, calling for deliverance, begging to be spared. Whereas monsters like the Silent Ones were slivers of Na'lek's rage, the six Titans were shards of its soul itself. There was nothing in the Fury more dangerous, hateful, or feared as the Titans. Their names, and the slaughter they had brought to Lantrelia, were branded forever into Kaven's memory, spoken to him as legend and history as a child.

He forced himself to look up and into the distance, to where Na'lek himself might have stood, watching him with loathing. Which Titan was this? Each was taller than the Wall itself, a giant of terrible strength and power, yet each was different, embodying a separate aspect of Na'lek's rage.

*Which one is it?* he wondered. It didn't have the writhing flames of Death or the terrible jaws of the Gorger. Instead, he saw two pinpricks of red light in the Titan's distant face, glowing eyes the color of blood. That marked it as the Watcher.

The Watcher was the strangest of the Titans, for it had never attacked before. It had been spotted many times, but it was only ever seen far out on the Fields of Glory, watching the Wall with those horrible red eyes. The other Titans always brought savagery and death, killing hundreds in their random, unpredictable onslaughts. But not the Watcher. It was waiting for something, but Kaven couldn't say what. Was this the day its long vigil would end? Was this the day the Watcher would bring terror and misery to Regelia?

He begged Na'lek that it wouldn't be so. *Don't let us die. Please don't let us die.*

Mayn was the first to recover her composure, but she still trembled visibly. "Rise up, men! Raise your weapons and stand your ground. Sound the alarm in the city, let them know that a Titan comes. Go!" Roused by her words, the soldiers scattered in different directions, some departing from the Wall to run south toward the city, while others returned to their posts.

Bravery was futile in the face of a Titan. It was better to flee, to hide and pray that they didn't find you. If the Watcher attacked, everyone would die. *So why am I still here?* Kaven wondered, his panicked thoughts wild and fearful. Yet he held his ground and did not run. *I'm not a coward,* he told himself. *I will die for Regelia. I cannot fail.*

Kaven knew that there was no weapon for fighting the Titans. No machinery or magic or blade could counter the Fury's ultimate constructs. If it was the Ravager who stood in the Watcher's place now, or any of the others, he would already be dead.

He stood with bow raised, barely able to stand with the way his knees knocked together. Kaven stared into the Titan's crimson gaze, unable to look away from the fearsome specter. *I'm sorry,* he prayed to Na'lek. *Spare us, please.*

The Watcher remained motionless, true to its nature. Even so, Kaven waited for the attack to come. Would it shatter the gates, as the Ravager had done? Or would it snap them up with bladelike fingers, as the Gorger preferred to do?

The fervent cries of the priest rose into the Fury, a frenzied song of desperation, as the Watcher's eyes remained fixated upon them. The soldiers on the Wall cried out as one, pleading for mercy as the Fury thundered in the distance. Howling like a dying man, the wind returned, slamming against them with incredible strength. The violet clouds boiled, rumbling the deep laughter of their vengeful god. The Watcher stared on as the Fury raged above it, wondering, deciding.

The thunder then quieted, and the wind grew still. The Watcher turned, swiveling back toward the Eternal Storm, and strode out onto the far, deadly reaches of the Fields of Glory, where it disappeared from view. Na'lek had listened to their prayers; they were saved.

The soldiers' cries turned to rejoicing, and they threw their hands up toward the Fury, praising Na'lek for his mercy. Kaven found that he was crying, but he didn't care. Their god had decreed that their lives were worthy. They would live to fight another day.

"By Na'lek's rage and the Fury's shadow," Mayn whispered, her eyes wide as she stared after the Titan. "We are saved!" She wept softly too, murmuring her own thanks to the Fury and the god who had created it.

As the cleanup resumed, Mayn removed her helmet and started back toward the command post. "By the Fury," she murmured, "I don't know how long I can do this for him."

Kaven forced his legs to move and hurried after her. "Captain?"

"Hmm?" Mayn turned back to regard him.

"Shall I return to the watchtower?" he asked. He had no desire to go back to the Fields, instead he wanted to go home. *I can't do anymore of this today,* he thought.

Fortunately, Captain Mayn shook her head. "No, lad. The Titans are too dangerous; I'm going to recall the watchmen for a few days. We'll need to rebuild those Portal-Towers too." She frowned. "I believe you volunteered for the reserves?" Kaven nodded, and she continued. "Good. In that case, go home and get some rest; I'll need you on duty tomorrow afternoon."

"Thank you, ma'am." Kaven saluted, relieved.

Mayn nodded and turned away. She ran a hand through her hair, muttering to herself in a frustrated tone. "Titans take me, a tower down, more killed in the east, and my scribe has come down with fever. I'll have a queen's share of paperwork to do tomorrow."

Kaven cleared his throat. "I'd be happy to help you out tomorrow, if you wish; I've got a good hand." Scribes earned good coin, and Kaven could use the additional pay. Besides, there was no danger to that task.

"Really?" Mayn turned and looked him up and down. "Well, I'd certainly appreciate the help. All right then, I'll see you at noon. Give my regards to your mother."

"I will." Kaven gave her another salute. "Have a good evening, ma'am." As Mayn stepped away, Kaven turned to descend from the Wall. Another battle fought, another battle won. Despite the harrowing Titanic encounter, he'd still managed to kill a Silent One. *Father will love to hear about that,* he thought excitedly.

Kaven still couldn't believe how fortunate he was to be alive. Few men survived encounters with a Titan, and the Watcher hadn't been sighted in a few years. *Na'lek must be pleased with me.* It was a comforting thought, and it helped to quell his fears.

Several wagons resided near the Storm-Gate of the Barrier Wall, where men waited to transport weapons, supplies, and other soldiers back to Regelia's capital city, Redwind, which was only a twenty-mile ride south of the Wall.

Climbing into one of the wagons, Kaven waited to be taken home. After placing a bag of his equipment in his lap, he glanced back at the sky, where the outer reaches of the storm stretched over the Wall. The Fury's rage had been countered, and for now Kaven's home was safe. But soon, he knew, the Fury would lash out again, with the eternal hatred of Na'lek and all his supreme power. The Eternal War would continue, and perhaps tomorrow Kaven wouldn't be so fortunate.

# THREE

*"The Fury is eternal, as is our remorse."*

—From the Tomes of Regret, Verse 3 of Sorrow

KAVEN WALKED THROUGH the open gates of the walls that protected the city he had helped to defend. At first glance, the capital city of Regelia seemed small and forlorn. Dull gray buildings sat hunched in large clumps, and slate-gray streets ran through them like rivulets in a stream. The structures were all single-storied, as anything higher would attract the Fury's lightning. Yet atop them flew proud banners, waving in the strong wind. These displayed the lightning-wreathed sword of Regelia on crimson. The flags were what gave the city its name—Redwind.

Regelia was a kingdom of scientific genius, and Redwind was the most advanced city in Lantrelia. Gates and doors could open by themselves, and powerful mechanical golems wandered through the streets, set about tasks that no human could complete alone. Kaven had even heard rumors of a new experimental siege weapon that could use explosive powder to launch an iron ball through the air.

As Kaven walked across the cobblestone streets of the market, he watched the smiling people go about their daily business. Women haggled with shopkeepers over the price of clothes or food while their children played with toys or dogs beneath their skirts. Men laughed in inns or worked on roofs, filling in holes left by lightning strikes while scientists showed off the latest household gadget. Golems, looking like faceless men formed of wood or metal, moved among them, ignoring the populace as they marched obediently to unheard orders.

At street corners, burly guardsmen watched the goings-on with wary eyes, tasked with keeping the peace within the city. Kaven saluted them as he walked by, and the gesture was returned respectfully.

Kaven navigated through the busy populace, moving quickly through the familiar streets. He passed a Church of Na'lek as he went and paused to kneel on the steps that led up to the imperious black tower. The church dominated the sky, twice as high as the Barrier Wall itself. The Zealots and their priests did not fear the storm.

*Na'lek,* Kaven silently prayed. *Thank you for saving us from the Titans. Thank you for delivering us from the Silent Ones.* He hesitated, trying not to think too hard about the portal. *Accept the souls of those who died today. Allow them into your city, Na'lek.*

Dark clouds were beginning to form overhead as Kaven departed from the church. They were only regular rainclouds, thank Na'lek. Thunderstorms were common here on the continent of Stormvault, especially in Regelia. However, the farther north one went, the less rain there was. This made the kingdom of Venedeis particularly dry. Kaven had always wondered what would happen if a thunderstorm merged with the Fury. Unfortunately, the storms were typically scattered by the Fury's winds before that could ever happen.

As the lesser storm gathered, the people of Regelia began to disperse from the streets, especially the technicians, carrying away delicate equipment. Kaven did not quicken his step but continued at an unhurried pace. He loved the rain. Kaven yawned suddenly and began to fully appreciate just how relaxing tonight was going to be. *I could sleep for an eternity,* he mused.

A light drizzle misted through the air as Kaven rounded the corner of the street leading to his home. Well . . . what had been his home. These days, it was more a place to spend his nights, eat a couple of solid meals, and bathe. Interspersed with a few lectures for good measure, of course. Time spent in the watchtower dominated the rest of his life.

It had been a long time since he'd really lived here. Though he had spent the better part of his childhood in this house—playing in this neighborhood—he left at age fourteen for the Regelian University for Scientific Advancement. Many children and young adults applied to join the college, but unless they were particularly gifted, few were allowed admittance. Kaven certainly hadn't met any criteria, but his mother was quite influential among the Regelian nobility. And so, for six years, Kaven had studied with the greatest minds of Regelia, hoping to one day join them.

Upon his recent completion of college at age twenty—not graduation, but completion, as his mother constantly reminded him—he had enlisted in the Wall-Guard. With no hope of a career in the enviable field of Regelian Science, Kaven could only hope to make a name for himself on the Wall and secure a prosperous position in the military.

And yet, even with that one hope, he still fell woefully short. There were two facts about Kaven that were unavoidable: he had no skill with science and no prowess in battle.

*Fury take me, just a little luck in battle would make me happy,* he thought. His one kill today was pathetic, and yet it was the best he'd ever done.

Besides wanting to succeed for his own sake, he wanted more to make his parents proud. Sometimes having a renowned scientist for a mother and a war hero for a father made his failures quite unbearable. This was why he was now standing on a street corner, with his gear soaking in a puddle, hesitant to enter his family's manor.

The building had two stories, which was a dangerous risk, as lightning could leave gaping holes in the walls or roof. Yet his parents had quite a fortune—not that they ever shared it with him—and could afford the luxury. As with most structures in Redwind, it had additional floors beneath the ground, outside of the Fury's reach.

With a sigh of resolve, Kaven mentally prepared himself. Having just weathered one storm, he hefted his bag onto his shoulder and prepared to face another.


Kaven made his way around the back of his house. There, in the large yard behind his home, Kaven found his garden. Two large, full bushes flanked a pathway of red stone that led into a veritable forest of flowers, shrubbery, and vegetables. Kaven smelled the sweet aroma of his cultivated plants and felt at peace. He loved to tend his garden, to watch the flowers bloom, and to taste the produce he'd grown. Ever since he was little, he'd loved plants, and even today, his garden was perhaps his greatest accomplishment.

He looked up at the dark sky as the rain watered the garden, and he paused before each plant, making sure the soil was full and wet. Kaven quickly trimmed away a bothersome branch that had been creeping out toward the pathway. Once he had finished, he surveyed his work with satisfaction, and then hurried back toward his home.

Kaven entered through the back door leading to the kitchen. He hoped to avoid the initial onslaught of questions from his mother and his father's criticisms by covertly making his way to his bedroom without going through the more heavily travelled portions of the house. If he could at least avoid them until the morning, he could face them with a full night's sleep.

Luckily, before he began to move through the kitchen, he remembered to remove his military boots. This would aid him in avoiding his parents and save him from a potential tongue-lashing from whichever servant was responsible for cleaning the floor these days. Kaven's parents ran a remarkably loose ship when it came to their household servants, and it wasn't uncommon for his mighty father, the hero of the Chasm War, to be seen cowering from the wrath of a cook whose baked goods had just been filched. Kaven preferred to avoid those types of interactions at any cost.

Kaven left his cloak outside in the rain, purposefully ignoring the crimson blotches dotting it. He would never wear the tainted thing again. He tried to ignore the memories of the day's events. Silent Ones, portal detonations, Titans—how much more could a man endure?

Gliding silently across the flagstone floor on his stockinged feet, Kaven caught sight of a tray laden with freshly baked pastries for tomorrow's breakfast. *Titans, I'm famished,* he thought. Taking two of the delicacies and hiding them gently in the palm of his right hand, he reached out with his other hand to open the swinging door that led to the servants' stairs and granted easy access to the family bedrooms on the upper floor.

Just as he was about to open the door, it burst open with incredible force, slamming his outstretched arm into the wall and spinning him slightly. The force of the blow caused him to cry out in pain and grab his wrist with his other hand, dropping the stolen pastries in the process.

"I'm just going to have one or two, Moira," he heard his father shout back to his mother. "They'll never even notice if I rearrange them." He added in an undertone, "It's like you think I've never done this before, woman."

Kleon Fortis strode into the room, shoving the door open farther. Kaven cried out despite himself, trying to squeeze out from behind the door's crushing grasp. Kleon noticed Kaven's cry, and the look of surprise on his face turned quickly to confusion.

As his father slowly turned to regard him, Kaven looked up expectantly. His father had never been the type to show concern over hurts that Kaven had taken. Instead, Kleon had seen them as an opportunity for a lesson—if he showed any interest at all. Most times, the injuries were simply ignored. An inevitability of life. But rarely had his father been the cause of those injuries.

It was easy to see the resemblance between the older man and his son, with his square nose, brown hair and eyes, rigid chin, and stern expression. His mother had often wondered how she would ever tell them apart. Unfortunately, their similarities did not extend beyond physical ones.

His father advanced toward him. Was that pity in his eyes? Kaven raised his arm a little higher to show his father the scope of his injury. He knew it wasn't that bad, but a little concern from his father could go a long way for his self-esteem.

Kleon pulled the door away, releasing Kaven from his wooden prison. "Moira!" he bellowed. "The boy's home!"

Kaven heard a muted thud from upstairs. His mother had dropped whatever she was working on and was heading down to greet him. Kleon turned back and resumed his journey to the pastry tray.

"Hello, boy," he said as he went.

"Hello, Father," Kaven said, standing up straighter and wincing at the pain in his bruised arm.

"You got into the cakes first, I see," Kleon grumbled. "Four missing cakes will surely be noticed by the cook. Well, spoils to the victor, I suppose." He looked down at the two on the floor, raising a finger to pursed lips as he considered them.

Kaven couldn't help but admire his father. Kleon was an impressive figure, tall, solid, and stocky, if perhaps a tad squishy around the middle. What little of his hair remained was white. He wore an eyepatch over one eye, a souvenir from the Chasm War, but the other was hard, brown, and unwavering.

Kaven was still massaging his arm, though it was just for show now. Yet it paid off, as his father finally took notice.

"Injured in battle, eh? Now, that's some progress!" Kleon said, a smile beginning to stretch across his normally stony face.

"Not in battle, Father," Kaven replied, suddenly wishing he'd let the matter drop. "The door hit me."

The smile ceased in midstretch.

"The what hit you?" he asked.

"The d—"

"Thank Na'lek you're safe!" Moira Fortis bustled through the door and over to Kaven, wrapping him in a warm embrace. "But you're hurt!" she said, pushing him gently out by his shoulders to inspect his arm.

"It's nothing, Mother," Kaven began. "I just got hit by the d—"

"Oh, I don't know," Kleon said loudly, cutting him off. He bent down to pick up the fallen pastries. "You can never be too careful with those door injuries. Mighty fearsome creatures . . . doors."

"Father, I was in a real battle and . . ."

"Certainly," Kleon exclaimed, beaming with mock pride, "and the creature is dead where it stands. Hail Kaven, Mighty Vanquisher of Doors!"

"Kleon," his Mother admonished, "leave him be."

"There was a real battle, Father," Kaven began to explain. "I spotted the Silent Ones coming and brought warning to Captain Mayn. I fought to hold the Wall . . . and we even saw a Titan."

His father perked up at this.

"How many did you kill, son?" Kleon asked. "Have you finally proven yourself to Na'lek?"

Kaven sighed, reluctant to answer. His father never understood just how difficult it was for him to fight. Kleon was a war hero whose place in Shilanti was assured. He was strong, skilled, and powerful. Kaven wasn't any of those things. "I killed one, Father. But that is all." He'd been excited about this small victory, but he knew his father expected much more.

As expected, his father scowled at this, but Moira quickly intervened.

"Come, dear," she said. "I am sure you're hungry, and I want to hear all about the Titan. I must have a hundred questions for my research. Maybe you can answer a couple of them?"

"Sure," Kaven replied.

"Come to dinner tonight," Kleon instructed. He put the wasted pastries beside the tray, hungrily eyeing the fresh ones. "I don't want you digging around with your plants while important things are happening in Regelia. Now go wash up."

Kaven nodded. "Yes, sir."

"Love you, dear," Moira said. She took her husband by the arm and escorted him through the door, leaving Kaven behind.

# FOUR

*"The Zealots will guide us. The Church will show us how to make amends with our lord Na'lek. Trust them above all."*

—From the Tomes of Regret, Verse 2 of Repentance

KAVEN COULDN'T HELP but feel disappointed in himself as his parents departed. His father was a difficult man to impress, and with good reason. In the Chasm War, Kleon Fortis had saved hundreds of lives when he slew the Bloodfiend, lord of monsters, in single combat. For his service to Regelia, he had been granted a title and given an estate. A man like that had high expectations, and Kaven had never managed to live up to them.

Wishing he had a pastry to comfort him, Kaven turned to go, his thoughts brewing a bitter cup. What had he ever done that was worthy of praise? He wasn't a scientist, or an athlete, or even a good soldier. Kaven doubted that he could even bake a satisfactory pastry.

What his father wanted was a true-blooded soldier, preferably of Stormgardian stock, who would follow in his footsteps and spit into the Fury without fear. Instead, he had been cursed with a scrawny wimp of a boy who couldn't aim straight and spent most of his time sitting in a watchtower.

Even his mother was disappointed in him, though she pretended otherwise. Moira Fortis possessed one of the greatest minds ever to grace Lantrelia, and Kaven was . . . average. He slumped against the door that had so recently struck him, feeling agonizingly weary. Every day was the same, an endless cycle of failures. Ultimately, he was useless, and everyone knew it.

Kaven soon managed to drag himself upstairs and into his room. His living area, if it could be called that, was a sparse, square room with little in the way of furnishings or decorations. Kaven was never here, so he hadn't had the time to personalize his dwelling. But what small amount of furniture did exist—a drawer, nightstand, and bed—were well-kept and cleaned regularly by the servants. Green curtains hung over the single window, and a lamp was burning on the stand, lit by servants when they learned of his arrival.

Kaven paused beside his bed and peered into the small mirror resting beside the lamp. His pale face was smudged with dirt, and his wild brown hair was unkempt and ragged. His clothes were a wrinkled mess and smelled strongly of smoke and sweat.

With yet another sigh, Kaven took a quick detour and cleaned himself in the washroom. After his stench and appearance were made tolerable, Kaven retreated to his bedroom and shut the door. He eyed his bed longingly but decided against going to sleep. He had work to do, after all.

He stepped over to his drawer and swiftly dug through the content until he fished out a small metal object. It was oblong, like a slightly oversized egg. The edges were smooth, cool metal, but the top and bottom were a mess of gears, bolts, and other various machinery.

Kaven sat down on his bed and took a wrench from his nightstand and set to loosening the bottommost bolt. The Fury-cursed contraption refused to work, no matter how hard or long Kaven worked on it. He had designed and crafted it himself, which was probably part of the problem.

He had even submitted it for his final exam, but it had failed him then, and years later, it still proved troublesome. Kaven liked tinkering, though he had never made anything that worked. Passion was no substitute for talent, especially in Regelia.

Kaven was soon lost in his work, and the hours slipped away as he fiddled with the device. Multiple tests ended in failure; he couldn't even coax it to utter a single sputter of protest.

He wasn't frustrated, despite the machine's insistence at remaining inoperable. The process of the work soothed him, and after the fourth failed test, he felt the stress and the terror of the day fade away like the morning dew. He twisted and changed and shifted, but the device refused to work. Kaven knew that one day it would. He felt it in his soul.

"Lord Kaven?" Someone was knocking on his door, and the jarring sound broke his concentration.

With a sigh, Kaven set his project down and called out, somewhat irritably, "Yes? Yes? Come in."

The dreadful knocking ceased, and a servant poked her head into the room. "Lord Kaven? It's evening, sir, and your parents would like to know if you're coming to dinner?"

"Tell them I'll be down soon." Kaven regretfully stowed his tools away and put his device back into the dresser.

The servant curtsied. "As you wish, Lord Kaven. I will inform them."

"You do that," Kaven grumbled. He considered abandoning the meal, but his parents would never stand for it. He also wasn't looking forward to his upcoming conversation with his mother. By now, she was certain to have noted the Watcher's appearance and probably had prepared a hundred pages of notes with questions for him. The worst part of it would be that Kaven wouldn't know the answers to her inquires. She always hungered for details, and Kaven had barely been able to look at the Titan. Moira would be disappointed.

Kaven pulled himself out of bed, bemoaning his fate with dark mutters. He chose his evening outfit and changed quickly. His apparel was simple: a long-sleeved black shirt with matching pants. He hated dressing up, and he certainly wasn't going to do it for a dinner like this.

Stifling a yawn, Kaven descended from the upper floors and made his way toward the formal dining room. The wide, square-shaped chamber had a large table in its center, which could seat up to ten people. Kaven was never here when his parents invited friends or colleagues over. He didn't want to embarrass them.

Three plates were set upon the table, one at each end, and the third was placed near the middle. That last one was for him, of course. His mother and father were already seated at the opposite ends of the table. Three servants were in attendance this evening, and they chatted amiably in a corner while they waited for Kaven to sit down. After taking his assigned seat, he looked down at his already-filled plate. Today's meal was a simple affair: mashed potatoes, steamed carrots, and smoked ham served with a rich, dark beer and accompanied by warm bread rolls.

Kleon looked down at his plate longingly, but he paused as his wife stood. When Kaven and his father joined her, Moira spoke the blessing. "Lord Na'lek, watch us from your throne in Shilanti and preserve us from your Fury."

Immediately after Moira concluded the brief prayer, or perhaps slightly before, Kleon sat and began gorging himself on the steaming meal. Mother took her seat and began eating at a more measured pace. Kaven took a few bites, and though the food was delicious, he wasn't in the mood for it. The beer, at least, went well with every mood.

They ate in silence for ten minutes, but it was then that Moira's inquisitive nature could be contained no longer. "Kaven, dear," she said at last. "I wanted to ask you a few questions about today's skirmish on the Wall."

Kaven suppressed a groan. *Thanks, Na'lek,* he thought. *The quiet was nice while it lasted.* "Yes, Mother?" He tried to sound polite, but the wrinkling of Moira's brow told him that he hadn't been entirely successful.

"I was able to get a full report of today's events while you slept," she said, reaching into her lap and bringing up a thick notebook. She always carried that book with her, no matter where she went. "However, I could not interview any of the soldiers who encountered the Titan, so I'll need a thorough analysis from you."

Kaven's father snorted from around a mouthful of ham, eyeing the notebook with disdain. "Really, Moira? You're going to drag that thing out now?"

Moira gave her husband a dry look. With a chuckle, he returned to feasting on a second helping that the servants were piling onto his plate. Mother continued. "If you please, Kaven, describe every detail about the Watcher you can recall. I need everything, even if it's the most minute, insignificant observation."

Kaven stared down at his plate, thinking. He could see his mother, tapping her notes with a silver metallic quill and watching him expectantly. All he could really remember about the encounter was how frightened he was, and that he'd felt like he was going to die. But he couldn't say that, not with

Kleon sitting nearby. He didn't need his father thinking any less of him.

"Its eyes were red," Kaven finally said.

Moira frowned. "Yes, dear, I know that."

"That's really all I know," he replied truthfully, feeling ashamed.

"There's nothing else you can recall?" his mother pressed, leaning forward. "Nothing specific? Were there any deviations to its normal routine? How close to the Wall did it come? Was it alone?"

"I don't know," Kaven said. "I mean, it was alone, but it was really far away. I didn't see anything."

Moira frowned and sat back in her chair, furiously flipping through her book.

Kaven wished there was more that he could say, but there truly was nothing more. There was nothing he could say about the Watcher that Moira didn't already know. Of course, if it had been the Devourer who had come, or the Gorger, there would have been far more to see. Although, if it had been either of those, Kaven would probably not be seated here but would be instead experiencing the torture of a Titan's digestive system.

Kaven had heard too many stories about walls painted crimson with blood, or watchtowers torn apart like twigs, or the Fields littered with corpses slain by the immortal enemies that lurked within the Fury. The other Titans were ruthless and powerful, and they did not understand concepts such as mercy or honor. Only the Destroyer had ever seemed to understand human emotions, and it had exploited them to devastating effect.

Watching his mother, Kaven felt sorry for her. Moira Fortis had more reason to hate the Titans than most. Before Kaven was born, perhaps twenty-five years ago, Moira's mother had been devoured by the Gorger, dragged into the Fury while on patrol along the Wall. And two years later, her cousin had been snatched up by the Ravager, who had burrowed under the Wall and destroyed the city in which she had lived. Since then, Moira had made the Titans the focus of her research. She had spent years studying them, trying to learn their attack patterns, habits, and weaknesses. Armed with one pivotal fact, that the Titans could be killed, she struck out with a personal vendetta to end their menace. However, after long years of tireless work, she had never discovered anything of value or import. Na'lek had made his harbingers powerful and unknowable. They came like sudden storms, striking with swift brutality and merciless efficiency, before disappearing back into the Fury long before a counterattack could be raised.

In her defense, the Titans were the ultimate manifestations of Na'lek's wrath. The pure will of a god does not die easily. The Titans were known as the Hands of Na'lek, and the name suited them well, for they delivered his wrath with extreme force and deadly power. Kaven had never seen the Destroyer's skull, which was said to be on display in Stormgarde, though it was proof that they could die.

Moira closed her book, face troubled as she stared down at it. Wordlessly, she stood and departed. Kleon, realizing too late that she was upset, leapt from the table and hurried after his wife, leaving a clean plate behind.

Kaven lingered, only half-finished. He took a few more tentative bites, trying to blot out the image of the Watcher that kept appearing in his mind. The Titan's terrible eyes were like bores, and the mere memory frightened Kaven. By the Fury, the eyes were so red, like the blood of those destroyed sorcerers. Kaven put his fork down, unable to eat anymore.

Without another thought, he hurried back upstairs and put himself to bed. Sleep came quickly, but it was not the dreamless, peaceful sleep he'd desired. Instead, Kaven ran through the mutilated, twisted corpses of Regelian soldiers while Silent Ones pursued him across the Wall, led by Death itself. And all the while, the Watcher looked on from the distance, through eyes that glistened with murderous intent, the sound of his dark laughter drowning out the Fury's thunder.

Dawn banished the nightmares as its light spilled through the window and fell upon his face. He rose, groaning with discomfort as his sweaty clothing stuck to him. Fear gradually slipped away, replaced instead by exhaustion. "I really could have used more sleep," he murmured, rubbing his eyes.

He swiftly refreshed himself, dressing in his military uniform. He had to return to the Wall today, though he wouldn't be in combat. The uniform was simple and utilitarian, a plain long-sleeved tunic with matching brown pants. His leather armor came next, consisting of shoulder guards, sturdy boots, and armor on the front and back. Over this he wore a bright red tabard, displaying the crest of Regelia. Today, Kaven would be in the reserve force, and he wouldn't have to see action unless there was an emergency. Hence why he wore leather and not steel.

He then slung his full quiver and bow over one shoulder and went downstairs. His mother was seated at the table, hunched over her notebook as her quill darted across the pages. "Good morning, dear," she said without looking up.

Kaven sat down beside her. "Morning."

Moira's hand zipped across her paper quicker than an arrow, and her eyes darted from word to word. "Early shift today?"

Kaven shook his head. "I'm not going out to the towers. One of the portals was destroyed yesterday." He shuddered.

"Besides, no one wants to chance a meeting with one of the Titans."

Moira paused for a moment. "Does Captain Mayn think that the Watcher may reappear? Perhaps I'll take a trip to the Wall myself. What will you be doing today instead?"

"I thought I'd go to the archery range and get some practice in before noon," Kaven replied. A servant bustled into the room and placed a steaming bowl of porridge in front of him. "Afterward, Captain Mayn wants me to take care of some bookkeeping at the Wall."

Kaven failed to notice that his father had entered the room behind the servant until he had finished speaking. Kleon snorted irritably. "Why is she having you do that? You're no scribe, boy!"

"I'm in the reserve force today, Father," Kaven replied. "It's protocol for the tower guards when the towers are inoperable. I thought I'd lend her a hand while I waited."

Kleon's face darkened. "You should've volunteered to stand with the rest of the Wall-Guard."

Kaven frowned. The Wall-Guard had plenty of soldiers, Kaven would be put to better use elsewhere. "I'm not needed today. If there is an emergency, I'll be called to take up a sword."

"Na'lek above!" Kleon gazed upward, annoyance plain on his face. "There was a Titan outside the Barrier Wall! The queen should have all available soldiers on duty today. I tell you, the military is becoming more disorganized with each passing day."

Moira nodded. "I'm forced to agree. When the Titans are close, we need extreme vigilance. However, I do believe that we are more than equipped to handle any other attacks."

"The Four Kingdoms have grown soft," Kleon growled, and he unconsciously touched the empty slot on his belt where a sword had once hung. "It's been decades since we've had a real attack. The Titans are quiet, as is the Fury. Every day there are minor skirmishes, but we're only seeing scores of monsters. When I fought for Regelia, we faced thousands of Fury-spawn and lightning so black it turned day to night! They would rip the Wall down from underneath our feet and slaughter us by the dozens. Men like Matchless Gorshol and Lord Tren would lead us to glorious victory." Kleon took his seat as the servant brought his breakfast. "Mark my words, Moira, Lantrelia has forgotten how to fear the Fury. That's what happens when your enemy is silent for a long time; you forget what it's capable of doing. The Eternal Storm may be silent now, but it will strike again, and we'd best be ready for it!"

"You've spent far too much time in Stormgarde, my love," Moira replied. "Did you ever think that Na'lek might simply be pleased with us? We fight the Fury diligently, and the Church guides us down the path of righteousness. Why, just last week I spoke with Zealot Jana, and she told me that Na'lek has been merciful this year."

"Times change," Kleon grunted. "Humanity will fail again, as it always does. You know the Day of Reckoning must come."

Kaven ate in silence, but he listened intently. The Day of Reckoning was prophesied in the Tomes of Regret, Na'lek's divine scripture. The Day was supposed to be one final assault from the Fury, one last test for humanity, and it would be a battle that would involve every monster within the Eternal Storm. Kaven had never read the Tomes, as only the priests or the Zealots were permitted to do so, but he'd heard verses quoted by the priests during their monthly services. It foretold a great cataclysm and a battle unlike any Lantrelia had ever seen. Kaven wished he knew more—he'd always wanted to read the Tomes—but he laughed silently at the thought of himself as a priest.

Moira closed her book and put her pen aside. "I don't see the Day coming within our lifetimes. None of the signs have appeared. For example," she began to quote from the Tomes of Regret, "'the stars will bleed fire and paint the skies red, and at Na'lek's command, the earth shall break and swallow the seas.' Last I checked, the Expanse is still an ocean and the stars are where they should be."

Kleon still looked unappeased as he chewed on his porridge and eggs. "The Day could come tomorrow, or perhaps in a hundred years, I don't know. All I'm suggesting is that our queen shouldn't underestimate the Eternal Storm's power."

His parents' argument soon changed from the Wall's defense to a discussion of what his mother should wear to a ball they were planning on attending that night. When the topic switched, so did Kaven's interest.

"I'm off," he said, rising.

"Where to?" his father asked, looking away from his wife.

"The training yard," Kaven replied. "I figured I'd get some practice before I go back on duty."

"With your bow?" Kleon eyed his weapon.

"Yes," Kaven said, wondering what this sudden inquisition was about.

Kleon chortled and took another bite of his porridge. "Na'lek knows you need the practice."

Moira frowned, but Kaven was used to this sort of reproach. "Perhaps he'll lend me the skill I need."

"Miracles can happen, eh?" Kleon grumbled.

"I will do you proud, Father." Kaven hoisted his bow and met the old war hero's eye. "I will."

"I would hope so."

Kaven resisted the urge to argue. No good could come from it. "Goodbye, mother," he said, and promptly left.

Kaven wondered if today was the day he could prove that he was a good son, one worthy of pride. Not likely, since he was in the reserves. Besides, he wasn't a good soldier, or a good student, or even a good shot. *Please, Na'lek,* he silently prayed as he stepped outside. *Give me a chance here.*

Almost immediately after exiting his home, Kaven noticed how dark it was outside. He glanced skyward and shivered. Violet clouds rolled overhead as a strong wind buffeted him. From the north, the Fury reached over Redwind and the city seemed to hold its breath, waiting in the storm's shadow.

Kaven wished for a cloak but didn't want to go back inside and face his father. This was a bad time to be outside, as the wind could whip a storm band into the city at any time, and Kaven would face the threat of being burned to dust.

*Better than being stabbed by a Silent One,* he supposed, grateful to be on the reserves today.

Kaven steeled his nerves and set out into the streets of Redwind. Even though it was late morning, the streets were oddly vacant, which made the city seem much bigger than it actually was. The most sensible of people were tucked away indoors, knowing the wisdom in waiting out the storm in the shelter of their homes. But Kaven was a soldier, despite what his father said, and he would march beneath the Fury without fear. He endured the outskirts of the Fury every day, and that was what threatened the city now. It was by far the least dangerous part of the storm.

To go deeper, there was the real danger. Men who went beyond the edges of the Fury never returned, and Kaven often feared what would happen if the storm grew large enough to cover all the land. Most days the storm stayed within the Barrier Wall's confines, but though it was a sound defense against the Fury-spawn, it was ultimately useless against the Eternal Storm itself.

He made his way to the edge of the city, taking advantage of the emptiness by moving at a quick jog. He did pass a few people along the way, guardsmen, hopeful shopkeepers, and city officials. He returned the occasional smile or friendly wave, but he was otherwise alone. It seemed there was only himself and Na'lek, which made the Fury's shadow all the more oppressive.

The training yard was situated near the barracks, positioned by Redwind's northernmost gates. This was as close to the storm as one could get without leaving the city limits. The barracks itself was composed of five rectangular buildings, built much the same as the rest of the city, a single story with a flat roof and lightning rods atop them. The training yards were flat stretches of dirt about fifty paces long and wide, and one was positioned before each barracks building.

There were more people here, soldiers like himself who didn't go on duty until later in the day. They waited here until their shifts began, or until the Wall had need of them. An attack could come at any time, day or night, and it could be a score of enemies or thousands of monsters. There was no telling how large a force of Fury-spawn would be arrayed against them until it was almost too late. Some soldiers rested in the shelter of the buildings, laughing and chatting over ale, while others sparred or practiced their archery.

The other soldiers didn't talk to him, but he didn't know any of them beyond recognition. Sometimes he felt as if his only friend in the army was Captain Mayn, who was technically a friend of his mother's. But Kaven wasn't a lonely person, such things didn't bother him. He found most often that he preferred himself as company rather than others.

Once he set up a target for himself, Kaven began shooting at thirty paces. He had only minimal success, striking the target twice for every ten misses. He continued to practice for a full two hours, but his aim never improved in the slightest. On the bright side, it didn't worsen either. Hurray.

Disappointed, Kaven dismantled the wooden stand that the target was balanced on and put it back in one of the buildings. Suddenly, thunder crashed across the sky, and the ground trembled as it burst into the city like a battering ram. Kaven jumped and instinctively dropped to the ground. The world turned black as the Fury's raw power struck somewhere nearby, blinding him momentarily despite his shelter. Thunder boomed from the Fury continuously, shaking the ground like a frenzied drummer striking over and over as the light continued to vanish around Kaven again and again as lighting assaulted the city.

Kaven trembled, shaking with fear, though he knew he was safe within the barracks. The Fury went silent again, and the lightning band vanished as suddenly as it had come. The thunder was replaced by the howl of the wind, and the darkness faded entirely. Kaven stood and began a slow, silent count to twenty. The Fury did not rise again.

He poked his head outside the barracks door and looked up tentatively. The violet and black clouds still blanketed the sky, dancing with the wind of the Eternal Storm. He was safe again, for the time being. He steadied himself and joined a nervous band of soldiers who were moving toward the gates. The Fury loomed before them, and Kaven was even more grateful that he wouldn't be doing any fighting today.

# FIVE

*"Greatness is defined by none other than Na'lek. No man can hope to be anything without his blessing."*

—From the Tomes of Regret, Verse 29 of Power

HAVING CROSSED THE barren stretch of land that separated Redwind from the Fury, Kaven climbed the stairs that ran parallel to the Barrier Wall. The walk was wearying, due to the Wall's tremendous height, yet Kaven preferred it to risking a portal. Not after what had happened yesterday. Pieces of that woman falling from the sky, splattering the ground with red—*Stop it!* Kaven shook his head to rid himself of the dark thoughts.

When he stepped atop the mighty Wall, he saw dozens of soldiers standing in formation along its outer edges, watching the storm carefully. Several poles rose from the balustrades, and the crimson banners of Regelia flew in the wind. Kaven could see a dozen holes marking the wall top, showing where the lightning had recently struck.

Kaven left the new battalion of soldiers as he advanced across the Wall. He passed over the massive, iron-wrought Storm-Gate that protected the land of Regelia. The Storm-

Gates were seldom opened, and Kaven's father hated their existence. He saw the gates as the weakest part of the Wall, and though he was probably right, Kaven knew it was sometimes necessary to go out onto the Fields of Glory. Each of the Four Kingdoms had only one Storm-Gate.

Ahead, Kaven saw a squat structure rising from the Wall. The command center, where Wall-Captains could handle their business sheltered from the Fury. There were ten command centers spread out across Regelia's portion of the Wall.

He nodded to two guardsmen who opened the door for him. He had never been inside of a command center, as it was reserved for the Wall-Captains and their scribes. The building was built like the barracks back in Redwind and was just as large.

Captain Mayn was inside, seated at a desk at the far side of the single-roomed structure. She looked up and motioned him forward. Kaven walked past two smaller desks—both empty—and saluted. "Good morning, Captain," he said.

Mayn nodded. "Morning, Kaven. Thanks for coming down to help me out."

"My pleasure," he said. "Just tell me what you need done."

The Wall-Captain nodded toward one of the other desks. "Take a seat and start going through those reports. I need the troop statistics to send back to the queen, so if you could compile them into a single document, I'd appreciate it."

Kaven nodded and took his seat. He set a fresh piece of parchment in front of him, along with a writing spear, which appeared to be a silvery, metal quill. The writing spears could hold ink within their iron frames, eliminating the need for traditional writing tools. They were a relatively new Regelian invention but had already replaced ink and quills entirely within the kingdom. The scribes of the other nations were slowly beginning to integrate them into their own use.

Kaven then looked over at a hefty stack of papers sitting on the edge of his desk. These would be the reports from all fifty Wall-Captains stretched across Regelia's portion of the Wall. The reports would contain data from the last week, everything from supplies expended, soldiers lost or wounded, damages sustained to equipment, and countless other details.

Since Mayn was only interested in the statistics involving soldiers and their skirmishes, Kaven wouldn't have to comb through the entire stack. It was a simple task, although time-consuming. Kaven didn't mind, however. This sort of work suited him.

He got right to it, pulling out the relevant reports and copying the necessary data onto the new sheet. However, with each word he wrote, the writing spear became heavier, and his heart began to beat faster, and the blood drained from his face.

*Under the command of Captain Tora—Ten skirmishes within the last seven days; fourteen casualties.*

*Under the command of Captain Sen—Five skirmishes within the last seven days; nine casualties.*

*Under the command of Captain Noseth—Six battles within the last seven days; twenty-five casualties.*

"Na'lek preserve us," Kaven whispered as he read on.

More reports followed, and few sections of the Wall were without loss. It was easy to forget how deadly the Fury was after a lucky streak. Kaven's regiment hadn't suffered a single causality in recent memory, and many men spoke of how calm the storm had been of late. Yet, when Kaven saw souls claimed by the Fury, he realized that, even when Na'lek was silent, he still demanded a hefty price. Eleven casualties. Thirty casualties. Four casualties. More.

A certain report caught Kaven's eye, from a Wall-Captain positioned far away from Redwind to the east, at the border where the Barrier Wall crossed from Regelia into the kingdom of Fulminos.

*Nineteen battles within the last two days: two hundred casualties, possibly more. Fulminos sends support in the form of three hundred soldiers. In need of immediate reinforcements.*

"Have you seen this, Captain?" Kaven asked, holding up the report.

Mayn narrowed her eyes, squinting at the document. "Oh, yes. Terrible thing, that. It just came in today, though I was informed earlier by General Naveer. Hundreds of Silent Ones emerged from the Fury at sunset; the battle continues even now."

Kaven felt a chill of fear crawl up his spine. "Are we sending reinforcements?"

"It's already been done," Mayn replied, looking down at her work. "Stormgarde sent additional troops and our engineers supplied the Fulminites with the finest weaponry. The Silent Ones should be dealt with soon enough."

Nodding, Kaven returned to his scribing, feeling guilty for sitting at a desk while men died on other parts of the Wall. A part of him wanted to take up his bow and march down the length of the Wall, joining the men who fought to protect the kingdoms. But, what good could he do? Slay a single Silent One before he was killed? No, it was best to stay here. He was doing work that was important, even if it couldn't compare to the sacrifices being made in the east.

*Skritch, skritch,* went the writing spear, scrawling in time with the ever-passing seconds. It wasn't until several hours later that Kaven finished finding and transcribing the military reports. He stood and handed the completed report over to Mayn.

She smiled at him. "Thanks, lad. The queen likes to pretend that she cares about us soldiers, so she has all of these forms delivered to her." Mayn rolled her eyes. "As if the Fury-spawned woman could tell a Firerod from a bow."

Kaven winced at the curse Mayn uttered. To be called "Fury-spawn" was one of the most grievous insults one could receive. She often complained about Queen Helia, but Kaven couldn't say that he agreed with Mayn. The queen had been on the throne long before Kaven was born, and she struck him as a wise and capable ruler.

"Is there anything else you need, ma'am?" he asked.

"No, no." Mayn glanced upward. "Na'lek is busy at the border, so all is quiet here. The watchtowers will be operational again tomorrow, so I expect you here early in the morning. But until then, head on home."

Kaven saluted and gave his Wall-Captain a quick smile before excusing himself from the command center. He stepped back out in the Fury's wind and—*kacrack!* Thunder split the sky, crashing with the sound of a hundred explosions. All went dark as a gigantic bolt of lightning arced downward, hurtling from the sky directly above the Wall and falling onto the city far beyond.

With a yelp, Kaven scrambled toward a nearby bunker, little more than a squat, dome-shaped hut. Hundreds of these bunkers were scattered across the Wall, as they could only hold two people. He ducked inside the meager shelter as more thunder erupted overhead, heralding the Fury's deadly lightning.

Nearby, standing on the Wall's edge, violet-robed men stood with their arms stretched skyward, chanting in words that Kaven couldn't hear over the Fury's roar. These were the

Wind-Guard, sorcerers who mastered the powers of the sky. They spent their time forcing the Fury back, and often they could tear storm bands apart before any damage could be done. Now they fought the storm on a primal level, magic versus rage, but it seemed that they weren't faring well.

"Knifemen!" a soldier shouted from a bunker near the Wall's edge. "Titan's teeth, there must be dozens of the Fury-spawn!"

Captain Mayn emerged from the safety of her office, hurriedly sliding her helmet onto her head and releasing a string of curses that must have made Na'lek cringe. Another bolt of lightning struck nearby, and as always, the world grew black as the shadowed lightning blinded soldiers momentarily.

Soldiers scrambled from their cover, and the Firerods slowly began to ascend from the Wall. The Fury roared and spat black fire down upon the Wall, with three bolts falling less than a mile from the gates. A fourth struck a Firerod; one instant the weapon was there, humming with radiant power, and the next it was gone, vanished, turned to dust so fine that it could not be seen by the naked eye.

Kaven had his bow ready, arrow nocked, yet he still crouched behind the bunker, hating himself for every moment he stayed still. He was too scared to move. Silent Ones were terrifying, but Knifemen were so much worse. Kaven had never seen one, but he had heard enough.

With Knifemen below and the Fury above, Kaven was terribly afraid. If his father could see him now, he would be more ashamed then he already was.

The screams and cries of soldiers rose above the crashing thunder, along with orders barked from Mayn. "Keep away from the edge!" she yelled above the cacophony of god and man. "There are too many!"

Kaven peeked around the bunker's protective shell, and he saw corpses. Draped across the battlements, and lying beside them, were several dead men, their red tabards a mirror of the blood pooling around them. Metal glinted black as more lightning struck the ground, reflected by the bodies of the Knifemen. He quickly pulled back into shelter.

The Firerods hummed, charging while the Wind-Guard chanted against the Fury's terrible lightning. A strange humming sound rose amongst the panicked cries of men. It was the tune of a song that Kaven didn't recognize. In fact, it sounded so utterly foreign he had trouble comprehending it. The sound had such a low pitch that he had trouble hearing, and there was an odd waver to it, like a voice within a hum.

The eerie sound was coming from the Knifemen. Kaven knew a lot about them, having read his mother's notes numerous times. She wasn't sure whether this song was a means of communication or simply a war cry.

Kaven then heard the familiar buzz of electricity and knew that the Firerods had begun to discharge on the Knifemen below. The thunder was growing softer, and the chants of the Wind-Guard became less frantic. Gingerly, he stepped out of the bunker and looked up. The clouds were still there, black crashing into violet as the wind propelled the Fury in an eternal circle, but the storm band seemed to be fading.

His fellow soldiers were nearby, standing well away from both the Wall's edge and the glowing Firerods. Twelve of the magical weapons were lined up behind the battlements, periodically discharging a bolt of blue energy down onto the ruined fields below. There was no way to aim these giant Firerods, but their attacks covered a wide area in deadly swaths of electricity.

And then everything grew quiet, save for the buzz of the Firerods. Mayn nodded to her soldiers. "Well done; victory is

ours once more. Lower the Firerods and see to the wounded"
—she hesitated—"and the dead."

The Firerods soon became dormant and sank back into
the Wall. Volunteers wearing gray went forward to retrieve the
bodies of the slain men. Kaven felt a deep sense of loss and
respect toward the fallen. He wished that he hadn't hidden.

Even though he was a soldier, Kaven moved forward to
help with the dead. He gingerly lifted the legs of a slain soldier
while a stern-faced woman grabbed the man's arms.

"We're going to take him down the stairs," she said in
a tone that matched her expression. While Kaven was barely
holding back tears, she didn't seem fazed at all. "Move yourself,
soldier."

Kaven grunted and began moving backward with his burden. The body dropped from the woman's hands, causing him
to stumble as something warm and wet splattered his face. The
stern-faced woman dropped too, a jagged metal blade jutting
from her forehead, still spraying blood as she toppled.

He froze in sudden fear as three more men dropped, blood
shooting into the air as shards of steel whistled by, cleaving
both armor and flesh. Kaven was brought out of his trance by
the sound of the monsters' hum, coupled with a sharp curse
from Captain Mayn. He spun to see numerous Knifemen
standing atop the battlements, raising more blades to throw.
Kaven dropped to the ground as more projectiles shot overhead. Another man went down—an archer, running to the
edge—bleeding from his neck.

The Knifemen had not been killed by the Firerods; they
must have hugged the sides of the Wall, only to then scale it like
terrible lizards. "Wind-Guard to me," Captain Mayn roared.
"Fall back and strike them from above." She stood nearby, her
sword drawn as she crouched behind a bunker. Archers and

sorcerers assembled behind her, moving to avoid the seeking blades of the Fury-spawn.

The barrage of steel knives ceased, and Kaven—on all fours—began to back away from the carnage. The twisted song of the monsters rose from a muted hum to a roaring crescendo. And then they stepped off the battlements, trodding carelessly across the dead.

They were strange creatures, the Knifemen, and Kaven found them awful to behold. They were humanoid in shape, much like the Silent Ones or the Eye-Takers, but that was where all similarity ended. Covering the entirety of their forms were hundreds and hundreds of small, glittering knives. From every inch of their frames, a wicked blade jutted forth, and then two more sprouted from these knives. Possibly more. Some knives were short, like those that grew from their chests and head, while others were quite long, like the six wide blades emerging from all sides of their arms. It reminded Kaven of crystals growing from a rock. The Knifemen's fingers were pointed, and they walked on many thin blades. As one, they snarled with pointed teeth behind angular, beak-like lips and raised their arms high in challenge. In the center of their heads, nearly concealed behind knives that pointed sideways, were solitary blue eyes.

The archers loosed immediately, and Kaven dropped flat with a startled yelp. The Knifemen didn't hesitate either as they ripped blades from their chests and arms and flung them like javelins at the soldiers. Alarmingly, Kaven noticed that as soon as one blade was pulled free, a new, identical blade grew from the Knifemen bodies.

Spinereaver arrows struck the Knifemen with lethal accuracy but bounced harmlessly off their seamless armor. The monsters were far more effective. Dozens of steel blades slammed into the bunkers, and two archers collapsed, screaming as knives sliced through legs and arms.

Mayn emerged from behind the bunker, and a score of spear bearers followed her. Five Regelians died instantly, struck down by oncoming blades, yet the rest evaded behind bunkers, only to leap over and charge ahead, spears pointed forward. The blades of a Knifeman were brittle around the face and neck; there they could be broken.

Only a single Knifeman was taken by surprise as two Regelians shoved their spears through its head. Flimsy metal broke like glass, and the Knifeman collapsed, its song ending. The rest of the monsters—nearly twenty of them now—blocked the oncoming spears with wide swings of their arms.

One Knifeman grabbed the haft of a spear and yanked its bearer closer, before driving one of its arm blades through the soldier's heart.

Mayn rushed the monster, swinging her sword toward its neck while it was distracted. She struck a powerful blow to the side of its face, and shards of metal flew into the air as the Knifeman collapsed, head partially decapitated.

The spearmen used their weapons like clubs, wildly keeping the Knifemen's many blows at bay. *When fighting Knifemen,* Kaven had heard his mother say, *a soldier should focus on keeping himself out of the monster's reach until he could find an opening to strike at its head.* Spear butts served this purpose well.

Kaven lay prone as the monsters and soldiers dueled above him, useless information running through his head at breakneck speed. His mother's perfect observations and detailed knowledge. His father's many stories and battle experiences. All of this was useless while he was frozen in fear's powerful grip. Fervently, he prayed that a Knifeman wouldn't step on him with its sharpened feet.

The wind turned from bitter cold to blistering heat as fire roared above Kaven. Streaking from the Wind-Guard and hurtling above the battling soldiers, massive fireballs struck the Knifemen not engaged with Mayn's men. The monsters glowed with a deadly heat that penetrated steel and the flesh beneath. Over a dozen Knifemen dropped as one, reduced to little more than smoldering metal and flesh.

Only seven Knifemen remained, engaged in furious battle with the Regelians. The archers and Wind-Guard waited nervously, ready to cut down the monsters if they broke through.

Each time Kaven tried to lift himself, the image of the stern-faced woman's bloody corpse flashed in his mind, and he fell again. Yet, somehow, he finally forced himself upright. He drew his bow and pulled forth one of the few arrows that hadn't fallen from his quiver when he fell. He retreated behind a bunker, where four more archers waited, and readied his shaft.

More Knifemen climbed over the Wall, replenishing the numbers of Fury-spawn as they advanced. Scores were leaping up into the fray, extending the field of battle farther down the Wall as they rushed the Regelian defenses.

Captain Mayn and her men were superb warriors, and they worked methodically. Two spearmen kept a Knifeman busy while Mayn circled and cut the monster down from behind, and then they moved on to the next one. They brought down another seven Knifemen this way.

Kaven looked to the right and left and saw other battles down either side of the Wall. More Knifemen had climbed to the top, but the Wall-Guard was keeping them back on all fronts. Soldiers were rushing in their direction from other portions of the Wall, realizing the severity of the attack as men below blew war horns. Then Kaven saw a Knifeman that hadn't been noticed by any soldier. It stood over five dead men, its claws and arm blades dripping red.

The Knifeman turned toward him, its single eye glittering behind countless blades. It started toward him. Kaven frantically yelled toward the Wind-Guard, trying to catch any one of the sorcerers' attention. But at that moment, a spear bearer fell far from Kaven, struck down by a pair of snarling Fury-spawn, and the Wind-Guard turned their magic on the briefly victorious Knifemen, turning them both to cinders while failing to notice Kaven's plight.

The archers nearby moved quickly away from the advancing Knifeman, retreating behind the Wind-Guard. But Kaven didn't move. He held his bow at the ready, arrow trained on the Knifeman. He didn't want to flee anymore. He didn't want to lie down while men and women died. He could not do it again. Not again!

*Please, Na'lek,* he silently prayed. *Give me the strength to make this shot!* He aimed for the Knifeman's eye, hands sweating and heart pounding. He released, and the Spinereaver arrow whistled through the air at a dizzying speed.

The arrow struck the Knifeman straight in the head . . . and bounced off. Kaven threw his bow down with a growl and glared at the Fury. He drew his shortsword and stepped toward the Knifeman, driven by a rage like he had never known. He felt as if the Fury itself flowed through his veins, and he was prepared to match his anger against Na'lek's.

The Knifeman tore a blade free from his arm, flinging it with deadly force. Kaven ducked, and he felt the knife whistle past his hair. He closed the distance swiftly, before the monster could throw again, and slashed at the Knifeman's throat. The monster stepped into the blow, lazily raising an arm to deflect it. Kaven bounced back and swung again, but the Knifeman effortlessly batted his shortsword away, no matter how he attacked.

The Knifeman suddenly twisted its arm when Kaven connected with it once again, and one of its arm blades caught his weapon between several other knives. The monster gave a great yank, and Kaven lost his grip on the shortsword.

Idly, the monster flicked his arm, sending Kaven's weapon clattering some distance away. The Knifeman's hands closed into deadly fists, and it hummed all the louder. It swung at Kaven with a swift right hook, and Kaven staggered backward, barely dodging the lethal blow. But the Knifeman was quick, and its next swing caught Kaven on his left side, directly under his ribs.

An incredible pain burst through his side, seeping through his bones and into his marrow like spilled paint. Kaven dropped like a stone, clutching his throbbing side and crying out. How many blades had stabbed him? Too many. *By the Fury.* He groaned, clenching his teeth. *This is* real *pain.* Everything else he had ever felt was nothing compared to this frightening, blinding agony.

The Knifeman towered over him, Kaven's own blood dripping from its fist. Kaven shut his eyes, waiting for the monster to split his skull. But the blow never came. Had Na'lek spared him? He forced himself to open his eyes and suppressed a groan as he looked up. The Knifeman was still there, humming angrily. But there was another man as well, and he was battling the Knifeman.

This newcomer did not wear the armor of a Regelian soldier, but a suit of black steel with a long violet cape. He wore no helmet and had close-cropped blond hair. He held a kite-shaped shield in one hand and a thin sword in the other.

He stood with his back to Kaven, using his body as an impenetrable phalanx while he dueled with a shard of Na'lek's Fury. The Knifeman no longer battled with a sense of boredom, as it had with Kaven, but fought like a whirlwind of slashing blades. With fists and kicks, the monster cut at the soldier using every knife it had. But each blade bounced off the man's shield or was deflected by his armor. With only a single blade, the man thwarted every attack the Knifeman could muster. And with a final heroic heave, the man pushed into an opening and cut through the Knifeman's head.

The soldier raised his shield as the monster's head exploded, sending shrapnel flying for his face. The pieces of steel fell to the Wall, followed by the rest of the Knifeman's corpse.

Sheathing his sword, the man turned toward Kaven. He was tall and powerfully built, much bigger than Kaven in every regard. "Are you hurt, child?" he asked, his voice deep and rich.

Kaven failed to answer; he was too stunned. He recognized this man, and it was someone he had never expected to meet. It was the mask that gave the man away. Covering the entirety of his face, the mask was composed completely of violet rose petals. The man was Zealot Stonearm, Figurehead of Na'lek, leader of the Church. Kaven again tried to force out a reply, but was still unsuccessful. This time, he realized that it was probably because he was bleeding to death.

Zealot Stonearm's face was unreadable behind his mask, but he waved to someone nearby. The Zealots of the Church all wore masks, so people wouldn't see them as mortal men, but solely as the messengers of Na'lek.

A portly man in violet robes hurried to the Zealot's side. He would be a priest, then. The priests were nowhere near as close to Na'lek as the Zealots, but they were still holy men. They were some of the few individuals that could read the Tomes of Regret.

The priest bent over Kaven and pried his hands away from the wound. Kaven groaned, but the priest held him with a firm grip. Something like a static shock ran through his body, and a terrible pain replaced the throbbing, as if the knives were being pulled free once more. But then it was gone.

Kaven blinked in surprise, looking down to see that his wounds had fully healed, leaving not even a scar. He stood slowly, with the priest helping him stand. He tried to give Zealot Stonearm a little bow but almost fell over again. "Th-Thank you."

Na'lek's Figurehead nodded. "Our god smiles upon you this day, boy. Thank him, not me. Now, can you direct me toward your Wall-Captain?"

Kaven looked around and noticed that the battle had at last concluded. All of the Knifemen were dead, and Regelian soldiers were working again to clear away the corpses. There were also many Zealsworn—soldiers of the Church—on the Wall. He spotted Mayn nearby, addressing three members of the Wind-Guard.

"She's there, sir," he said, pointing her out.

"I thank you," Zealot Stonearm set off after her, trailed by the priest and three Zealsworn.

Curiosity aroused, Kaven followed him. He knew there was a great deal of cleanup to do, but he was trying desperately not to dwell on the people he had seen die. Besides, how often did one get to listen to the most powerful man in Lantrelia?

Mayn spotted Zealot Stonearm quickly, and her face paled at the sight of him. She bowed regally, drawing her sword and spinning it in a graceful arc until its tip touched the ground.

"You are the commander here?" Zealot Stonearm asked.

She straightened, a smile on her face. "Wall-Captain Mayn, sir. Thank you for your timely assistance."

The Zealot scanned the Wall. "Mm, yes, it is fortunate that my journey brought me here. But you did well today, you and your soldiers. Our Lord Na'lek is well pleased."

Mayn's grin widened and she looked up at Stonearm with admiration. "Thank you, Lord Zealot! Is there anything I can do for you?"

"Continue to stand here," said Zealot Stonearm. "Safeguard our kingdoms and prove yourselves against the Fury. That is all Lord Na'lek asks of you. As for me, I am headed east along the Wall to lend aid to the battle against the Silent Ones."

"You can be sure that we will forever hold these gates," Mayn said proudly. "Would you like me to send a contingent of my own troops to join you?"

Kaven looked around doubtfully. Mayn's Wall-Guard could hardly afford to lose any more men.

Zealot Stonearm seemed to have the same thought. "That won't be necessary, Captain. My Zealsworn will be more than enough to handle the Fury's monsters today."

"As you wish," Mayn replied.

The Zealot turned toward his priest. "Begin the march; I want to reach the border by this time tomorrow." The kingdoms were narrowest at the Barrier Wall and could be reached rather quickly by traveling inland. Most of the major cities were farther inland. The Priest of Na'lek bowed and hurried off to the waiting Zealsworn. A man brought forth a black horse, leading it toward the Zealot.

Kaven was mildly surprised that Zealot Stonearm was choosing to travel to the battlefield by moving across the Wall. Wouldn't it be easier to use portals? They were dangerous, certainly, but useful. Perhaps Stonearm simply wanted to boost the morale of the soldiers he passed on the Wall. Kaven was certainly grateful the Zealot had come; Stonearm had saved his life.

"Until we meet again," Stonearm said to Mayn, "let your sword be swifter than the winds."

Stonearm turned but paused when he saw Kaven, regarding him from behind his rose-petal mask. "You look oddly familiar," he said. "There's something in your eyes that I recognize. Have we met before?"

Kaven nearly forgot his etiquette, shocked to be addressed directly by the Zealot again. He awkwardly bowed. "I've never had the honor. But you may know my father, Kleon Fortis?"

"Ah!" Stonearm's crystal-blue eyes lit up with understanding. "Of course—the hero of the Chasm. You are his only child, yes?"

"Yes, sir." Kaven ground his teeth in frustration. Everyone seemed to know his father. No matter where he went, the name Kleon Fortis followed. It wasn't surprising, considering his father's legacy, but being yoked to the name had begun to chafe.

"Na'lek has his eyes on you," Zealot Stonearm said with a knowing tone. "You are destined for true glory, much as your father before you."

"Thank you, Lord Zealot!" Kaven said. He couldn't help but beam at the man's words. Did Na'lek really have his eyes on him. Even if he wasn't destined for glory, the compliment elevated his spirits despite the day's events.

"You would make a fine Zealsworn," the Zealot said.

Kaven grinned. "I'd like that, sir."

The Zealot nodded with approval and then turned to mount his horse. The Zealsworn marched eastward across the Wall, beginning the slow curve to the north toward Fulminos. Kaven watched him go, feeling happy and victorious.

"Kaven." He turned toward the sound of Mayn's voice. The woman was frowning at him. "Go home," she said. "Your shift is over."

He saluted and departed from the Wall. Mayn probably saw how exhausted he was, and his shift *was* over. However, he couldn't help but feel like he had been purposefully dismissed. The walk back to Redwind was long, and the walk back home was even longer. Over dinner that night, he told his parents that there had been a Knifeman attack, but he didn't tell them about Stonearm. And he didn't tell them that he'd failed again.

# SIX

*"The Tomes are for none but the humblest of Na'lek's servants.
Those who would blaspheme these sacred pages will be cast
into the Fury and devoured."*

—From the Tomes of Regret, prelude to the first book

THAT EVENING, KAVEN received a missive from Mayn
informing him that his watchtower had been destroyed in the
Knifeman attack. Because of this, Kaven spent the next three
days at home. He managed to get plenty of rest and tended his
garden carefully. Kaven also put several hours into his project,
but the secret to his own device continued to elude him.

After a long, late night of tinkering, Kaven had given
himself over to the merciful oblivion of sleep. He floated in
a restful, dreamless void, and he saw fields of brilliant stars.
Na'lek's presence was there, just out of reach. Kaven pressed
forth through the void, stretching out a hand, but Na'lek began
to laugh.

Kaven awoke with a slight jolt, and the sound of loud, raucous laughter followed him into the waking world. Sighing, he
sat up and dressed himself. The watchtower wouldn't be fixed
for another few days, so he slipped his device into a pocket,
intending to work on it after breakfast.

The laughter continued, and he recognized it as the rasping bark of his father. His parents had company over. He exited his room and stalked through his house quietly, peering around corners as he sought out his parents. The servants eyed him with confusion, but he ignored their stares. Lately, his mother had taken to inviting young noblewomen over, in the hopes that they'd take a fancy to him. Kaven wanted no part of that, so he hunted for his mother, trying to find her before she found him.

He poked his head around a corner and peeked into the living room. He quickly withdrew. It was worse than he had first feared. His parents were both there, and sitting across from them were two men.

One of the men was a dark-skinned Fulminite named Haz who had fought alongside Kleon in the Chasm War. Haz wore a permanent glower on his battle-hardened face, and Kaven doubted that he'd ever heard the man say more than two words in the same breath.

It was the second man who terrified him, but only because Kaven feared he might die of embarrassment. The other man was an old fellow named Gane, who also happened to be the headmaster of the Regelian University for Scientific Advancement. This was the most prestigious college for technological learning in the entire world. People traveled from all Four Kingdoms and across both continents for the chance to apply. Few were admitted. It also happened to be the college from which Kaven had failed to graduate. Several times.

He never would have gained admittance if not for his parentage. Kaven's mother was one of the most respected scholars of the modern age, and her intellect was unmatched across all Lantrelia. Many professors at the college had expected the son of Moira Fortis to follow in his mother's footsteps. No such luck.

Headmaster Gane had personally ordered that Kaven be ejected from the university forever. The man was also, of course, a good friend of his parents, which meant that Kaven had to endure Gane's eternally disappointed gaze at least once a week.

Carefully, Kaven turned to creep back toward his room and wait out this storm.

"Boy," came his father's voice. Kleon Fortis had the hearing of a Spinereaver. He also had a mouth like a grannoc—noisy lizard-like creatures from the Fury that constantly dueled the rats of Lantrelia for the coveted position of Lantrelia's greatest pest. They liked to gather by trash bins or merchant shops and squeal loudly for scraps.

Kaven sighed, knowing defeat when he heard it. He turned and stepped into the room. "Good morning, Father, Mother." He glanced at the bearded old man. "Headmaster," he said, not meeting the man's eye. He looked at the Fulminite instead. "Haz."

Haz glowered.

"And a good morning to you as well," said the headmaster cheerfully. Kaven brought himself to look at the man and found that he was smiling. It was a warm smile, though he could still see the disappointment in Gane's rich, dark eyes.

Headmaster Gane was well along in his years; his short hair was white as fresh snow; his face was leathery and his hands were gnarled like old tree branches. Yet, there was still great strength in his form and in his mind. Gane was a renowned genius and inventor. The Firerods that protected Regelia's Wall were his creation, along with a plethora of other wondrous feats of science. The man had known Kaven long before he'd ever attended the college, and Gane had always been kind and affectionate toward him, like a wrinkly old uncle. Perhaps that was why Kaven felt ashamed in his presence.

"Have a seat, dear," Mother said, gesturing to a place beside her. She sat on a wide couch, looking petite next to her muscular, if slightly rotund, husband. Haz and Gane sat across from her in separate cushioned chairs.

Kaven did as he was bid, saying nothing to his father. "It's a little early for all of this, isn't it, Mother?"

"Nonsense!" She waved toward a servant, who brought Kaven tea and a bowl of porridge. "It's never too early for your friends."

"Which you'd know if you had any," Kleon muttered.

Kaven ignored him, and his mother quickly changed the subject. "Haz was just telling us that he's leaving for Stormgarde City with his son in a few hours."

"That's what was so funny?" Kaven asked, glancing at his father from around his mother.

"That was something else," Kleon said, sounding annoyed, as if Kaven had asked the stupidest question in Lantrelia.

"I heard there was a Titan outside the Wall," Headmaster Gane said suddenly. "Moira, were you able to see it?"

She shook her head sadly. "The Watcher was gone before I could make a trip to the Wall."

"That's unfortunate," the headmaster replied with a frown of his own. He looked strange when he frowned, somehow unnatural. A frown wasn't meant to be on that kindly face. "The Fury certainly has been active these past few days."

"That's what I warned about just yesterday," Kleon boasted, nodding vigorously. "I tell you, if things continue the way they have, Na'lek will catch us with our shields down. The Day of Reckoning will come soon, if we're not careful."

The headmaster and Haz exchanged looks before Gane smiled again. "Regelia will not be broken by the Fury. Believe me."

Moira nodded. "Na'lek will always protect us."

"Speaking of which," Kleon began, "Stonearm announced that he was going to Fulminos yesterday. The fighting has only grown fiercer in the past few days."

Moira patted his arm. "That reminds me of what Priest Gillan said in his last sermon . . ."

Kaven pulled out his device and set to working on it, and the conversation between his parents faded to a dull buzz. He switched it on, nothing. He made a few adjustments and tried again, but still there was nothing. He didn't give up, though; he knew he was getting closer.

"Must be going now," said the voice of the headmaster. "But I'd like a word with Kaven, in private."

At the sound of his own name, Kaven looked up, pocketing his device. His parents stood and walked out of the room with Haz, chatting with the silent man as if he were the most engaging person in the world.

Now alone with the headmaster, Kaven fidgeted, but managed to meet his gaze.

"You are a remarkable boy," the headmaster said with another small smile. "I've seen you fail time and time again, yet you never give up. I admire your seemingly eternal persistence."

Kaven nodded slowly, unsure of how to react. "Thanks?"

Headmaster Gane smiled. "Ah, I believe I'm starting to ramble. We old men like to do that from time to time." He cleared his throat. "Kaven, simply put, I need your help."

"You need my help?" Kaven couldn't quite believe his ears.

"You sound surprised." The headmaster's eyes twinkled above his smile, as if he knew the funniest jest and couldn't wait to tell it.

Kaven nodded again.

"That's one of your greatest problems," Gane said, staring deep into Kaven's eyes. "You doubt yourself."

Kaven shifted uncomfortably. "How . . . how can I help you, sir?"

"I need you to deliver a message for me," he replied, "to Stormgarde City."

"Really?" A hundred different questions and problems popped simultaneously into Kaven's head. Deliver a message into another kingdom? Why send him? He had a duty to perform. "I'm expected at the watchtower in a few days," he said.

"I've already cleared things with Captain Mayn," Gane said, his smile unwavering. "She has given you leave to perform this task."

Kaven had forgotten that Gane was a good friend of Mayn's as well. "Why not send the message yourself through a portal? Isn't Haz going to Stormgarde anyway?"

"Let's just say that I would risk neither the lives of a creature, nor the contents of this missive, with something as dangerous as a portal."

"Fair enough," Kaven replied. "But why—"

The headmaster interrupted him. "Kaven, stop giving excuses where there are none to give. I assure you, if you do this for me, I will make it worth your while."

"How so?" he asked.

"I will let you reapply to my university," Gane replied. "One full term, tuition fully paid."

Kaven's mouth fell open, and he stared at the headmaster in complete shock. Had the man gone mad? Had he forgotten the Kaven's abysmal failure? "Sir," he began, "you know what happened last time—"

But once again, he was interrupted. "I don't care for your past failings. As far as I'm concerned, the past is as dead as the Destroyer. This is a chance to redeem yourself, and I offer it freely to you."

"I can't, sir," Kaven said, trying to be honest. If his own project was any indication, he really was hopeless in the field of science. "You should know better than most that I don't deserve another chance. I failed."

Gane nodded. "I know. Yet, there are different avenues we may take. You may not have the makings of a scientist, but why not a scholar? A degree from my college is a valuable possession, Kaven. I have faith that you will not fail again."

Kaven hesitated. Could he really succeed? After all this time? Kaven didn't think he could. But if a man like Headmaster Gane could have faith in him, maybe Kaven could have faith in himself too.

"All right," he finally said, nodding to himself. "What do I need to do?"

Gane reached into the cloak he wore and withdrew a slender gray tube. Kaven instantly recognized it as Spinereaver bone, just like his arrows. This bone was highly resilient and strong, ideal for packaging along with weaponry. The end of the hollow tube had been replaced with a wax seal.

"Take this to Stormgarde City and wait outside an inn called the Widow's Hope," the headmaster said, proffering the tube. "You'll know it; it's in Victory Square. A man will be waiting for you when you arrive. Give him my message and follow his next instructions."

Kaven took the message and pocketed it. "How will I know this fellow?"

"You won't," Gane said simply. "He will know you. Now, you must leave immediately. Bid your parents farewell and take the horse that is waiting for you outside. Travel atop the Wall, don't go over land, and do not take a portal. This is important, Kaven."

Kaven leapt to his feet, excitement fueling him. He saluted the headmaster crisply. "By the Titans and the Fury itself, I won't let you down."

"I wouldn't expect anything less," Gane said warmly. "Oh!" He reached back into his cloak. "There is one more thing I want to give you." He withdrew an iron rod and held it out to Kaven. "A gift from me to you, for your safe travels. Any journey close to the Fury is a perilous one."

Kaven accepted the rod with reverence. It was about the length of his forearm and had a reflective silver color. It was topped with a sphere connected to the rod by a tight coil. It was a miniature of the mighty Firerods of the Wall. Though not nearly as powerful, it was more accurate, and deadly in close quarters. These were extremely expensive, not to mention difficult to obtain, and as they were crafted by Gane's own hand, it was a grand gift and a fearsome weapon.

"Thank you, sir," was all he could manage to say.

Gane nodded. "Now, off with you! I expect to see you soon, and I'm eager to correct your past mistakes."

"I will," Kaven said, cradling the Firerod. "Thank you, Headmaster!"

Kaven sped from the room, leaving Gane behind as he pursued his parents. Elated and giddy with excitement, Kaven felt joyous for the first time in a long while. He silently thanked Na'lek and held tight to this feeling of glory. Perhaps Zealot Stonearm was right; perhaps he was destined for glory.

# SEVEN

*"The monsters are things of pure rage. They are manifestations of Na'lek's divine anger. Stand against them. Fight. Bleed. Die. Prove that you are worthy of mercy."*

—*From the Tomes of Regret, Verse 89 of Power*

THERE WAS NO greater glory than to give one's life to the Fury. Every Stormgardian knew it to be true. It was the ultimate sacrifice. And yet, standing before the Storm-Gate that separated her from the Fury beyond, Shera was afraid.

Slowly, the gates of the Barrier Wall began to creak open, and the Eternal Storm rumbled its anger. Around her, Shera's sword brothers—the fellow soldiers of Stormgarde, noblest of the Four Kingdoms—raised spears and swords and yelled in defiance of the Fury.

Before the gates had even fully opened, the warriors of Stormgarde charged toward the gap, rushing the enemy that awaited them on the Fields of Glory. But Shera couldn't move.

The armor she wore was heavy, and she felt like she carried a mountain on her shoulders. Her sword and shield hung from her hands like lead weights as she stared after her sword brothers. She felt terrified and ashamed to be wearing the blue and silver of her people.

It wasn't that she was scared to fight or scared to be under the Fury. She had used the sword all her life and had dueled countless times. She had been a Wall-Guard for eight years and could kill a Spinereaver at a hundred paces with her bow. She was a skilled soldier but lacked an attribute that was vital to being a warrior. Shera was not brave, and knowing that made her feel worse. She had never faced the Fury-spawn on the Fields before; this would be her first time. *Maybe my last time,* she thought.

She feared death and she feared what awaited her after it. And so she stood, virtually alone on the grounds in the Wall's shadow, as the clamor of battle erupted beyond the gates. Shera tried to step forward, tried to lift her sword, frozen as a man left to die in the northern wastes.

A man came up behind her and put a hand on her shoulder. Startled, Shera turned to look at him. He was a soldier, like herself, dressed in silver armor and wearing a blue tabard over his breastplate. This displayed the sigil of Stormgarde: a gauntleted fist raised against a darkened sky. Shera knew him as one of the many Wall-Captains, but she couldn't place his name.

"What's your name, sword-sister?" he asked.

"Shera," she replied nervously. Beyond her, men screamed as they were cut down by Fury-spawn.

"My name is Orlan," the Wall-Captain said. "Is this your first time?"

She nodded mutely. *Na'lek give me courage,* she prayed silently. *Titans, why am I so terrified?*

"Shera, I am curious," Orlan continued. "Why are you standing here?"

"I'm afraid," she said simply. "I cannot move."

"Fear does not give you cause for inaction," Orlan said. "If anything, it should make you fight harder. Forge fear into strength, because I will not tolerate it amongst my soldiers."

Shera swallowed hard. "I've never been outside the Wall, sir. I've never had to fight monsters with my own sword."

"You should be excited," Orlan said. "There is no greater honor than to fight Na'lek's rage beneath the storm itself. This is your highest calling."

"I know it is," Shera said, attempting to steel her nerves.

"Then stay by my side." Orlan raised his sword. "The Fury calls us forward!"

He charged toward the gates, and Shera forced herself to follow. They rushed out of the Wall's shelter and onto the Fields of Glory, where Shera faced complete chaos. The Stormgardian ranks had broken, leaving soldiers and monsters scattered at random as they battled.

Then one came at her. These were Eye-Takers and they were some of the most intelligent monsters of the Fury. They were squat, muscular humanoids, with thick violet skin and black armor. Wielding spears and one-handed axes in sharp claws, the Eye-Takers were fierce, terrible warriors that delighted in bloodshed. Most horrifically, after slaying an opponent, Eye-Takers would tear out their victim's eyes. They even tore the eyes from their own dead.

The Eye-Taker roared as it rushed toward her, baring cat-like fangs and pointing a spear toward her heart. Shera raised her shield, preparing to deflect the monster's blow. She momentarily forgot her terror when she saw how short the Eye-Taker was. Its head barely reached her shoulders. Shera couldn't help but smile in amusement. *Why was I so afraid?*

Then the spear came, stabbing for her heart, and she remembered. But Shera swung her shield and deflected the weapon to the right. She then slashed at the Eye-Taker's neck, but the monster spun around her sword and rammed its spear toward her side. Shera quickly sidestepped and the spear flashed by her harmlessly. She swung again, but her sword bounced off the haft of the spear. As the Eye-Taker stabbed again, Shera leapt past it and shoved her shield into the beast's face. The Eye-Taker stumbled and Shera quickly rammed her sword into its chest. There was a sharp tug as Shera's sword bit deep and the monster's flesh split, spraying white blood like a split water sack. The Eye-Taker went down with a scream, nearly dragging Shera to the ground.

She pulled her sword free and stared down at the dying Eye-Taker, panting. Shera had killed monsters before, from afar, and was no stranger to death. But this? This was the first time she had cut one down with her own blade. It terrified her and thrilled her at the same time.

Something hit her from behind, and she fell with a cry. Another Eye-Taker loomed over her, raising its bloody axe with two hands, but the Eye-Taker toppled, its head bouncing into a nearby pit.

Orlan stepped over the corpse and held out his hand. "Are you all right, soldier?"

Shera took his hand and got to her feet. "I think so."

"Good." Orlan turned, his dark eyes searching for more monsters. "These things have drawn breath long enough." He sped off again, and Shera hurried to follow him.

Passing through the chaos, Orlan cut down three Eye-Takers with ease, lopping off their heads from behind. Shera stumbled around corpses and pits, her every instinct demanding that she run from this place. She tried not to look down at the eyeless corpses of her sword-brothers.

Thunder suddenly burst from the Fury, loud and close. As one, the Stormgardians pulled back warily. But not the Eye-Takers; they roared with a renewed vigor and pushed forward. Those near the back of the lines hovered close there, ripping out the eyes of corpses they came across.

Orlan rushed toward where the battle was fiercest. He slammed into the Eye-Takers, a storm in his own right, ramming his sword down into a monster's head as thunder crashed again, closer now. But Orlan ignored the storm, focusing on the true threat. He was unstoppable, his sword becoming a blur as he slashed at the monsters. Yellow eyes alight with hunger, the Eye-Takers leapt at him with black axes swinging.

"For Stormgarde!" Orlan slammed his sword downward and was met with a plume of white blood as a clawed arm fell to the ground. Shera rushed in beside him and finished it off with a heavy blow to the head.

Thunder crashed nearby, heralding imminent lightning. Orlan ignored the Fury, disemboweling an opponent with a swift right slash. He danced from Eye-Taker to Eye-Taker, dropping the astonished monsters before they had a chance to react.

Shera fought beside him, flanking the monsters while Orlan held their focus. Ducking under an axe that bounced off Orlan's shield, Shera rammed her sword into an Eye-Taker's neck. Blood spattered her face, armor, and tabard. She retched, stumbling forward as her false bravado faltered. For a moment, Shera had almost believed that it was real. Another Eye-Taker loomed before her, and the world went black as lightning struck nearby.

Shera felt a rush of air swoop by her, and she cried out and fell to the ground. A different blackness clouded her vision as her head struck stone. She cringed, waiting for the axe blow to come. Something heavy struck her shoulder, and she flinched violently, but no pain followed. She opened her eyes, and her vision cleared so that she could see the severed Eye-Taker's head staring back at her through lifeless eyes. Shera looked up, but Orlan was already moving on to a new enemy.

Standing quickly, Shera managed to retrieve her sword and hurried after Orlan. Around her, the soldiers of Stormgarde battled with an unchecked vigor, shouting warcries as they cut down monsters. Even as her sword-brothers died, they praised Na'lek and perished with shouts of glory on their lips. Shera envied them. How did they do it? How could they fight, even die, with such valiance? Why couldn't she?

Men fell, hewn apart by Eye-Takers or shot from afar with arrows. As soon as soldiers fell, the monsters leapt on them like vultures, clawing at their eyes. Shera tried not to look down as she stumbled through the battle, tripping over eyeless corpses. A black bolt of lightning suddenly struck a nearby man. He didn't have time to scream. Shera's world was blanketed in shadow as the lightning dissipated, the outline of the man burned into her vision. But when her eyes cleared, the man was gone. Obliterated.

But everywhere she looked, the noble soldiers of Stormgarde prevailed against the Fury's monsters. Their blue tabards were like radiant beacons across the desolate Fields. Though soldiers died, they did so proudly, and their souls would soon be welcomed into Shilanti. The Eye-Takers were thinning, and the Stormgardians continued to push back their now outnumbered foe.

*I can do this,* she told herself. She took a deep breath, drawing inspiration from her sword-brothers. *I can be valiant.* She located an Eye-Taker nearby, hunched over a corpse, claws digging curiously.

Shera rushed toward the creature, whose back was toward her, shield ready and sword held high. She yelled the war cry of her people: "Stormgarde stands!"

The Eye-Taker pivoted suddenly, straightening with the speed of the lightning above. The short monster effortlessly went under her sword, grabbed her by the neck with its long arms, and threw her forward. Shera hit the ground hard, slitting the palm of her hand on a pointed rock as her shield bounced away.

Fear took hold of her again. Raw, primal fear. Oblivious to her gashed hand, she rolled onto her back, still gripping her sword.

The Eye-Taker stood over her, spear clutched in its hands and a wide grin on its lips. "Such pretty eyes," it said softly, voice a gruff drawl.

The monster rammed the spear downward, but Shera was already moving, fueled by nothing more than blind terror and adrenaline. She rolled to the side and the spear bounced off stone. Shera threw herself to her feet as the monster turned to face her. Shera attacked viciously, swinging her sword in wild, heavy arcs. Some part of her knew, deep down, that this was foolishness. She attacked with the madness of a feral cat and the skill of a novice. Any man who could hold a sword would have cut her down in an instant. Yet this Eye-Taker was unprepared for such a savage assault, and all it could do was block her rapid strikes with its spear haft.

Shera seized control of her panic and forced it down, and then took advantage of the surprised Eye-Taker. While the monster stumbled back from her mad barrage, she swiftly pivoted around the spearhead and drove her sword into its neck. The Eye-Taker dropped soundlessly, and this time Shera was not dragged down.

Shera stood still a moment as four claps of thunder crashed overhead in rapid succession. Shame gradually took the place of fear in Shera's heart. She had never lost control of herself like that. But this was her first true fight, and these things took time and experience to learn. That had been the first monster she had slain directly. Shera allowed herself a small smile of satisfaction, knowing Na'lek was pleased. Her father would've been proud.

Tearing a strip of cloth from her tabard, she made a make-shift bandage for her bleeding hand. The rocks here on the Fields were incredibly rough and sharp, and many men had sundered their armor by falling into rocky pits. This fall had split the chain mail of her gauntlet but hadn't penetrated deep. Still, she wouldn't be using her shield anymore today.

She heard yelling behind her, and seven Eye-Takers charged toward her, breaking away from the main force. "Get down!"

Instinctively, Shera obeyed, falling flat on her stomach. Arrows suddenly flew over her head, killing the Eye-Takers as they advanced. She leapt to her feet, brushing blood and sweat from her lip. She nodded her thanks as nine bowmen, led by a few spear bearers, hurried past.

Where had Orlan gone? Shera didn't even remember where they had separated. She looked about but saw no sign of him. "Captain Orlan!" she called, but no response came. In fact, she could barely hear any sounds of battle at all. Glancing back at the Wall, she realized that she was now a good distance away from it. She continued to move farther out, looking for her commander. Thunder boomed overhead, and a dark bolt streaked to crash into the Wall beyond. This was a weak storm band, sporadic and infrequent, yet still dangerous. When caught by a storm band on the Fields of Glory, you were supposed to take shelter in a pit. It was safer than being out in the open. But, in the middle of a battle, Shera doubted it would do her much good.

She soon realized that she was alone. Shera could still hear ringing metal, but it was distant. The battle had moved north, leaving her alone with the dead. She heard an odd scratching sound coming from behind a nearby pile of rubble that was nearly as tall as she was.

Shera moved to where she could see around the rubble and found Orlan behind it. He lay on the ground faceup, his sightless eyes staring at the Fury as his blood began to spread across the broken rocks. The haft of a spear protruded from Orlan's chest, ignored by the Eye-Taker crouching over him, examining his eyes with a pointed claw.

Shock was Shera's first emotion, seeing such a powerful warrior dead. Then came a surging sorrow, which she momentarily swallowed. The Eye-Taker didn't seem to notice her, and she crept closer, sword raised.

Leaning closer, the Eye-Taker suddenly plucked out Orlan's eyes with deft fingers. The monster held up the stolen orbs, grinning victoriously.

*No, that wasn't how it should be.* Slowly, Shera's fear and sorrow and pain merged to form a terrible, terrible anger. *No! No!* Orlan would not be defiled in such a way! He was a hero! He had saved her life! He had . . . Rage consumed her.

Shera closed the distance between herself and the monster in four hurried strides. Not hesitating for an instant, she slashed wildly at the Eye-Taker's head and was rewarded with a spray of milky blood.

The Eye-Taker fell back screaming, and Shera kicked it in the side, sending it toppling into a pit. "Titans take your soul, Fury-spawn!" She growled, standing protectively over Orlan.

Much to her surprise, the Eye-Taker stood slowly, hand clutched over one eye. It removed its trembling claws, revealing a large gash running from its forehead, through its right eye, and down to its lip. "How dare you?" the Eye-Taker hissed, its voice low and guttural. "H-How dare you?"

Shera felt no pity for this creature, a shard of her god's anger made flesh. "I'll do worse," she growled. *They are given mouths to mock you*, Shera thought, remembering a quote from the Tomes of Regret. *They will lead you astray.* She couldn't let the Fury-spawn goad her.

The Eye-Taker turned, obviously pained, looking with a not-so-subtle glance at its spear, which was still implanted in Orlan's body. Shera stood still, meeting the monster's single eye. Then the Eye-Taker bolted.

Shera sprung toward the spear, knowing that the Eye-Taker had to scramble out of the pit. Reaching the weapon, she kicked it hard as she could, and the spear snapped right in its center, clattering to the ground, as Shera spun toward the charging monster. But the Eye-Taker wasn't there.

Instead of trying for the spear, the Eye-Taker had rushed to a nearby corpse of one of its brethren. The wounded monster had retrieved both the axe and the eyes of its fellow Eye-Taker. Wearing a wicked grin on its pained face, the Eye-Taker stalked toward her, moving in a wide circle.

Furious at being tricked, Shera rushed the monster, trying to take advantage of its blind spot and catch it off guard. But the Eye-Taker was ready and anticipated her charge with a wide swing to the right.

Shera cried out, barely managing to deflect the axe from taking her head. The Eye-Taker pressed the attack, face contorted with rage and snarling. The axe whistled through the air as the monster spun it expertly, hacking at Shera with heavy overhand chops. Each time Shera blocked the axe, shockwaves reverberated through her arms and chest, and they soon became laden with pain. On the defensive, Shera could do nothing but backtrack.

The Fury thundered again as the Eye-Taker chased her, hammering her with wide, damaging swings. Shera was in a panic, and it was becoming harder to breath. Knowing that she couldn't hold much longer, she rushed the Eye-Taker in desperation, trying to drive her sword through the monster's defenses and into his heart, but the Eye-Taker simply dodged and, with a smooth pivot, drove his fist into Shera's face. The blow came in time with another clap of thunder, and Shera fell.

The Eye-Taker kicked Shera's sword and sent it flying. Then, with strong arms it rolled her over onto her back and placed its leg on her neck. The monster hovered over her, framed against the Fury, blood dripping from its stricken eye.

"S-Stupid pale-skin," the Eye-Taker rasped, raising its axe. Shera squirmed, but she could barely breathe, much less get away, as the Eye-Taker increased the pressure on her neck. "I'll let your miserable eyes *rot!*"

The axe came down. Day turned to night. Cool wind turned to blazing fire. Shera found air and screamed as she felt her flesh boil in a terrible heat, as if she were aflame. Blind, she writhed on the ground as pain consumed her. Slowly, the pain faded, and her vision returned. A vertical black line was branded into her vision, and the axe lay discarded beside her. A lightning bolt had struck the monster, turning it to less than dust in an instant. The Eye-Taker was gone, snapped up in the Fury's unending rage. Na'lek had spared her, withdrawing his hand.

The afterimage of the lightning faded, and Shera's vision finally returned to normal. On her knees, Shera trembled, every ounce of her strength drained. She didn't thank Na'lek for saving her, as death would've at least rewarded her honor. Instead, she would live on, and perhaps her life would end by some other means.

She stood near Orlan for a moment, paying her respects. She'd known him for barely an hour, yet he had saved her life twice. He rested in Shilanti now, surrounded by heroes like himself. Giving one's life to the Fury was the greatest form of redemption that a mortal could obtain. Only the Zealots could hold more honor.

Orlan was at peace, having achieved the highest of goals. Yet Shera remained, and she suffered. She had failed to defend him, failed even to avenge him. If not for the Fury's will, she would be dead beside him. Adrenaline faded, and exhaustion took its place. Burdened by the memory of her cowardice, she began the weary walk back toward the Barrier Wall.

She passed dozens of Eye-Taker corpses, and the number of dead monsters far outstripped the slain Stormgardians. But the sight of slain men was still harrowing, especially with their eyes torn out. She tried not to look.

The sound of cheers guided her back toward the Barrier Wall, where the victorious battalions gathered before the gates and roared their triumph toward the Fury. The men were depleted and weary and had left friends behind on the Fields of Glory, but they rejoiced in their sacrifice.

The Storm-Gate, which had been shut after the battle had begun, opened to admit the soldiers back into Stormgarde. Shera joined the other soldiers as they returned home, and the gates that shielded the kingdom from Na'lek closed once more.

Fresh, rested soldiers marched toward the Wall to replace those that had served today. A group of twenty more soldiers approached, though these wore deep turquoise tabards and plumed helmets. This was the royal guard, and they were escorting one of the most powerful figures in the kingdom. Benehain Dawndancer, regent-lord of Stormgarde, was a tall, powerful man with a long mane of black hair and a clean-shaven face. There was a great ferocity in his eyes as he gazed upon his soldiers.

Lord Benehain ruled the kingdom on this continent— Stormvault, the land forever burdened by the Fury—in place of the king. King Essain himself ruled from the heart of

Stormgarde on the continent called Far and believed it necessary to have a regent-lord oversee things across the ocean. Even though the four Stormgardian Zealots were more than capable of running things, they had more important duties, and Lord Benehain was the perfect man for the position. Stormgarde prospered on the Fury's doorstep, thanks to his rule.

"My sword-brothers," Lord Benehain called, raising his own sword high. "Once more, Stormgarde triumphs!" He paused, as the soldiers cheered. Shera felt some of her old vigor return as she joined them. The regent-lord continued. "I first must express my gratitude for the Wall-Guards in our watch-towers, as they gave us time to prepare for this attack. The Eye-Takers are a brutal foe, and they brought with them a storm band spawned from the heart of the Fury itself. Yet, every brave man and woman here rose to the challenge and have bloodied their blades on Na'lek's hate. Stormgarde stands, thanks to you."

Benehain paused again, and silence fell across the assembled soldiers. "Our brothers have fallen today; the Fury has claimed their lives as the price for our sins. Yet, they now feast in Shilanti and enjoy the fruits of their sacrifice. Do not mourn the dead, but instead envy those who go before you! Praise their courage, and remember what Na'lek demands of us. Now, come with me to the city, and dine with me in honor and victory. May this food sustain us until we too are claimed by the Eternal Storm. Stormgarde stands!"

"Stormgarde stands!" echoed the soldiers. Shera felt a rush of pride for her people, both the living and the dead. The other kingdoms scoffed at Stormgardians, calling them suicidal fools. Were they suicidal? Maybe, but never could they be called fools. Stormgarde merely had a more active interpretation of the Tomes of Regret. It was their belief that the only way to gain Na'lek's forgiveness was to fight, and then die, in the war against the Eternal Storm. A man's death not only secured his soul but helped to elevate the souls of his children and wife. The other kingdoms believed that the war was important, but preached that there were other ways to atone. Perhaps by serving the poor, or absolving of sin, or maybe even spreading the words of Na'lek to the island folk. They were the fools. The only honor was to fight the Fury, even when it took your life.

Shera couldn't imagine what would happen to her if she didn't fight the Fury. That would be truly terrifying. Her soul would not go to Shilanti after she died but would rather be forever destroyed, consumed by Na'lek's hate.

The regent-lord led the march back to the city, escorting the two hundred or so soldiers that had participated in the battle. Shera didn't feel like she was part of this victory, but she knew that was foolish too. She glanced back at the Wall, feeling regretful. The dead would be mourned and buried, but the celebration of victory always came first. That was the Stormgardian way.

Stormgarde City was very close to the Wall, closer even than Regelia's capital, and they were within its shadow after a ten-minute march. The walls that surrounded the city were just as impressive as the Barrier Wall, white and massive. The hefty, iron-wrought gate was open, just as it always was during the day, and a wide moat surrounded the entire city. A wide wooden bridge crossed the moat in front of the gates.

Volunteers, mostly the mates and children of the soldiers, had set up many long wooden tables in the grassy fields just beyond the moat. They had already set immense platters of food upon them. Trays laden with steaming pork and chicken sat next to bowls filled with the freshest apples, pears, and grapes. Crystal pitchers of water, red wine, and malted beer stood next to dozens of matching cups, and there were plates of frosted pastries stacked in neat little pyramids.

Grannocs were already advancing toward the food, watching with beady eyes as they skittered forward on scaly legs. They dominated the land between the Wall and the city, a race of Fury-spawn that could never be defeated. The tiny scavengers licked blue scales with tiny tongues, but volunteers guarded the tables, armed with brooms or trays as they kept watch over the food. The grannocs waited, cowering from the wrathful servants. Their patience was infinite, for they knew that one day their time would come.

Shera smiled at the tiny creatures. As a girl, she had often wanted one for a pet, but her father had forbidden it. Grannocs could have a rather fierce bite if provoked, proving them to be true creatures of the Fury.

The soldiers took their pick of the food provided by their regent-lord and began talking about the battle in earnest. Shera took her seat at the end of one of the tables and began to slowly chew on a piece of blackberry pie. She wasn't especially hungry. She listened quietly as her sword-brothers boasted and jested about their actions in the battle. A large, red-bearded man sitting beside Shera claimed to have cut an Eye-Taker in half with one swing.

A short girl, no older than Shera herself, with a smooth face and wild dark hair, said that she'd slain three Eye-Takers with a single arrow. A behemoth of a man leaned over from farther down, laughing uproariously. Raising a tankard of beer, he boasted that he'd killed no less than six monsters with a single blow. His battle axe, which was propped up beside him, was still smeared with a sickening amount of Eye-Taker blood. Of all the tales, his seemed most credible.

Shera wondered how they could be so brave. Why were they undisturbed by what they had witnessed? Yes, the souls of the fallen would be honored, but Shera's stomach flipped inside of her. She was not pleased with herself; no, not at all.

She silently thanked Na'lek for another chance to prove herself. What if she had died after performing so cowardly? Her soul certainly wouldn't have been honored.

Shera was becoming so uncomfortable that she wanted to leave right then, but to do so before the celebration was over would dishonor the slain. She nibbled at her pie and sipped water while the other soldiers grew louder and louder with every beer they drank.

Finally, Lord Benehain excused himself, formally ending the celebration. Only a few left, though, as the rest were content to stay awhile, putting off the worries and grief that would come later. Shera was the first to leave.

As she stood, she heard her own name.

"Shera Lacer?" A woman had walked to the table and was watching Shera with bright gray eyes. Taller than Shera by a good six inches, this newcomer wore her black hair back in an ornate bundle of curls, as was fashionable among the Stormgardian noblewomen. She wore a silk dress, light gray with a lacy trim, and her pale complexion seemed white compared to Shera's sun-darkened skin. The woman was beautiful, older than Shera by a decade or more, with delicate, mature features. Some of the men at the table glanced her way.

Shera studied the woman, unsure of how to address her. "Yes, ma'am? I'm Shera."

The woman looked to the table, which caused the men to quickly turn back to their food. "Walk with me a moment," she said. "I have something to ask of you." The woman walked away without waiting for a reply.

After a brief pause, Shera hurried after her. She caught up to the woman, who walked with a calm, regal air, but since she did not stop, Shera decided she should probably inquire about the woman's intent. "How may I assist you?" Shera asked.

"My name is Lyra; I am head of House Sunfeather," the woman said.

"I'm pleased to meet you," Shera said untruthfully. They seemed to be heading toward the city.

Lyra gave her a brief, sideways glance. "I came to the Wall to pray for your victory. I was a soldier like you once."

Shera said nothing, feeling her dislike of the woman rise. Some Stormgardians believed that the war was not eternal and that they could retire after serving for a few years. It was a popular practice among the nobles. Shera detested the lot of them. The only exception to this were the priests, who retired to continue service to Na'lek in a way that was just as important. The nobles liked to come and pray over the battles; it made them feel like they were doing something to appease Na'lek without risking their own lives. They made a spectacle of the war, and they did not fear the Fury. Na'lek would burn their souls.

Lyra continued. "I saw you, when the battle began, and then later as you fought on the Fields. To be quite honest, it was an abysmal display of swordsmanship."

Flushing, Shera frowned. What was the woman talking about? She wasn't the best swordswoman, certainly, but she wasn't poor by any stretch. It was her courage that eluded her. "Lady Lyra, I am aware that there are problems. But surely you didn't just come here to—"

The woman spoke over her. "The worst I've seen in all my days!" Lyra glanced at her again, and this time there was no mistaking the scorn in her eyes. "Why they gave you that sword, I'll never know."

"This was my father's sword," Shera said defensively, temper rising. It had been the last thing he had ever given her. She had been too young to lift it then and barely old enough to understand why the Fury killed. She'd vowed to bring her father glory with this sword, and no one would stain his honor.

No one! "If you've come here simply to mock my family's name," she spat, "or to lecture me on the art of swordplay, then you can take your haughty airs and expensive silks and go jump off the Wall!"

Lyra gave her a half smile. "If—"

Shera cut her off. "Be quiet! I don't want to hear another word from you."

The noblewoman stepped onto the bridge and they began to cross the moat. "My, my," Lyra said. "What a temper. The mark of a fighter, for certain. Direct more of that rage toward the Fury, Shera. There it will be put to better use."

Shera couldn't believe that this woman was still insulting her. "Titans take you, can't you hear? What do you know of the fight? Listen—"

This time, Lyra interrupted her. "No, you shall listen to me, child! Put that warrior's spirit to rest and quiet your rage. By the Fury, you're more easily roused than a rabid Spinereaver."

"What do you want then?" Shera asked, her patience worn thin.

"Do you know why you froze?" Lyra asked. "Why your fighting was so poor?"

Shera nearly stumbled, caught off guard by that question. That was the question that gnawed at her heart, eating her away piece by piece. She was afraid to ask it, though she knew the answer already. "I'm afraid."

"I will destroy your fear." Lyra paused, standing before the gates, right before they crossed the threshold into Stormgarde City. "If you follow me, I will make you the bravest woman in Lantrelia."

# EIGHT

*"Na'lek eradicates whom he wills. Nothing can withstand him. Submit, and be spared from his dark power."*

—*From the Tomes of Regret, Verse 50 of Repentance*

THE HORSE'S HOOVES pounded against the Wall, heavy clops ringing in a rhythmic counterpoint to the thunder in the distance. Lightning loomed ahead, dark streaks against the purple clouds, as one of the Fury's storm bands swirled along the horizon making its uncertain journey along the outskirts of the central storm. The unpredictable bands could appear at any time, seemingly from nowhere, and they always brought thunder . . . followed by black death.

Kaven was safe for now, stretched low along the back of the horse that Gane had loaned him from the university. The band was far enough away that it posed little threat. He glanced out across the Fields of Glory to where the Fury waited. The Eternal Storm loomed over him, ominous and black. The violet, shadowed clouds rippled in the winds while flashes of black light burst from the distance. The Fury rumbled and growled, its winds whipping against him as he rode onward. He felt the Eternal Storm's gaze on him always.

He was frightened, certainly, but also excited. He had a chance to reenter the Regelian University of Scientific Advancement. He hadn't heard of anyone else being offered such an opportunity. Kaven had already decided that he wouldn't study mechanics or science, as he had last time, but rather choose scholarly pursuits, like his mother before him. Perhaps there he'd find success.

The pavement along the Wall stretched interminably—its rounded, scroll-worked crenellations broken only by alternating guard towers and Firerod shafts every hundred paces. Many of the guards manning their stations stared as Kaven rode past, his cloak billowing out behind him. *They're probably wondering what sort of dire news I am carrying,* he thought. *I wonder the same thing.*

The traveling cloak, as well as the horse, had been loaned to him by the headmaster. He reached into his cloak and patted the tube of Spinereaver bone that was nestled in a pocket next to his device.

"You'll soon be to Stormgarde, lad!" one of the Wall-Guards called as he passed. It was hard to hear him over the roar of the wind. "Keep your sword arm clear!"

Kaven continued without looking back—even prodding his horse to gallop. He didn't know if the advice was given to be friendly or if the soldier was gibing him for not being one of them. Messengers were the lowest-ranking in the Regelian army, but they could go anywhere without too many questions. Probably because of their total lack of intimidating qualities.

*That suits me just fine,* he thought. His excitement was mounting. Would he be able to start tomorrow? He wouldn't have to serve in the watchtower anymore, that much was certain. This only served to heighten his anticipation. And the college had a beautiful orchard too. Kaven could recall several times he had been late for class because he had fallen asleep beneath the apple trees.

Kaven's excitement lessened somewhat when he saw the border station approach. It was here where the kingdom of Regelia ended and that of Stormgarde began. Every point of the Wall where two kingdoms met had a border station. Each station, in turn, was dually controlled by both powers.

The Barrier Wall was immense, crossing through all Four Kingdoms to completely encircle the Fury. Its only purpose was to serve as the first and primary defense against invasion. Here, at the borders, the kingdoms worked together to safeguard their lands. For the most part, relationships between the kingdoms were good; however, Regelia and Stormgarde held some animosity toward each other. Kaven wasn't quite sure why, but he did not share in the mutual dislike.

Still, Kaven thought that the sight of men in blue tabards standing next to Regelians in red seemed odd. However, at the same time, it testified of Lantrelia's unity against the Fury.

The bunker on the Regelian side of the border station rose into view ahead of him. He slowed his horse to a walk and one of the Wall-Guards, hearing his approach, stepped from his place at the edge. The other guard stayed where he was, facing the Fury. No part of the Barrier Wall was ever left unwatched. The swirling storm could spawn a wave of monsters without warning and send them toward any part of the Wall. Some places were more frequently attacked, warranting heavier guard. Yet, each section of the Wall had horns and fires to light should an attack come, signaling for reinforcements from more fortified positions.

The Regelian men were handsome soldiers, with long brown hair, brown eyes, and coppery skin that was common in their people. The Stormgardians, on the other hand, were taller and stronger than the Regelians, with black or gray hair and paler skin.

Kaven approached the Wall-Guard, who rested his spear on his shoulder and stepped up to Kaven's side.

"Made someone angry, eh, lad?" the guard asked good-naturedly, a smile peeking through his grizzled beard.

Kaven returned the smile. No one from Regelia really enjoyed journeying into Stormgarde. Not only was the kingdom's Wall bluff and aesthetically discordant, but the people tended to be as well. Stormgarde was a kingdom that had focused on military power and might for so long that they had forgotten how to be . . . pleasant. True, they produced the greatest warriors in all of Lantrelia, but it would be nice if they had some manners.

"Just doing my duty, sir," Kaven said. "I have a message to take to Stormgarde City. It's not military. I'm technically off duty."

"Hmm . . . supposed to be off duty, but on a mission. That's dedication," said the guard.

"I don't know about that, sir. Could be I'm just a pushover."

The guard's smile revealed a hint of teeth. He looked out to the Fury and the storm band in the distance. It was still far out, rumbling with distant threats.

"Pushover or not, you've got a fair amount of courage, son. Coming out on the Wall with a band headed this way. And into Stormgarde, to boot. Real guts. And you can stop that 'sir' business—the name's Kresler."

Kaven glanced at the sky ahead. Lost in his thoughts, he hadn't noticed that it was looming closer. There was still a chance it would dissipate—the bands came and went so quickly. It would be best to avoid any possibility of lightning, but he had a mission to accomplish and he was supposed to complete it with all speed.

"Sure you don't want to lie up here for a while?" asked Kresler.

Kaven cast one look at the protective interior of the guard hut. Then, fixing his eyes on the horizon, he shook his head determinedly. *I must do this quickly,* he thought. He wanted to start his new opportunity as soon as possible.

Shaking his head in return, the guard turned and began to walk to the Stormgardian side of the border station. "Well, let's get this over with, then."

The Regelian border guards were not there to keep people from getting out of Regelia. They would make sure that only people with the correct credentials got in, whether from Stormgarde or the more distant kingdoms of Venedeis or Fulminos, although anyone from Fulminos would enter via the border station on the other side of Regelia, since they shared that border. There were only a handful of places that one could enter another nation legally, and this was probably the least-trafficked one. Why such security was necessary, Kaven didn't know, but it was commanded by the Church of Na'lek.

The border guards served to ensure smooth passage into the other kingdoms. Still, Kaven was slightly hesitant to approach the Stormgardians. Even though Stormgarde and Regelia had a strong trade alliance—Regelian weapons were the most sought-after in the world—that didn't stop bored soldiers from trying to make some excitement for themselves by bullying messenger boys. Kaven dismounted his horse and followed the guard to the Stormgardian border station.

The four blue-clad Wall-Guards, standing at attention, barred any advance across the border. The two in the middle faced toward Kaven and his escort while the two on either end stared into Stormgarde, watching for anyone leaving. There were two more guards on the edge of the Wall staring into the surging winds. If there was one thing Stormgarde had plenty of, it was guards. Their armor was silver, and their blue tabards showed the sigil of their kingdom. They carried rounded shields on their backs, swords at their waists, and spears in their hands.

As they drew up to the borderline, they stopped walking. There was certain to be interrogation. One of the central guards called out, "Captain, two approaching . . . Regelian side."

The door of the Stormgardian bunker opened and a burly man came out. His dress was like the others, except he had several red slashes across his tabard, just over his heart. The slashes, regardless of color, marked him a Wall-Captain. He was taller than Kaven, but not quite as tall as the other guards.

He walked to where the four guards were standing and exchanged a few words with the guard who had called him out, then he turned and began walking toward the border. As he came nearer, Kaven could see that this man had the look of a grizzled veteran. Though his thick beard was black, there were streaks of gray that stood out more distinctly than just age could allow for. This man had taken battle scars. He was an accomplished warrior.

"What brings a couple of dainty Regelian flowers out on such a fine night?" the Wall-Captain asked. In the distance, thunder boomed, and a few seconds later the sky was darkened by a pulse of lightning. It was closer now.

"The boy has a mission that's taking him to the city," Kresler said in a no-nonsense sort of way.

"If it's the boy's mission, then let him speak of it himself," said the Wall-Captain.

*I don't have time for this!* Kaven thought. He reached into his cloak, seeking the bone tube. "Look here, Captain. I have . . ."

But at that moment, the Wall-Captain burst into action, fluidly pulling his sword free from its scabbard. In less than a second, Kaven looked down to see the length of a sword extending to his throat. Kresler began to reach for his own sword, but the gruff Stormgardian growled. "You keep reaching for your sword and I'll keep pushing on mine." The sword point dug ever so slightly into the skin of Kaven's throat and he leaned back. The Stormgardian directed his gaze to Kaven's right hand, still nestled in the front of his cloak.

"Sword . . . ?" Kaven said, continuing to cringe away from the blade digging into his neck. "I don't even have a sword."

Kresler stepped in between them, placing one hand to push gently on Kaven's chest while he put his other hand firmly on the Stormgardian's sword blade to move it from Kaven's vicinity. The Wall-Captain bristled at the move but did not resist. Instead, he redirected his ire at Kresler.

"Don't you teach your messengers about border etiquette?" he asked, casting an irritated look at Kaven.

Abruptly, Kaven knew what the fuss was all about. He had been trained, but in his rush to get through, he had forgotten. One of the soldiers had even reminded him just a few minutes earlier. Whenever you were attempting to cross a border, your sword arm was supposed to remain free. It was meant to signify a peaceful approach and was mostly ceremonial, but it was still technically an expectation. And, like an idiot, he had reached into his cloak with his sword arm.

"I'm sorry, sir!" Kaven said to the guard. "We were trained. I just forgot . . ."

"You forgot?" The Wall-Captain demanded, scowling.

"Look here," said Kresler, obviously attempting to salvage a quickly deteriorating situation. "It doesn't have to be like this. The boy is obviously not a threat. He was just going to show you what he's meant to deliver."

"That's easy for you to say, but how am I supposed to know that? You Regelians can hardly be trusted. This boy could be a dire threat."

"Threat?" Kaven shouted, unable to contain himself. "How could I possibly be a threat to you?"

The Stormgardian looked him up and down, an apathetic look on his face. Then with a shake of his head and a shrug, he said, "It's true. You don't look like much, but we know your kind. Regelians are always fiddling with some experiment or another, and we won't be caught unaware."

Kresler sighed. "You've had your fun, Captain. Let him pass."

"Afraid I can't do that." The Stormgardian seemed to be containing a smile. "I'm gonna have to take him inside. He needs to answer some questions, and we'll need to check him over for hidden weapons or other threats. Now that he's made the first aggressive move, it's our right."

"I don't have time for this, Captain," Kaven said through clenched teeth.

"You'll have to make time, boy, unless you want to pay the peace tax," said the soldier.

"Peace tax?" asked Kaven.

"A monetary gift to show your goodwill to the kingdom of Stormgarde."

"You've been angling for this 'tax' the whole time, haven't you?" said Kresler, glaring at the soldier who was wearing an ugly smile.

"A soldier has to make ends meet somehow." He sneered at the Wall-Captain, lifting his palms in a half-shrug.

"How much?" asked Kresler, digging into his pocket. "I'll pay for the boy."

"Either way, as long as someone pays. One golden mark."

Kresler fished a gold coin from his pouch and flipped it to the captain, who caught it nimbly. He cast a quick glance at it before depositing it into his trouser pocket.

"Thanks, Kresler," Kaven said meekly.

"Yeah, thanks, Kresler," said the Wall-Captain, grinning more widely. "Come on, boy. Time for the most dangerous part of your journey." He stepped to the side, gesturing with his sword.

Kaven began to move past the Stormgardian Wall-Captain, but he heard Kresler whisper, "Watch your back," and thought better of it. He fell in beside the man, who set the pace as they walked to the Stormgardian side of the border station. As they neared the far side, the Wall-Captain broke away from Kaven to talk with the waiting guards. Kaven took the opportunity to mount his horse, checking the saddle and tack before mounting, just as he had been trained.

From the side, he heard the guards break into laughter.

"A full mark?" one of them said, loudly.

"You sure took them good, Captain," said another, laughing and pounding the back of his officer.

"I told you. It was easy as crushing a grannoc," said the Wall-Captain. "Now pay up. My mug needs filling."

Each of the guards dug into their pockets and handed what were presumably coins to the captain.

*Great. Nothing like being the laughingstock. Glad I made a good first impression.* Shaking his head, Kaven continued into the approaching storm.

# NINE

*"Only in Shilanti is there peace. In Lantrelia, we will all be broken. We will all die."*

—From the Tomes of Regret, Verse 15 of Sorrow

THE WIND WHIPPED through Kaven's hair and caused his cloak to billow behind him as he rode. Unfortunately, these effects were not due to the intense speed with which he was riding, as he had not been able to achieve more than a quick walk since his entry into Stormgarde. No . . . the storm was picking up, and he was moving slower than ever.

His slow pace was due to the configuration of the Barrier Wall. Whereas Regelia's Wall was wide and spacious, an effective thoroughfare for the nation's military, the Stormgardian's maintained a Wall lined with obstacles, to prevent would-be invaders from making quick progress into the kingdom proper. There were stone barricades staggered every thirty paces, alternating from the right to the left sides. Each barricade was topped with a wooden panel, and each panel was lined with long spikes to prevent an opposing force from climbing over the barricade.

As it passed through Kaven's homeland, the Wall was a thing of beauty—from the intricately designed parapets, to the smooth, painted pavement, to the technologically advanced Firerods with their access holes—it was impressive to behold. The Wall of Stormgarde, though still impressive, was plain due to the utilitarian approach of design. The crenellations were blocky. The sides of the wall were rough and uneven. The floor was marred with gaps and crevices where the stone had been chipped away. Certain spots bore signs of construction, but it was obvious that there had been no concern with making the repairs look seamless. How could a people take pride in a thing that was so carelessly maintained?

Kaven slowed his horse as he passed one of the stone barricades to get a better look at the construction. He noticed that there were hinges on either side of the wooden panel, presumably used to raise the lid, pointing the spikes in the direction of an oncoming force. He thought such a thing was unnecessary, especially when Firerods were involved.

Each of the Four Kingdoms had its own specialty. Stormgarde was known for perfecting the art of war, even if they lacked the technological advantages harnessed by the other kingdoms. However, for a less-advanced people, the traps were ingenious. Kaven could recognize and respect that.

Stormgardians trained for war at an early age. Their battle schools began accepting students when they were only five or six years old. The only criteria for admission was the ability to obey. If a child could understand orders and follow them without question, they were considered ready for training.

Because of this, many in Regelia believed that they were an uneducated lot. Kaven's mother was particularly scornful, often claiming that the only Stormgardians who could read or write were those in politics. That was probably nonsense, of course.

Kaven didn't have as much exposure to the other two kingdoms in Lantrelia. Regelia and Stormgarde had many dealings with each other, but his knowledge of Venedeis and Fulminos was much more cursory, obtained through classes at the college rather than experience. He had seen Venedecians plenty of times in Redwind; they had a love of learning that rivaled Regelians, but he hadn't ever spoken to one. Fulminites were a lot less common in the city, as they preferred their own kingdom to visiting foreign lands like Regelia. Haz was the only Fulminite Kaven had ever met.

Fulminos was a kingdom entrenched in espionage, stealth, and the art of politics. They had little time for science or magic, and even cared little for the Wall, though they still did their part to defend it. Fulminos was also the only kingdom in Lantrelia not to be governed by a single person—but rather by a secret group of individuals known as the Council of Shadows. Before the Council was formed, kings had ruled openly, but the political figures of the kingdom grew greedy, and it was from this lust for power that the Dagger Wars had begun, bathing Fulminos in blood. Yet from the ashes of war the Council had grown, quelling the conflicts scattered across the kingdom with a shadowed hand. Now they ruled in secret, their judgments delivered by officials known as Dark Executors.

Kaven was intrigued by such a system of government. Could you trust rulers who never showed their faces, never revealed their names? He remembered asking one of teachers how one became a member of the Council of Shadows if it was such a secret organization. His teacher hadn't been able to tell him. Fulminos hid its secrets from the other three kingdoms, and perhaps that was necessary. The Dagger Wars, though five hundred years gone, still served to frighten the people of Fulminos with threats of its return.

Where Fulminos was a nation of secrets and quiet sub-terfuge, Venedeis brandished its trade boldly for all the world to see. The kingdom's magic arts were complex and wonderful to behold. The people of Venedeis wanted everyone to see and marvel at them . . . and they *were* marvelous, there was no denying that. Venedeis produced the strongest sorcerers in all of Lantrelia, and they accomplished magical feats that even the greatest Regelian scientist couldn't even begin to comprehend. Venedeis was ruled by a queen, much like Regelia, but also had four advisors known as the High-Mages. These four individuals were the most powerful sorcerers alive.

Kaven often wished that he was a sorcerer. His grand-mother had been able to touch the magic deep within Lantrelia, though she hadn't been powerful. No other member of the Fortis family had any magic in their blood.

He didn't know much about magic, though he knew it was a thing of Na'lek. The priests often spoke of it in their sermons, how the sorcerers carried a bloodline that came from a time before the Fury. The priests speculated that once, long ago, every person had been able to cast spells to some degree. But ever since Na'lek had sent his Fury, magic was slowly dying out, weakening from generation to generation. It was yet another punishment for humanity's sins.

A crash of thunder jolted Kaven out of his reverie. The violet clouds flickered black and his horse reared slightly. Kaven expertly reined him in and pointed him forward, but as he looked to the sky, he felt the blood drain from his face. The storm band had moved in close. Too close. The black and violet thunderheads dominated the sky above him, surging and churning with unspeakable power. At any second, the light-ning would fall.

Kaven looked around for a bunker. The Regelian Wall had them spaced frequently along the Wall for just such an

emergency, but there was nothing but barricades and crenellations on this wall. *Fury-cursed Stormgardians and their mis-
guided bravery.* They probably thought it was the epitome of
courage to set their teeth against the lightning and spit in the
face of the Fury. *Stupid.*

The band was moving toward him. He couldn't turn
around and run away. The Eternal Storm was faster than he,
and it would chase him east, prolonging his exposure to the
storm. He needed to try and move through it. It would be
quicker that way, safer. *Na'lek, shelter me,* Kaven thought, *and
give these Stormgardians the sense to build decent protection.* With
a wary eye watching the roiling clouds above, Kaven shivered
and kicked his horse forward.

Kaven would have liked to have said that his heart pounded in
time with his horse's hoofbeats. Unfortunately, his horse had to
keep slowing down to pass the cursed obstacle boxes along the
Wall. Meanwhile, his heart felt like it was relentlessly attempting to escape from the confines of his rib cage. This part of
the Wall would take an infernally long time for invaders to
conquer, but finding freedom from a rogue storm band was
proving equally difficult.

The thunder and lightning were coming almost on top of
each other—causing Kaven's horse to pull at the reins to escape
the sensory overload. A streak of black lightning struck a catapult propped up against the edge of the Wall. The entirety of
the wooden weapon disintegrated. There was no smoke or fire;
it was simply gone.

Kaven tried not to imagine what would happen to him
if he were struck. He looked for a guard, wondering what
their orders were during a storm band. But he didn't see any
Wall-Guards. Weren't there supposed to be hundreds of soldiers

in Stormgarde's Wall-Guard? Where were they? How did the Stormgardians guard against invasion with no guards stationed along the Wall? He shook his head as he pulled his horse close to the edge of the Wall overlooking the Fields in order to go around another contraption. It certainly seemed like an opportunity for disaster. Perhaps his father would have some insight when he got . . . *CRACK!*

Thunder rang around him. His horse screamed abruptly as the world shook and darkness enveloped them. Kaven suddenly knew how the clapper inside a bell felt. He reacted as quickly as possible to gain control of his horse. He pulled the reins back—hard—but they were suddenly yanked from his hands. Before he could register the strangeness of this, Kaven became aware that he was falling off his horse. Panic blanketed his mind as he felt a jolting pain in his knees—followed quickly by his elbows—as he crashed to the ground and continued to skid forward, crashing into one of the hinged barricades.

Kaven scrambled into as tight a ball as he could manage as another bolt of lightning struck the Wall directly in front of him. A chunk disappeared leaving a jagged rend in the stonework. Looking back, he saw a much larger gap in the Wall. With a groan, he stood, using the crenellation for support as he peered over the side. His horse was there, sprawled at the base of the Wall. The lightning had torn away the stones they had been walking on, leaving the horse to fall to its demise below. It was a wonder that Kaven hadn't been taken with it.

*CRACK!* Another bolt of lightning drilled into the crenellation directly in front of him—the one he was leaning against. It gave way with a groan, remnants spilling to the ground far below. Kaven shifted his balance just in time to keep from suffering a similar demise, momentarily blinded by the darkness. His ears were ringing. He dared not move . . . he dared not stay where he was. What could he do? He was experiencing the full force of the Fury, enduring the storm just as it had been intended to be, suffering for the sins of his forebearers. Na'lek was neither just nor holy. He was vindictive and cruel, and he would pluck Kaven from Lantrelia as carelessly as a man pulls away a bothersome flea.

"Na'lek! Help me!" Kaven cried out, as the lightning struck yet again. The swirling violet clouds glared down at him, like Na'lek's unrelenting eye, watching him perish.

"Please! I don't want to die! Help me!"

Over the cacophony, Kaven heard a faint *whoosh* followed by what sounded like hundreds of voices joined in anticipation. The ground around him was enveloped in what looked like the shadow of a man, and suddenly he felt himself being lifted from the ground. Were those hands grabbing his arms? What was happening? He began to struggle, tearing at the hands that held him. He was being pulled backward. First up, then down . . . and he struggled.

He quickly grabbed for his shortsword and the hands on his arms released him. Jarring pain followed, over and over again . . . and then there was only darkness.


"You should have left him out there to die," Kaven heard a rough voice say. He was in a comfortable bed, layered in several blankets. His head felt like it had been used to sound the war horns.

"Always you seek the hard course," said another voice, rich and deep.

"And always you seek the noble one. When has it ever given you something in return?"

Kaven opened one eye narrowly, to merely a slit, and peered at his surroundings. He was in a small, rectangular room with a fairly low roof. Assorted weapons decorated most of the wood-paneled walls, and a single bookshelf with several books sat next to the bed. On the other side of the room, a fireplace was crackling merrily with two men seated in armchairs beside it.

One of the men stood from his chair to stir a pot hanging over the fire. "Nobility is not about what you might receive from an action. It is about seeing a need and meeting it. Your failure to understand this is what has kept you from further promotion, my old friend." The man stirring the pot glanced to his companion. Kaven couldn't see either man clearly. The shadows from the fire caused them to be silhouetted forms against the far wall. The other man cleared his throat roughly. Kaven decided that he would rather not continue his eavesdropping and be caught in the middle of an uncomfortable conversation.

Preparing himself for the worst, he turned over on his bed and released a groan suitable for a person just waking from a sound sleep. At least, that's how it started. As he moved, he suddenly realized how much pain he was truly in, and his groaning swelled even as he attempted to cover the burning agony in his bones and muscles.

"Ah, our charge awakens, Kralak!" said the man standing over the fire. He strode over to the bed, a smile of concern becoming clear on his face as he emerged from the shadow of the fire and into the light of the torches hanging on sconces on this side of the room.

As the man drew nearer, Kaven could see he was an older man. His mostly gray hair was peppered with black and his face was covered with wrinkles. No . . . those were scars. They made him look much older than he likely was. He was dressed in an off-duty officer's tunic of the Stormgardian army—blue with gold embroidery—but no rank was visible. The man in the armchair didn't move.

"How are you feeling?" the approaching officer asked.

"My body feels like it's been trampled by a herd of Bouncers," Kaven mumbled through gritted teeth.

The officer's smile went from one of concern to genuine humor. That simple change seemed to erase most of the scars from the man's face and shed a dozen years from his apparent age. He laughed. "That's usually how a person feels when his horse falls out from under him and he slides into a spike barricade while charging through a storm band. Titan's teeth, boy, I dread to think what would have happened if we hadn't pulled you to safety."

The rough voice from the armchair spoke up. "Not to mention, he bounced down a flight of stairs as you pulled him to safety. That's bound to account for a great deal of the bruising and swelling."

Kaven looked up at the officer in confusion.

The officer shrugged apologetically. "It's true. When I began pulling down, you struggled and started reaching for your sword. I lost my grip and you sort of . . . slipped. I feel bad for that, but it's still better than the lightning."

"Where am I?" Kaven asked.

The officer blanched, suddenly apologetic. "I'm sorry. Where are my manners? My name is Gorshol and these are my quarters. Though they are small, I figured it would be the most restful place for you to recover."

Kaven thought he recognized that name. Hadn't he heard it somewhere recently?

"You're being modest again." The figure in the armchair stood up.

Gorshol cut him off. "Modesty has nothing to do with this, Kralak. Bring a cup of tea over for our young friend. It should be ready now."

Kralak moved to obey, not reluctantly, but with the snap and polish Kaven had heard the Stormgardian soldiers possessed. As Kralak brought the tea over, Kaven was surprised to see that he was even older than Gorshol—with many more scars, if that was possible. The frown wrinkles around his mouth made it easy to assume that Kralak rarely smiled. His snowy white hair was pulled back in a tail at the back of his head. His tunic was similar to Gorshol's except the gold embroidery was not nearly as fine.

"The boy shouldn't be here," Kralak said, handing the tea to Gorshol who passed it to Kaven.

Kaven accepted the tea from Gorshol readily and took a large swallow. He smiled. "Thank you, Captain."

Kralak sputtered, his eyes wide with surprise. "Captain? Captain! Boy, this man is no mere Wall-Captain!"

Gorshol put a hand on Kralak's shoulder. "It's all right. Let it be."

But Kralak shrugged his hand off. "Boy, you are in the presence of War-Leader Devin Gorshol, Matchless of Stormgarde!"

Kaven—who had been sipping his tea at the time of this announcement—nearly spilled the hot liquid down his chest. *War-Leader! Matchless!* Kaven was stunned. Stormgarde was a nation where rank was far more important in a man's life than his own breath. Ranks were either achieved through success on the battlefield or through a special system of dueling. The title of Matchless, the rarest and most coveted of monikers, was bestowed on warriors of unsurpassed skill who successfully won two hundred duels. Consecutively. Matchless were honored by all Four Kingdoms and were respected as Lantrelia's greatest swordsmen. The only other way to claim the title was to defeat a Matchless in a formal duel in which you could take their title for yourself.

Gorshol's first title, though not as notable, was far more important. He was the War-Leader, and that meant that he was the commander of the entirety of Stormgarde's military, overseer of the kingdom's entire portion of the Barrier Wall, and second only to the king and his regent-lord. Forget meeting Zealots, this man was far more impressive!

"Who I am is hardly important to this situation," Gorshol said.

"Not that important?" Kaven said, his voice cracking embarrassingly. He continued unabated. "It's amazing! I've never met a Matchless before. And you're the War-Leader too?"

"He commands the Wall from the border of Regelia to Venedeis," said Kralak. "He leads both the Wall-Guard and Stormgarde's army."

Gorshol nodded. "Though I'm hardly ever needed elsewhere in the kingdom. I rarely even go into Stormgarde City anymore."

Kaven bolted up in bed, wincing at the pain in his back and sides, only now remembering his mission. In his excitement of meeting one of the most powerful men in Lantrelia, his assignment from Gane seemed pale in comparison. Yet he quickly remembered its importance. "Stormgarde City! I need to get there as quickly as possible."

Gorshol calmly attempted to ease Kaven back into a resting posture. "Easy, my friend. Stormgarde City isn't going anywhere. It will still be there when you're rested and ready to travel."

Kaven shook off Gorshol's hand, not in an unfriendly way, but still with some force. Kralak's eyebrows seemed to climb up his forehead. "You don't understand," Kaven insisted. "There's someone waiting for me there. I have a message that I have to deliver quickly."

"Ahh, I see. A mission, is it?" said Gorshol, nodding appreciatively. "Never let it be said that I have stood between a man and his mission. An important quest should not be delayed." He pursed his lips thoughtfully, pulling at the lower one with two of his fingers. "Unfortunately, you've been unconscious for several hours. And I don't know if you are in any condition to continue on the Wall alone."

Kaven sighed. Would Gane's messenger still be waiting for him? How much time had passed? "I really should be going, sir. I've wasted too much time already."

Gorshol frowned. "As I said, you shouldn't be traveling alone so close to the Fury. You must allow Kralak and I to escort you."

Kralak looked up from pouring himself a cup of tea. "What?" he demanded. "Sir, I heartily object to this waste of time when . . ."

"It won't take us long, Kralak. We'll be back within the hour. Besides the storm band, the Fury has been quiet today. I'm sure Stormgarde can survive without us for that short period of time. Regardless, I need to travel toward the Storm-Gate anyway. The Wall-Captain there perished less than an hour ago."

Kralak scowled. "Permission to speak freely, sir?"

"When has that ever stopped you, my old friend?" Gorshol said, throwing a smile in his direction.

Kralak gave a not-so-subtle nod toward Kaven. "Present company is making this conversation difficult, sir."

Gorshol nodded in understanding. "You may speak openly, Kralak. I'm sure . . ." Gorshol trailed off, directing the conversation toward Kaven with an apologetic smile. "I just realized I introduced myself, but we still don't know your name."

"It's Kaven, War-Leader," he said, and feeling that wasn't quite enough information, he added, "from Regelia." After seeing Zealot Stonearm's reaction to his family name, he decided that he didn't want this encounter to be overshadowed by his father.

"It's nice to meet you, Kaven from Regelia," the Matchless said. "And please, call me Gorshol. As I was saying, Kralak, I'm sure that Kaven will be amenable to keeping this conversation private, if you so desire."

"Sir, I have no desire to see this boy ride topside to the Fury when he might be injured." Kralak spoke the words quickly, as if eager to have them out of his mouth. "But the Regent-Lord clearly stated that no one can . . ."

"So, Lord Benehain is the source of your worry," Gorshol interrupted, waving a hand dismissively and turning toward a small writing desk in the corner of the room. "I should have thought of that myself. The Underwall will not be a problem."

"How will that not be a problem? That is the core of the problem," Kralak said.

"What's the Underwall?" Kaven asked.

"It's a secret . . . you shouldn't even know it exists," Kralak growled under his breath.

"Be at ease, friend," said Gorshol. Seating himself at the desk, he picked up a writing-spear and began writing with quick, decisive strokes. "Technically, we've already broken the Regent-Lord's command just by bringing him here. You don't fix a breached wall mid battle—you just defend it until the threat is gone."

"I won't tell anyone about anything I'm not supposed to," said Kaven.

Gorshol folded up the finished note and walked over to his wardrobe. From within, he withdrew a blue cloak and walked over to Kaven.

"What are you doing, sir?" asked Kralak, a hint of unease in his voice. It seemed so strange to hear that tone coming from a person with such a dominating presence.

"Nothing that will do any harm if we do it right. Stand up, lad," Gorshol said. He threw the cloak around Kaven's shoulders and fastened it with a brooch he pulled out of his pocket. The brooch was in the shape of a shield, a raised fist rising across the center. Gorshol handed him the letter. "Put that in your pocket. Do not lose it. If anyone questions your identity, show them the letter. When you arrive in Stormgarde City, destroy it." Turning to Kralak, he added, "See that it's done."

Kralak saluted. "It will be." He looked angry.

Gorshol nodded, smiling. "Kaven, you have just been made the personal envoy of War-Leader Devin Gorshol—a post that will make you the envy of many Stormgardian soldiers . . . and one that would never be granted to an outsider. Many of my own soldiers have applied for this position, but I have not yet found one worthy. You will be scrutinized and judged by any soldier you meet. Wear it well!"

"I don't know why all of this is necessary," Kaven said. "Once we're on the Wall, there won't be anyone to tell. I haven't seen a single guard since I crossed the border."

Gorshol ushered him to the door, which he pulled open with a flourish. "I would venture to say your experience won't be the same going forward."

Looking through the open door, Kaven was shocked by what he saw in the hallway outside.

Dozens of soldiers moved about with military efficiency. Lone soldiers carried messages or ran errands. Groups of soldiers marched in troop formations. When the three of them stepped out into the wide corridor, none of the soldiers appeared to notice, but Kaven was certain the messengers moved a little more quickly and the troops' backs became slightly straighter at the appearance of their War-Leader.

Even though he was wearing the Stormgardian colors, Kaven felt exposed in the cloak and the insignia. He couldn't help but feel like the passing soldiers were looking at him out of the corner of their eyes. Who was this youth who had received the honor and commendation of their champion and leader? Kaven stepped slightly to the side and behind Gorshol.

"Don't hide, boy," Kralak growled at him.

"He's right, lad. What sets a Stormgardian apart is our arrogance. If you are going to be successful at this masquerade, you must wear the costume proudly."

Kaven stepped up and to Gorshol's right. Now that he was over his initial shock at being thrust into the midst of a Stormgardian encampment, he took the time to inspect his surroundings. The hallway he was in seemed to stretch interminably to the left and the right. The walls and ceiling—even the floor—were constructed with massive granite stones.

"Are we . . . inside the Barrier Wall?" Kaven asked, a hint of wonder in his voice.

"Indeed, we are," said Gorshol, "and you may be the first outsider to ever be permitted a glimpse at the actual depth of our defensive perimeter."

"This is amazing," Kaven said. "Is this why I never encountered any soldiers on the Wall after the border station?"

"We try to avoid the tops of the Wall unless we have to defend against a wave of Fury-spawn," Gorshol explained. "The spike barricades serve a dual purpose in that they open in either direction to help defend against offensive assaults on the Wall, but they also contain stepladders from within the wall to allow easy access to the surface."

"You're going to give away everything?" Kralak asked, displeasure plain on his grizzled face.

Gorshol glanced at his disgruntled friend and sighed. "Kralak, you know that I do not believe in keeping secrets from the other kingdoms. Regelia and Stormgarde have bickered for too long. We are all allies in the Eternal War, yes?" He shook his head. "But perhaps Lantrelia is not yet ready for complete unity. Kaven, it is important that you don't share what you see here with anyone. The Underwall is a closely guarded secret."

"I won't tell anyone," Kaven promised.

"That's good enough for me," Gorshol said with a smile. "Now, let's go see about finding a horse you can borrow to complete your quest."

Doors lined both sides of the hallway and there were signs above each door with distinct red lettering. The door directly opposite them was labeled clearly—"Stables." Kaven began moving in that direction, but Kralak took hold of his arm and pulled him to the right and into the stream of soldiers.

"This way to the stables, boy."

Kaven looked back at the labeled sign in confusion.

Gorshol looked back and chuckled. "We mislabel the signs to deter invaders from disrupting our supply chain effectively in the event of a raid."

"You really are going to tell him everything," Kralak mumbled.

Kaven looked up at Gorshol. "I don't understand."

"Our signs are written in code," Gorshol said, ignoring Kralak completely. "If you had gone into the room labeled 'Stables,' you would have found a barracks full of resting soldiers."

"Resting . . . but ready at a moment's notice for a fight," Kralak corrected, seeming somehow offended.

"The horses are kept here," Gorshol pointed ahead to a door with the word "Latrine" above it.

Kaven smiled at the genius, but frowned an instant later when he realized the implication.

"But the Fury-spawn can't read," he said.

"They can speak, can't they?" Kralak retorted. "Who knows what power Na'lek can give them?"

Gorshol nodded. "He's right, Kaven. Stormgarde has often found it necessary to be prepared for any form of attack. I believe that the Fury is constantly changing, probing us for weaknesses and growing stronger. We must be vigilant."

Once inside, Gorshol had a young stable hand prepare a sturdy-looking mare for Kaven to ride. "This is Stormdancer; she has been my horse for many years. She's from the Isles of Stars, and a champion's blood runs through her veins. She may be getting old now, but she'll carry you all the way to Stormgarde City." The Matchless ran a hand through the horse's rough black mane.

Kaven hoisted himself into the saddle, patting the mare's neck. Stormdancer whinnied appreciatively.

"This is where I leave you," Gorshol said. "Keep riding until you come to the dead end. There's a gate that will let you out, and the road to the city is right outside. If anyone questions you, simply show them the papers I gave you. Kralak will see to it that you depart safely. Now, where exactly are you delivering this message?"

"An inn called the Widow's Hope," Kaven replied.

Gorshol smiled. "Perfect. Leave Stormdancer there, and I'll send someone to retrieve her. Unfortunately, you'll be on your own for the return trip."

"I can manage," Kaven said. "Thank you for your assistance, sir. I'll never forget it."

"It was my pleasure, Kaven," the War-Leader replied. "Take care."

With a final wave to the Matchless, Kaven flicked Stormdancer's reins and brought the horse to a trot. Kralak rode beside him at a brisk pace, mouth shut and expression grim. As he rode the rest of the way through the Underwall, soldiers cleared a path for him. No one tried to stop him; one glimpse of his insignia cut off any remarks or complaints, though the insignia earned him a few unpleasant stares. Kaven wondered if his skin, which was a shade darker than most Stormgardians, would arouse suspicion. However, it wasn't uncommon for men of all kingdoms to join Stormgarde's military, rather than their own, to receive superior training.

He felt cramped in the confines of the Underwall on his horse, especially with the silent Kralak riding nearby, and he mumbled apologies to the men and women he inconvenienced. At the slower pace, it took Kaven an hour but he did at last reach a point where the tunnel suddenly ended. A wooden gate was installed in the side of the Wall, and after showing two guards his paper, they opened it for him.

Kaven was surprised by the brevity of the trip. A journey from Redwind to Stormgarde City would take several hours by riding. Gorshol had said he'd been unconscious for some time. They must have moved him farther through the Wall during that time.

He rode out into a mighty gust of wind, blinking at the sudden assault of cold gusts. Looking upward, he could see violet clouds boiling overhead. The Fury was reaching far over the Wall today. Thunder rumbled in the distance, the herald of lightning to come. Not wanting to lose another horse to the Eternal Storm, Kaven kicked Stormdancer into a gallop across the hard-packed earth. In the distance, he could see the walls of Stormgarde City rising high against a blue sky. Beyond that, the sun slowly sank toward the horizon, reluctantly giving way to the night.

The ride to the city was much shorter than the path through the Underwall, as Stormgarde City had been built close to the Barrier Wall. It was much closer to the Wall than Redwind was. Typical Stormgardians. After a ten-minute ride, he crossed the gate that spanned the moat around the city and rode in. The gates wouldn't be closed until the sun had set fully.

Kralak cleared his throat and rode close. His voice was a low growl. "You are not to speak of the Underwall to anyone. Understand?"

"Yes, sir."

Kralak snatched the papers Gorshol had given Kaven and gestured toward the city. "Off with you, then."

Kaven rode away without a second glance, and he was immediately greeted by a crowd of people filling cobblestone streets between square, utilitarian stone buildings, all of which were only a single story in height. Taller buildings, of course, led to increased risk of lightning strikes.

Stormgarde City was massive. It was far larger and more widespread than Redwind could ever hope to be. Though it lacked the crimson banners of his home, the structures were built the same way. The city stretched so far westward that some of the buildings had two stories, as they were far enough away from the Fury that it never touched them.

Slowly, he navigated through the masses of Stormgardian citizens, all of whom only parted for him with begrudging mutters. He couldn't recall exactly where he was supposed to go, so he asked a passerby for directions to Victory Square, and the man pointed him toward the center of the city.

He slowly made his way to the center, and he saw what was undeniably Lantrelia's greatest trophy. Victory Square was a circular intersection between four major streets, and it was surrounded by many different businesses, all proudly painted blue and gold. Six poles rose from the streets, each adorned with the banner of Stormgarde. Yet the true wonder was in the center of Victory Square. Perched atop a massive stone slab was a massive skull larger than Gorshol's horse, yellowed with age but still fearsome.

The Destroyer's skull was positioned with its wide jaws agape, long fangs sharpened to razor points. The skull was serpentine, like some giant viper. Kaven didn't know if the Destroyer had actually been a snake, but regardless, he was quite grateful that he had not been in Stormgarde three hundred years ago when the Destroyer had come. The Titan had slaughtered thousands before finally being killed.

Shuddering in the presence of such ancient power, Kaven turned away from the skull and looked for the Widow's Hope. *There!* He saw a weathered old building with a large sign that had the name scrawled in bold golden paint. The inn appeared sturdy despite its obvious age, and the yard was well-maintained and the soft glow coming from the lights seemed welcoming. He steered Stormdancer into the inn's yard and gave the horse to a scrawny boy to stable.

Kaven grinned to himself as he stepped into the inn. *I did it,* he thought proudly. *I braved the Fury and made it to Stormgarde City!*

The Widow's Hope was a cheery place. Loud, raucous Stormgardians sat at smooth wooden tables and laughed over tankards of beer. A hearth blazed merrily near where a young woman played a lively tune on the flute. Kaven eyed the beers disdainfully. Nothing could compare to a vintage Regelian wine.

He brought the sealed tube out of his cloak and began looking around the common room. Kaven had no idea what the recipient of his message would look like. *Headmaster Gane said he'd know me,* he thought. *I hope he's still here.*

At that moment, he heard a voice. "Ah, you are my messenger."

He turned to see a woman coming toward him. She was tall and pale, with curled black hair and a regal expression, dressed in a silken blue dress. "My name is Lyra."

Kaven frowned. "Headmaster Gane said I'd be meeting with a man."

Lyra's stoic expression dissolved into a wry smirk. "Typical graybeard. That's his idea of a joke. The poor man's humor died with his youth. Well, are you ready?"

Kaven held out the sealed tube. "Here's your message."

*Ready for what?*

"Oh, that?" The woman snatched the tube and broke the seal. She pulled out the message and unrolled it. Kaven saw that the parchment was blank. "There is no message," she said, crumpling the paper. "Do you really think that's why Gane sent you here? Follow me."

"Why am I here, then?" Kaven asked distrustfully. But Lyra didn't reply, instead heading to the stairs that led down toward the bedrooms. He didn't like going underground, but in Stormgarde City where the Fury was such a constant threat, rooms needed to be beneath the ground. Warily, Kaven followed her.

# TEN

*"The Fury is but a foretaste of what is coming. The Day of Reckoning shall be the final culling."*

—From the Tomes of Regret, Verse 100 of Power

"WE ARE THE Deliverance," Lyra said as they descended, disregarding his question.

"Okay . . ." Kaven followed the woman as they stepped into a long hallway. "What's the Deliverance?"

Lyra glanced back at him, a pensive look on her face. "The Deliverance was formed to put an end to the Fury. We believe that humanity can be redeemed from Na'lek's rage and end this Eternal War."

"You want to bring about the Day of Reckoning?" Kaven asked, aghast. The day would be an apocalyptic final battle. Thousands would die before the war finally ended.

"No." Lyra sounded amused. "The Deliverance wants a peaceful resolution to this conflict."

Kaven frowned. "The Tomes of Regret clearly state that the only end is through the Day of Reckoning."

"Perhaps you do not know as much about the Tomes of Regret as you think," Lyra said.

Kaven was silent a moment, knowing that she was right. "Why haven't I heard of the Deliverance before?" he asked.

"There are many who would find our beliefs foreign," she replied. "Like yourself, they have a literal view of Na'lek but are unwilling to pursue different solutions to the Fury. We have another interpretation. As a people, we have fought the Eternal Storm for thousands of years, and nothing has changed. For Na'lek to display his vast mercy, it is we who must first alter our ways." Lyra looked back at him again, eyes narrowed. "And there are other reasons for secrecy. Some men profit from the Eternal War, and they would go to great lengths to protect the Fury. The Deliverance would have enemies among these fools."

Kaven wondered what kind of men would protect the storm. He couldn't imagine another human using such terrible means for gain. The thought of it made him shudder, as if Na'lek's gaze were on his back.

They finally reached the end of the hall and came to a wide, gray, featureless room. Two torches hung on the walls, only partially lighting the area. Kaven couldn't see any kinds of furnishings. Why would an inn need a room like this?

Three figures stood in the room's center. They wore voluminous white robes with cowls drawn over their faces. Something glinted in the folds of their robes. Knives? Kaven hesitated at the room's threshold, suddenly fearful.

"Why are they here?" he asked nervously.

"Don't worry," she said calmly. "They're here to protect you."

"From what?"

Lyra took his hand and guided him into the room. "As I said, the Deliverance has enemies."

Kaven tried to watch all three of the robed guards at once. Titan's teeth, what had Gane mixed him up in? "What do you want from me?"

STORM OF FURY, WINDS OF LEGEND


"We'll get to that," Lyra said. "But first, you must meet your companions."

"My companions?"

Even as he spoke, Kaven heard footsteps coming up the hall behind him. A fourth robed figure strode into the room, taking position at the edge of the wall.

Following behind the figure came a dark-skinned youth. He wore a black leather suit and had six knives strapped to his waist, along with a second belt with dozens of small pouches. His head and face were shaven, and his gray eyes locked onto Kaven immediately, appraising and then dismissing him in the time it took to blink. He wasn't any older than Kaven but was certainly taller and stronger. His jaw was thick, his nose was small and square, and his lips were turned down in a grim frown.

Kaven studied him carefully, confident that he knew this man's profession, not that it helped settle his nerves. The Kingdom of Fulminos trained the best assassins in Lantrelia. Judging by his garb and disposition, this Fulminite was a master of subterfuge and stealth. Kaven was instantly wary of him.

Kaven looked back to the stairwell as someone else came into the room, led by a second guard. A short girl poked her head into the room, looking left and right before stepping in. She wore a white dress that looked a tad too big for her. She had waist-length red hair and big, dark eyes that studied both men with a timid gaze. She smiled shyly in greeting and went to stand out of the way.

Kaven's first impression of the woman was that she was pretty. Her pale skin seemed to glow in the torchlight, her face was youthful and bright, and her figure was full and appealing. She looked younger than either Kaven or the Fulminite. She was a Venedecian, judging by her long hair and pale complexion. Kaven wondered if she was a sorceress. What if he only thought she was pretty because he was under an enchantment? He edged away from her.

Once again, footsteps resonated from the hall, and they all turned toward the door where another guard entered the room, leading a second woman. Where the Venedecian was small and wiry, this woman was stout and strong. With her black hair tied back in a short bun, and adorned in the gray and blue armor of her homeland, the woman possessed the air of a soldier. A highly trained and experienced soldier. Another distinguishing characteristic, at least in Kaven's mind, was that she was *beautiful*. The sorceress was pretty, but this young woman was stunning. Everything about her seemed perfect, from the proud way she wore her armor to her tanned skin and flawless features. She studied them all with an imperious gaze.

Kaven watched blankly as they took each other in. The assassin gave them each a judging look, the sorceress watched with curiosity, and the Stormgardian seemed disdainful.

"Hello!" the sorceress said suddenly, and the sudden noise caused Kaven to jump. Her voice was clipped and hurried, as if she didn't have enough time to say everything that needed to be said. "My name is Tasi'a! Who are you?"

"Uh, Kaven," he replied awkwardly.

The Fulminite could've been a statue, if not for the gruff sound of his voice. "Toyon."

"I am Shera Lacer," the beautiful woman declared, her voice surprisingly arrogant. "My sword belongs to Stormgarde."

Kaven frowned, unsure of what to make of the proclamation. Stormgardians certainly were an odd lot.

Tasi'a didn't seem fazed. "It's a pleasure to meet you all," she said, beaming.

Lyra's voice put an end to any further conversation. "There will be time for introductions, but now we must speak. I'm sure you are eager to know why you're here. The Deliverance has an important task that requires completion, and the four of you have been chosen because you share a similar quality: failure."

Kaven decided that he didn't like this Lyra person. What right did she have to call them failures? It certainly caused a stir among the others, because Toyon shifted, Shera glared openly, and Tasi'a nodded in agreement.

He wondered what kind of task needed the support of a sorceress, a soldier, an assassin and . . . well, whatever Kaven was. Certainly not a technician. Lyra hadn't made any mention of how big the Deliverance was. Perhaps they didn't have access to many resources. If he was the one being chosen for important tasks, then the Deliverance must be truly desperate.

Lyra continued, not noticing their silent responses, or not caring. "However, I believe that your failures are merely the precursors of success to come. You may think yourselves weak in the fields you have chosen, or perhaps insufficient in other aspects of life. I do not. You will have an opportunity to prove once and for all that you are not failures. And in return for your service, the Deliverance will grant you whatever you desire."

Kaven scratched his head, wondering why she was giving them a motivational speech. He still wanted to know what this task was, because now he certainly didn't want to work with these strange people. *What does she mean by anything I desire?* he wondered. *Headmaster Gane is already going to give me what I want.*

"I didn't come here to listen to encouragement, Lyra," said Toyon. "Are you going to tell us what you want from us? Or can I walk away now?"

Lyra gave Toyon a knowing smile. "This will be your last opportunity to 'walk away,' as you put it. Leave now, if you wish, or stay and prove yourselves."

Kaven considered the offer briefly, but his curiosity won out and he did not move. Nor did anyone else.

Lyra nodded once, still smiling. "Excellent. You've all made a wise choice. The four of you are going to do something that men have only dreamed of for centuries." Her voice rose with excitement. "You will go into the Fury itself and travel to Shilanti. There, you shall beg Na'lek to spare us from his Fury."

# ELEVEN

*"The monsters know you are sinners. They are built within Shilanti itself, forged by Na'lek in the heart of his Fury. They know nothing but anger and hatred for you."*

—*From the Tomes of Regret, Verse 4 of Power*

SAIPHIN SCREAMED UNCONTROLLABLY as his flesh was burned from his bones. He began to shake violently and was ripped from the ground, thrown away as if by a huge, invisible hand. He was tossed about like a small leaf caught in a gale. A leaf that was on fire. He had felt this pain before, and he knew how to survive it. There was a power that surrounded him, and it struck at him like whip. He sensed a darkness through the pain, a deep and terrible anger. The force struck him again and again, threatening to tear him into thousands of tiny shards and scatter him into this wind. It was Abyss, striking out from beyond the veil of death. Saiphin held himself together, resisting the terrible onslaught by the winds. He curled into a ball as he hurtled through the unknown, twisting and turning as the force pushed and tore at him.

And then the heat was gone, the wind vanishing as suddenly as it had come. Saiphin hit the ground hard, rolling onto his back. He gasped as a rib cracked.

The dark presence of Abyss faded and everything was still. The worst mistake his people had ever made was giving the Shadowed One the mercy of a soul death.

Saiphin opened his eye and blinked groggily. His other eye was sealed shut with blood and throbbed in time with his heart. Saiphin feared that it was punctured beyond repair, and that was a harrowing thought. "Father," he said, wincing in pain, "I've lost half my soul." The words shocked him, frightened him beyond expression. Even so, it seemed a fitting addition to his sufferings.

Still groggy, Saiphin searched for his weapon and found the handle lying a few feet from him. The ax-head had been sheared off somehow. With a sigh, he left it where it was.

Slowly, the memories of the past few minutes began to return. He recalled that he'd been forced into a battle and that a girl had taken his eye. She'd taken half his soul. Such a barbaric creature was deserving of a cruel, painful death, but even that satisfaction had been robbed from him.

Quickly, he looked around, but he did not see the strange gray and brown landscape of that horrific place. Instead, Saiphin was standing on broken blue stones and the sky above him was darker than Abyss. A red sun was descending toward the horizon, so big that it almost filled the entire sky. Saiphin wiped the sweat from his brow as an intense heat settled upon him. Desolation surrounded him, and he knew that he was in Tana once more. He was home.

In the distance, a grand city of the Tana'kel lay sprawling over the ruined terrain. Through the fog of heat, Saiphin could see the earth breaking apart as magma boiled up through crevices and slowly consumed the city. No one screamed, for there was no one left alive.

Then the ground began to shake, causing Saiphin to trip and fall. The land split, opening like the jaws of some great

beast, and the entire city met its fiery demise in the belly of
Tana. The quake subsided and all grew still once more. How
many cities had perished in this way? Far too many.

Saiphin grimaced, sending a prayer for the soulless who
had died. However, he did not despair, for the gods had shown
him something wonderful. Something that could perhaps save
the Tana'kel from their fate. There was a new world out there,
a cool, lush land filled with weak, primitive creatures. And
Saiphin knew how to access it. He had to find the Champion;
he needed to know of this miracle.

Saiphin set off at a run. He wasn't sure where he was, especially now that the only recognizable landmark had just been
destroyed. But he knew that if he followed the sun, he could
find the coastline and follow it north to the Grand Arena.

And so he ran across his dying world, passing the ruin of
the Tana'kel's once proud civilization. He avoided any of his
people that he saw and kept his defenses up as he sprinted. To
his relief, he saw that some cities still stood, and they even had
active arenas. These Tana'kel spent their days pretending that
Tana wasn't about to die. They played their games and lived in
relative luxury, acting as if the land might not swallow them
at any moment. Some tribes were so apathetic, or perhaps so
ignorant, that they still waged wars across the Lakes of Silver.
Saiphin had heard that entire armies had been devoured by the
fiery chasms that crisscrossed Tana, opening at random to consume anything unfortunate enough to be overhead.

Night had fallen across Tana by the time Saiphin reached
the coastline. Despite running for hours, he did not feel tired.
That was the blessing bestowed upon the Tana'kel warriors.

He blinked, wincing as his dead eye throbbed, as he looked
out at the massive ocean. It was all but gone now. All that
remained were a few large puddles far out in its center. They
would soon be gone as well. Gazing out across the dry seabed

he noticed the dry bones of monstrous sea creatures. They had died quickly once the water levels began dropping. These creatures, who had once been the strongest and most feared beasts in all of Tana, had been reduced to shriveled husks, which the Tana'kel had fought to harvest. But just like the livestock and other wild creatures, their meat had run out months ago. The forests and jungles had been consumed by wildfire, while farms and gardens had withered away. There was precious little food and water left. It wouldn't be long before the Tana'kel began to starve. Of course, Tana might be destroyed completely before that happened.

The ocean was a much more recognizable landmark, and Saiphin could determine that he was four hours south of the Grand Arena. As the world grew darker, so did it grow cooler, which put Tana in a relative state of calm and tranquility. Eruptions seemed less frequent during the nights, which was a small mercy. Saiphin ran northward with all the speed he could muster. The Champion would want to begin working immediately, and taking advantage of the night would go a long way to saving the Tana'kel.

Soon, Saiphin arrived at Tana's crowning jewel: Tanar. An immense sprawling city of square golden buildings and large palaces with domed towers, Tanar was the last of the great cities. It was now only half of its original size; a large portion of it had been devastated in a terrible earthquake two months ago.

When he entered the city, Saiphin finally let his guard down. Some of the smaller wild tribes had begun capturing travelers and refugees. These unfortunate souls were devoured by their brethren. Saiphin was safe in the city, where large numbers of Tana'kel gathered, but out on the roads, he could be prey for the most desperate of his people.

Saiphin dreaded what he would find at the heart of Tanar, as he feared that the Grand Arena could be gone, destroyed along with the Champion and all the Tana'kel ruling hierarchy. To his immense relief, he found that it still stood. Rising proudly from the center of Tanar, the Grand Arena was a gigantic amphitheater capable of seating hundreds of thousands of Tana'kel. The oval-shaped building had four main entrances on the ground floor from which the spectators could enter to ascend the stairs to their appropriate seats. Spyglasses were supplied for the highest seats, hundreds of feet above the ground.

In the days before Tana had started to die, different tribes would send dozens of their greatest warriors to the arenas scattered across Tana. But only the most noteworthy and skilled soldiers could fight here, in the presence of the Champion. During the duels, teams would work together to slaughter enemy troops in glorious battle. When only thirty warriors remained, the arena would become a free-for-all, and the last ten standing were declared the winners. But the battles weren't just about survival, they were also about killing. While avoiding being slain, the warriors had to collect the eyes of their opponents as proof of an honorable kill. Of the final ten, the five with the smallest number of eyes would be executed and the remaining survivors would be the true victors. The tribes they represented would receive many tributes, such as land, soldiers, and wealth. The winners themselves would receive great stature and praise for completing the trials of the arena, and they would live like kings. Saiphin had never been chosen to fight in an arena.

As the cataclysm destroying Tana worsened, the tribes had stopped dueling for wealth and had instead fought for food and water. Kingdoms would offer up supplies as rewards, and the victors would eat well rather than starve. But now, everything was horrifically scarce, and the tribes guarded their dwindling resources jealously. Today, the arenas were simply places for frightened farmers and nobles to throw away worthless money while they waited for their imminent deaths. Saiphin shuddered as he walked through the wide tunnel toward the stands, knowing that it wouldn't be long now. Every day, the sun grew larger and the ground heaved in torment. Tana writhed in her death throes, and soon she would fade entirely.

Saiphin heard his people before he saw them. They screamed and roared and cheered as they watched the battle from the stands. When he emerged onto the grounds, creeping forward through the shadows, he saw thousands of Tana'kel above him. Five large globes of light hovered in the air above the battleground, flooding the arena with light. Saiphin knew that this had once been a simple spell, but now it took twenty sorcerers to maintain a single orb. He quickly found the Champion's box, situated at ground level at the arena's front, two hundred feet away from him. Scattered across the dusty ground of the amphitheater were at least fifty corpses, each with their eyes plucked out, having died honorably. Saiphin continued to creep closer.

Ten Tana'kel stood near the Champion's box, bare to the waste, wielding bloody axes and holding up cloth bags. The crowd hushed as five Tana'kel officials walked out onto the grounds, dressed in white robes. They took the bags from each warrior in turn and began to count the contents. The crowd grew silent as they waited for the announcement.

In loud voices, the officials bellowed the counts of each warrior, voices amplified by magic to echo across the arena. Another spell that took multiple sorcerers to accomplish. A big soldier with a scar down his chest had forty eyes in his bag, and a sly-looking Tana'kel dripping with sweat had twelve. The officials nodded to one another and then drew knives from within their robes. They met the eyes of the five soldiers with the lowest scores and cut their throats. The five did not protest or scream, even as they perished. Once the warriors had stilled, the officials bent down and gently plucked out their eyes.

A murmur swept through the crowd as thousands of voices prayed in unison. With their souls released, Saiphin knew the warriors were now at peace.

In his box, the Champion rose from his seat. Even at this distance, Saiphin could make out his impressive, muscular figure. The Champion's eyes glimmered as he looked down upon the victors with an imperious gaze. He wore a resplendent black robe, which accented his violet skin, and a golden crown rested upon his brow, fitted with a large amethyst. Saiphin had seen the Champion plenty of times, but that amethyst always caught his gaze. It was the eye of Abyss himself.

In one hand, the Champion held a large leg of some unfortunate beast, which gave off a tantalizing steam, and he also had a golden goblet filled with cool, clear water. He took a bite of the meat and swallowed, savoring its flavor. Saiphin wet his lips unconsciously, watching the food longingly. It had to be the last of its kind.

The Champion finally swallowed and leaned down to get a better look at the five exhausted Tana'kel. "You have proven your might before me and this audience. You have fought bravely and killed honorably." His voice reverberated throughout the arena, powerful and magnificent. "I find you worthy of victory in the Grand Arena!" The crowd broke into thunderous applause, and the Champion waved them all to silence. "Now, as you deserve, I shall . . ." He trailed off, eyes bulging. The crowd followed his gaze and gasped in unison.

Saiphin had strode out onto the arena, walking purposefully into the light and toward the Champion's box. The Champion would have to hear his words, no matter what traditions Saiphin had to break. This might be Tana's only hope.

The Champion dropped his goblet in utter shock, precious water spilling onto the thirsty ground below. "H-How dare you!" he sputtered, and pointed toward one of the warriors in the arena. "Kill this fool and bring me his eyes!"

The scarred Tana'kel, the one who had just claimed twenty souls, turned toward Saiphin and smiled, spinning his axe between both hands expertly. "Looks like he's only got one to pluck," he mocked. "Pity."

With his right eye, or what was left it, ablaze with pain, Saiphin continued forward, resolute. Half-blind and weaponless, Saiphin knew he should have been afraid, but he had just defied Abyss, and all of Tana rested on his shoulders. He knew that he would not fail here.

"You're really not going to surrender?" The soldier was close now, and Saiphin could see the blood smearing his axe. "You've got guts, half-soul."

Saiphin said nothing.

The soldier suddenly charged, blade swinging in a wide arc toward his head. Saiphin ducked under the blow, stepping around the Tana'kel as he charged and punched him in the liver. The Tana'kel warrior fell, reeling from Saiphin's blow, but he quickly forced himself to his feet.

Though staggering somewhat, the warrior roared in challenge and swung again. Saiphin sidestepped the first and second swings, staying just out of the soldier's reach. The infuriated Tana'kel rushed Saiphin brutally, relentless with his wide chops. Then Saiphin rolled under another swing and came up behind the warrior. Startled, the soldier tried to turn, but Saiphin caught the warrior's axe arm and forced it backward. Bone snapped audibly. The soldier cried out, dropping like a stone, and Saiphin kicked him ruthlessly, striking his face. Blood spattered the ground and leaked into his gaping mouth, but the Tana'kel did not stir.

Saiphin bent down, picking up the fallen Tana'kel's axe with one hand. Without hesitation, he slammed the axe-head down into the warrior's neck, severing his head with one blow. Saiphin realized he was holding his breath and exhaled as he calmly gouged out the warrior's eyes. A sense of peace settled on Saiphin as the slain warrior's soul escaped from the fleshy confines of his skull and was released into the sky. Saiphin stood slowly, restraining a wince.

Saiphin dropped his bloodstained spoils and turned toward the Champion. He reached into himself and tapped into the reservoir nestled in Tana's heart. He grunted as his very bones quivered, for the magic came to him sluggishly. It was like trying to pull a hammer out of tar, and it strained his body horribly. Tana's life force was nearly dead, so dead that it took many sorcerers to perform the simplest of spells. Yet Saiphin was one of the most powerful sorcerers of his generation, and Tana slowly obeyed his commands.

Finally, the magic was his to command, and he used the small trickle he had seized to amplify his voice, making it a hundred times louder. "My name is Saiphin," he shouted, "and I have come here to speak not only with our Champion, but every Tana'kel here. I have a message of hope. Hope to save us all!"

The Champion, conqueror of a hundred tribes, enemy of Abyss, stared down at him impassively. As Saiphin met his solid gaze, the Champion nodded slowly, a gesture for him to continue.

"I was stationed with a hundred of our brothers east of Tyrant's Keep," Saiphin proclaimed. "Last night, we suddenly found ourselves swept up by the foul violet winds and were taken away by the black light. But we did not perish; instead we wandered out of the storm. To my surprise, we had entered another world, inhabited by primitive creatures who butchered us without provocation. Despite our courage in the face of this new threat, I was the only one to survive, and I was cast back here to Tana by the same black light. They took my eye," he pointed to the dark point of his vision, where half his soul had perished. "But before I was blinded, I saw opportunity. This new world is a soft land, ripe with food and water. It is a world much younger than Tana, safe and secure from the fires that ravage this place. The natives are weak and sluggish; we can take it for our own. We need not meet our end here with Tana, but instead, we can find life again on this new world!"

Slowly chewing on his hunk of meat, the Champion raised an eyebrow, apparently interested. "You claim to have rediscovered World-Walking. But tell me, Saiphin, how is this possible? Tana is far too old for such mighty magic, and the black light is of Abyss. How can we use it?"

"Lord Champion." Saiphin smiled. "This storm, it is a thing of gods! Its magic is young and greater than anything I've ever felt before. Our people killed Abyss once, and we can do it again. We can World-Walk once more."

# TWELVE

*"The Fury is death. To fight it is to fight Na'lek himself. An impossible task. Instead, focus your attacks on the monsters it spawns, for slaying them garners you favor in Shilanti."*

—From the Tomes of Regret, Verse 25 of Repentance

LIKE WIND SUMMONED from the deepest parts of the Fury, a sweeping cold raced through Kaven, and with it came a tingling fear that numbed his heart and dried his tongue. He stared at Lyra in disbelief, barely comprehending the true weight of her proclamation. She wanted them to go into the Eternal Storm and speak with Na'lek himself? It was impossible. One couldn't meet with Na'lek. *Not in this life, anyway*, Kaven thought.

Toyon cleared his throat and spoke up. His speech was slow and measured, each word considered and approved before they left his lips. "It cannot be done. No man can enter the Fury and hope to survive."

Shera nodded, the dark shadow of worry clouding her face. "There are thousands of monsters within the storm. Hundreds of thousands. We'd be butchered as soon as we passed the watchtowers."

"And there are the Shredders to consider," the sorceress Tasi'a said. "Those terrible, magic-infused winds can tear men apart in a matter of hours. Of course, the full potential of the Shredders has never been accurately tested, but I do believe it's safe to say that we could not endure it."

Kaven frowned. "There's another problem too, right?" The others turned to regard him, and Kaven was bolstered by the attention. "Shilanti is not on Lantrelia. It's in the sky, beyond the reaches of mortal men." That's what he'd always been taught, anyway.

Lyra smiled at him. "Tell me, Kaven, have you ever read the Tomes of Regret?"

Kaven shook his head. Of course, he hadn't. There were few men who were allowed to read the sacred scriptures. It was said that the secrets Na'lek had woven into the Tomes were not meant for the eyes of common folk. By Na'lek's decree, only the priests, the kings, the Zealots, and wise scholars could delve into the lore concealed within the Tomes. Kaven had heard fragments before, as the priests would quote from the book in their sermons, but his own knowledge of the Tomes was limited. Kaven's mother had been allowed to read it, as she had a friend among the Zealots.

"I have," Lyra said, her smile confident beneath bright, knowing eyes. "And the Tomes often describe Shilanti as being located within the Fury's heart."

Kaven almost chuckled at that notion, but he held himself back. He'd always believed that paradise would be somewhere far away from Lantrelia and her troubles. Na'lek hated mankind beyond anything else, so why would he choose to dwell among them? Kaven didn't think it made any sense.

"What if it's really not there?" Shera demanded.

"That is not in question," Lyra said, her voice firm. Whatever the truth of it, Kaven could tell that she believed her words. "Lord Na'lek penned the Tomes himself, and I trust in his words without question. Shilanti is there."

"If I may interject?" Tasi'a asked suddenly. She continued without waiting for a reply. "Assuming that Na'lek's city is truly located within the Fury, there is still no way that we can reach it without being destroyed. No being can survive the storm, so unless you plan on sending us to Shilanti by cutting our throats, we will not be going."

She laughed at her own joke, but Kaven didn't find it amusing. There was a grim truth in that statement; if the Deliverance wanted to send him to Shilanti, they could just strike him down. Sure, he wouldn't be able to return, but he could still bring their message to Na'lek.

"Considering that the Deliverance has been preparing for this a long time," Lyra said, slightly irritated, "you can assume that we are aware of this problem, Tasi'a. Fortunately, none of you know as much about the Fury as you seem to think. We have accounted for the dangers of the Eternal Storm, and we have a method to counter them."

"How are we to fight the hordes of monsters?" Shera asked. "We four cannot hope to face an army."

"The monsters will not be a great problem," Lyra said. "They are spread out over the Fields of Glory and only form in great numbers when they are preparing to assault the Wall. Remain vigilant and careful, and you shouldn't be in any great danger."

Toyon nodded. "I agree, but the lightning is a greater problem. There is little protection out there."

"This is true," Lyra said. "Try to move away from any storm bands, but if you are caught in one, take advantage of the pits. That's all you have."

Shera mentioning the monsters had reminded Kaven of the Watcher. Those terrible crimson eyes still haunted him. "What of the Titans?" he asked.

Lyra looked at him, and a small flicker of doubt washed across her face. "If you should encounter a Titan . . . run. Run until your legs collapse beneath you, and pray they never find you."

Silence fell across the chamber, and Kaven felt as if he was being watched. He didn't look back, knowing that there was nothing but a stone wall. *But what if there is something?* Kaven still didn't look.

Tasi'a didn't let the silence linger long. "Monsters and Titans we can evade if we are clever enough, but what of the Shredders? They will certainly kill us if the Titans don't."

Kaven had heard that there was a Stormgardian custom where old or dying soldiers would venture out into the Fury alone in a final act of defiance. Sometimes they went in small groups, and sometimes they went unarmed, but all went to die. On some occasions, their bones blew back out of the Fury, stripped clean of flesh by the Shredders. Other times nothing came back at all.

"We've solved that problem too," Lyra said. That small glimpse of doubt was gone, replaced by confidence. "We have a potion devised for this purpose."

"A potion?" Tasi'a scoffed, wrinkling her nose at the notion. "Alchemy is fool's magic. It's nothing more than oil and water, more often than not."

"Fear not," Lyra said with a reassuring nod. "This isn't an alchemist's brew. This potion is very real, and it will shield you from the Shredders."

"Has it been tested?" Kaven asked. He didn't know much about magic, but he knew of alchemists. They often had shops in Redwind's market area, advertising potions that could cure sickness, mend broken bones, enhance strength, and even cause feelings of love. His mother called them frauds and thieves. The last thing Kaven wanted was to step into the Fury with a potion purchased from an alchemist in some back alley of Stormgarde City.

"Many times," Lyra said. "It's perfectly safe and reliable, so long as you remember to reapply."

"It's not a permanent solution?" Tasi'a asked, brow furrowed in concern.

Lyra shook her head. "No, it only lasts a few days. We discovered this the hard way."

Kaven frowned, wondering if the Deliverance had gotten anyone killed doing this. A harrowing thought crossed his mind. *What if we're not the first they've sent out? What if that's why they chose me? They're tired of killing off their best people, so now they're moving on to outsiders.* A second chance at the university was not worth his life. Kaven decided that he was not going to go through with this.

Shera snorted, her tone disapproving. "If we were meant to walk under the Fury, then we would have the strength to resist on our own."

"You will use our potion nonetheless," Lyra said sternly, giving Shera a pointed look. "You can prove your own strength another time."

"So that's it?" Toyon asked. "We walk right into Shilanti and march up to Na'lek without a care, and simply ask him to let go of his hatred? Na'lek's Fury has scoured us for thousands of years. If he doesn't kill us right then and there, I doubt he will be partial to our pleas."

"That is why we believe this will work," Lyra said. "We have fought the Fury since before memory can recall, and we have yet to prove ourselves worthy of sparing. Na'lek now desires a different approach, and I firmly believe that this, going to him and pleading for humanity, is his will.

"You may die, certainly. But you may save all of mankind from the Fury. When you return, you will be heroes. You will put an end to the Eternal War, and you will live like kings. Songs will be sung of you, the saviors of Lantrelia, and you will be rewarded beyond measure by a grateful people."

Kaven didn't care for riches. His family was wealthy enough, and such things had never interested him anyway. The fame, the recognition, however, caught his attention. Far too often as of late, he'd found himself praying for his father's approval, praying to be more successful. Perhaps this was Na'lek's answer. This was what Na'lek wanted. Kaven had faith in the headmaster, and if Gane could trust the Deliverance, then so could he.

But death waited for him in the Fury. If not the monsters or the lightning, or even the Shredders, then the Titans themselves would certainly hunt them down. Na'lek was said to be merciless, and his Fury was a terrible, murderous thing. Was the recognition worth it? After all, if Kaven stayed in the watchtower, where it was safer, he could eventually work his way into notoriety. But Kaven knew, somewhere deep within himself, that he couldn't do that. It didn't work, it had never worked. He needed to change something if he wanted to be noticed by his Father or by the headmaster.

When Na'lek gave you such an incredible opportunity, you did not ignore it. Fear was a roiling, churning beast inside him, but Kaven quelled it. "When do we leave?" he asked, trying to keep a waver out of his voice. Was he really doing this?

"Tomorrow morning," she replied. "For now, take some time to get to know each other and then retire and rest for the night. Any room will do." With a final nod, Lyra departed, and the other cultists followed after her.

Following the Deliverance's departure, a suffocating silence settled over the room, and Kaven frowned. He didn't like these kinds of awkward silences, and there was no way he'd let the entire trip be like this. *Best to get this over with now.* "Well . . ." Kaven hesitated, wetting his lip. In fact, his whole body felt dry. "As you know, my name is Kaven. I look forward to traveling with you."

He winced at his own words. To put something like going into the Fury itself in such a simple term as "traveling" made his heart twist fearfully. *Titan's teeth, I'm really going to do this!*

Tasi'a smiled, and she stepped up to shake his hand. "A pleasure. I've never met a Regelian before. Is it true that you drink beer with breakfast?"

Kaven nodded. "Usually, though sometimes I prefer wine."

Tasi'a wrinkled her nose but still smiled. "That is curious! No other people in Lantrelia drink alcohol so early in the day."

"I don't see why the other kingdoms don't," Kaven said with a shrug. "It's not like we drink to get drunk. We simply enjoy good beer."

"You don't think it's strange at all?" Tasi'a asked.

"No," Kaven said.

"Curious indeed," Tasi'a replied. The sorceress's eyes constantly darted about, rarely focusing on any one thing for long, as if she were constantly searching for something new and exciting. Her eyes settled on Toyon, who was standing apart from them, silent and stoic as an old statue. "Excuse me a moment, would you?"

Kaven nodded, and Tasi'a moved away. Kaven eagerly turned his attention toward the stunning Stormgardian.

"So, your name is Shera?" he asked. She nodded but said nothing. Kaven cleared his throat. "That's a nice name. Does it mean anything?" Once, long ago, Lantrelians had spoken a completely different language. Now called the Ancient Script, only fragments of the dead tongue still existed. Some people liked to name their children using broken words from the Ancient Script. Kaven's own name meant "Footsteps," which once more highlighted how hopeful his father had once been that Kaven would take after him.

Shera seemed interested by this question. "It means 'Heartblade,'" she said proudly. Kaven nodded appreciatively, but Tasi'a introduced herself to Shera before he could say anything further.

Sighing, he turned to Toyon. "What about you? Does your name have any meaning?"

The scrawny assassin shrugged. "Not in the Ancient Script," he said softly. "But I was named after my great-grandfather."

"Nice," Kaven said brightly. But Toyon said nothing to further the conversation.

Fortunately, Tasi'a seemed eager to step in. "I was named after Na'lek's consort."

Shera raised an eyebrow. "Na'lek has a consort?"

Tasi'a blushed. "Oh right. I often forget how few of us have read the Tomes."

"How much have you read?" Toyon asked.

"The entirety of Power," she replied. "It details much of Na'lek's strength, along with that of the Fury."

Silence took hold again, so Kaven changed the subject. "Where did you go to school, Tasi'a?"

Tasi'a beamed. "The Venedecian College for Magical Properties. Despite my less-than-average magical abilities, I still managed to pass with a degree in Pyromancy. I have skill in other fields as well, of course."

Kaven had heard of that school. It wasn't the best college in Venedeis, but it was still notable. "What about you?" he asked Toyon.

"Narat's Academy of the Stealth Arts," the assassin said. Kaven had never heard of that university, and since Toyon looked down, he guessed that it probably wasn't a good one.

"And you, Kaven?" Tasi'a asked.

"The Regelian University of Scientific Advancement," Kaven said. *That* caused a stir among his companions. The college was the most prestigious school Regelia had to offer. Tasi'a beamed and Toyon's eyes widened in surprise. Even Shera seemed impressed. Kaven grinned despite himself, but he quickly deflected the subject off himself, lest they discover his humiliating expulsion. "What about you, Shera?"

Shera held herself up higher, pride radiating from her like a Regelian with a newly crafted invention. "I trained under the greatest blademasters of Stormgarde."

This surprised Kaven. "You didn't go to college?"

Shera stormed toward Kaven, who backed away hurriedly. "*College* does not need a building or a fancy name!" She turned and stalked out of the chamber, and Kaven heard the door to one of the many bedrooms slam shut.

Kaven stood frozen, bewildered, and thoroughly confused. Toyon was immutable, but Tasi'a's smile slipped away as she watched Shera's expeditious retreat. Kaven stared after, wondering what under the Fury he had done to offend her. Even though it had been accidental, it seemed that all chance of a rapport with her had been lost.

"What did I say?" Kaven asked the other two, hoping for some insight on the supposed insult.

Toyon gave him a flat look. "The wrong thing."

"That's not fair," Kaven protested. "I was just surprised she didn't attend college, that's all."

The Fulminite shrugged. "You might want to employ some tact when speaking to women."

Kaven felt a flash of anger appear inside him. Maybe it was brought on by fear of the Fury, or perhaps it was left over from his father's scornful words. Whatever the reason, the anger grabbed hold of his tongue and lashed out. "At least I can speak to women."

As soon as he spoke, Kaven regretted it. Toyon said nothing; instead he raised an eyebrow and then followed Shera, disappearing out of the room.

*Great,* Kaven berated himself. *Well done.* He looked to Tasi'a for help. "I didn't want to start anything," he said apologetically. "I especially didn't want to fight before we've even left Stormgarde."

Tasi'a sighed. "I'd leave it until tomorrow, Kaven. Good night." She departed, leaving Kaven alone.

Kaven stood still a moment, regretful and confused, but soon went into the hall and chose one of the unlocked bedrooms. He threw himself into a stuffy, square bed and fell asleep.

# THIRTEEN

*"All glory belongs to the Zealots, who give it to Na'lek."*

—*From the Tomes of Regret, Verse 26 of Repentance*

KAVEN AWOKE TO the sound of Lyra's voice proclaiming something about breakfast. He didn't really care enough to listen. The woman entered his room, and Kaven let out a cry of dismay, pulling the blankets up to cover himself. Lyra didn't seem to mind, placing a bundle of clothes at the foot of his bed.

"Hurry now," Lyra instructed before she quickly departed. Kaven rose slowly and dressed himself. The Deliverance had supplied him with a sturdy pair of trousers and a shirt, all plain brown, along with a traveling cloak.

He made his way upstairs and into the common room, where Tasi'a, Shera, and Toyon were all sitting at a table. The elderly innkeeper was placing plates of toasted bread and fruit in front of them as Kaven took his seat. Shera ate in a brooding silence, casting venomous glances in his direction. Toyon was silent too, his expression placid and his eyes still. Tasi'a was uncomfortable by the animosity displayed, and she attempted to start up several conversations, all unsuccessfully.

Once they had finished, Lyra led them back downstairs. As he followed, Kaven was suddenly gripped by a powerful nervousness as the realization of what he was about to do began to seep into his bones. The Fury had killed thousands upon thousands over the generations, and Kaven was about to go into it. Willingly.

Who knew how powerful the wind was within the Fury's heart? It might be able to snatch him up from the ground and cast him thousands of miles back into the Barrier Wall. With the wind, there would be much more debris, and finding shelter from the lightning storms would be difficult. That wasn't to mention the armies of monsters that marched across the ruined lands: Eye-Takers, Silent Ones, Spinereavers, Bouncers, Knifemen, and more. Yet the one thing that Kaven feared above all else lurked upon the Fields of Glory. The five Titans waited, constructs of pure rage and destruction. They were powerful, immortal, impervious, and hungry. The vivid memory of the Watcher's eyes still lingered in the back of Kaven's mind.

What would Headmaster Gane tell his parents about this? Would they be proud? Would they be angry? Would they even care at all? Kaven's thoughts were still on his parents when Lyra gave a brief command, and the Deliverance rolled in a giant vat, filled to the brim with a strange golden substance. At first glance, Kaven thought it was a solid material, like ice, but he noticed that it was rippling slightly as the vat moved.

"This is it"—Lyra gestured to the vat—"our protection potion. Please take a goblet from one of my companions and fill it. Then go into one of the side rooms, strip, and pour it over yourself. *Every inch* of skin must be covered!"

Shera was the first to step forward. She grabbed a goblet that a member of the Deliverance offered her and dunked it into the vat. The golden surface broke when the goblet touched it, allowing large chunks of the half-liquid potion to slide in.

She withdrew the goblet and strode down the hallway and into one of the bedrooms, slamming the door after her.

Kaven went next. "Thank you," he said to the robed woman who offered him a silver goblet. He scooped out a large portion and hurried into another room. After shutting the door, he pulled off his clothing.

He frowned at the potion, somewhat relieved that he wouldn't have to drink it. He lifted the goblet over his head and poured it over himself. Upon touching his head, the chunks instantly liquefied and surged down his body. It was shockingly cold and Kaven began to shiver. Once the goblet ran out, he put it aside and began to rub the liquid, which had now turned into something like glue, over his body. He had some trouble with his back, but eventually he was successful. The liquid began to harden even as he spread it about, and he felt his skin tightening, as if he were being encased in a shell. But soon Kaven could no longer feel it at all. However, the biting cold remained. He put his clothes back on and exited the room, still shivering violently.

Toyon and Shera stood with Lyra, but Tasi'a was absent, presumably applying her dose of the potion. To Kaven's surprise, he saw that whenever Toyon or Shera moved, their skin gave off a golden sheen. It was a beautiful thing to behold.

Lyra turned from a hushed conversation with a cloaked man when Kaven returned. She looked him up and down briefly and gave a curt nod of approval.

When Tasi'a reemerged into the room a few moments later—her skin sparkling too—the robed men and women departed, taking the vat with them. Only Lyra remained, and she gave them one final look of appraisal.

"Rest a few moments and make ready," Lyra said. "I will be waiting in Victory Square." She departed then, and the robed men took the vat with them. Shera and Toyon did not hesitate, following immediately after Lyra.

Kaven watched them go with narrowed eyes. This was entirely not his fault. The anger in Shera's eyes sickened him.

Tasi'a suddenly moved in front of him, startling Kaven out of his bitter thoughts. "You know you should apologize," she said.

He sighed. "I know."

"Come on, then!"

Despite his protests, she grabbed him by the hand and dragged him after Shera and Toyon.

Kaven mentally kicked himself all the way through the inn, ashamed at having put himself at odds with half of his party within the first five minutes. He'd always lacked a mannerly aptitude, which he assumed was purely the fault of the soldiers he was often around. He'd never been very good with people, especially women, either on the Wall or at the college. At least he hadn't insulted Tasi'a too.

When they reemerged into the city, Kaven saw Lyra standing by the Destroyer's skull, looking up at one of the Titan's long fangs. Four large packs were lying at her feet. Toyon and Shera stood by her, not talking to each other.

*Where are the other Deliverance cultists?* Kaven wondered as he wove through the many pedestrians that clogged the courtyard, only stopping when he stood beside Lyra.

The noblewoman eyed him up and down. "That was sooner than expected. Much sooner." She glanced at the others. "I assume you have all gotten to know each other?"

Shera glared at Kaven, and the heat of her eyes could have melted the armor she wore. "More than I would have liked."

Kaven sighed. "All right, I'm sorry I offended you. Truly, it was not my intention." He nodded toward the Fulminite. "And I didn't mean to snap at you either, Toyon."

Shera's stare did not abate, but Toyon nodded acceptingly. Tasi'a smiled and let go of Kaven's hand, trotting closer to get a better look at the Destroyer's skull.

Lyra raised an eyebrow but said nothing on the matter. "It is time; you must leave Stormgarde now, while the day is still young." She pointed to the packs by her feet. "There's one for each of you. They have enough supplies to last three weeks, along with an equal amount of the potion. Reapply every couple of days and the Shredders won't touch you. You'll also find sleeping equipment and more clothing. Stay together, stay safe, and may Na'lek guide your steps and guard your souls." Lyra bowed her head gracefully. "The Deliverance thanks you for this service. Now, leave immediately." Then Lyra turned and vanished into the crowd.

Toyon looked eastward, toward the Fury that surged so closely to the kingdom's walls. "It's calm today. At least as calm as the Fury can be. This is the best time to leave."

"Let's not linger then," Shera said, and she grabbed a backpack and strapped it to her back. Without another word, she set off toward the gates of Stormgarde.

Kaven quickly grabbed his pack and hoisted it across his back with a grunt. Toyon and Tasi'a hurriedly followed, and Kaven wondered if the diminutive sorceress would have trouble with her pack. He would've offered to help, but he felt as if he'd topple over himself. Tasi'a seemed fine as they hurried after Shera, so Kaven decided that it would be wise not to mention it at all.

It quickly became apparent that Shera thought herself their leader and guide, and Kaven didn't feel like arguing with her. Toyon and Tasi'a didn't seem to mind it either, and Shera led them through the city with little difficulty. She knew of many side streets and alleys to cut through, and before he knew it, Kaven was once again facing the iron-wrought gates that led across the moat. After they left the city, they jogged across the plain and came to the Barrier Wall. The Storm-Gate of the Wall was wide open, revealing the broken landscape beyond.

Kaven eyed the Wall-Guards doubtfully. "Will they try to stop us?"

Shera glanced back at him, a look of bemusement on her face. "Stormgardians will not impede those who wish to fight against the Fury."

"That seems foolish," said Toyon as they walked through the gates.

"It's not," Shera snapped. "Taking the Path of Faith is a right granted to every soldier, no matter their health or status."

Toyon raised an eyebrow. "That's entirely beside the point."

Kaven, though he dared not say anything out loud, agreed with Toyon. The Path of Faith was legalized suicide. It was Stormgarde's oddest custom, allowing dying or old soldiers to go out into the Fury alone, in a final attack against the storm. Those who walked the Path of Faith never returned. Except when the wind blew their bones back across the Wall.

Shera bristled with anger, but she said nothing more on the subject. Silence fell over their little group as the world suddenly grew darker. They had passed beneath the Fury's shadow. Kaven looked up slowly, as the terrible violet clouds of the Fury spun high above them. He wasn't scared yet, as the watchtowers were farther out than this. Yet being beneath the Eternal Storm was a harrowing experience, and it was the ultimate display of Na'lek's power. The god's anger was made unmistakably apparent in the clouds of the Fury.

The wind buffeted Kaven, blowing back his cloak and hair, making him shiver. A faint crash of thunder rolled across the Fields of Glory, and a flash of black split the distant clouds, illuminating strange shapes in the sky, like the shadowed faces of the Titans themselves. Kaven glanced to the side, noting various pits in which they could take shelter if the lightning came close. There was no telling when a storm band could come upon them. They were erratic, random—sudden and fickle as the wind itself.

Kaven watched the horizon carefully, but he saw nothing other than the storm on the horizon. He had no desire to fight monsters today, or any day. He instinctively touched the hilt of the shortsword strapped to his waist and then made sure his bow and quiver were in place. Lastly, he patted the miniature Firerod tucked into his belt.

He noted the others, wondering if they were also feeling uneasy. Shera had a hand on the pommel of her sword, and a round shield was strapped to her back over the large pack she wore. Toyon was carrying no visible weapons, but if Kaven's guess was right regarding his profession, he would have a few blades on his person. Tasi'a only had a small knife, but then, she did have a magical arsenal that would respond to her commands.

If any observer may have seen them, they would think them prepared. But could they truly survive within the Fury itself? If no other man had ever done so in the past thousand years, how could they hope to? How would Na'lek react to their trespass? Would he destroy them within the hour? Or would he let them approach? And if, by some miracle, they reached Shilanti, what would Na'lek do? Would he come and talk with them? Or would he simply kill them, as he had with all the heroes who'd come before? The Deliverance believed that he could make it, and some part of Kaven had to as well. If not, then he was fool for coming here. But if . . . if they could speak with Na'lek and convince him to spare Lantrelia from his anger, then Kaven would finally prove himself. It was a risk worth taking, no matter the outcome.

They were silent as they walked forward, moving against the wind and onto the treacherous and broken landscape of the Fields of Glory. They traveled for an hour, passing beyond sight of the watchtowers. Kaven was now deeper within the Fury than he had ever been before. In fact, the watchtowers marked the end of the Fury's outskirts, which were by far the safest parts of the storm. More thunder boomed in the distance, this time behind them. The Barrier Wall was in for yet another storm band. It was good that they'd left when they did. The wind was starting to pick up now, but Kaven found that it didn't impede him too much. They were still safe, but for how long Kaven did not know.

Kaven jerked, grunting in surprise as a strange tingling sensation spread across his entire body. The others flinched as well. They were in the Shredders, those strange, violent winds that tore apart any that dared ventured too deep into the Fury. The Shredders could tear the flesh off a man's bones in a matter of hours, but one would probably bleed to death before that happened. Oddly, the Shredders only affected living creatures, not inanimate things like food, clothing, or weapons. Kaven's mother had often noted that some of the monsters bore slices inflicted by the Shredders. Kaven exhaled slowly, relieved that his skin remained intact. Whatever potion the Deliverance had concocted, it had the desired effect. Moving forward, Kaven began to feel slightly better about their chances.

Immune to the Shredders, the four traversed deeper into the Fields of Glory, traveling directly east in as straight a line as the winds would allow them. They walked in a tight clump, Shera at the head and Toyon and Tasi'a behind. This helped buffer against the winds and kept them close together. Some Fury-spawn were swift, and they might be able to snatch one of them if they didn't stay close.

It was Shera who broke the silence at last, rubbing at her skin irritably. "I still can't believe that Shilanti is here, inside the Fury itself." Her tone was surprisingly friendly, though the wind made her hard to hear. "Wouldn't you think that the Fury would tear it apart?"

"I don't think Na'lek would let his own kingdom be destroyed by the storm," Kaven said.

Tasi'a nodded in agreement. "It has long been theorized that there is a large radius of calm directly in the Fury's center, forming a perfect circle. If Shilanti is a physical place on Lantrelia, I would suspect it would to be there. Assuming Na'lek is even there at all, of course."

Kaven frowned. "I've never heard that theory before."

"I'd be delighted to explain," she said with a smile. When no one denied her, she began. "This theoretical place of calm is referred to as the Point of Origination. The High-Mages have often hypothesized that the Fury is magical in nature, and that the Point is where the Fury originates. This is the spell's source."

"Why would it be magical?" Toyon asked. "Na'lek is a god; he wouldn't need to use magic."

Tasi'a laughed. "Na'lek is magic. He is the water, and he is the air. He is everything from our lifeblood to the insects to the Titans themselves. He didn't craft the natural laws of order; he *is* the law. Everything he does translates to something physically possible to our limited human perspective. The Fury is magic because Na'lek is magic." She looked about, confident that she had explained everything perfectly.

This was far from the truth, at least in Kaven's mind. "That," he declared, "makes no sense."

Tasi'a sniffed. "It's scientific. Of all of us, I thought you would understand it best, Kaven."

Kaven cleared his throat to avoid having to reply to that. He still wasn't going to tell them that he had been expelled. *Shera and Toyon already think little of me.*

Shera snorted in response to that statement. "Science has nothing to do with the nature of Na'lek."

"It is not a difficult concept to understand," Tasi'a said defensively.

"Have you studied this theory before?" Shera asked. "I certainly have not. I think dueling is simple, even easy, but I wouldn't expect you to grasp it quickly." Tasi'a hesitated and Shera smirked.

That was the first time Kaven had seen Shera smile. *Titans, she's beautiful!* He determined that he'd get her to do it again.

Hours passed, and soon it was time for the midday meal. Kaven had no idea how Toyon could determine what time it was with the Fury blanketing the sky for as far as he could see. It wasn't as dark as the night, but it certainly was close. Kaven gladly set his pack upon a smooth stone and sat down with his back to it. His legs already hurt, and it was still the first day.

Tasi'a murmured something unintelligible, and a small fire burst from the rocky ground. The fire was eerie; it did not flicker like it was supposed to, and it was not affected by the wind. It just sat there like a glowing sculpture, almost as if it was dead. A dead fire. Kaven did not like it. But it still radiated a welcome warmth and the four of them huddled around it. Opening his pack, Kaven removed the bedding and was met with a gust of cold air. Shocked, Kaven withdrew quickly and viewed his pack from a safe distance. His food was tucked away in the back, surrounded by chilling fog. The Deliverance had cast some sort of spell on the pack to keep it cold. There were boxes that did the same thing in every Regelian home.

For their first meal, they had dried meat, cheese, and hard bread. It was filling but awfully bland. Kaven finished quickly and relaxed on his rock, pulling out his device and tinkering with it absentmindedly. Immediately, his exhaustion drained away as he worked with a small wrench he had packed.

"This reminds me of the food they served at the College of Magical Properties," Tasi'a said around a mouthful of food. "I was there for two years, along with my brother."

"You have a brother?" Toyon asked, looking up from a knife he was sharpening. Kaven hadn't even seen him draw it.

"Oh yes," Tasi'a said, absentmindedly scratching her wrist. "He was there with me, nearly three years ago now. Ah! Let me tell you a story. It's superb!" She settled in against a rock and launched into her tale. "As you may already know, my spellcasting is . . . less than adequate. It was even worse when I was a student in the college. I could barely make a spark, much less a fire, and I was teased constantly, much to my brother's chagrin.

"One day, during lunch, I was eating in the cafeteria. My brother, who was already an adept sorcerer, was sitting across from me, when a group of young men entered and took their own lunches, sitting in the table adjacent to ours. They were loud boys: rude, raucous, but frustratingly cute. No sooner had they sat down than they began pulling faces in my direction, as my brother's back was turned. I observed their rude gestures and sneers and simply raised an eyebrow. And, in a feat of magic I had previously not thought I was capable of, I summoned a cup's worth of water and promptly dropped it on my own head.

"My brother has always had a short temper." Tasi'a smiled a twisted smile that was surprisingly sinister. "When he saw me soaking wet, he turned upon the boys like a Spinereaver on a nest of grannocs. They pleaded and begged, insisting that they were not to blame, but it was too late. My brother unleashed a typhoon of water the likes of which Lantrelia hasn't seen since.

The boys fled, soaked so thoroughly that their robes clung to them like a second skin."

They all laughed as Tasi'a finished—even Toyon. "I never would've expected such a thing from you," Kaven said in between chuckles.

"What do you mean?" Tasi'a asked, eyes wide and proclaiming her innocence. "My brother is clearly the one to blame."

When they had finished eating and talking, they packed and prepared to move out. Kaven would have preferred to camp there for the night, but Shera and Toyon both insisted that they should put in a few more hours of walking.

"All right," Shera said as they set off. "We have no way of knowing when we'll encounter monsters, and in fact, we may have already crossed into their kingdom, so I want to know your experience with the different kinds of monsters out here. Simply raise your hand if you know the monster and what it can do. If you've fought it before, that's even better."

Kaven and the others nodded. This was a good idea.

"Silent Ones?" Shera asked. Kaven raised his hand, as did Tasi'a. "Spinereavers?" Only Kaven raised his hand. He had once seen four try to climb his watchtower. "Knifemen?" Kaven kept his hand up, groaning softly as he remembered the stern-faced woman he'd watched die. *So much blood. She'd dropped like a stone.*

"Flamebringers?" No response. "Bouncers?" Toyon raised his long arm into the air. "Eye-Takers?" Only Toyon again.

"That's not as bad as I expected," Shera said, despite sounding somewhat disappointed. "Let's go over them so that you know what to expect. Eye-Takers." She paused, face suddenly shadowed by some memory. "These creatures are tough and brutal, and they have a knack for picking off the weaker soldiers. They *always* pause after making a kill to harvest their victim's eyes. If one of us dies, we need to bring down the distracted Eye-Taker quickly. The more eyes they take, the more vicious and determined they become. It's like some sort of bloodlust."

Kaven shuddered. Eye-Takers were horrible creatures. The greatest of their kind, the legendary Bloodfiend, had taken his father's eye.

"The Silent Ones," Shera continued. "As their names imply, these monsters never make any noise of any kind. They are capable of some rudimentary magic, casting spells such as flight, and they grow their weapons straight from their arms. The Silent Ones are merciless killers, hounding their chosen victims with unwavering purpose until their prey has been slain. Their carapace can be hard to break through, so aim for the necks or shoulders."

Kaven was well-acquainted with the Silent Ones.

Shera went on with her lecture. "Bouncers are tiny rodent-like creatures with a venomous bite. It is not particularly potent, but it can leave you paralyzed within an hour. Bouncers are quick and nimble, making them tricky to hit. They also always travel in packs, so if you see one Bouncer, there will be more. Probably many more."

"Knifemen." Shera hesitated, coming to a halt. "I've never fought these monsters in battle, but I've seen what they can do. The Knifemen are made from razor-sharp blades that make up the entirety of their form. They are the ultimate weapon and can kill you from any direction. They're renowned for being hard to kill unless you have a heavy weapon like a hammer or an axe, and they can remove their blades to throw at ranged opponents."

Shera nodded in agreement. "They are." They started walking once more while she continued. "Flamebringers are one of the rarer species. I've never even seen one before, let alone fought one. From what I've heard, they are a grotesque amalgamation of flesh and fire."

"Question," Toyon said. "Amalgamation. What does that mean?"

"It means the combination, or process of combining, two or more things," Tasi'a supplied. "In this case, the Flamebringers are a twisted fusion of fire and flesh."

Kaven shivered. "That does sound grotesque."

"If I may continue," Shera said irritably. "The Flamebringers are usually unarmed, but they can breathe fire and launch fire from their right hands. Their blasts are much stronger than the fireballs that most sorcerers can compose. Luckily, they have a limited supply of fire, as they draw it from their own bodies, and they must recharge. As you can imagine, getting punched by a fiery fist will kill you. Fortunately, their fleshy parts are weak, and they can be killed by normal means."

Shera glanced back at Kaven, looking directly at his quiver. "Spinereavers are little more than animals; they have no real intelligence. They walk on all fours and are rather slow. Despite this, they are clever hunters. They are especially dangerous because hundreds of long, sharp spines line their backs, which they can launch at their enemies with incredible speed and accuracy. Even when they run out of spines, they have sharp teeth and claws. They can only launch their spines forward, so I recommend attacking from behind. Luckily, their hides aren't terribly tough, so a good blade stroke or arrow will put them down."

Kaven touched his quiver. All of his arrows were crafted from Spinereaver quills. They were the best quality shafts in Lantrelia. The arrows that men made could not compare to those of Na'lek's Fury.

"And there could be more monsters we don't know about." Shera glared up at the storm. "Just stay alert. I don't need to mention the Titans, do I?"

A chill swept through Kaven and his eyes darted across the horizon, searching for a towering shape. The Fields of Glory still seemed empty. The five most terrifying creatures on Lantrelia were somewhere here, waiting beneath the Fury, perhaps already hunting them. Shera didn't say anything more, but Kaven mentally ran through the Titans fearfully.

The Gorger, also known as the Insatiable, was the Titan who devoured everything that moved, regardless of size or quantity. The Ravager destroyed everything in its path, not noticing who was being trampled beneath it. The Devourer was the dreaded Titan who literally fed on magical energy and anyone unfortunate enough to be wielding it. Death, the Silent Father, seemed to find genuine pleasure in killing. Death had been known to taunt its victims, pulling them apart slowly before finally crushing their skulls beneath its feet. And finally, there was the Watcher, whose predilections could not be predicted as it had never made an aggressive move against the people of Lantrelia. Kaven feared him above all, as he worried that the Watcher would become like the Destroyer. No man had ever seen the Destroyer until it had arrived at Stormgarde's gates, leading an army of thousands of monsters. The Destroyer might be three hundred years dead, but the Watcher lurked on the Fields, waiting and learning from his predecessor's mistakes.

"If we see any sign of the Titans," Shera said suddenly, jolting Kaven out of his fearful thoughts, "we'll take whatever precautions and detours are necessary to avoid a confrontation. We *will* die if a Titan finds us."

On that morbid note, they set off at a brisk trot, which was soon slowed to a normal walk by the wind. Here, where the winds became increasingly more chaotic, terrible gales surged high in the air. The angry clouds of the Fury were pushed low in the wake of the wind, seeming to reach down toward them, like fingers reaching for a tantalizing treat. But Kaven would not be consumed by the storm. No, instead he would defeat it once and for all.

# FOURTEEN

*"The Destroyer is a conqueror and a tyrant. When he comes,
know that the Day of Reckoning shall soon follow."*

—From the Tomes of Regret, Verse 32 of Power

THE NIGHT WAS cold and windy, and Kaven had to endure
Toyon and Shera fighting over whether they should light a fire
or not. Shera argued that a fire at night would attract monsters,
but Toyon protested that the darkness would prevent them
from noticing something like a Silent One, which had no need
of sight to kill and hunt. Eventually, Shera had relented. After
that, Kaven spent a fitful night trying to sleep on rocks, coupled by a late shift keeping watch.

A storm band had materialized while Kaven was on watch,
bringing thunder and lightning so black that it had made the
darkness around them seem bright. He had awakened his companions so they could take cover, but the band had been broken
apart by the winds and dispersed before it could reach them.

Kaven spent the rest of his night in a futile attempt to
work on his device. Although his efforts were again useless,
he did decide on a name: Animus. The name filled him with

a deep feeling of excitement. Kaven *would* get it to work. He knew he would.

When morning came, they dined on oatmeal and water, and everyone was far too tired to speak.

After eating, they set off across the pitted terrain as the Fury churned above them. The Eternal Storm was surprisingly . . . placid. Kaven wondered why the monsters of the Fury hadn't yet risen up to defend their domain. Perhaps their presence was still unnoticed by Na'lek, or he was testing them somehow, trying to get them to lower their guard. As midmorning approached, Kaven resolved to be more alert, but he could see nothing but the flat landscape and the terrible clouds.

*Perhaps Na'lek had decided to allow us to see him,* Kaven thought, smiling to himself. He wasn't nearly as afraid as he thought he would be. That lack of fear livened his step as he marched across the Fields of Glory, taking deep, refreshing breaths of air.

They made good time, despite the scarred, hazardous terrain and strong winds. Kaven was exhausted; this wind was hard to struggle against, and he'd received far too little sleep. He hoped that he would never have to fight a battle in these conditions, but he was certain the odds were stacked against him.

Thunder rumbled, far away and faint. Kaven couldn't even see the lightning. The Fury was almost calm.

"This is unnerving," said Toyon as they settled down to lunch. "Why are there no monsters? We should have at least seen scouting parties by now."

Tasi'a lit another fire in a small hole carved out by lightning. "Maybe they haven't spotted us yet?"

Toyon shook his head. "That doesn't make sense, Tasi'a. Every kingdom is attacked by monsters at least twice each week. Sometimes they come daily. It stands to reason we should have stumbled over a raiding party heading to Stormgarde by now."

"We may not be traveling directly east anymore," Kaven suggested. "We may have drifted off course."

Shera snorted. "This is a blessing from Na'lek. He wishes us good fortune on this journey. The fewer monsters we face, the better."

"Isn't that why you came here?" Kaven asked with more than a little contempt. "To kill monsters? Perhaps die in a blaze of glory?"

Shera spun toward him and gave him a look of pure anger. She gripped her sword hilt and set her jaw. "Listen well, boy," she spat. "If you keep pushing me, I'll give you the first real fight of your life! And you will lose . . . badly."

Anger flashed through Kaven, but he suppressed it, meeting her stare with a cool expression. After a moment, she turned and led them farther into the Fury. Kaven watched her go, frowning. He had no desire to fight Shera, but he was quickly growing tired of her. Toyon and Tasi'a had nothing to say on the matter.

They marched until dusk settled onto the Fields, extinguishing what little light existed beneath the storm. Tasi'a lit another magical fire and planted it in one of the pits, limiting the light it cast.

Kaven sighed, pulling his cloak around him as the wind buffeted him, increasing his misery. Were those torches on the horizon? The sound of a trumpet blasted through the night air, and Shera was instantly on her feet, only to drop back down again. "Get into a pit," she hissed. "Quickly! And put out that fire!"

Kaven ducked into a pit and was quickly followed by Shera and Tasi'a, who extinguished the fire. Toyon tossed their packs into a separate pit before taking shelter himself. Kaven peered over the edge of his pit, not daring to expose anything other than his eyes.

The torches on the horizon grew larger and larger, as more trumpet blasts punctuated the night. He could see the fire now, moving steadily forward. Not torches after all. Flamebringers. The monsters marched forward, moving southward in a path parallel to their own. As they drew closer, Kaven could see that they looked like men, except they were ablaze. Armor composed of narrow iron bars covered them, except their faces and right arms. Their arms were composed of pure fire, and the metal they wore glowed red with heat. They held long spears, both haft and blade forged of metal. Their faces were almost perfectly human, with dark or light skin, multicolored hair and eyes, handsome and ugly. However, patches of magma grew from their face like spores, differing in size on each monster. One Flamebringer's entire left face was bathed in lava, while another had only a single patch of fire on his cheek. There were scores of them—at least three hundred in number—with a dozen marching in the back and sounding the trumpets.

Kaven waited, trying to breathe silently as the Flamebringers marched past, a mere twenty paces in front of him. It seemed that Na'lek looked upon him with favor, for not one monster turned in their direction. The Flamebringers passed, and after an eternity of waiting, the glow from their fire and the sound of their trumpets faded into the night.

Slowly, Kaven emerged from the safety of the pit. Toyon appraised the situation, carefully watching the horizon, and deemed it safe to drag their packs out of the hole.

"Should we stay here?" Tasi'a asked nervously. "Is it safe?"

"As safe as any place may be under the Fury," Toyon said. "I'll take first watch."

Tasi'a didn't light another fire, and so Kaven lay down in total darkness as the Fury's winds continued to strike at him. He closed his eyes and listened, but he did not sleep.

Kaven opened his eyes groggily and found that he could see. The Fields were always entrenched in shadow beneath the Fury, but some sunlight reached him. Sleep had eventually come to him, in flitting fragments, like moths darting from tall grass. His restless body had caught too few.

Toyon was awake already, changed into a new set of gray clothes. He was chewing on some dried meat. Kaven sat up slowly and packed his sleeping equipment. The girls were still asleep, so Kaven grabbed a piece of breakfast and sat down beside the Fulminite.

"Good morning," he said, trying to sound cheerful.

"Morning." Toyon didn't look up, as clearly the ground was much more fascinating than Kaven.

"It's going to be a long day," Kaven said, hoping to start a conversation.

"Always will be," the assassin said flatly.

So much for conversation. "You're not still mad about what I said, are you?"

"Should I be?" Toyon glanced at him.

"Are you?"

"No."

Kaven frowned and coughed loudly. This had the desired effect, as Tasi'a awoke with a start. "Morning!" he said cheerfully.

Tasi'a rubbed her eyes and gingerly touched her hair, which had transformed from wavy lines to a tangle of matted locks. "Morning . . ." She yawned loudly.

Unfortunately, Shera woke up too. She greeted Kaven with a flat stare and sat up. Without speaking, she donned her armor and began to go through a series of stretches and exercises. Kaven wondered how she could do that in her heavy armor.

"Sleep well?" Tasi'a asked to no one in particular.

"Not really," Kaven said, offering the sorceress a strip of meat.

"We should head north," Shera said suddenly.

"Why?" Kaven asked. "The quickest way is east."

"I'm aware of that," Shera said darkly. "However, those Flamebringers were right on top of us last night. I think we should head off the path for a bit and make sure we're still safe."

"But the monsters came from the north," Tasi'a pointed out.

Shera shrugged. "South, then."

"We'll lose valuable time and supplies," Toyon said. "It is foolhardy to change direction, even if it might be safer."

"Why don't you want to go forward?" Kaven asked. "Are you scared?"

*Whack!* Shera spun and backhanded Kaven across the face. He fell hard, striking the rocky ground. Shera towered over him, face alight with anger. "How *dare* you! Stormgardians are never scared to venture into the Fury, fool! It is our birthright, our honor, and our duty. We sacrifice ourselves willingly to *end* this madness. I wouldn't expect a foolish Regelian runt to understand the meaning of our sacrifice. Stormgarde is a kingdom of bravery and truth. I came here to save the lives of my kinsmen, to die by the sword for them. Why did you come here, Kaven? What honor drives you?"

Kaven stared up at her, stunned by what had just happened. He put a hand to the red mark that burned on his cheek. She had hit him! Anger and confusion danced a jolly tune in his mind. Titans take her! He'd had enough of her Fury-spawned bullying! He . . . what had she said? Why had he come here? She'd come to fight for Stormgarde. He'd come to prove himself to his father, of course. Kaven felt a chill in his bones as he realized that wasn't right.

His father hadn't fought in the Chasm War for fame or honor; he'd done it to protect Regelia and the family he loved. The Deliverance was founded to save humanity from Na'lek's Fury. But Kaven had always fought for himself. He'd always lamented his own lack of prowess, but he'd never considered why he was fighting. The Eternal War was about saving mankind from destruction, about proving that they were worthy of redemption. But Kaven had always made this war about his own worth. The Church did not honor that, and Na'lek did not listen to it. Perhaps that was why he'd never been successful. Perhaps Shera was right. He was a fool.

The name Fortis was Kaven's legacy, as it was that of his parents. But perhaps a name or a title wasn't what made someone great. Rather, the actions of a man define him, whether they are remembered or not. Kleon Fortis had given his all for Regelia. He was great. Shera was prepared to fall by Na'lek's hand for Stormgarde. She was great. Kaven wanted nothing more than to be recognized. He was wrong. He was going to change that.

*How many monsters have you killed to protect others?* he asked himself, knowing the answer before he even finished. *To save those who cannot fight? To save the innocent? What about those who do not deserve to perish? How many monsters have you killed, Kaven, not to prove yourself to your father, but to protect Regelia?*

"I have no honor," he said quietly, looking up at the furious Stormgardian.

Shera was taken aback. "What?"

"You're right," he said, standing slowly. "I am a fool. If I'm honest, I came here to make a name for myself. I came to make my father proud."

Shera watched him warily, confused and still angry.

"I'm sorry," he said. "I insulted you, and I insulted Stormgarde. I'm also sorry that I've been a fool and a moron." He glanced at Tasi'a and Toyon, who had edged away from the fight. "And that goes for you as well." He turned back to Shera. "Please, forgive my stupidity, and thank you for showing me how wrong I was."

And then Shera was smiling. Really smiling. "You know what, Kaven? I do forgive you. I'm sorry I hit you."

"You can do it again if I continue to insult you." Kaven returned the smile.

Shera clasped his hand and shook it. Titans, she was beautiful when she smiled! "Let's start over, shall we?"

Kaven nodded. "Yes, please."

She turned on the spot. "All right, troops, fall in! We've lingered here too long!" She marched forward, still smiling.

Toyon and Tasi'a fell in behind Shera and in front of Kaven. They exchanged wary looks. "What was that about?" the Fulminite asked in his soft voice.

"I believe," Tasi'a said cautiously, "that one of our companions has ceased to be spiteful and cold, and the other has stopped being an idiot."

Kaven couldn't contain himself, hearing Tasi'a call them out like that was too much. He started laughing loudly, and the other three soon joined in until their sound rose over even the howling wind.

The howling. Kaven froze suddenly, listening. The wind was singing. "There's something coming," Kaven hissed to the others.

Thunder boomed in the distance, and Kaven began to count. One. Two. Lightning struck on the horizon, soon followed by more thunder. "Take cover!" Shera commanded. Immediately, everyone attempted to find a hole to hunker down in. There was no other available shelter.

Kaven crouched into a pit that was just large enough for him to slide into. He had to put his head between his knees to keep it from sticking up above the top. Kaven began to pray.

Thunder crashed overhead, followed immediately by lightning that blackened his vision as it struck down. Lightning fell like rain, heralded by continuous ear-shattering thunder. Kaven hoped that no monsters wandered through this band. Though it was rare, lightning and monsters sometimes came at the same time, even though the lightning did not spare monsters from its wrath. Wherever the lightning struck, more of the land vanished, obliterated completely in an instant.

Every time the lightning hit the ground, Kaven's vision turned black, repeating in a terrible cycle, his vision returning only to be snatched away again. Clear. Black. Clear. Black. Thunder crashed, and it sounded like Lantrelia itself was being torn apart as the Fury flung bolt after bolt at them. But the wind was still incredibly strong, bearing the band away to continue its journey toward one of the Four Kingdoms.

Kaven pulled himself out of his hole and looked around fearfully. Many new holes decorated the shattered ground, but, thank Na'lek, Tasi'a, Toyon, and Shera all emerged from their own pits, faces pale and bodies trembling.

"Is everyone all right?" Kaven asked, realizing that his voice was shaky.

"I am unharmed," Tasi'a said, dusting herself off and quickly regaining her composure.

Shera swiveled to watch the band and make sure that it wouldn't return. Sometimes the winds could completely switch direction, bringing lightning bands back around for another bombardment. "I'm fine."

Toyon nodded. "Honestly, we were overdue for that."

"I think it's getting late," Tasi'a said. "Why don't we camp here for the night?"

"How far into the Fury are we now?" Shera asked. "In miles, I mean."

Tasi'a shrugged, "I'm not exactly sure."

"Wait." Kaven's eyes widened in mock surprise. "I thought Venedecians knew everything."

Tasi'a laughed. "Clearly, there's a difference between the knowledge of a Vendecian and a Regelian. For example, I understand the nuances of humor, but you do not." She smiled cheekily.

Kaven snorted. "I doubt that, Tasi'a. Everyone thinks I'm funny." He smiled at Shera, who was giving him a dubious stare.

They made camp, laying out their sleeping bags as Tasi'a started another fire. They cooked lamb, of all things, and it turned out that Toyon was quite the cook. He carried a bag of spices with him at all times, though Kaven had initially wondered if they were poisons. The evening meal was delicious, and they had real conversations and laughter for the first time. Even Toyon joined in. After eating, they settled down into their bags as Toyon once again took the first watch.

Kaven drifted off to sleep, watching the still fire. Shera was sleeping on the other side of it, and she was still smiling.

Kaven slept soundly until Tasi'a woke him. "Your turn for the watch," she said.

Nodding and yawning, he stood and grabbed his bow and quiver from where he had placed them by his pack. "Sleep well, Tasi'a." The sorceress smiled and was soon sleeping soundly in her bedding.

Nocking an arrow and letting it hang slack in his hand, Kaven stood at the edge of the camp and looked out into the darkness. All was silent—even the wind wasn't making much noise, except when it rustled his cloak. Kaven scanned the horizon, making sure to look around the entire circumference of their small camp. Nothing moved. That was good. He didn't want to fight in the darkness. He yawned, but he would get another chance to sleep after his two-hour shift was over. Then he would wake Shera, who had the final shift until dawn.

Kaven reflected on the day's revelations. Shera had shown him the truth of his actions in the Regelian military. He had fought to prove himself, fought for the sake of pride. He had fought with arrogance and apathy. He had worn selfishness like a cloak, concealing it from everyone, including himself. But no longer. He would never fight for those terrible reasons again.

He jogged around the perimeter of their camp to stay awake. Kaven was careful to stay quiet as he moved; the others needed their sleep. This was the worst part of his journey in the Fury thus far. The first night hadn't been so bad, for exhaustion had only just begun to rear its ugly head. But nine hours of uncomfortable, restless sleep, followed by fifteen hours of continuous walking, did not make for pleasant nights. His legs grumbled in protest of their continued use as he jogged, and his arms threatened to revolt as he swung them in a crisp, military style. He quieted his quarrelsome body, gritted his teeth, and continued through the pain. If his time in the military had taught him anything, it was that the more he did this, the better he'd get. And the day that his limbs stopped aching during a march like this would be a good day indeed.

Every couple of times around, he would pause and search the surrounding area, as well as the horizon, but there was no sign of any Fury-spawn, or of a storm band building. After these periodic checks, he would return to his exercise.

Once an hour had passed, his body simply could endure no more without a rest, so he crouched down onto his sleeping bag and focused his attention on watching for any threats. Still there was nothing, and Kaven began to feel uneasy. Toyon was right; the fact that they had traveled for so long under the Fury's baleful watch without any real incident was . . . odd. They were in the Fields of Glory, fully in the grasp of the Shredders, the deadliest part of the Fury.

They were also far deeper into the storm than anyone had ever gone before. This place was supposed to hold the grand empires of the Silent Ones, Flamebringers, and other monsters. But the terrible armies of the Fury-spawn were absent, leaving the Fields silent and empty. All they had experienced was one lightning band and one raiding party. It was foreboding and made Kaven suspect that something, or someone, was frightening the monsters off. Tasi'a seemed to think that Na'lek was taking a direct hand in all of this, guiding them down a safe path. But Kaven decided to trust his mother's words: *All things fear the Hands of Na'lek.* The Hands were the Titans, and he did fear them. Even the Fury-spawn were terrified of the Titans. Kaven worried that a Titan might have been hunting here recently; he couldn't think of any other reason for the monsters to be missing. If they were found by a Titan . . .

Kaven shivered, suddenly glad that no one else was awake to witness his apprehension. He scanned the horizon once more, watching for the colossal, towering shapes of the Titans. The Watcher's terrible red eyes lurked in the corners of his mind, threatening to consume him with fear. Those dark, haunting eyes had seemed so dangerous from the Wall. So hateful.

The next hour crawled by at an incredibly slow pace, and Kaven jumped at every tiny sound, even though the Titans would not be that quiet in their coming. In the few times they had attacked the city, the ground had trembled with each step they took, and they could be seen from miles away before they were close enough to hurt anyone. That always gave the kingdoms time to prepare. Not that it did them any good, of course.

Kaven was so worried about the massive monsters that he forgot to scan the skies and keep a close watch on the ground. He had lost track of the time, but luckily, Tasi'a had found a solution to that eventuality. A clear little orb floated above the fire, untouched by the winds and emitting a soft blue light. Every two hours, the color changed. When Tasi'a had created it, the orb was gray. Then it had turned green for Tasi'a, and then red for Kaven. Now it was blue, announcing that it was Shera's turn.

Still shaking, Kaven hefted himself up and walked over to where Shera slept. He patted her on the shoulder until she awoke, which didn't take long. She opened her eyes and looked up blearily. "It's your shift now, Shera." Kaven tried to sound pleasant. "Time to get up."

Shera rose, grumbling slightly and putting a hand to her disheveled hair. "Blasted wind. Does it ever still?"

"I doubt it." Kaven chuckled, his fear submerging now that he had company. "But the wind is all that's out here tonight. All else is silent."

The Stormgardian unsheathed her sword. "Na'lek sends that it stays that way." Shera nodded toward him. "Get some sleep, Kaven. We will be safe until the morning."

Kaven smiled. "Good night." He quickly slipped into his sleeping bag and surrendered to his exhaustion, and despite the hard, jagged rocks that served as his bed, sleep came quickly. It was a dreamless sleep, devoid of monsters, the Fury, or the Watcher.

Kaven groaned when morning came and Shera shook him awake. He sat up and looked around groggily. Tasi'a was hunched over the fire, hair fluffed like a cat's tail and eyes half shut. She was magically suspending a frying pan over the fire, which contained sizzling bacon. Tasi'a looked ready to fall over sideways and sleep the day away, and the bacon was beginning to burn.

Shera was moving on to wake Toyon, who sprang to his feet silently the moment his shoulder was touched, a thin knife suddenly in his hand, as if summoned by magic. But when he saw that all was well, he slid the blade back amongst the others on his belt and sat down beside Tasi'a.

Kaven took his seat, which was nothing but a stone that was slightly less uncomfortable than others in the area, on the other side of Tasi'a as Shera sat down next to Toyon. Tasi'a did not stir when they took their seats.

Toyon nudged her. "Tasi'a, that bacon looks a little charred, don't you think?"

"Huh?" Tasi'a jerked, as if being startled out of a trance. The pan wobbled and fell into the fire.

"Hey!" Shera, who had just slid on her leg armor and breastplate, kicked the pan out of the fire and ran to scoop up the bacon. Using her foot, she turned the pan right-side up and grabbed the hot meat, tossing it from hand to hand until she could deposit it into the pan. "Be more careful, Tasi'a. We can't afford to lose any of this food."

Tasi'a looked about, startled. When she realized what had happened, she blushed a deep crimson. "Sorry! I . . . sorry. I'm just so tired."

Kaven laughed, patting Tasi'a on the back. "Aren't we all? No matter. I prefer burnt bacon anyway."

"Really?" Tasi'a asked with a small frown.

"It reminds him of Regelian beer," Toyon said with a smirk.

They others laughed, but Kaven didn't think it was funny. There was nothing cheap about Regelian beer. They ate quickly, as they had a long way to travel today, and Shera wanted them to get an early start.

And so they set off, heading in a direction that they hoped was east. Tasi'a tried to determine which way the winds were blowing as they packed their bags and started walking, but the streams of air were so chaotic that Tasi'a couldn't get a proper read from them. So, they were going off Toyon's instincts and Shera's supposed sense of direction.

Kaven had no knowledge of directions, but he dearly wished he did. He also hoped that Toyon and Shera knew what they were doing. Tasi'a, meanwhile, seemed disgruntled at her exhaustion. The scowl was an odd expression for her.

They chatted as they pushed against the winds, keeping a watchful eye on their surroundings. Toyon was curious to learn about the Regelian University for Scientific Advancement, and Kaven was happy to supply him with details.

The soft-spoken Fulminite had considered attending the college and had an interest in the science and mechanics used in Regelia. Unfortunately, Toyon hadn't enough expertise to be accepted into the college.

Kaven was pleased to be able to provide useful information about his college. He spoke of the different classes, dealing with various branches of technology. There was Ironmancy, which involved working with metal and stone for construction. There was Firework, creating technology that ran on heat and Output, crafting machines that used magic, such as the Firerods. Kaven's own device, Animus, would be an Output machine if he could ever get it to work.

Toyon shifted his backpack so it rested more comfortably on his shoulders. "I would have chosen Ironmancy, I think. Fulminos produces some of the finest blades in Lantrelia, and I have always been interested in the craft. What did you major in, Kaven?

"Well . . ." Kaven hesitated, dreading this conversation, but hiding it was pointless now anyway. "I wasn't proficient in any of the branches, so I sort of hopped between them to avoid being expulsed from the university."

Shera glanced back at him. "How did you even get in?"

"My parents are sort of famous," Kaven said, his cheeks growing warm. "And Headmaster Gane, the man who runs the university, is a good friend of theirs."

Toyon chuckled dryly. "So you attended for free?"

Kaven blushed again. *By the Titans, this is humiliating.* It was a relief to know that the other three had come from similar backgrounds, fraught with numerous occurrences of incompetence. "Basically."

"I wish my parents could have done that," Toyon said wistfully. "They had . . . other goals in mind."

They walked in silence for a time until they stopped for lunch. This lunch was an affair of fish and onions, which Tasi'a chose to omit in favor of some strawberries.

"I don't know why you hate these," Shera said to Tasi'a over a mouthful of the crunchy bulb. "Onions are filled to the brim with—"

"I am aware of their benefits," Tasi'a interjected. "Yet I prefer not smelling like a grannoc has died in my mouth. I will be eating my berries instead, thank you."

Kaven joined Shera in feasting on the onions, lauding their great taste, while Tasi'a watched with a look of supreme distaste as she nibbled her berries. "Amazing," said Kaven, leaning close to Tasi'a. "You should try some!"

Tasi'a quickly pulled away from Kaven's offending stench but found herself confronted by Shera, who offered a half-eaten onion toward her.

"They have such a unique taste; are you sure you don't want any?" Kaven smiled at the look of disgust that blossomed on her face.

Toyon ate in silence, watching their antics with a look of blank apathy. Kaven couldn't decipher what the grim man was thinking. He didn't seem disapproving, but nor was he laughing.

When the meal came to its conclusion, they packed up once more and set off. By Toyon's estimate, it was well past midday. "We can walk a few more hours today," Shera shouted over the wind so Tasi'a could hear her. The sorceress was walking a few paces behind the others, remaining adamant that she would stay far away from them until the stench of onions was eradicated entirely.

"If we get out of this alive," Kaven said, "I'm going to throw a huge feast, but I'm only going to serve onions."

"Count me in," said Shera.

"Count me out," Tasi'a declared.

Toyon frowned. "How are you going to throw a party? I doubt you can afford it."

Kaven chose not to mention his parents' considerable wealth, instead shrugging. "We'll be the men"—he glanced at the girls—"and women who put an end to the Fury. They'll shower us with riches and treasures."

"Public recognition is probably the most we'll get," Shera said, shrugging. "Not that wealth is why we are doing this. But we might get away with a feast."

"We'd better," Toyon grumbled. "No way we're doing all of this and not getting a proper feast."

They walked on as the hour grew later and later. Kaven looked up at the storm doubtfully as they marched. Again, the Fury was oddly calm today, and there were *still* no signs of any monsters. The whole thing was discomforting, yet he couldn't complain.

"Something was here recently," Toyon announced, stopping suddenly. He bent low to the ground and picked up a tiny tuft of white fuzz that had been caught on a rock.

Shera hissed at the sight of it. "Spinereaver!"

Toyon nodded. "Only one."

"How long ago?" Tasi'a looked around nervously.

Kaven stared at the fur. Spinereavers were clever hunters, perhaps even better than wolves. If a Spinereaver was hunting them, they could be in serious danger. Spinereavers often traveled in packs, and Kaven had no desire to face dozens of those beasts.

Toyon released the tuft and it was taken by the wind. "It was a few days ago, unless I'm mistaken."

Kaven opened his mouth, but Shera spoke first, asking the question he had been about to say. "Are we being tracked?"

"I don't know." Toyon scanned the horizon but evidently saw nothing. "I believe it's ahead of us, but I cannot be certain. We should be more vigilant from now on."

They saw no sign of the Spinereaver, or any other monster, throughout the rest of the day as they traveled. Dinner that night was a quiet event of cheese and leftover fish, and much to Tasi'a's relief, there were no onions to be had.

After they finished dining, they went to bed with Kaven taking the first watch. The two hours passed uneventfully, and as the little orb changed from red to gray, Kaven bent down to awaken Toyon and swiftly went to bed. But he was restless for an hour, his nervousness chewing at him, before he finally went to sleep.

Kaven was alone. He stood under the Fury as the dark storm raged over him. Thunder boomed in the distance, rolling toward him with the wind. He had to move, or the lightning would take him. But where were the others? Their sleeping bags and supplies were still here, but the three had been gone when he had woken.

He ran from the Fury and its dark lightning, calling the names of his companions. "Toyon? Tasi'a? Shera?" He ran frantically, never stopping or looking back, even as the thunder grew louder and the sky darkened behind him. Where had they gone? Had they sensed the storm and fled? No! They never would have left him! *Or would they?* Kaven crushed that small voice quickly. He knew that they would not abandon him.

Kaven rushed forward, knowing that the Fury was chasing him, hunting him. He pushed his tired body to new speeds as he called out for his friends. "Shera? Toyon? Tasi'a?" But no answer came, and the only sound was that of the oncoming thunder.

He looked back, and he finally saw the darkness that was brewing behind him. Thousands upon thousands of Silent Ones were marching toward him under a tortured sky, surging forward with blades raised high. Even as they rushed toward him, they made no sound. They came forward with a dark purpose. Above, the Eternal Storm cackled and screamed with thunder and lightning, and something huge and black moved behind the Fury. Na'lek himself.

The Silent Ones had killed his companions. That was the only possibility! Kaven felt dull as he came to understand that they were all dead. They were slain. Killed by the monster, devoured by the Fury. A face appeared in the clouds above, stormy features twisted in a roar, eyes burdened with the wisdom and rage of countless eons. Na'lek had taken them, and now he came for Kaven.

But he had to keep moving. The Fury swiped at him with lightning like claws, slashing and tossing up great chunks of stone in its violent pursuit. He had to dodge away from the blows and switch directions constantly to avoid being vaporized. And all the while, the Silent Ones were coming ever closer. Kaven knew what was happening now; the Fury was herding him somewhere, like a farmer with a pitchfork guiding his cattle. And the Silent Ones were the sheepdogs, ensuring that he couldn't try to go back. But where was the Fury sending him? The slaughterhouse.

There was nothing Kaven could do. Perhaps he could stop and launch a couple arrows into the advancing army, but the lightning would take him almost immediately. All he could do was delay the inevitable and keep running. The Fury was victorious once more; Na'lek had won.

Then the specter of his own death materialized before him, personified in an immense black form with terrible red eyes. The Watcher bent down, observing him with a hateful gaze, laced with a dark amusement. The corpses of Toyon, Tasi'a, and Shera were draped across the Titan's feet, faces pale and eyes wide with their final expressions of shock. Their throats had been torn open, spilling their lifeblood across the broken ground.

Kaven skidded to a halt in front of the behemoth's feet, staring up at the terrible Titan. The Watcher stared back, and then it opened its immense maw, revealing thousands of razor-sharp teeth. Horns reached up from its shoulders and head, streaked with red and brushing the clouds. Its steel armor reflected the darkness of the lightning bolts as they struck. And then the Watcher began to laugh, a terrible, malevolent sound that shattered the ground and caused the Silent Ones to flee in terror.

Kaven collapsed to the ground, screaming and covering his ears. He looked up at his enemy in horror, calling for Na'lek to deliver him. But it was too late now; death had come for him. The Four Kingdoms would be consumed by the Fury, and he had failed one last time.

Patches of steel rose from the Watcher's leg armor and began to turn white. The chunks grew legs, tails, and long spikes from their backs. Spinereavers. One of the beasts leapt down from the Titan and crouched in front of Kaven, ready to pounce. Kaven cowered away from the beast, and the Spinereaver lunged for his throat. Saliva spilled over Kaven's face, neck, and chest until he felt like he was drowning under the Spinereaver's onslaught.

Kaven came awake screaming. He sat bolt upright, panting as he looked around in a panic. It was still night and he noticed that Shera and Toyon were sitting upright as well. They were both soaking wet. Then he noticed that he was wet as well. How in the Fury . . . ? Then he saw Tasi'a standing over them, a wide grin on her face.

"I also prefer water to onions," she said wickedly.

*Just a nightmare.* Kaven sighed with great relief. That relief quickly changed into annoyance. He shivered as the cold wind assailed him and rushed toward the fire, with Toyon and Shera quick to follow. The three of them huddled around the motionless blaze, trembling and shooting glares at Tasi'a.

Tasi'a smiled widely, immensely proud of her revenge. "I don't suppose you'd like a drying spell?"

"I *would*, actually," Shera spat from where she crouched over the fire, nearly leaning into it. Kaven noticed that a large layer of ash was covering the ground around the fire, and most of their camp as well. The fire must have flared up during the night.

The sorceress sniffed daintily. "Well, I'm sorry. I'm feeling kind of tired right now; I should probably conserve my strength."

Kaven snorted. "Yes, that'd probably be best." Kaven should have seen something like this coming, especially after hearing that story about her brother. But she didn't have to go this far.

Toyon crouched into a hole to change out of his wet clothes. He now wore black pants and a matching shirt, along with a brown cape and a leather belt, openly adorned with his knives and pouches. Kaven counted twelve blades. He looked much warmer now.

Kaven eyed him jealousy. He should probably change too. It would definitely be warmer. But he didn't relish changing out here in the open either.

Shera stood suddenly and rushed toward Tasi'a. "How about a hug?" Tasi'a screeched and leapt backward to avoid the wet assault. Shera pursued the sorceress around the camp, insisting that Tasi'a be given a nice, warm embrace.

Suddenly, Tasi'a tripped and fell to the ground. Shera, laughing the whole time, stopped and helped her to her feet. "Very graceful, Tasi'a." She had fallen into a depression of some sort.

Toyon came over, shaking his head. "This is what happens when you're not caref—" He stopped, eyes widening.

Kaven rushed over, ignoring a new wave of shivers. "Toyon, what's wrong?"

He pointed at the girls. "Look at what they're standing in."

The three of them gasped as they arrived at Toyon's observation; Tasi'a had tripped into a massive, four-toed footprint that was at least eight feet long and six feet wide. Shera was the first of the three to speak. "A Titan . . ." she murmured in disbelief.

Toyon nodded slowly. "That thing wasn't there when we made camp here."

Kaven's fear quickly returned. He stared at the print in absolute horror. Toyon was right; that hadn't been there. The Titan had walked by just a couple of hours ago, maybe less, and no one had noticed.

"Kaven, did you see anything during your watch?" Shera demanded, not looking away from the footprint pressed into the stone. Only something of immense weight could have put such an impression into solid rock.

"No," Kaven whispered. "I saw nothing." He could see the monster's other prints. It had come up from the south and had walked right by them as it continued northward. Kaven looked to the north, following the line of massive footprints, but the Titan was already so far gone that there was no sign of it in the distance.

"I didn't either," Shera said, confused. "Tasi'a? It must have come during your watch."

Tasi'a shot her a glare. "Do you really think I would have missed a *Titan* walking past our camp?"

"Let's not argue," Toyon said calmly, trying to pacify the sorceress. "The important thing is that we are still alive and the Titan is gone."

"I vote we get an extra-early start today," Kaven said, still watching the horizon warily. What if it came back? He shuddered. What if it was the Watcher? What if it influenced his dreams? "Just in case it decides to return."

Shera nodded. "That is a good idea, Kaven. Everyone pack up so we can get out of this dark place."

They quickly put out the fire, gathered their things, and practically ran away from the massive set of tracks. They didn't slow down again until midday when they had to stop for lunch.

Kaven was hungry because they hadn't eaten breakfast in their haste to flee from the Titan's path.

Tasi'a started another fire in what they all hoped would be a secure location. It was a shallow depression in the area and would provide some protection from the enemy's visibility and the Fury's lightning. They set out their supplies, but Kaven was still terrified. How had a Titan snuck up on their camp? That didn't make any sense!

Kaven chewed on a scoop of beans slowly. They did not taste appetizing at all, with a rubbery texture and cold center. Were they not cooked all the way? "Can you pass me a canteen, please?" he asked.

Toyon obliged, handing him the round water carrier.

"In case some of you haven't noticed yet," Shera announced as Kaven drank deeply, "we've stopped shining. That means our protection potion is about to run out. We need to reapply before we continue."

Kaven squinted at his companions. He *hadn't* noticed, but that golden sheen was gone. This meant that the chaotic, deadly energies of the Fury would begin to slowly cut them to pieces.

Shera reached into her backpack and pulled out one of several vials of the protection potions. "Everyone find a secluded area and put it on. Remember, every inch of your skin must be covered. I'll go first while you're all eating." She walked away from the camp to find a deep pit.

Kaven tried to eat quickly. Though grateful for the respite, he was eager to keep moving. The more distance they put between themselves and that Titan, the better.

By the time Shera had returned, Kaven had finished his beans and was ready to go. So he went next. Leaving the camp, but not going too far away, Kaven went into a pit with a bottle of the potion.

Stripping, Kaven quickly poured the freezing, golden liquid over himself. Once it had hardened and faded away to a shimmer, he redressed and returned to the camp. "All right, Toyon, you're up," he said as he entered. Everyone was ready to go now and the fire had been put out.

"I'd like to go next," Tasi'a announced. She hurried forward but then paused. "If you don't mind, Toyon."

The lanky assassin waved a hand. "By all means, Tasi'a. Go ahead."

The sorceress disappeared amongst the rocks. Kaven watched her go. "Do you think this is dangerous? No one is out there to keep an eye on her."

Shera scoffed. "We don't really have a wide variety of privacy options under the Fury, Kaven. If we want to maintain some sort of decency, we have to take that risk."

"You could still go with her," Kaven mumbled. It really was a dangerous thing to do. He wondered why he hadn't asked Toyon to go with him.

"If she asked it of me," Shera said, "I would."

Proving Kaven's fears unfounded, Tasi'a returned, shining gold and shivering. Toyon set out to reapply, and Kaven called after him, "Do you want me to watch your back?" He probably didn't, but it didn't hurt to ask.

Toyon glanced at him flatly. "I'll manage." He went out into the rocks and was lost to sight.

Soon, Toyon reemerged, safe and protected from the Eternal Storm, and the four of them set off once more. Two more hours passed and they were all in cheerful moods, despite that dreadful scare in the early morning. Kaven was feeling much more tired today, however. It felt as if he'd been here for months already. "How far away are we?"

Tasi'a raised an eyebrow. "From the Fury's heart?"

"Yes."

Toyon scratched at the black stubble growing on his chin, a result of not having a razor and an unwillingness to use his knives for this task. "Unless I'm greatly mistaken, I'd say we have another four days of travel ahead of us."

"Na'lek sends that the Fury remains this calm for the remainder of our journey," Shera declared, looking up at the raging sky.

Kaven nodded. "And for our return trip?"

"Silly Regelian." Tasi'a giggled. "When we return, there won't be a Fury to walk through!"

*Unless we fail,* Kaven thought. But he decided to keep such grim thoughts to himself. There was no point in bringing down their optimism. Or his own, for that matter. To his own surprise, Kaven felt good. For once, it seemed to him that this suicidal mission had more than a decent chance at success. He didn't know what had brought this mood on. Perhaps it was his companions, or the beans, or Na'lek's will. Whatever the reason, Kaven was grateful for the air of good cheer.

Stone crunched from behind them. Kaven, who was taking up the rear, paused, knowing that the sound had not come from his companions. He turned, and the other three spun with him. Shera had her sword and shield out, the air around Tasi'a shimmered, and Toyon held a knife in each hand. Kaven hesitated between his Firerod and his bow, but he had never used Gane's gift before, so he drew his bow and readied a shaft.

From behind a large boulder came a four-legged creature the size of a Lantrelian wolf. From a wide, spade-shaped head, four black eyes studied them with a hungry gaze. Short fangs glistened in a long snout as it raised its lips in a snarl. Long yellow claws clicked against the stone as it crouched, its long, whiplike tail pointing straight upward, emphasizing its short white fur. Its back was lined with hundreds of gray spines, each as long as Kaven's forearms and as thick as his thumb.

Kaven reacted immediately. His only thought was to kill this creature before it could attack. However, the Spinereaver was quick. It rolled like a crocodile, spinning onto its back to dodge the arrow, and then came back up onto its feet. The monster's spines retracted upon meeting the ground and reemerged when the beast was upright.

"For Stormgarde!" Shera rushed toward the Spinereaver, Toyon following behind as Kaven readied another arrow.

The creature thrust its back forward, arching to heave its quills toward them. A dozen razor-sharp spines launched from the Spinereaver, swift and powerful. The spines slammed against Shera's shield, slowing her charge. Most of the spines clattered to the ground, but two were driven a fourth of their length into her iron shield.

Shera met the Spinereaver head on as Toyon leapt to the side of her. Kaven found his aim blocked by Shera and ran to find a better angle while Toyon stabbed a knife into the creature's shoulder, but he accidentally blocked Shera's sword blow and the monster scratched at her shield furiously, dragging long gouges into it.

Shouting another war cry, Shera raised her sword to slam it into the Spinereaver's head and Kaven launched another arrow. Kaven suddenly felt an intense heat as a ball of fire slammed into the ground next to the Spinereaver, exploding in a brilliant burst of heat and flame. The monster was tossed back, along with Toyon. Shera hit the ground hard and Kaven's arrow barely missed her head.

The Spinereaver fell on top of Toyon, and the Fulminite only avoided death because the monster landed on its side. Ignoring the downed assassin, the Spinereaver stood and charged toward Shera as it dislodged a second volley aimed at Tasi'a.

"Be more careful!" Shera roared at Tasi'a.

Tasi'a said nothing, instead spinning her arms in a circle, as a shimmering, purple orb materialized to encompass her. The spines struck the barrier and snapped, falling to the ground in pieces.

Shera raised her sword, slashing at the Spinereaver even as the monster lunged at her. The blade caught the monster across its front leg, painting a long line of red across the white fur. The creature yelped, swatting at her with wide paws. The blow was deflected by Shera's raised shield, and she thrust her sword back into the Spinereaver, stabbing it in the chest. Unfortunately, the blade did not go in far, only an inch or two disappearing into the beast's flesh. The Spinereaver reared back on its hind legs, kicking Shera in the jaw. She collapsed, and the Spinereaver sank low to feast on her.

"Hey!" Kaven launched another arrow, which took the Spinereaver in the right flank. The monster turned on him and arched its back, launching a dozen spines at him. Kaven rolled to dodge but felt a wetness spatter his face.

Kaven collapsed, bleeding. He looked down at his left forearm; a hole had been bored straight through it, and the offending spine was lying beside him, glistening and wet. Then . . . came the pain. Kaven felt like a Flamebringer had grabbed his arm and was squeezing as hard as it could. He tried to stand but fell back, dizzy and disoriented. He was losing too much blood.

The Spinereaver was stalking slowly toward Tasi'a, who had her shield up once more. The monster launched dozens of spines at the sorceress, slowly chipping away her shield and coming closer and closer. Tasi'a couldn't fight back; it was taking all her concentration to maintain her faltering shield.

Kaven had to do something! It couldn't end like this, not now. They were so close to Na'lek. The Fury *would not* win like this. Kaven tried to sit up and felt a wave of nausea wash over him. He was holding his bow, but he couldn't sit up enough to reach into his quiver. The spine was still lying next to him. He grabbed it and positioned it on his bow, but it wobbled in his shaking hands. Trying to steady himself, he shot the spine at the Spinereaver, but then he fell over, blood spilling into his mouth as it pooled around him. Consciousness fled from him.

# FIFTEEN

*"Defiance of the Fury is commendable, but defiance of the Church is blasphemy."*

—From the Tomes of Regret, Verse 22 of Repentance

KAVEN OPENED HIS eyes, blinking tears from them. His left arm was throbbing and it hurt to move even in the slightest way. He looked down at the wound; it was wrapped in white bandages stained with his blood. Kaven was honestly surprised to still be alive, but he sent a grateful prayer to Na'lek as he sat up.

He judged by the darkness around him that it was night-time, and the wind assailed him, howling as it pushed the Fury ever forward. Was a storm band brewing? Kaven could barely make out the storm, it was too dark and he felt groggy. He found that he was sitting in his sleeping bag next to a fire, Tasi'a and Toyon sleeping nearby.

"You're awake!" Shera was suddenly kneeling beside him. "Keep still, Kaven. You lost a lot of blood."

"Is everyone okay?" Kaven asked slowly, feeling dizzy as he looked up into her face.

She smiled. "Everyone but you. You'll live, though. A spine went right through your arm and you fainted from blood loss. Tasi'a tried healing you, but she couldn't drive out the Spinereaver's poison completely. When we get back, you'll need to see a professional healer."

Kaven groaned. "It burns like fire."

"I'd imagine so." Shera stood, giving him a sad smile. "Unfortunately, there's not much we can do for you."

Kaven suppressed another exclamation of pain. "What happened to the Spinereaver?"

"You killed it!" Shera beamed at him. "You put its own spine right through its skull. It was one of the wildest shots I've ever seen!"

"Guess I'm just lucky," Kaven muttered. So that was his first real kill then, and he hadn't even been awake to see it. He didn't feel particularly jubilant.

Shera raised an eyebrow. "Luck is a foolish concept. Na'lek himself guided your hand."

Kaven didn't feel like arguing the point. "How long was I out?"

"Several hours," Shera said. "It's almost dawn."

Kaven sighed, knowing he had cost them about half a day's travel. "I'm sorry. How pathetic is it that one monster nearly killed us all?"

Shera nodded, smiling wryly. "I do believe that we're simply unaccustomed to working with each other. Do you want something to eat?" She began to rummage in his backpack.

Kaven shook his head. "No, thanks." He felt exhausted and his arm throbbed. "If you don't mind, I think I want to get some more sleep."

"No problem." She put the pack down and resumed watching the surrounding landscape. "We'll be leaving in the morning. Good night, Kaven."

"Night." Kaven put his head back down and surrendered to sleep's cool mercy.

"I don't believe you understand how difficult it is to pinpoint precisely where my spells will strike to create a tactically accurate attack against my opponents!" Kaven came awake to the unfamiliar sound of Tasi'a yelling. He moaned and kept his eyes closed, unwilling to join in the cacophony. His arm hurt worse than it had before, and the throbbing had become more distinct.

"I would not call throwing a massive fireball into our midst a 'tactically accurate' attack," came Toyon's soft voice.

"Says the one who spent half the battle unconscious!" Tasi'a retorted angrily.

Toyon chuckled dryly. "Only because of the aforementioned fireball."

"Can you both be quiet?" Kaven said, sounding even more exasperated than he really was. "You're giving me a splitting headache."

"Shut up, yourself, Shera!" Tasi'a snapped.

"Please stay out of our argument," Toyon said, his tone calm and steady. "It only involves Tasi'a's failure."

"Failure!" The sorceress sounded ready to strangle Toyon. "*I'm* the failure?"

Shera, who had been cooking breakfast over the fire, stood up. "All right, that's enough! Toyon is complaining and Tasi'a isn't speaking and it's beginning to scare me. I'm far too tired to deal with you both being strange, and I certainly don't want to listen to you fight. We messed up during that battle, all of us. But it's done, and we're still alive. Now *everyone* shut up and sit down so we can eat together as *friends*."

"And Shera's being the voice of reason," Kaven grumbled. "We all might be going crazy."

Tasi'a and Toyon were standing on opposite ends of the fire, glaring at each other. But their anger melted when they saw Kaven, and they rushed over.

"Kaven!" Tasi'a exclaimed. "You're awake!"

"How do you feel?" Toyon asked, clapping a hand on Kaven's shoulder. His good one, thankfully. "You still look pale."

Kaven smiled. "I'm fine. My arm hurts like you wouldn't believe, but I'll be able to manage. Thanks for asking."

Tasi'a smiled. "Thank you for saving our lives."

"Careful now," Shera called. "Don't forget all that blood you've lost. It's going to be a little while before you're ready to fight a Spinereaver again."

"Thank you all for making sure I didn't die," Kaven said, staring up at them. Was this what it was like to have friends? It felt . . . wonderful.

Toyon sniffed. "With my luck, I would have ended up being the one to haul your corpse back to Regelia."

Kaven laughed. "You could have just dumped me in a hole."

Toyon smiled, a strange expression to see on his face. "I'll keep that option in mind next time."

"In all seriousness," Tasi'a said, "a Spinereaver's poison is nothing to laugh about. You'll be fine for a couple of weeks, but if you don't get magical aid, you will die."

"I've got time, then," Kaven said. He wasn't worried; if the Fury couldn't kill him out here, then what chance did a Spinereaver have?

"We need to finish what we've started here," Shera said, beginning to serve them a breakfast of eggs. "I don't intend to leave Shilanti until the Fury has been vanquished. However, we need to learn how to fight together, otherwise we will never make it."

Kaven nodded. "We have to work on finding the balance between our specific skills." Kaven didn't mention that he didn't know what his skill might be. If he could get his device, Animus, to start working, it would be marvelously useful, but he doubted that he'd be able to do that out here. Still, Kaven was the only one who knew how to operate a Firerod, and that was perhaps their most powerful weapon.

"Toyon," Shera said after they had finished eating. "Do you think the Spinereaver we killed was the same one we saw signs of previously?"

The assassin shrugged. "Impossible to tell. The monster didn't have any distinguishing characteristics."

They quickly packed and got ready to leave. Kaven carefully slid his backpack on, taking extra care not to hurt himself, and the four of them set off once more, beginning their fifth day under the Fury.

Every time Kaven took a step across the rocky landscape, it sent a jarring pain up his arm. He hoped that he wouldn't tear it open again; the last thing he needed was to collapse and start bleeding.

"Shouldn't we see Na'lek's city soon?" Tasi'a asked.

Toyon shook his head. "We're still about three days away from the Fury's heart. If Shilanti is as immense as the priests claim, we'll see it tomorrow."

"Shilanti! Shilanti! Tomorrow! Tomorrow!"

They all froze as a strange, high-pitched voice echoed around them. Tasi'a hissed, "How is that sound echoing?"

"How! How!" came the loud voice, speaking so quickly it was hard to make out the repeated sound. "Echoing! Echoing!"

Shera drew her sword. "Bouncers!"

Kaven pulled out his Firerod, a chill creeping up his spine. The magic weapon would be more effective against the little creatures than his bow, and he could hardly use that with one arm.

Bouncers were terrible creatures, so named because they constantly hopped about, never once walking or crawling. They traveled in massive packs, overwhelming small bands of soldiers and stripping them of flesh in a matter of seconds. Moira Fortis's notes claimed that the largest recorded pack was six thousand strong. Bouncers also often mimicked sounds with near perfection. They were even able to replicate complex sounds, like that of a sword being drawn or loud footsteps.

"Bouncers! Bouncers!" A small, blue-furred shape leapt out of a lightning pit. Toyon spun, stabbing a knife into the Fury-spawn while it was still in midair. The Bouncer let out a high-pitched squeal and thumped to the ground.

Kaven looked down at the tiny creature. With four legs, long yellow buckteeth, fluffy fur, stubby ears, and a short tail, the dead Bouncer looked somewhat like a rat, but twice as large and wide.

Toyon wiped sticky green blood from his blade on a white cloth. "There are more in the holes," he whispered to them. "Be silent; they're waiting for their companion to return."

They all stood still, not daring to move or speak. *How long will the Bouncers wait?* Kaven wondered. *How many are there?* Then Kaven was struck by inspiration. These creatures obviously were not intelligent; if they were waiting for the dead Bouncer, he could fool them with a simple trick! He kicked the Bouncer corpse back into the hole.

Shera glared at Kaven. "You idiot . . ."

"Idiot! Idiot!" Bouncers sprang out of the surrounding holes by the dozens, gray eyes flashing and teeth chattering in unison. "Idiot! Idiot!"

Tasi'a extended her hands toward the farthest pit from which the monsters were spilling. "*This* is a tactically accurate strike!" A massive fireball erupted from her hands, crashing into the hole and obliterating the Bouncers in that area, leaving nothing but ashes. Some of the monsters were not killed, but ran in little circles, squealing as they tried to outrun the flames that enveloped them.

Tasi'a turned and smiled at Toyon.

He shrugged, flinging a knife to spear two monsters midbounce.

Shera swung her sword, striking down three Bouncers that hopped too close. "Don't let them bite you. Form up and stay close!"

Kaven backed up until he bumped into Shera, and he pointed his Firerod toward another pit, flipping the switch on the weapon's side. The rod hummed and began to vibrate in Kaven's hand, and then it unleashed a net of blue lightning that fell over the swarming rodents. Bouncers halted mid-squeak, fur burning as they were instantly cooked by the attack. Kaven directed the Firerod's assault, sweeping it over dozens of Bouncers. They dropped in large clumps, struck down before they could come close. The acrid stench of burning fur and flesh filled the air, but it was dispersed by the wind wherever it arose. The problem was that the stench kept coming, as did the Bouncers.

They still poured from the pits by the score, coming from what must be some underground nest. They darted between Kaven's legs, where the Firerod could not be safely used. He whipped out his shortsword and began hacking at the masses of blue-furred bodies swarming about him.

The Bouncers leapt up at him, razor-sharp teeth snapping and tiny claws scratching at him. Wherever he lashed out with his sword, he felt the resistance of tiny bodies being cut apart.

Bouncers clawed at him, leaving scrapes that were not deep enough to bleed but still stung. So far, he was avoiding their dangerous bite.

Around him, his companions fought their own endless waves of Bouncers. Toyon seemed to be participating in a dance, flowing from one Bouncer to the next, moving so fast that Kaven couldn't keep track of his movements. He stepped around each rodent, daggers darting to intercept each Bouncer as they leapt for his throat. He gutted them effortlessly. His attacks were precise stabs that felled dozens of monsters. Where Kaven saw chaos in the Bouncers, Toyon saw a pattern, and he took advantage of it with supreme skill. Not a single Fury-spawn touched him, and he inflicted death wherever a Bouncer appeared.

Tasi'a was disintegrating scores of Bouncers with blasts of emerald energy. None could get close, much less bite her. The Bouncers were beginning to shy away from the sorceress, becoming hesitant to come near her spells of death. But Tasi'a was merciless in her hunt, purging the Bouncers with great sweeps of magic, destroying Na'lek's creatures with measured skill.

Bouncers fell before Shera like wheat before the farmer's scythe. Using her shield to block their bounding attacks, she cut swaths through them as she advanced toward one of the pits, pushing the Fury-spawn back.

Robbed of his Firerod, it was all Kaven could do to stop the Bouncers from ripping into him with those dangerous, long teeth. He hacked at them with his shortsword as they bounced up to nip at him. It felt like he was hitting apples out of the air with each swing. *Titan's teeth, there are so many of them!* If even one of those things bit him, Kaven knew he would be a dead man. The bite would go down to the bone, and Kaven would stagger, losing his concentration. Then another would latch on,

then another, until dozens of Bouncers were tearing away his
flesh piece by piece. He had to hold on.

Finally, the numbers of Bouncers began to thin. Toyon
was at his side, striking Bouncers as he broke their rush against
Kaven. Taking advantage of Toyon's aid, Kaven rushed to cut
them down in their confusion. Soon, the ground was covered
with still, silent Bouncer corpses.

Tasi'a was staring at the small corpses, eyes wide with horror. "They're so small . . . Titan's teeth, I can't believe they're so
dangerous."

Toyon put a hand on her shoulder. "I've seen many men
die to Bouncers, Tasi'a. This was a small pack; we were lucky."

Eyes still as wide as the moon, Tasi'a stared down at the
tiny bodies. Toyon's words had done little to soothe her.

"By the Fury." Kaven coughed, trying to catch his breath.
"That was utter chaos! How in Na'lek's name can there be so
many of them?"

Shera wiped her sword on the furry bodies. "As Toyon
said, this was nothing. A large pack would have overwhelmed
us with ease."

Kaven stared at her in amazement. "What? Really?" He
couldn't imagine that many Bouncers. He knew such packs
existed, of course, but the hundreds of corpses here were still
stunning.

"Sure," Toyon said. He sounded a lot less winded than
Kaven. "There's a reason we usually need an army to fend them
off."

Kaven shook his head, looking at the dead Bouncers in
astonishment. How could so many of these creatures exist out
here? What did they eat or drink? "A population of this size
proves that Shilanti is out here. Or at least that there's some
kind of oasis in the Fury's heart."

Toyon shrugged, sheathing his knives. "We'll see."

"Kaven." Shera glared at him. "Next time we face any kind of monster, please refrain from tossing the corpse of one of their own back in their faces!"

"Sorry," Kaven mumbled. "I wanted to scare them away." He really had thought that plan would work.

"The monsters of the Fury do not 'scare.' They only become angry." Toyon began walking away.

Tasi'a and Shera followed after him, with Kaven bringing up the rear. "What about the bodies?"

Shera glanced back at him. "What *about* the bodies?"

"Are we just leaving them there?" Kaven gestured to the mounds of Bouncers behind them.

"Yuck." Tasi'a grimaced. "I'm not burying a bunch of vermin corpses. No way!"

Kaven frowned. "What if another monster can trace them to us?"

Shera shrugged. "The most another monster will do is make a meal out of them."

Kaven didn't want to argue over a bunch of dead Bouncers, so he let the subject drop. But he really didn't think it was a good idea. There were many monsters that could hunt by smell, and many smart enough to see that those Bouncers had been killed with swords and magic. The facts weren't hard to put together. But, if Shera didn't want to waste time hiding their tracks, Kaven wasn't going to bother her about it any further.

With the wind battering them around like leaves caught in a gale, they surged forward unyieldingly. The scratches Kaven had sustained by the Bouncers were minor but stung badly enough that he nearly forgot about his arm. Nonetheless, he did not ask to stop and rest as the next hour passed.

Kaven wasn't sure what made him turn around as they prepared to stop for lunch. It certainly wasn't the crunch of armor on stone, for if that sound had existed, the wind drowned it out. And it certainly wasn't any battle instinct he possessed. Perhaps it was blind luck, a sheer coincidence, or even Na'lek's divine will. Or maybe it was the feeling of lethargy that began to overtake him. Whatever the reason, the action saved his life.

He turned around to see a Silent One standing behind him, bladelike arm raised and ready to strike. Had it heard their battle? Or had it simply come upon them by happenstance? It didn't matter . . . not really. What *did* matter was the razor-sharp weapon being thrust toward his throat.

Kaven fell to the ground, so shocked he didn't even cry out, causing the Silent One's blade to go over his head. The Silent One stumbled but quickly brought both of its built-in weapons down on him. Kaven scrambled backward, drawing his shortsword.

The Silent One advanced toward him, four arms extended and ready to tear him apart. Out of the corner of his eye, Kaven saw his companions turn slowly, too slowly. They were under the Silent One's spell. He didn't have time to wait for them. The Silent One was going to kill him right now. Sword raised, Kaven kicked a stone, sending it skidding to his right.

The gambit worked. The Silent One turned its eyeless head toward the sound, weapons plunging down toward the rock. Kaven swiveled to the left, keeping a wide berth from the blow, and rammed his shortsword into the Silent One's neck. The Fury-spawn went down, oozing purple ichor down its cheek.

Kaven stood over the dead Silent One, panting heavily as the spell broke. His companions came upon him, weapons and spells at the ready.

"Titans take me, Kaven," Tasi'a said, eyes wide. "That was superb!"

Shera kicked the Silent One in the head. "That was well done, Kaven. I have never seen a man distract a Silent One so quickly." She shook her head as if clearing her thoughts. "By the Fury, it had us under its spell!"

Toyon nodded in agreement. "Yes, it did. Well done, Kaven. You've just saved our lives."

Kaven smiled, raising his sword. The ichor of the Silent One ran off the blade like water, leaving the blade clean. "I . . . I killed it!"

"That's the best a soldier can do on the battlefield," Toyon said. "Shall we continue?"

Kaven hesitated for a moment, looking down on the dead Silent One. He had killed it. He had killed a Fury-spawn! Sure, he'd slain the Spinereaver and the Bouncers, but this monster he'd bested in a duel with the sword! He'd defied the Fury itself! It was exactly what his father had always wanted. A small part of him wanted to shout, *There's another one, Father!* Even though Kaven had decided to fight this battle for his home, he couldn't help but feel a great deal of pride over this victory. He grinned down at the slain Silent One and then hurried after his companions.

# SIXTEEN

*"Oh, how we bemoan our failings! Better to throw ourselves into the Fury than to defy the Church's will!"*

—From the Tomes of Regret, Verse 43 of Sorrow

THE REMAINDER OF the day, along with the entirety of the next, was uneventful after the Silent One's attack, and they made good progress. There was no sign of Shilanti, however. Sometime the following afternoon, a storm band surged toward them, but it dispersed moments before arriving. So evening came again and they all relaxed around a fire as the land darkened rapidly.

"I'll take the first watch," Kaven told the others. "Toyon, do you want the second?"

The assassin nodded and Shera spoke up. "I'll take the last."

They did not take their time eating, as they all wanted to get some sleep. Kaven took off the bandages wrapped around his arm. The inside of the cloth was purple with dried blood. He discarded them and examined the wound. It was a perfectly round puncture, no wider than his smallest finger, and the spine had completely passed through his arm. It had been sewn shut with makeshift stitches. What had Shera used? Maybe fishing wire? The wound was scabbed over, which was a good sign, he supposed, and didn't seem to be infected. It would probably be fine.

He bade the other three good night as they sank into their sleeping bags. His companions quickly fell asleep, signaling that Kaven's two-hour watch had begun. Kaven set his Firerod on his lap and retrieved Animus from his pocket. He began to tinker, keeping an eye on the horizon as he did so.

Yawning, Kaven fell into his usual routine of adjustments, tests, and then readjustments. Nothing fixed Animus, of course, but the ritual was still soothing. He glanced up at the shadowed clouds above and frowned. The threats of the Fury still seemed nonexistent, despite the recent encounters. They hadn't even seen any strange debris either. Even though he had taken a serious injury and almost died twice, he still felt as if Na'lek wasn't even trying. Not that he wanted him to.

Still, Kaven remained vigilant, watching the Fields of Glory with acute attention. He also made sure to periodically check the skies, as he wouldn't put it past the Fury to spawn a storm band right on top of them.

*Is this your worst?* Kaven wondered. Na'lek didn't respond.

The cold wind stung as it brushed the many scrapes crisscrossing his legs, arms, and torso, pushing his rough clothing against the cuts uncomfortably. Kaven resisted the urge to scratch them. He wished Tasi'a could heal them, but the battle had exhausted her, and she still wasn't fully recovered. Kaven could endure, as it was much smarter to save Tasi'a's magic for a real emergency. Perhaps Shera could . . . Kaven froze in his watch. Something was casting light in front of him, something much brighter than the magic fire. He realized he could hear the fire crackle and pop, but Tasi'a's flames made no noise.

Kaven turned slowly, heart hammering as fear snaked through his bones, turning his blood to ice. Rising behind their camp was a stone wall, which had certainly not been there before. Then he looked up. The wall was a leg, attached to a body that rose nearly high enough to touch the swirling clouds above. It was a Titan. Kaven fell back, screaming in panic.

Standing on two legs, with long arms that ended with vast claws, the Titan looked down upon him with dead black eyes over a short, wide snout. Teeth longer than Kaven's arm jutted down from red lips. The Titan's black hide was pitted and scarred from countless lightning strikes that had assaulted it over long years. Some scars looked suspiciously like claw marks. Wounds from another Titan? The Titan's back was stooped so that the head and neck pointed forward like that of a beast.

Thousands of tiny flames danced across the Titan's frame, bouncing through holes and across ridges like tiny fleas on a dog, no flame touching another. These fires fluctuated, growing periodically dimmer and brighter. Some winked out altogether, only to rekindle elsewhere. Ash poured from the Titan like dark waterfalls, piling around its immense, four-clawed feet.

Even as he cried out in alarm, trying to get his companions to rise, Kaven knew which Titan he faced. The puzzle seemed to click into place now; the Titan had moved so silently that they hadn't even noticed it, and the Titan had left a layer of ash over their camp. How had he not seen it before? Magical fires didn't create ash! There was only one who could do such things: Death, the Silent Father.

And even their survival through that night made sense now. Death enjoyed stalking its victims before attacking. Sometimes it would come right to the edge of the Barrier Wall and just watch for hours, ignoring any spells or projectiles the defenders threw at it. Death had come to their camp, unnaturally silent as it was now, with its fires extinguished, and had stood over them, observing them. And now it had come to kill them.

"Death is upon us!" Kaven screamed, activating his Firerod. "Death is here!"

Shera burst to her feet, drawing her sword. She had slept in her armor tonight but had to grab her shield from where it lay atop her supplies. Looking up at Death, who was still standing by impassively, Shera screamed. "A Titan! Na'lek, preserve us; flee for your lives!" And she took off running.

Toyon was on his feet too, a knife in each hand. He met the Titan's eyes and took off after Shera as she yelled her command. Toyon was fleet of foot and quickly outdistanced Shera, who was much slower in her heavy armor.

Kaven wasn't sure why, but he didn't run immediately. Instead, he met Death's gaze and was afraid. The Titan's eyes were darker than the night, just like the Fury's lightning. This was the closest he'd ever come to seeing a god, and it was a harrowing sight. His Firerod hummed, and Kaven attacked without thinking, unleashing lightning upon the Titan. The night flashed with an actinic blue light as the Firerod struck Death's shin. The Firerod's blast made no mark on the Titan's rocklike skin. Death roared, and Lantrelia trembled with Na'lek's rage.

Out of the corner of his eye, Kaven glimpsed Tasi'a sitting bolt upright in her sleeping bag, frozen, staring up at Death, eyes wide with terror. Kaven didn't think; he didn't remember he was afraid. He simply acted. Abandoning his useless attack, Kaven leapt toward Tasi'a as Death raised a monstrous foot that was longer than Kaven. Scooping up Tasi'a, Kaven threw himself out of the way as Death slammed his foot down.

*Boom!* A shockwave like thunder raced through the ground, throwing up giant chunks of stone high into the air. Still holding tight to Tasi'a, Kaven felt himself be thrown upward as ash filled his mouth, nose, and eyes. Blinded, Kaven felt like he was floating. He did not know how high Death had thrown them, only that he wouldn't survive hitting the ground. But the wind was so very strong up here, and the Fury took hold of them, shaking and hurling them about within its torturous winds. And it threw them away like worthless refuse, tossing them aside to places unknown. Death roared again, but it was a distant sound, and darkness poured into Kaven's mind, and he knew no more.


Shera ran as fast as her tired, gauntleted legs would carry her. Death! Death had found them! She didn't think of anything but survival as she ran, only vaguely aware of Toyon a little way ahead of her. *Oh Na'lek*, she thought, on the verge of panic, *make it go away! Make it go away!* Death roared behind her. Why wasn't he chasing her? Thank Na'lek for that! She wondered why Kaven and Tasi'a hadn't overtaken her. They should have been faster than her. They might be too exhausted to keep up. What if they had tried to fight Death? Kaven might be foolhardy enough to try something stupid like that. *Protect us all, Na'lek!* Shera thought she had known what terror was, but she was so wrong. This was pure fear! It crippled her, drove her like a maddened beast. *I'm so scared!*

She ran, not daring to look behind her, only watching the landscape ahead for holes or bumps. Tripping now would mean dying. Death roared his challenge again and thunder boomed somewhere ahead of her. Now the Fury would participate in their destruction. Na'lek had declared that they die.

Finally, she summoned a hidden reserve of strength and looked behind her but immediately moaned in despair. Death was rushing toward them, taking massive strides and rapidly closing the distance she had accumulated. Even more terrible was that neither Kaven nor Tasi'a were behind them. They were dead. Death had killed them both. Her fear vanished, replaced instead by a horrid numbness that seeped through her. Titan's teeth, they were her friends! They were her friends!

Teeth bared in a horrific snarl, flames dancing about his black eyes, Death surged toward her as the thunder crashed again, closer now. And Shera stopped. Tasi'a and Kaven were dead, and she knew that she could not outrun Death now that the fiery Titan was charging right at her. If she were to die here, then she would die fighting the Titan. She would die as Orlan had, gloriously and honorably. To the Fury with fear! She would spit in Death's face, even as the end came. That was the Stormgardian way. *Na'lek, deliver me . . .*

She turned toward Death, raising her sword and shield, and shouted in defiance, "For Stormgarde!"

"Glory to Fulminos!" To Shera's surprise, Toyon was at her side, brandishing his knives and shouting his own war cry.

Together, they stood in the face of Death as the Titan slowed to a stop, towering over them and grinning. A rumble emanated from deep within Death's throat.

Shera felt mild surprise in the dim, small corner of her mind that still held feeling. Was that laughter?

Toyon looked at her, sadness in his eyes. "They're dead."

She nodded, and the dull calm burst into hateful flame. She glared up at Death, a sneer curling her lips. "Let's avenge them."

They charged toward the Titan, and Death did not attempt to stop them. Understanding crawled into her heart like a poisonous worm. Tasi'a and Kaven had died too quickly; but Death still wanted its sport. Hot, angry tears streaked down her face, but she did not fear the Titan. She'd never have to fear them again.

Toyon leapt upward, landing on Death's foot. Shera followed, stabbing her sword into the Titan's heel. To her immense astonishment, her sword went right through Death's skin. Despite its appearance, it was not stone at all.

Death bellowed and kicked its leg outward. Shera was dislodged and hit the ground several yards to the left of the Titan. Toyon had landed beside her, the blow knocking him unconscious. And so it would end. They had done better than Shera had expected; Death was hurt, golden blood oozing from the three stab wounds in its heel. Shera had never thought they could make a Titan bleed. But Death seemed furious, bending down to observe the tiny wounds in its supposedly indestructible hide. The wounds closed instantly, leaving no trace of ever being opened at all. The Titan bared its teeth, growling loudly. Yes, they had angered Death.

Then there was a new sound. Deep *booms* shook the ground around them, but it wasn't thunder. Shera tried to sit up and managed to see a new, massive figure bounding toward them from the south. A second Titan.

This new Titan was pitted and ruined just like Death, the result of thousands of storm bands raging through the Fury. This Titan stood a head taller than Death, had the same black and rocky skin, but a flat, humanlike face, complete with ears and a mouth. All it lacked was a nose. This Titan was shaped like a man and had humanlike feet and hands. A brilliant crimson light poured from its eyes, shining in Death's face. Shera gasped, realizing that she was seeing something that no man or woman had seen up close before. She was looking at the Watcher. *So the Titans are going to fight over their prey?* she thought bitterly, watching the two colossal monsters.

Death looked up, eyes widening in surprise. The flame-and ash-coated Titan hissed, claws opening wide as it crouched, ready to spring. But the Watcher struck, hand curling into a fist that slammed straight into the other Titan's throat.

Reeling backward, Death collapsed onto its hands and knees. Wheezing, it put a claw to its neck. The Watcher was on top of its foe in an instant, kicking Death in the side. With a loud wail, the defeated Titan scrambled to its feet and fled.

As Death disappeared into the distance, the Watcher turned toward them, red eyes blocking most of Shera's vision. The Titan's hand extended, reaching toward her. *Time to die.* Shera let her head fall back. Even as she surrendered her life, Shera was not afraid.

# SEVENTEEN

*"Na'lek has made Death incarnate. It walks the Fury, garbed in ash and flame."*

—From the Tomes of Regret, Verse 70 of Power

KAVEN OPENED HIS eyes, rubbing his hands across the soft, fluffy pillow his head rested upon. He sat up in his bed and groaned. Light streamed through his window; it seemed to be morning. His legs and arms were extremely sore and they itched, and the wound on his arm was pulsing again. He attempted to stretch but had little success. He looked down—when had his pillow become so furry? Then it all came back.

Death. Tasi'a. The wind. Pain. Kaven leapt to his feet and saw to his horror that the "bed" was actually the belly of a dead Spinereaver, crushed by his fall out of the Fury. The monster had saved his life. He shuddered, wondering what would have happened had the monster been upright. Tasi'a was also draped across the Spinereaver, the beginnings of a large bruise forming on her face and legs. He ran over and examined her, not bothering to conceal his worry. She was alive, thank Na'lek, and had no critical injuries; she was simply unconscious.

To be honest, Kaven was shocked to find that both he and Tasi'a were still alive. Na'lek himself must have guided them through the Fury, sparing them from the Titan's grasp. The Fury thundered nearby, reminding Kaven that they were not safe. He searched for his weapons and found the short-sword and the Firerod nearby, both unharmed. Animus was still stowed safely in his pocket, and fortunately Kaven had not crushed it in his fall. He shook his head, thanking Na'lek again for his mercy. If Kaven lost Animus, that was years of work forever destroyed.

*Where are the supplies?* he wondered before remembering that he was nowhere near the campsite. They had no food and no water. They were lost in some unknown part of the Fury, with no sense of direction and no . . . no Shera. No Toyon.

Kaven groaned, only now noticing their absence. Shera and Toyon had not been swept up by the same wind that carried him away. Either they were lost in the Fury, or . . . the Titan had taken them. Death was a merciless killer. It did not spare any being. Kaven fell on his knees, head bowed. *Na'lek,* he thought, *hear my prayer. Please protect Shera and Toyon. Please.*

*They're dead,* a small voice within him whispered. *You failed to see the Titan. You let Death take them away.* And he wept. Their time together had been so brief, and half of it was spent hating each other. Yet, they had traversed half the Fury together, something no man had before achieved, fighting the monsters that called this wasteland their home. Their quest had been one of peace—to end the ceaseless fighting against the Fury and to appease the almighty Na'lek. But it was over; they had failed. The Fury was victorious. It had needed only to unleash one of its greatest weapons, and the quest had failed. Toyon and Shera were gone, stranded in the wasteland or torn from this world by Na'lek. It was over.

"Why?" he screamed, throwing his head upward. "Why, Na'lek? If you're the god you claim to be, the god who wishes for our repentance, then why would you let them die?" Thunder rumbled and the Fury churned above him. Tasi'a came awake suddenly, looking up at him with shock, but he kept on yelling. "We were trying to fix this mess, monster!" Thunder crashed again, but he paid it no mind. "Why did you send this storm against us, Na'lek? You are a god; what do you have to prove? After thousands of years of death and destruction, you couldn't even let us come and beg for mercy? Is your thirst for our blood so great? Are we so far beneath you that you don't care anymore?" The thunder crashed again, and the clouds of the Fury churned and spun, mirroring the seething rage of the god far above. Yet, Na'lek stayed silent.

"You're supposed to be our creator!" Kaven fell, lying against the cold stone, tears pouring freely. "Why," he whispered softly through the sobs. "Why are you our destroyer?"

Something touched his shoulder, and he looked up to see Tasi'a's face staring at him, tears making streaks through her dirty cheeks. "Sometimes," she said softly, slowly, "sometimes we cannot understand what Na'lek wishes. In the same way that a hound cannot comprehend the ornate principles of magic, so too can we not fathom the imperceptible will of the divine."

Kaven snorted. "So we're hounds now? Dogs bred to fight for Na'lek's amusement?"

"Kaven," Tasi'a cautioned, "you border on blasphemy."

"Perhaps he is deserving of blasphemy," Kaven snapped. "Why else would he let Shera and Toyon die? Why else did he strand us out here with no supplies? For what purpose butcher dozens of us each day? Na'lek is *not* a loving god, Tasi'a! He does not care for Lantrelia, no matter what the priests say. He's vain, greedy, bloodthirsty, arrogant, and hateful!"

"You're wrong, Kaven!" Tasi'a protested. "You should know that everything happens for a reason." She was beginning to cry harder now, though she retained some composure. "I do not believe that it is Na'lek who is killing us."

"Then who is?" Kaven asked bitterly.

For an answer, Tasi'a simply pointed upward. Thunder boomed once more.

Kaven laughed, but he felt no humor. "The Fury is Na'lek!"

"The Fury is Na'lek's rage," Tasi'a replied calmly. "It has always been our duty to pacify it."

"His anger does not justify our deaths!" Kaven yelled.

Tasi'a smiled sadly. "We all do awful things when we're angry. Na'lek is not a perfect god."

Kaven shot a glare at the Fury. "Why doesn't he end it?"

"Because he needs us to ask."

Tasi'a looked so sure of herself that Kaven couldn't bring himself to argue anymore. How could he argue about anything when Toyon and Shera were lying dead in some hole?

"But it's over now," he said. "We've no supplies, no sense of direction, and no one to watch our backs. We have to go back to Stormgarde."

Tasi'a shook her head, pointing somewhere ahead of them. Kaven looked and saw massive footprints. "Death, again," Tasi'a said. "We've been blown back the way he came." She turned to the left. "Shilanti is southwest of us. We can still make it."

Kaven shrugged. "So? It doesn't matter. We have to go back or we'll starve."

Tasi'a shook her head. "No, we can't. Kaven, it's a five-day journey back to Stormgarde, but only two more days to the Fury's center. We'll run out of the protection potion long before we reach Stormgarde. We must go to the Fury's heart and pray that Shilanti is there."

"So that Na'lek can kill us himself?" Kaven shook his head. "We can make it back to Stormgarde."

"No." Tasi'a sighed in annoyance. "But even ignoring the fact that we have no food or water, the Shredders will tear us apart in a few days. We'll be stripped to the bone before we can reach the outskirts of the Fields. Our only chance is to go to Shilanti and beseech Na'lek."

Kaven took a deep breath. *So, death behind and death ahead.* Should they perish in the Fury, or let the terrible god do it himself? Oh, what *wonderful* decisions Na'lek was giving them! Well, the wind had picked them up for a reason, so if Na'lek wished to see them suffer more, then they should oblige him. "Fine," he said. "Let's finish this in Shilanti."

"Excellent." Tasi'a set off immediately. "I believe Na'lek is guiding us toward his embrace! That's why he sent a Spinereaver to cushion our fall."

They marched, moving hopefully toward the Fury's heart. Kaven couldn't hear any more thunder, but he kept a careful eye on the storm.

The silence was deafening. "Tasi'a," Kaven said suddenly. "Should we do something?"

"About what?" she asked, striding around a wide pit.

Kaven frowned at the sorceress. He couldn't understand why she seemed so cheerful. "For Shera and Toyon, I mean. A memorial or something?"

"Oh." Tasi'a glanced back at him, her face stoic. "I don't think they're dead."

"That's foolish," Kaven said sharply. "The Fury destroyed them."

"Hope is never foolish," Tasi'a retorted.

Kaven shook his head. "It doesn't feel right. If they're dead, they should be honored."

Tasi'a sighed. "All right."

They stopped and Tasi'a put two small fires, one blue and one gray, in a deep pit. They both knelt and Kaven silently stared into the motionless flames. Tasi'a waited patiently while Kaven watched the fires, lost within his mind. His mind was in a dark place now, tinged with sorrow and hate. He finally found his voice. "I'd like to say a few words."

Tasi'a nodded slowly. "Okay."

Kaven cleared his throat. "Shera of Stormgarde. She was a champion of her kind, the pinnacle of a warrior and the envy of all women. Her deadly grace and beauty were unmatched in all of Lantrelia. There were none who were as brave, loyal, or strong as Shera. She was a leader and stood against the Fury longer than most men could. In the end, Shera stood resolute against the most feared and terrible creatures the Fury could conjure. She looked Death right in the eye and laughed. She didn't fear death; for Shera, it was simply a new opportunity. Even though she is gone, I know that Shera's courage will never be forgotten."

Kaven grew silent again, but he managed to continue. "Toyon of Fulminos. He was strong, courageous, and superb in all he did. He was a master of silence and shadows, and even though he could have easily looked out for himself, Toyon constantly put himself in harm's way to protect us. He truly understood the meaning of sacrifice and friendship. Though a Titan, Death himself, stood in his way, Toyon would *not* let him touch us. Not while he still had breath. I am proud to have known Toyon, and I pray that we will see him again when we reach Shilanti." He smiled at that thought, and his heart quickened with excitement. The Fury's heart, and the kingdom of the fallen, was so close. "Na'lek, with that hope—the hope of seeing them again—we continue onward."

Kaven looked to Tasi'a expectantly. She met his eye, and he saw defiance within her. "I am proud to call them friends," she said, voice strong. "Shera and Toyon, wherever you are now, we'll see you again."

Kaven nodded in satisfaction. He didn't believe her; he didn't think that they could have survived. But hope was important. It always was. "Come on, Tasi'a. Let's finish this once and for all."

Tasi'a let the fires in the pit wink out. She sniffed softly and nodded. "Yes, we must go. Too much time has been lost already."

Kaven let Tasi'a lead the way, as his sense of direction was pitiful. Silence descended on the Fields of Glory again, much to his annoyance. Despite the wind, the air seemed deathly still, and the black and violet clouds were ominous and quiet. The only real sound was that of their feet pounding on the gray stone. Kaven was tired of the unpredictability of the Fury. At the Wall, it was consistently violent. But out here, it had lured them into letting their guard down. Shera and Toyon might still be here if Kaven had watched more carefully.

"I wonder what Shilanti will be like?" Tasi'a said, musing out loud.

Kaven ignored her. He wasn't interested in hearing about Na'lek or anything remotely religious. He nodded every now and again, blotting out Tasi'a's lecture even as the hours passed by. The Fury began to slowly darken as night settled across the Fields, and that was when the itching began . . .

# EIGHTEEN

*"Fear is an illusion, soldiers of Stormgarde! Your task is to bleed the Fury dry."*

—From the Tomes of Regret, Verse 4 of Duty

SHERA WAS ALIVE. And she was terrified. Where was she? She opened her eyes, but only darkness greeted her. Was she alive? Was she in Shilanti? Na'lek above, she had seen Death! The darkness began to fade the longer she kept her eyes open, replaced by an odd white glow. Awareness came upon her, and Shera found that she was lying on a flat stone slab about ten feet wide. Toyon was seated beside her, his eyes red-rimmed. "Don't look down," he said.

Despite the warning, Shera went to the edge of the slab and did look downward. The ground below was over thirty feet away, and it seemed to be completely submerged in water. There was no telling how deep it was, or if such a plunge would be fatal. Where on Lantrelia were they?

Shera then looked up and furrowed her brow in further confusion. There was a stone roof ten feet above them, shaped like a dome and sloped downward in every direction, meaning that they were in some sort of underground cavern. Large stalactites dangled down, drops of water falling from them in continuous streams. Large mushrooms grew from the walls and the stone, glowing pale white and illuminating the cavern.

"Where are we?" Shera asked, surprised at how hoarse her voice sounded.

Toyon shrugged. "I don't know, but we're trapped. It's too far to jump, and the stalactites are beyond my reach. I held myself over the ledge, and this slab is fused to a thin pillar. I fear that too much movement will cause us to tip, and I cannot reach the pillar regardless."

Shera grunted. One problem at a time. "Where are our supplies?" She still had her sword and shield, and Toyon had his knives, but their bags were missing.

"Gone," the assassin said. "Left behind."

"How did we get here?" Shera asked, looking around the cavern as her voice echoed through it.

Toyon chuckled coldly. "Isn't it obvious? Look at this place. We are the Watcher's prisoners."

Shera blinked. That couldn't be right. When had the Watcher ever attacked? Perhaps this Titan only sought those foolish enough to enter the Fields of Glory? She looked back to the immense tunnel that led out of their cavern. It was large enough to accommodate a Titan. It was true, then. The Watcher was going to torture them for days before they were finally allowed to die. Did this mean Kaven and Tasi'a were still alive? Perhaps the Watcher was with them now, ripping them apart. As terrible as that thought was, Shera found herself hoping that her friends had died in Death's initial attack. It would be an easier fate. Either way, they were all going to be dead soon. Perhaps they could still plead humanity's plight once they'd perished. Maybe that's what they should've done in the first place: simply cut their own throats and skipped past the Fury to reach Shilanti. It would've been simpler.

"Do we fight?" Toyon asked, his voice soft in the immensity of their prison.

Shera paused, and that all-too-familiar icy fear took hold. She wanted to shy away, to perhaps jump down and escape, but then she thought of Kaven and Tasi'a. Two more souls sacrificed to the Fury. Shera drew her sword and faced the cavern. "We fight."

Toyon nodded, stepping up beside her. "Perhaps there is still a chance we can leave this tomb alive."

"Tomb?" A deep, booming voice reverberated from the tunnel and echoed around them, shaking the cavern. Shera cried out in pain as the awful sound assaulted her, but the terrible voice continued. "Tomb? This is no tomb! This is my home! I would appreciate it if you gave it some respect. I worked so hard on it, you see."

The cavern began to shake repeatedly, and Shera recognized the rumbles as the sound of a Titan approaching. "Stay away, monster!" she shouted, drawing her sword. "Though my strength may not compare to yours, I shall still strike you down!" Toyon was at her side, knives ready.

"Oh, come now," the Titan's voice replied. It was quieter now, so Shera could bear to listen to it. "I am not a monster! Perhaps you could say I am out of place, but certainly not a monster." A large, terrible shape emerged from the entrance of the tunnel, head nearly scraping the roof. It was indeed the Watcher who entered the cavern, sloshing through water that was ankle deep to a beast of its—his?—height. The Watcher was so tall that if Shera looked straight forward, she would be staring directly at his neck. Surprisingly, she noticed the Watcher was wearing pants made of some ragged brown material.

"Release us from this prison, Watcher," Toyon demanded.

"Prison?" The Watcher blinked his large red eyes slowly, seeming confused. "Oh no, you misunderstand! You are both my guests, you see."

Shera laughed despite herself. "Oh yes, I'm sure that being trapped up here is merely coincidental. After all, everyone knows the Titans are the harbingers of Na'lek's mercy."

"Oh!" the Watcher boomed. "I see your confusion. Yes, I do! I apologize, but I put you there so that I didn't have to look down upon you. I thought it polite, you see. Now, you called me both 'Watcher' and 'Titan.' I've heard your people's name for me before." The Titan leaned over the ledge, looking down on them with his glowing eyes. "But what does that mean?"

"We're . . . not prisoners?" Toyon asked, confused. "But you're supposed to be a killer. A destroyer."

The Watcher's humanlike face became downcast. "Ah, you are referring to the other giants that wander the storm? I am not like them, you see. They are mindless killers. I had to carve out this cavern so I would not be constantly hunted by them. I suppose that 'Watcher' is a fitting name for me. It is all I've done for the past several hundred years. As there is not much else I might do, I have studied your kind for my research."

"I don't understand," Shera said. "You're telling me that you aren't like the other Titans? You're not like Death or the Ravager?"

"Hmm." The Watcher rubbed a large finger to his chin. "What interesting names. Which one is Death and which is Ravager? Ah, but I'm rambling. I can ask my questions after I've answered yours. I am just so excited to be able to talk with some of you! I have never been able to do this before, and that is thanks to my fellow giants, the Titans, I believe you called them. That is why I've always watched from a distance." The Watcher smiled at them, looking eager. "Now, your questions. My, I do go on sometimes. It comes from having no one to talk to, you see. I am not a killer like these other Titans. I've never killed anyone! I am a scholar, not a warrior. That is why I wasn't able to bring down the brute who attacked you." He paused. "Oh, that reminds me. I was not able to locate your friends, but they are still alive."

Shera's eyes widened. "They're alive?" Beside her, Toyon sighed in relief.

"Yes," the Watcher said. "I went looking for them, you see, but I could not find them. I did, however, find their tracks, and they are heading toward the center of the storm."

"The Fury's heart?" Toyon said. "Good. We'll be able to find them."

The Watcher's eyes widened. "The Fury's heart? That sounds fascinating! You must tell me more."

Shera was hesitant to trust this being, and her old fears still harried her. But, as their conversation continued, she found herself more comfortable in the Watcher's presence. Shera did not know how long they talked with the Watcher, but it must have been several hours. They talked about the Four Kingdoms, the Fury, and Na'lek's anger. They talked of the Barrier Wall and the Fury-spawn that attacked them and their quest to travel to Shilanti.

The Watcher had spoken truly when he said he was a scholar. His thirst for knowledge regarding their lives, their culture, their *everything* was insatiable! Shera wryly thought that Tasi'a would have enjoyed meeting this Titan. She was so relieved that they were all alive! Time was still essential, however, and she was eager to set off again. Shera still wasn't sure where she was exactly, and without the Watcher's help, she couldn't get down. Unfortunately, the Watcher seemed fully engrossed in the conversation.

"It is superb, you see. I find that I quite enjoy your naming system," the Watcher was saying, bringing up the subject for the fifth time in their discussion. "I simply love the moniker of Watcher; it is a fascinating name. And so true! Tell me, do you name all of your creatures in a similar fashion? What does your name mean? *Shera*, it sounds like 'share.' But that's not your intention. Or is it?"

"Not exactly." Shera shook her head. "My name means 'Heartblade.'" The Watcher seemed confused, so she explained. "A soldier's heart."

The Watcher grinned. "I could have guessed that. You have the look of a soldier, you see."

Shera nodded, a modest smile on her face. "I've always been a soldier."

"How intriguing," the Watcher exclaimed. "And you fight against the monsters of the storm?"

"We all do," she said in reply.

"And you?" the Watcher asked, turning his lamp-like gaze on Toyon. "Are you a soldier?"

"I'm an assassin of sorts," Toyon replied.

The Watcher nodded. "Many of your kind seem to be warriors. I understand why you fight against the monsters out here. I've watched you do it for centuries, you see. But what I cannot understand is why these beings attack you over and over again."

"Aren't you one of them?" Shera asked.

"Goodness, no!" The Watcher chuckled. "I am not a monster."

Shera blinked, confused. "So why did Na'lek make you?"

"I apologize," the Titan said. "I know you have mentioned that name before, but who is Na'lek?"

Toyon and Shera both exchanged surprised looks. The Watcher didn't know who Na'lek was? How was that even possible? "Na'lek is our creator," Toyon supplied. "He made us all, including you."

"No, no," the Watcher said slowly. "I do believe you are wrong. If he is what you would call a god, then he certainly did not make me."

"Then who made you?" Shera asked, now quite confused.

The Watcher laughed. "What an amusing question! You have such strange ways here, you see. I was made by the True God, and no other. Although, of course, my parents chose my birthstone long before—"

"What do you mean, 'True God'?" Toyon interrupted.

"Many claim to be gods, you see," the Watcher said. "Or at least, others see them as such. But there is only one creator, and he is the True God. It is not surprising that false deities have arisen here as well. They seem to grow throughout Life's Cradle like shrooms beneath a tree."

Shera rolled her eyes. This Titan was obviously not a monster of the Fury at all. He must be from a distant island, perhaps the far north. All of the Island Folk were heathens, and legend held it that they bred monsters alongside cattle. "From which part of Lantrelia do you come from?"

"Is that the name of this realm?" The Watcher looked around at his cavern, a considerable feat, since he nearly filled it. "No, I am not from this world, you see."

"What?" Shera exclaimed. "What does that even mean? Where do you think you are from?"

"Ah! A fascinating question, Heartblade. I am from Melan'anon." The Watcher's gaze became unfocused, staring into some unseen distance with a deep longing. "In that beautiful land, I lived in a grand library and spent my days learning. There, I am not a giant, and I was often teased for my short stature." The Watcher sighed with longing. "It is a grand place to live, filled with nothing but peace and harmony. Of course, the Blood Wars are a dark part of our history, but we have outgrown the barbaric ways of our past and—"

Toyon interrupted again. "But how did you get here, Watcher?"

The Watcher paused. "I do not know. One night I went to bed, and I suddenly awoke under the storm. Back then, the lightning hurt a lot." He scratched at his pitted, stonelike skin. "For years, I have tried to figure out how I got here. If I can discover how, perhaps I can go home. I do not like it here, you see."

Shera suddenly felt sorry for the Watcher. This poor being, whatever he was, didn't deserve to be trapped in this cavern, hunted by monsters and humans. He should be in a library, reading books all day.

Toyon's face was blank, not at all feeling the same pity for the Watcher. "That explains everything. Na'lek summoned you here to act as one of his Titans."

"Your Na'lek does not sound courteous," the Watcher grumbled. "He should have asked me first, though I would've declined. Perhaps that's why he didn't ask. Hmm."

"Watcher," Shera began, putting an end to what most likely would have been a long conversation about etiquette. "We thank you for saving us from Death, but we really must get to the Fury's heart and find our friends. And we'll have to go find our supplies, else we'll starve."

"Starve?" The Watcher brightened. "Oh no, you won't starve! I've already packed for your trip, you see. And you'll love the Fury's heart. It's so warm and sunny compared to this storm, this Fury, as you call it." The Titan rushed out of the cavern and down the tunnel, sending water careening in every direction as the sounds of his monstrous footsteps bounced around the cavern. Soon, the echoes of his movements faded as he went farther away.

"Can we trust him?" Toyon asked, sounding wary.

"I think so," Shera replied. "He seems like a decent fellow. Besides, what choice do we have?"

Toyon sighed. "None, I'm afraid."

Shera thought over their position. The Watcher seemed to be safe, but he was also an incredibly intelligent creature. And no matter what he might say, he was still a Titan. What if this was a clever trap? Honestly, if this was a trap, then they were already dead. There was no escape. They had no choice but to believe this Watcher was who he claimed to be, that their mission could still end in success, and that Kaven and Tasi'a were still alive.

The Watcher returned to the cavern, still as loud as ever. In one monstrous fist he held two large bags made out of some strange, leathery material. He placed them on the platform and stood back, looking at them proudly.

Shera gingerly took one of the bags—it was heavy, but not overwhelmingly so—and opened it. Inside, she found their original packs, along with Kaven and Tasi'a's. There was also a large assortment of fruits and vegetables.

"Why isn't this heavy?" Shera asked, hefting one of the packs. "Titan's teeth, I shouldn't be able to lift this!"

"It is blood cloth, you see," said the Watcher. "It comes from Melan'anon. I did not have much with me when I came here, but fortunately my clothing was made from it. It is incredibly useful and innately magical. You can lift anything that is wrapped in blood cloth."

Shera had never seen anything like it, not even in Regelia, but she slung the too-light pack over one shoulder and decided it was best not to question it.

"Where did you get the produce?" Toyon asked, lifting a carrot from his sack.

"I have to eat too," the Watcher said simply. "I have immense gardens within these caves. I have to make a lot, you see, because your food is so tiny. It is hard to harvest small plants. I have my own water too. It runs through the entirety of my home. I couldn't get you any fish; they're rare down here and tricky to catch without squashing them."

Toyon eyed the offering of food with disapproval. "Where did you get the seeds? And the water?"

"The storm blows them in sometimes," the Watcher said proudly. "And it rains out here occasionally too. This is the culmination of many years of work." The Titan gestured around the cavern. "I did almost starve when I first arrived, but I managed to survive. I can go several years without eating, you see."

Toyon nodded to the Titan. "I can't say I understand why you're helping us, but I thank you for your generosity."

"It is the right thing to do!" The Watcher beamed. "Besides, you've taught me so much about your kind. It is the least I could do in return." The Titan paused, looking flustered. "Actually, there is one little favor I could ask of you, if it is not too much trouble."

"We'd be happy to help you," Shera said.

The Titan's smile widened. "If you could inform your people that I am a peaceful man, perhaps they would let me come into their land. It would be lovely to come out from under this storm, you see."

Toyon smiled. "We would gladly do this for you, Watcher."

The Watcher's face lit up with joy. "Thank you! Oh, I'm so excited! To leave this wretched hole behind and return to the wonders of civilization would be glorious. Perhaps then I will discover a way home."

"We'll come back and let you know when it's safe," Toyon said with a nod.

"We must hurry," Shera said. "We have to catch up to Kaven and Tasi'a before their potion runs out."

"Potion?" The Watcher blinked. "What potion?"

"There are strange winds out here," Shera explained. "We call them the Shredders. They can tear us apart within a couple of hours. We have a protection potion, but without our supplies, Kaven and Tasi'a will soon run out."

"Ah!" The Watcher nodded sagely. "I had often wondered why there were so many bones out here. I've found them scattered all about, you see."

Shera flushed. "Yes, those would be my kinfolk."

"I'm sorry." The Watcher hung his head. "I did not know."

"It's all right," Shera said with a small smile.

Toyon put a hand on her shoulder. "Time to go."

"If you would allow it"—the Watcher placed an immense hand on the platform—"I will carry you out of my home. It can be quite the labyrinth if you do not know the way, you see."

"Gladly," Toyon said, climbing up the Watcher's arm, using the rocky breaks in his skin as handholds, until he was sitting on the Titan's shoulder.

Shera hefted her pack and joined Toyon, seating herself on the uncomfortable precipice of the Titan. She tried not to look down, knowing that a drop from this height would kill her.

"Hold on," the Watcher said, turning toward the tunnel. "I would not want you to fall. I'll go slowly and try not to bore you with my blather. Let's go!" The Titan trudged toward the tunnel, leaving the cavern behind.

The Watcher had not been exaggerating when he described his home as a labyrinth. At first, Shera tried to keep track of all the twists and turns in the tunnels, but she soon lost all knowledge of their path. Some intersections had twelve different tunnels, all partially submerged in water and tall and wide enough for the Titan to walk through. In these tunnels, there was a current to the water, and it moved along at a steady pace. Shera wondered if the current would be strong enough to knock her off her feet. But the Watcher moved through the streams as if they were little more than puddles. Now completely lost, all Shera knew was that these tunnels were moving steadily upward. *How deep are we?*

Throughout their journey, the Watcher did not stop talking. "It took me several years to dig these tunnels, and I did it all by hand. The monsters don't bother me much, you see, but the ones you call Titans are another matter. One of them followed me down here once. He was clever, but he's dead now, killed by your people many years ago."

"The Destroyer," Shera said with a nod.

"A fitting name as usual, Heartblade," the Watcher said as he walked toward a tunnel that visibly sloped upward. "Yes, the Destroyer followed me down here when I refused to join his crusade. I was able to sneak out while he hunted me through the darkness. The Destroyer became lost down here, you see, and I couldn't return until he managed to escape. He was so infuriated! And he made such a mess of my beautiful home."

The water ended abruptly as they climbed upward. The glowing mushrooms that lit the tunnels became scarcer as the caves grew dryer, plunging them into near total darkness. The bright gaze of the Watcher's eyes lit the way before them, until Shera could see daylight ahead.

The Watcher hefted himself out of the tunnels and they emerged back under the Fury. The familiar purple clouds bulged and writhed above them, driven by the ferocious winds. Shera and Toyon were suddenly assaulted by the incredible strength of the wind and had to hold on tightly to avoid being blown off.

"How long were we unconscious?" Toyon asked.

"Only through the night," the Watcher replied.

"Which way do we need to go?" Shera asked.

"Head north," the Titan said, pointing in the right direction. "There you will find the place you call Shilanti. If your friends survived, you may find them there." The Watcher bent down onto his knees and placed a hand on the ground. Shera and Toyon descended from his mountainous form.

"Thank you for rescuing us," Toyon said. "We'll be sure to get you to safety once this storm has been destroyed."

The Watcher straightened, looking down on them with his red gaze and a smile on his stony face. "It was my pleasure. I wish you the greatest of luck, and I hope to hear of your success soon." The Watcher hesitated. "Be careful out here. The one you call Death is a cunning hunter. He may still have your scent, you see, and he does not give up prey easily."

Shera nodded. "We will be careful."

Shera watched him go, already beginning to miss the Titan. "He is an incredible creature. We should have asked him to come with us."

"He walks on a path of peace," Toyon said, watching the sky. "We walk on one of destruction. He should not be bothered anymore on our account."

Shera nodded, somewhat disappointed. However, the Watcher had said that Shilanti was there, in the Fury's heart. It really was on Lantrelia! They were a mere two days from Na'lek's kingdom. It would be over soon. She turned toward the north. "Our god is waiting for us. Let's collect our companions and see what he has to say."

# NINETEEN

*"The only path to Shilanti is paved with souls and drenched in blood."*

—From the Tomes of Regret, Verse 67 of Power

"FIVE HOURS," TASI'A said, gritting her teeth as she purposefully stared straight ahead. "We're only five hours away from the Fury's heart."

Kaven couldn't keep a grimace of pain off his face as he tried desperately to ignore the blood running down his arms, neck, and legs. Numerous small gashes crisscrossed his skin, some releasing small trickles of blood, others just marring his skin. It had started yesterday, beginning with an unpleasant itch, but in the morning, they'd found cuts on their skin. And it was steadily getting worse. Their protection potion was slowly fading, and the Shredders were starting to rip into them. It would only get worse. They had to reach Shilanti, and hope that the Shredders did not exist there. Otherwise, they would be torn apart. Yet the Fury's center was still some distance away, and the real question was if they would even last another five hours.

Each step Kaven took was agony, and it seemed to him that small patches of fire were burning on his skin. The cuts blazed with terrible pain, and Kaven was beginning to feel sick with it.

They were moving as fast they could, but the Fury loomed above them, striking with wind that threatened to knock them over backward. The Eternal Storm harassed them as they struggled forward in constant agony, racing for a shelter that might not exist. Kaven cringed whenever he looked at Tasi'a. Angry red lines blotted her face, across her nose, lips, ears—everything but her eyes. Similar slashes covered every other part of her exposed skin, and he knew clothing only concealed additional wounds beneath. How long until their eyes started bleeding? That was when they would be truly doomed.

Sometimes Tasi'a would glance back at him, her eyes determined. She would not give up, she would not be taken by the Fury, even if her face was twisted with agony. He knew that he must look like she did—as if someone had repeatedly cut him with a knife. New cuts were forming with each passing moment, and the existing ones grew deeper.

Tasi'a had refused to use any of her magic, and Kaven knew it was wise to wait until the cuts became truly threatening. They also had not eaten since they had encountered Death, and Kaven's stomach growled in discomfort. He had never been as hungry as we was now, and the pain in his stomach made him want to hunch over. But the cuts, at least, were not terribly painful. His arm hurt much worse, and the Shredders had not touched that wound yet. He feared when it did, he'd wish that Death had crushed him that night.

The Fury rumbled distantly, laughing at their slow mutilation. Tasi'a groaned as Kaven watched a new cut open on her neck, three inches long and trickling blood. At last, her determination was beginning to drain away. "We can't take this much longer," she said with a hiss. "We're going to be ripped apart!"

"We'll make it, Tasi'a," Kaven said through clenched teeth. "We'll be there before you know it. Just keep moving." He didn't know if that was true, but Tasi'a had shown him the value of hope. If she could not carry it anymore, then he would hold it for her, however long he could last.

*Titans take you, Na'lek,* Kaven thought bitterly, shooting a glare up at the Fury. *You're nothing but a monster. Why do you take pleasure in our deaths?* Na'lek, of course, remained as silent as ever. The heartless god felt no need to justify himself, but the Fury spoke for him with a loud crash of thunder. Tasi'a was agonizingly loyal to Na'lek, and even now she constantly reminded Kaven that Na'lek had some sort of plan for them. She would make a good Zealot, or at least a priest. But with the fates of Shera and Toyon still fresh in his mind, Kaven had little faith in Na'lek's plans.

"I didn't think it would end this way," Tasi'a said quietly, touching the back of her neck gingerly. Her fingers came back red.

Kaven reached out to touch her shoulder but stopped himself. "The Fury has always given us death. Why should our fate be any different?"

Tasi'a raised an eyebrow at him. "No, not that. I do not care about death. If we die, we reach Shilanti regardless." She raised an arm up in front of her. Four long gashes crossed her wrist. She wiped away the blood, and Kaven saw something silver under her skin. "There were simply . . . other things I had to do."

*What was that?* It had seemed metallic. Before Kaven could ask her about it, the Fields of Glory began to tremble.

Loud booms raced across the broken terrain, like thunder but with the frightening regularity of footfalls.

Kaven and Tasi'a turned, and they saw a Titan. The monster walked on all fours, balanced on short, three-clawed legs. Its eyes were blue and glassy, like unpolished diamonds. They almost looked fake, as if someone had thrust glass orbs into its head. The Titan's green skin was ragged and frayed from the lightning, and long spikes decorated its neck, back, and long tail in two rows. Black triangular teeth burst from long, reptilian jaws. Two pits on the end of its snout flared with each breath the Titan took as it crawled forward, a terrible forked tongue darting from its mouth to lap up scents carried by the wind.

The Devourer. The Titan who fed on magic and those who wielded it. Thunder boomed loudly, and Kaven saw a storm band forming beyond the Titan, heading straight toward them.

*This* was it—the ultimate irony. The Devourer would kill Tasi'a, leaving Kaven to die in the lightning. This was the end of their journey, Na'lek was killing them right here and now.

Tasi'a screamed, shouting unnecessarily. "It's the Devourer!" Fire erupted from her hands and she flung it recklessly at the Titan. The Devourer's tongue shot forth, lapping up the flames as they closed in. The Titan's head swiveled in Tasi'a's direction, and its tongue sought her.

"I know!" Kaven drew his shortsword as thunder heralded a lightning bolt, which struck the ground mere yards from the Devourer, darkening his vision. The Titan stepped toward Tasi'a, moving slow enough that she could keep ahead of it by running.

Tasi'a frantically fought the Devourer with magic, flinging spells of black and green. Orbs of violet light and cords of red power. But each time, the Devourer's tongue caught the magic in the air and pulled it into its waiting mouth.

Kaven didn't know what to do. His weapon was useless, and Tasi'a's magic even more so. What if they ran? How long would the Devourer pursue them? Could Tasi'a sate it with her spells? He doubted it.

Thunder crashed and black lightning hurtled toward—nothing. The lightning was just gone. The Devourer's tongued retracted into its mouth. Kaven blinked. It had eaten the lightning? More black lightning bolts arced downward, but the Devourer snapped them out of the sky. A fourth bolt finally found a target, hitting the Devourer's neck and plunging the Fields into darkness. Kaven heard the Titan roar in pain as he stumbled. When his vision cleared, he saw that the Devourer had given up feasting on the storm and had returned its attention to Tasi'a.

Kaven was thinking furiously. His mother had once told him of a documented encounter with the Devourer; sorcerers had chased it away by creating a trail of magical light leading back into the Fury. The Titan had hungrily followed it back into the storm. But he knew Tasi'a wasn't powerful enough to create a long enough trail.

Thunder crashed again and lightning followed, blanketing the Fields in darkness as the bolt slammed down. Kaven remembered the words of Headmaster Gane in his classes, *Output is the useful branch of technology when dealing with magic. Weapons like the Firerod gather magic from Lantrelia's surface, channeling it into a powerful blast as they charge up.* Kaven looked up at the black lightning and then down at his Firerod. *It could use a good charging,* he thought, grinning despite himself. He knew what to do. "Tasi'a!" he shouted.

"What?" she screeched in a panic, scrambling away as the Devourer stalked her. She kept it at bay with explosive bursts of fire on either side of its head.

"Listen to me," Kaven demanded. "I need the Devourer to stay low. Can you do that?"

"I don't know," she yelled back, voice weak with fear.

"You have to try," he said. "I have an idea."

Unsure of herself, Tasi'a complied. A brilliant purple streak surged from her hands and burst a few feet to the right of the Devourer, hovering above a pit—a swirling, fiery explosion of purple sparks. It was flashy, but nothing more than a display of light.

Kaven's assumptions were proven correct as the Devourer turned, bending down toward the light to drink it in. After the magic was consumed, it turned back to Tasi'a. "Keep doing it, Tasi'a," Kaven shouted, running toward the Titan. "I need the Devourer close to the ground."

The Devourer prowled toward Tasi'a, jaws wide and glassy eyes locked on her. Tasi'a hesitated no longer, flinging a second plume of light to strike the ground beside the Titan.

With a delighted bellow, the Devourer bent down and turned its long head toward the light. The Titan's two-pronged tongue lashed out, wrapping around the light as if it were some tangible thing, and dragged it back into its waiting jaws. Kaven rushed the Devourer, brandishing his Firerod, but the Titan had already finished its odd meal and was once more stalking the sorceress. The Titan was moving faster, its tongue darting forward faster and faster. The Devourer wanted more.

"Again!" Kaven commanded, running beside the Titan's giant leg. A tremendous crash of thunder split the sky, and lightning immediately hit the ground. The storm band was right on top of them. Another blinding bolt struck the Devourer's back, and the Titan hissed. Tasi'a unleashed another blast, but it went awry as darkness overtook them. Kaven rubbed his eyes frantically and gasped as a long gash opened across his back. The Shredders bit at him like Bouncers, tearing him apart piece by piece. A frightening warm wetness seeped down his back. Kaven's vision finally cleared, and he was greeted by a glaring purple light. He was standing in Tasi'a's magic.

The Devourer loomed over him, jaws agape, its tongue emerging from between the pointed teeth like a crimson snake. Kaven activated his Firerod, but he cried out as a terrible pain tore across his arm. The Shredders tore into his wound, and the white bandage he wore immediately turned dark red. The pain was blinding, but some part of him was aware of the Titan above him, and he instinctively flung the metal rod toward the Titan's maw, where it was snatched up by the beast's tongue.

The Titan roared in confusion, head swiveling toward Tasi'a. The Firerod was caught between the Devourer's teeth, blue electricity dancing around its mouth.

Kaven looked up from the ground on which he lay, watching as the enraged Titan abandoned him and charged Tasi'a. *Na'lek, let this work,* he silently screamed, glancing up at the Fury. *Let this work!*

The Devourer opened its wide mouth, fangs bared as it lunged toward Tasi'a. The sorceress fell, screaming as she fired useless magic at the Titan, simply feeding the Devourer all the more.

*Crack!* Thunder shattered the sky with a world-shaking explosion of noise and Kaven's vision grew dark once again. Vaguely, he could see the black lightning bolt that arced downward, striking into the Devourer's mouth, the Fury's magic drawn to the Firerod like metal to a magnet.

The Devourer's entire bottom jaw vanished, instantly disintegrated by the lightning's blast. The Titan shrieked, a terrible, gurgling groan that spewed from its throat. Golden blood cascaded from the gaping wound in a similar fashion, spilling across the Fields and flooding the pits. The Devourer trembled and began to fall, but Tasi'a was frozen in place.

Kaven ran toward her, heedless of the dying monster and the awful pain in his arm. Tasi'a finally came to herself, stumbling back in fear before tripping. Tasi'a toppled into a pit and sank beneath a massive pool of golden blood. The Devourer slammed into the earth, throwing up chunks of stone as Kaven leapt into the pit after her. The blood was surprisingly cold to the touch, and it engulfed him completely. He grabbed hold of the sorceress and pulled her free of the blood, and she gasped when she met the air. Above, the storm band blew onward, leaving the battle behind.

Kaven set Tasi'a down, and she shivered violently. He wiped blood from his eyes and turned swiftly toward the Titan. It couldn't be that simple; it couldn't be defeated so easily. He stared in awe as the Devourer twitched sporadically, his expression mirrored by Tasi'a's. Kaven feared that the Titan would rise again, but blood continued to cascade from its neck, and the twitching became slower and slower before it finally stopped. The Devourer was dead.

Kaven began to laugh through the pain. They had killed a *Titan*? That wasn't supposed to be possible! And yet the Devourer, butcher of hundreds, the indestructible hand of Na'lek, was struck down before them, lying in a veritable lake of its own blood.

"I told you," Tasi'a whispered, wide-eyed as she stared at the Devourer. "Na'lek will always protect us."

Kaven didn't answer; he was too stunned. A Titan was dead. The Fury roared in the distance, enraged yet not defeated. They were still going to die; the Shredders were growing stronger. Kaven's shirt was completely soaked with the Devourer's blood, but he fearfully remembered the feeling of his own blood leaking down his back. Kaven suddenly felt ill, and he stumbled, falling to the ground as his vision darkened.

He heard Tasi'a shout his name, but it was a distant sound. Kaven was fading, and he felt confused as sensation oozed away from his body. But then he gasped, realizing that he had stopped breathing.

Kaven sat up quickly, taking in huge gulps of air. Tasi'a stood over him, a golden glow around her hands as she watched him nervously. He quickly noted the absence of pain and looked down at himself. The gashes caused by the Shredders were gone.

Tasi'a's eyes were wide as she looked down at him, and Kaven saw that she had healed herself too. "Are you all right?" she asked, an edge of panic in her voice.

Kaven groaned as his arm sent a spike of pain through him. That wound was still there. "I think so," he said.

"Thank Na'lek," she said, smiling. Tasi'a stood, and when she did, Kaven saw a familiar golden sheen to her skin.

"Tasi'a!" he said, pointing at her. "Look at yourself!"

She did so and gasped in surprise. "The itch is gone," she whispered. "I don't feel the Shredders." She turned, staring at the Devourer's corpse. "By the Fury, Kaven, the blood is shielding us!"

Kaven stared at the Titan, awestruck. What in Na'lek's name had the Deliverance put in their potion?

"Kaven?" a voice called from behind the Titan's corpse, wrenching him from his confusion. Tasi'a and Kaven turned away from the Devourer as one—identical expressions of surprise blossoming on their faces as two figures climbed to the top of the massive body. *Titan's teeth,* he thought. Just when Kaven began to imagine that he had seen all the Fury's impossibilities, another approached. *It can't be!*

# TWENTY

*"Na'lek will not hesitate to kill you, should you break the Church's law."*

—From the Tomes of Regret, Verse 2 of Power

SHERA AND TOYON were standing behind them, shock and joy mingling on their faces. Kaven stared right back, his face a perfect painting of disbelief. They were alive! *But Death had killed them,* a small voice whispered, but Kaven crushed it, obliterating it from his mind. Never before had he been so happy to be wrong.

Tasi'a was the first to run toward them, but Kaven was behind her, sprinting like the winds of the Fury itself. Shera and Toyon waited, smiling as they watched them ascend the Titan's corpse. Tasi'a leapt into Shera's arms, and they hugged each other tightly.

Kaven cleared his throat and grinned at Toyon. "You're alive!"

The quiet man nodded, treating Kaven to a rare smile. "As are you."

"Are you all right?" Kaven asked.

"Yes." Another nod. "You?"

"As well as could be expected," Kaven replied.

Tasi'a laughed in exasperation. "Idiots." She stepped forward and embraced Toyon. "I'm so glad you're okay!"

Toyon returned the hug, albeit with a touch of hesitation. "Your company was missed, Tasi'a."

Kaven turned to Shera and grinned. But then he quickly put on an expression of mock seriousness. "Good to see you're alive; we needed someone to charge recklessly into battle."

"And I missed not having anyone to insult," Shera said with a smile. "Talking to Toyon is like talking to a rock, save that the rock is more interesting." They hugged briefly and Kaven didn't care that her armor bit into his skin.

"Now then"—Shera leaned against the Devourer's rigid claw—"I want to know how you have barely a scratch between the two of you. I'm also mildly interested in how you managed to kill one of the Titans." She gestured idly at the monstrous corpse, feigning indifference, but Kaven could see a blazing curiosity in her eyes. Now that Kaven thought about it, the death of a Titan was the most significant event of his lifetime. That was something Kleon Fortis would have to be proud of!

They sat down to eat, and Tasi'a proved to be all too eager to explain how the Fury's winds had whisked them away from Death's clutches. Unfortunately, she also mentioned the funeral Kaven had held for them. Shera found that hilarious, but Toyon simply nodded solemnly in silent thanks. When she arrived at the Devourer, Tasi'a gave Kaven credit for the kill, even though he tried to protest. He never would have been able to do it without Tasi'a distracting the beast.

"Now tell us what happened to you," Tasi'a said when she had finished, speaking excitedly between mouthfuls of food.

Shera and Toyon began their story, and Kaven was proven wrong for the third time today. Yet another impossibility—a Titan with no ill intentions. Kaven found the story hard to believe. The Watcher may have saved them, but perhaps there was some nefarious purpose behind the Titan's supposed good will.

Shera and Toyon had both been equally perplexed by the Watcher's nature, but they seemed to believe the story. Shera finished by saying that they had spotted the Devourer attacking in the distance and had rushed toward it, fearing the worst, only to watch the Titan die.

"Thank Na'lek that you killed that monster," Shera said. "I expected to find you both dead and stripped to the bone. But when we saw the Devourer die . . . Titans take me, I couldn't believe it! But now we've made it. Shilanti is so close now, I can almost see it."

"There's an old story in Fulminos," Toyon said. "The night is not the world of men, but of wolves. To walk into the forest in the dark is to risk never coming back out. Yet, if you see a light in the forest you will go to it and find shelter and safety. But, all too often, the wolves can also see the light, and they'll be waiting for you."

Kaven shivered. It was best not to forget how many lives Na'lek had taken. And if Na'lek was a wolf, then he made the Titans seem like crippled pups, and the light of Shilanti belonged to him. They were not safe yet.

Shera patted Toyon on the back, laughing. "This is why you aren't invited anywhere, Toyon. There's more to life than perpetual gloom. I vote we take a few hours sleep; night is almost upon us, and I haven't slept since we left the Watcher's cave. We can reach Shilanti by tomorrow."

Shera then tried to offer Kaven and Tasi'a the last of their protection potion, but Tasi'a quickly showed her the Devourer's blood. Toyon and Shera were just as amazed as Kaven had been by this discovery.

They made camp under the crook of the Devourer's arm, sheltered by the immense limb and the Titan's ruined head. Kaven took first watch as the other three went to sleep.

Alone, as the sky darkened, Kaven looked up at the Fury, feeling ashamed. "Na'lek?" he whispered softly. "I'm sorry. I'm so sorry. I shouldn't have despaired; I shouldn't have cursed you. I was just so angry; I thought you had taken everything from me. But now I see that you had a plan all along. I was just too stupid to see it. Please forgive me." Na'lek did not answer, and even his Fury was silent. But Kaven supposed he'd be able to ask again tomorrow, in person.

His two hours passed uneventfully, Kaven spending them in quiet contemplation of his actions and Na'lek's mercy. He woke Toyon and went to bed, instantly slipping into a dark, dreamless sleep.


Kaven awoke feeling refreshed for the first time in weeks. He stood and stretched, yawning as he shook sleep from his body. Shera turned and looked down at him from her vantage point on top of the Devourer's arm.

"Good morning," she said, sounding cheerful.

"Morning." Kaven smiled. "Ready to storm the gates of Shilanti?"

"As the Destroyer broke Stormgarde, so shall I do the same to Shilanti," she said, hopping down from the massive, stony limb.

Kaven nodded. "Today, we're ending the Fury."

"Na'lek willing, of course," Tasi'a said, packing her supplies before standing.

Toyon rose from his bedding with a rather loud yawn. "It appears that we are going to start early today?"

"Might as well," Shera said with a shrug. "It's probably not smart to keep a god waiting."

"'Na'lek is as patient as he is wise,'" Tasi'a said. "That's a quote from the Tomes of Regret, verse thirty-nine of Power."

Kaven frowned as he withdrew an apple from his pack. "That makes me wonder, what did our ancestors do to make Na'lek so angry?"

"Humans rarely change," Tasi'a said. "And we've been sinning for far too long."

They set off into the Fury once more, leaving the Devourer behind and marching under the Fury for what they hoped was the last time. Kaven was terrified more than he ever had been previously. He didn't exactly know what to expect in Shilanti, but the legions of monsters would surely be there, and Na'lek only knew what the other Titans were planning.

After about an hour, the Fields of Glory began to slope upward. It wasn't a particularly large hill, but big enough to obscure the horizon. Shera drew her sword, leading them up cautiously.

"Be careful," she said. "We cannot know what is waiting for us up ahead."

They crested the top of the hill and looked on. Kaven's heart leapt in his chest as he beheld the Fury's heart.

# TWENTY-ONE

*"Build weapons of war, stout Regelians, for the Day of Reckoning comes."*

—*From the Tomes of Regret, Verse 1 of Duty*

SUNLIGHT STRUCK KAVEN'S face, bright and warm. The Fury abruptly gave way to clear blue sky and the midday sun shone ahead of them. Kaven could see the Fury in the distance, but the storm formed a perfect circle around this patch of land, leaving many miles of land untouched by the Eternal Storm. Stone turned to grass and pits turned to trees, which swayed lazily, part of a gentle breeze that swept through the strange, untarnished circle.

There was a massive city built within the circle, but it was in ruins. Buildings were gray and lifeless, the wall around the city crumbled, and the wooden gates were gone. Many of the buildings lacked roofs, and some towers were sheared completely in half. Despite the ruin of this city, Kaven knew that this place had never been touched by the Fury. Age had claimed it. There was also a palace in the city, a massive, square structure that seemed to have once had four towers, one at each corner. Two were topless, one was halved, and the fourth was missing entirely.

A strange beam of white light rose from the palace in a straight line, but high in the air it split into six different beams, which streaked across the sky and connected with the Fury at six different points. Kaven didn't know what to make of it.

"What happened here?" Kaven asked, staring at the ruined city in disbelief. "This can't be Shilanti."

Toyon shook his head. "It makes no sense to me."

"Perhaps the city is disguised," Shera suggested, but she didn't sound totally convinced. "Designed to drive off those that lack resolve?"

"No." Tasi'a was studying the city intently. "I believe that this is Shilanti—or was, I should say. This place is man-made, a Shilanti in which our ancestors lived. I believe that this ruin was once the greatest city of our kind, but it is not the Shilanti from which Na'lek rules. Unless I am painfully mistaken, in that castle"—she pointed to the wreckage, specifically to the energy rising out of it—"is a portal to the real Shilanti . . . and Na'lek."

Kaven blinked in surprise. A portal in a city? Portals were incredibly unpredictable, and a collapsing portal could wipe out anyone too close. Why would they risk having something so dangerous inside their city?

Though Kaven had only seen one portal collapse, he knew one of the most infamous stories. When the Destroyer had invaded Stormgarde three hundred years ago, leading his armies on a rampage, a Zealot named Aeshe had stood against him. Though Stormgarde bested the armies of the Destroyer, the Titan himself could not be felled. Conventional weapons and magic could not break the Destroyer's hide, and the Titan butchered hundreds of warriors. Finally, only Zealot Aeshe stood against the Destroyer and Stormgarde's destruction.

Aeshe had exhausted his arsenal of magic and had begun to despair before he imagined a final, desperate plan. Aeshe opened a portal *inside* the Destroyer, and the portal collapsed. The resulting explosion claimed the life of Aeshe, but the Destroyer died too, ending the brief and bloody war.

"If that is true," Toyon said more than a little doubtfully, "then that is the greatest magical achievement of mankind."

Kaven hadn't thought of that. In order to operate with relative safety, a portal had to be maintained by at least four strong sorcerers. If this one had been around for hundreds—if not thousands—of years unattended, then it truly was a masterful work of magic. Though, it could've been created by Na'lek himself, and it would, of course, be beyond anything mortals could master.

Tasi'a smiled, bouncing with excitement. "Indeed. This will be one of the greatest sights we'll ever see!"

"Besides the kingdom of our god, you mean?" Kaven ruffled her hair.

Shera forestalled Tasi'a before she could retort. "Well, let's stop gawking and go find Na'lek. This is what we came to do. We made it to the Fury's heart!"

Kaven laughed aloud. They had survived. Despite all of the dangers and perils of the Fury, they had reached Shilanti alive and unscathed. The Fury rumbled, but it didn't have much time left in existence. They were going to save Lantrelia! He took off running.

"Hey!" Shera tore off after him. "Come back, you idiot." Toyon and Tasi'a hurried after the Stormgardian, laughing joyously. Kaven outran his companions, though he only beat Toyon by mere seconds, making him the first to cross into the ancient city.

Darkened, marred rock turned abruptly to the ancient, cracking cobblestones of a wide street with rows of tall, damaged buildings on either side. Kaven slowed and his friends caught up, everyone huffing from the sudden burst of energy and looking around at the city. Despite Shilanti's ruined state—if it even was Shilanti—it was once again comforting to be around things that were familiar. Even though it was withered with age, the presence of mankind's creations was comforting.

They walked through Shilanti, following the road that seemed to lead directly to the palace. The buildings were dark and empty, all furnishings and signs of civilization rotted away. Fountains stood dry and desolate, and statues slowly faded. The city was long dead, as were its people.

There were bones in the streets, a good many of them, in fact, though none of them were human. The squat, blunt skulls of Eye-Takers littered a small intersection of three streets, in what had probably once been a marketplace. Chitinous shell fragments littered another street like broken pottery, and several steel blades of Knifemen were thrust into a decrepit wall. The bones were all covered with gray dust, as was everything else in the city. The group left footprints behind as they walked, as if there were a thin layer of snow on the ground.

As they neared the castle, Kaven could see that the gates had rotted away long ago. He began to feel an increasing sense of foreboding. He had cursed Na'lek, called him hateful and vain. He had accused his god of murder and butchery. How would Na'lek react to his coming? Tasi'a had always insisted that he was a god of mercy and love. Kaven supposed that it was time to find out if he really was.

They crept into the castle silently, anticipating an attack at any moment. More bones were scattered about the courtyard: Spinereavers, Bouncers, Flamebringers, and more. Kaven wondered if they would be attacked in this place. They stood in the wide, empty courtyard, looking about at their surroundings. The yard was nothing but tall grass now, overgrown from years of being left unattended. Tall, chipped walls formed a square around the palace, enclosing it, and the towers seemed even more desolate up close.

The palace itself was a massive six-story structure. Large openings filled the tall building, some still containing stained-glass windows of red and blue. Odd, monstrous statues perched on ledges, looking down upon them with vile leers on their faces. The palace's roof was composed of three massive blue domes with red tiles between them that formed a slanting roof. A third of the palace was missing; the majority of the upper left corner was simply not there, leaving a curved hole behind, as if someone had scooped the walls out. That strange white energy was rising up out of the wrecked portion.

They approached the palace and walked up a short flight of stairs that led to the main entrance. The doors were still there, or at least a part of them. They were lined with iron, which was the only thing that remained. The metal twisted in intricate designs, forming the vague shape of two massive doors. Had the wood still been there, they might have been magnificent to behold.

Shera stepped forward and pushed on the doors. They swung open, creaking terribly. Kaven followed Shera into the palace, Tasi'a walking ahead of him and Toyon behind.

The castle opened into a massive chamber that must have once been a grand ballroom or a showcase of some kind. Kaven didn't have much knowledge of these things, so his deductions were probably way off. The walls, floor, and roof seemed to be colored a dull red and were covered with more dust and bones. At the opposite end of the long room were three corridors that led to other parts of the palace. One led upward.

"There's our way up," he said, pointing at the centermost passage.

Tasi'a looked around, eyes wide with wonder. "This place must have been beautiful in its prime! If only I could have seen it then."

Shera chuckled. "We're going to see an even more impressive city, Tasi'a. Today we dine in Shilanti!"

"That white energy seems to be coming from the top floor," Toyon said, looking up the stairs. "Let's start there and work our way down."

They began to walk up the stairs quickly, passing the second and third floors. When they passed the fourth floor, they came to a sudden stop as the sound of voices floated down to them from above.

"It's not my fault that Bore was an idiot," a deep voice said, tone strained with anger. "I told him not to touch it!"

"No, you told Bore that he was *supposed* to touch it!" a higher, angrier voice snapped, distinctly feminine. "Yath, you're a fool and a murderer."

The one called Yath made a sputtering sound of protest. "Azin, how could I have known that it would tear his arm and leg off? It wasn't my fault; he should have touched it with a stick first!"

Azin's voice rose in volume considerably as she yelled, "You should have told Bore that. You practically pushed him into it!"

"Well, you're the one who cut off his head," Yath said defensively.

"That's because he was bleeding out," Azin snapped. "I put him out of his misery!"

Shera looked back at them and mouthed the word, "Monsters." She slowly and quietly drew her sword and began to creep up the stairs. Toyon had knives in his hands and quickly rushed past Shera, silent as a shadow. Kaven drew his shortsword, careful to avoid bumping his bad arm as he climbed.

Tasi'a followed behind, her breath coming in rapid, nervous gulps. Kaven touched her hand to comfort her.

"Hey!" Yath's voice suddenly yelled out in a surprised tone. Surprise turned to fear, which was quickly echoed by Azin. Shera rushed up to the fifth and final floor, Kaven and Tasi'a fast behind her. Shera stopped suddenly, smiling.

Three Flamebringers lay faceup in front of Toyon, who was cleaning his knives on a rag. Their corpses blazed with fire and magma, merging unnaturally with humanlike flesh. One had been dead already, his right arm and leg both missing. Another's throat was slit while the third had been stabbed in the heart.

"Well done." Shera glanced down at the corpses with a look of satisfaction.

Tasi'a looked at the Flamebringers with distaste. "I'll assume that he was Bore." She pointed at the dismembered body.

"Good assumption," Kaven said softly. "But what killed him?"

The answer to that question was not clear. They had reached their destination; the roof above them ended in a jagged ruin, exposing a majority of the room to the sky above. They appeared to be in some sort of throne room; a stone dais stood proudly toward the back of the immense room. Two thrones stood upon it, but the rightmost one was broken and shattered, leaving only the base and seat behind. The thrones were carved from marble, and shallow grooves ran across their entire lengths in intricate patterns. Kaven guessed that was where gold inlays had been in some ancient day.

The most impressive display was the massive column of a pure white substance that rose from the ground and shot high into the air to spread outward toward the Fury. It was so wide that it filled most of the hole, and Kaven couldn't see around it without moving. The pillar was humming softly; the sound reminded Kaven of the Firerods back in Regelia as they charged up.

"What is that?" Her voice shrill with excitement, Tasi'a ran over to the pillar, leaping over the corpses and skidding to a halt inches away from the white column.

"Careful!" Toyon called. "It might be what severed this Flamebringer's limbs."

Shera walked over to the pillar, frowning at it. "Is it the portal you spoke of? The portal to Shilanti?"

Tasi'a leaned in closer, peering into the pillar. "It could be, but it's unlike any portal I've ever seen."

Kaven started to walk around the pillar and froze when he saw something on the other side. "Hey! Come look at this!" His companions hurried to join them and beheld the same grisly sight. Shera's face grew concerned, Tasi'a's disgusted, and Toyon's fixed with mild curiosity.

It was a human skeleton, but unlike any Kaven had ever seen before. The bones were a bright green, like emeralds. And they faded if you tried to look at them directly, disappearing from sight only to return when your gaze was averted. The skeleton was frozen in place, standing with its arms thrown wide, as if expecting an embrace. Its face was pointed upward, mouth agape. Its spine bent backward, as if something had begun to throw it, but the bones had frozen before actually lifting.

Tasi'a approached the skeleton, a look of fascination on her face. Toyon grabbed her before she got too near. "Don't touch that either."

But it was too late. Kaven had already touched the skeleton's hand. Instantly he felt a jolt of pain shoot through his spine and he stumbled backward. The pain faded almost instantly and Kaven straightened.

"You idiot!" Shera exclaimed. "Are you all right?"

Kaven nodded. "Yeah, I'm fine."

"Please don't touch it again." Tasi'a went up the skeleton and circled it, bending down to study the leg bones, standing on tiptoes to get a good look at the skull. "This was definitely a man," she said.

Kaven grimaced at the sight of the shifting bones. "I can't imagine this was a pleasant way to die."

Shera didn't look at the skeleton for long, either uninterested or repulsed by it. She bent down and grabbed a small chunk of rubble. Throwing it up once and catching it, she tossed it straight into the pillar.

Tasi'a leapt up as the stone left Shera's hand. "Don't!"

Toyon and Kaven turned suddenly to see the rock strike the pillar, going straight into it as if the pillar was made of mist. After going just a few inches in, the stone suddenly fizzed, as if coated with bubbles, and then it vanished suddenly, leaving nothing behind. The pillar stood still, undisturbed.

Shera smirked. "Does that answer your questions?"

"Not really." Tasi'a stood and left the frozen skeleton behind, coming up to observe the pillar again. "We still don't know if it is the portal to Shilanti, or if it's just a column of energy that vaporizes anything that touches it."

"What purpose would a vaporizing pillar serve?" Kaven asked, tilting his head so that he could get a better look at the glowing spire.

Toyon shrugged. "A method of public execution?"

"Waste management?" Shera suggested.

"A practical way to cut steel or precious stones?" Tasi'a put in, beginning to circle the pillar.

"Ancient torture device?" Toyon said next, searching the ground for another rock.

Shera grinned. "A place to toss your enemies? A food chopper? Pest control?" Looking down at her sword, she raised an eyebrow. "A way to sharpen weapons?"

"You'd need a deft touch, of course," Tasi'a said with just a hint of sarcasm.

"Nah, you just ram the blade through the center." The two women doubled over laughing at their shared joke.

Kaven cut in. "All right! I'm sorry I asked . . ."

Tasi'a sighed heavily as she came around the pillar and stepped past them, stopping to examine the skeletal remains again. "We're getting nowhere like this! Everyone spread out and look for something useful."

Toyon straightened. "Like what?"

"How should I know?" Tasi'a grabbed two fistfuls of her hair and yanked, cheeks blowing in and out as her face reddened in frustration. "Just start searching!"

The three parted to go carry out Tasi'a's decree. Shera moved beyond the pillar and Toyon bent back down to find another stone. Kaven decided to investigate the thrones—perhaps the last king's name was still there? Kaven walked over to the two statuesque chairs, dusty and fragile with immense age. He avoided the one that was already broken, not wanting to damage it further.

Kaven stepped up to them, putting a foot on the seat of the rightmost throne, which he assumed belonged to the ancient king. *Aha!* There was an inscription carved into the back of the throne. The writing was crisp and neat, preserved despite its age. Unfortunately, the inscription was written in the Ancient Script, which Kaven did not know how to read. One word seemed familiar though. *Naleck.* Interesting, it sounded like Na'lek.

"Tasi'a?" Kaven called. "Come look at this."

"Hmm?" Tasi'a was hesitant to leave her investigation, but she came over, head still swiveled toward the glowing bones. "What is it?"

Kaven pointed to the inscription on the throne. "Right here. Can you read that?"

Tasi'a came over to the ancient stone. "Does this hold any relevance to our search? If not—" She paused, brow furrowing as she peered at the writing. Toyon was by her side, bending down so that he could see it clearly. "Hmm. I'm not exactly sure if I can. Wait! There's some kind of magic rune etched under the writing. I think I can activate it . . . oh! There we go."

A green light erupted from a point under the words "Wizard King" and spilled into the room, pooling at the base of the throne before rising in a pile as large and wide as Kaven. The light shimmered and began to form into a more distinct shape. Blobs began to lengthen, forming arms and legs. Those indentations became eyes, and that protrusion was a nose. Wrinkles became elegant robes that draped the figure from chest to feet, obscuring even its toes. The clothing was grossly ornate; patterns covered the entirety of the sleeves, torso, and legs. Flying birds, wings outstretched. Strange catlike animals bearing long fangs. Ribbonlike fish with tails that stretched across his back to touch their own heads.

The shapeless mass of light had become a slender man of average height, with a mane of reddish-brown hair that appeared well-groomed. The entire figure of the man was tinged green, like an outline that allowed other colors to seep through. The man's high cheekbones and wide jaw wouldn't have made him the center of attention among women, and neither would the blunt fingers closed into a tight fist. However, the many jewels that adorned his hands could probably do the job just as well. Straight hair hung loosely at his shoulders, and a thin crown was perched upon his head, set with one large gem at the front.

His long, rounded beard, which almost touched his stomach, would have been considered unfashionable in Regelia.

Despite the man's quirks, his most distinguishing feature was his eyes. They were cold and sharp, and they seemed to resonate with a persistent demand for subservience. These were eyes that were used to obedience. These were the eyes of a man with a hard heart. These were the eyes of a tyrant. They were ancient and hateful, and their hue was the violet of the Fury itself.

The green-tinted man scowled, staring at nothing. "I am Naleck," the figure of light proclaimed dramatically, glaring directly forward. "Wizard-King of Shilanti, Lantrelia, and soon even the worlds beyond."

Tasi'a raised an eyebrow. "Now this is interesting. It's a Magiscroll, a permanent recording of image and voice, without any writing. We often use them in Venedeis in place of books." She glanced at the figure of the Wizard-King.

So this was Na'lek? Kaven studied the figure closely as the image of his god stepped forward. The throne room had changed too; the roof was whole and the floor unbroken. Both thrones stood erect and proud upon the dais. The whole room was now a translucent green as the light corrected what age had done to this once-grand place. This was what the throne room had been, countless years ago.

"This is for those that come after," the Magiscroll continued, voice imperious and haughty. Kaven could hear Na'lek's hatred. Titans, he was so arrogant! "This is for those who wish to witness the birth of a new age. This is for those who will exalt me above all else."

Na'lek walked forward, stepping through Kaven and toward the pillar. The pillar was not outlined in green like the restored throne room, so he supposed that it had not existed when this had been recorded. Kaven didn't feel anything as the

Magiscroll passed through him. "I stand here today burdened with immense hardship. The weight of this is heavy upon my heart. I cannot sleep at night, tortured by these dreams." The apparition's eyes narrowed, changing from a brief glimpse of pain to a dark heat in an instant. "I am not satisfied, but God has denied my prayers."

Shera was watching the Magiscroll with a look of bemusement on her face, standing next to the throne with her arms crossed over her chest and head tilted slightly. She was frowning. "Why did he say 'God'?"

Her confused question went unheard by the ghostly Na'lek, who was now standing before the pillar with his arms outstretched. "I am not satisfied with you. You are my people, you are my kingdom, my land and my wealth. But you are worthless. Lantrelia has given me much pleasure, but it has long since run dry. I am discarding you in favor of a riper harvest. My magicians have studied the great dark above and have found life and beauty on other worlds. These . . . shall be mine."

Tasi'a's face darkened, looking from the figure of light to the pillar and back. She had come up behind Na'lek and was looking over his shoulder, or rather through it. Something about the Magiscroll was bothering her. But what? Shera also looked concerned, but Toyon wasn't. Kaven didn't think anything about the Magiscroll was odd, though he didn't understand what Na'lek was talking about. He was instead surprised by how human Na'lek looked.

Oblivious to his spectators, Na'lek continued to rant. He was smiling now, a triumphant expression that, even though it proclaimed joy, still seemed to look down upon the world around him. "I've had my fill of Lantrelia and the paltry pleasures she affords. My armies shall pour into these new worlds and take them for me, and we shall not stop until the cup of my wealth overflows with wonder and splendor." Na'lek's fists unclenched, and he lowered his arms. "Ah! But you wish to know how my might grew so vast? How I will discover the path between worlds? Quite simply, I will use a portal."

Tasi'a began to nod, face grave. Toyon, who had sat down on the throne, suddenly stood, staring directly at Tasi'a. Shera only quirked an eyebrow, and Kaven still didn't know why the sorceress was so concerned.

Kaven realized that he was witnessing Na'lek open the portal to the true Shilanti. No mortal could ever open a portal vast enough to span across the skies. Na'lek's power must be truly grand.

Na'lek's face grew dark, brow furrowed in concentration. His eyes were still cold but focused. "My portal will surpass the wildest imaginations of all beings that have ever existed or ever will exist. My reign shall echo into the deepest reaches of history until all is undone at the end of time itself! My name shall be whispered by the greatest kings and lords in the ages to come. The name of Naleck, Wizard-King of a Thousand Worlds, shall be eternal, and my kingdom will exceed even eternity itself! Now, observe my ascendance."

The Magiscroll extended his arms in front of him, palms pointed outward. Green magical energy flowed from Na'lek's hands, growing and multiplying until the entire room was almost shrouded by rippling bands of magic that thrashed and writhed in the air as a twisting mass. The magic rushed about, singing like the wind until it became deafening. Kaven, not wanting to miss anything, rushed through the opaque magic until he could again see the emerald-rimmed figure standing amidst the chaos, sweat leaving wet streaks down his face and hands.

Shera, Toyon, and Tasi'a were there, crowding with Kaven around Na'lek, nearly pressed against the ethereal man as they watched with mixed feelings of anticipation. Tasi'a looked worried, Toyon doubtful, and Shera confused. And Kaven . . . well, he didn't quite know what to feel. He was excited, not worried or apprehensive. But there was something that tickled in the back of his mind. It was a small voice that whispered that something was not quite right. This dread had no cause that Kaven could find, but he still felt a small measure of nervousness nonetheless.

"Sire!" a small voice called out against the cacophony. "Lord Naleck! The Nexus is unstable! It's unstable!" Kaven started at the sound before realizing that the newcomer was part of the Magiscroll. He couldn't see the man through the chaos of the magic, despite its translucency. It was just too thick.

Na'lek grunted, his reply coming out broken as he strained to control the raging vortex of magic he had summoned. "Your worries . . . are pointless! It will . . . bend to . . . my will!" Anger tainted every word he spoke.

"The Nexus cannot be controlled!" the man shouted. "Sire, you have to close it!"

"Close it?" Na'lek bellowed back, eyes alight with fury. "Never! I've yet to even begin!"

Surprise was evident in the unseen attendant's tone. "Sire! The Council has forbidden such a use of—"

Na'lek's sharp retort cut him off; he was breathing heavily now, his voice strained. "The Council . . . is hereby . . . abolished! You've all . . . failed me."

There was a long pause before the hidden figure replied. "Lord Naleck, you've become enraptured with your own power. Sire, you have to close the portal before you harm yourself or others."

The power-mad god bared his teeth in a snarl. "Has that ever stopped me before? Simple fool, I am . . . the Wizard-King! I will rule all that I see. The universe . . . is mine—"

And then it happened. The world exploded. The rippling, twisting cords of magical energy were suddenly sucked inward, forming into a dense mass in front of Na'lek, and then rising to form a pillar, overlapping the already existing one. This happened in the space of a second, and in that instant, Kaven could see the frightened faces of dozens of green-tinged men and women, assembled a little way behind their Wizard King, watching with fearful eyes. Staring at this new pillar, Kaven grasped what it signified. But then the second passed, and fire replaced everything.

Stone was blasted apart above them; chunks of emerald marble and granite were thrown outward as the magical energy rapidly expanded. The roar of fire was deafening, and Kaven instinctively dropped into a defensive position, covering his head with his arms, even though the destruction had happened eons ago. Na'lek's back was snapped backward and he froze as what appeared to be strange, bubbling flames coated him. His flesh, clothing, and jewelry melted, and magical energy soaked into his bones, which were perfectly aligned with the real skeleton.

The fires spread outward, traveling faster than the winds as they consumed the people standing behind Na'lek, taking them so quickly that they barely had time to blink in surprise. The flames were beginning to take a more familiar shape: large, dark clouds that began to rise slowly into the air. A wind blew them higher and faster, and a crack of thunder filled the room. Black lightning struck the rightmost throne, erasing the majority of it as was reflected in the real world.

Then the Magiscroll faded, taking all the green light with it and returning the throne room to its broken state. The throne remained shattered and the roof was gaping wide, stonework eradicated by the explosion. The ground was pockmarked with numerous holes and cracks. And Na'lek's glowing skeleton was still in place, back bent and arms wide, empty eye sockets glaring up at the sky.

Kaven stood frozen, silent, and the other three were like statues in the wake of what they had just witnessed. Tasi'a finally moved, taking a step toward the throne, face a picture of horror. Tasi'a knelt before the inscription on the throne, reading it again and again.

And then she turned back toward them, tears beginning to slip down her cheeks. "'May his reign be long and prosperous,'" she read. "'Never before has Shilanti been ruled by so mighty a man. Long live the Wizard-King Naleck, ruler of all Lantrelia.'"

Kaven hesitated, too stunned to speak. Five words seemed to be branded into his mind, and they repeated themselves in an endless cycle. *Shilanti, Man, Wizard-King, Naleck . . .* Was it actually saying what Kaven thought? Could it really be saying that Na'lek . . . wasn't a god? Was Na'lek—or should he say "Naleck"—nothing more than a man? Perhaps . . . perhaps they were two different beings? Yes, that must be it! History couldn't really twist a long-dead man into a god, right? Right?

Kaven looked to Tasi'a, hoping that she would deny what the Ancient Script boldly claimed. Tasi'a, who had argued so fiercely on behalf of Na'lek's character. Tasi'a, who had made her study of the Tomes of Regret more extensive than any person that Kaven knew, would deny this outlandish claim. Surely, she could confirm their religion was built on the glory of Na'lek. She knew everything about Na'lek and his ways.

"It seems," she said softly, "that Na'lek as we know him . . ." —Tasi'a hesitated, her voice wavering—"has never existed."

Shera groaned out loud, sinking to her knees, and Toyon bowed his head. Kaven felt a weight drop onto his heart as he stared dully at Tasi'a, wishing that she had never activated that Magiscroll, that they had never come to this ruin. He wished he had never agreed to this fool's mission.

Na'lek was dead. Na'lek was long dead, consumed by age and the relentless, never-ceasing river of time. Time changed everything, like water eroding a rock, until something half-true was left—a smoothed, warped version of events. There was no god that had sent the Fury, no god that had protected them from the Devourer, and no god that was angry with mankind. There was only a long-dead king and his maddened scheme for conquest.

Kaven didn't know how to feel. Angry? Betrayed? Confused? But none of those emotions fit, because the situation made sense, a horrible sense. Why feel angry? Who was he going to be angry at? The Church? The Church was as unaware as he had been before today. And why should he feel betrayed? No one had betrayed him. Only time had affected them, hiding facts until they were disguised by a shrouded myth.

Tasi'a was surprisingly calm as she straightened, but her eyes betrayed the confusion and sorrow within. "We . . . we have nothing to refute that Magiscroll, nothing to defend Na'lek. I suggest that we operate as if . . ." She paused, grimacing sadly at her own words. "As if Na'lek was never a god."

Shera stood up, fury clouding her face like an angry fog. "This must be a coincidence! Look at the spelling! How do you know they're even pronounced the same?"

"Names can change over time," Tasi'a said, starting to sound like her normal, inquisitive self. "Both the spelling and pronunciation may have altered. You're right, Shera. This could just be a coincidence . . . bad luck. But I don't believe in luck."

Kaven sided with Shera, desperately wanting her to be right. "That's only because you thought Na'lek had a hand in everything!"

Tasi'a snapped, face going red as she stormed forward until they were nose to nose. Temper rising, she began yelling in his face. "Don't you think I want Na'lek to be real, Kaven? Don't you think I want my beliefs to be true? But the facts don't lie, and I'm sure that someone with even your *limited* intelligence should be able to discern that this all makes perfect sense!"

Kaven began backing away from the diminutive woman, wincing at the stinging insult and retort. "Tasi'a," he said, trying to be calm and cheerful, but failing horribly. Despair coated his tone; he felt like a farmer witnessing a wildfire consuming his fields just before the harvest. "I just . . . I can't believe that . . . that it's a lie."

"Not a lie," Toyon said softly. Out of them all, he was either the least affected or the best at controlling his emotions. Probably a mixture of both. "This was an event that happened so long ago that not even our ancestors can recall the vaguest details of it. How could all of the facts be expected to survive for so long? How can they be expected to remain unaltered? Na'lek was a mistake. Just because he is not our god does not mean that our god does not exist. Keep that in mind as we continue."

Kaven blinked, looking at Toyon blankly as he took in the assassin's words. Of course! That was the answer! Na'lek and Shilanti were merely misrepresentations of the real God! *But maybe they're not,* whispered a small, dark voice inside of him. *Maybe there is no god.*

"What of the Fury?" Kaven whispered, looking toward the pillar and Na'lek's corpse. The Fury wasn't even a storm; it was some type of monstrous portal gone horribly wrong. That explained why the monsters that attacked were random, and why there wasn't any form of empire in the Fury's heart. That was why strange debris always assailed them as it was blown out of the Fury; they were all taken from other worlds, ripped from their homes like Shera said the Watcher had been. And that made sense too: the black lightning was a gateway of sorts. It didn't kill or destroy but instead transported the things it touched to . . . where? Perhaps to Na'lek's other worlds?

He told these things to Tasi'a, and though she looked horrified, she agreed with him. Pulling his gaze away from Na'lek's horrible bones, Kaven stared into the pillar. In the Magiscroll, the unseen attendant had called it the "Nexus." The Fury wasn't a manifestation of their god's wrath and judgment, but instead it was the accidental creation of a mad tyrant.

"We have to tell the Deliverance," he said. He paused, feeling the blood drain from his face in shock. "By the Titans, we have to tell the Church!"

Toyon stepped forward aggressively. "No, Kaven. We cannot tell anyone about what we have found here."

"What?" Kaven stared back at Toyon, genuinely perplexed. "Why not?"

However, it was Tasi'a who replied. She was sitting down, back to the Nexus, eyes red with unshed tears. "Don't you see what this kind of news would do? The Church would collapse! The Tomes of Regret, which help us govern ourselves, would be worthless. There would be panic and riots. And who knows what would happen in the chaos that followed?"

Toyon was nodding. "So we must keep this secret between us. Only we shall be broken by this discovery." He paused. "And the Watcher knows."

Kaven saw the sense in keeping this dire discovery hidden from the populace. The news would ravage the people. They would be forced to think about their fruitless faith and of the monsters they had slaughtered, most of whom had probably attacked out of confusion rather than hatred.

Tasi'a stood, turning back toward the Nexus. "This portal was created using immense, unheard-of magic, but the years have made the Nexus weak. That's probably why the Fury has stopped expanding. I've been probing it magically, and I have discovered a critical decay in its stability matrix. Since it has weakened, I believe I can now close the portal. We can at least accomplish what we came here to do."

"No." Toyon's stern objection caught Kaven by surprise again.

Loathe to repeat himself, Kaven again had to ask, "Why not, Toyon? We can at least put an end to the slaughter that happens every day! And if the Fury remains, we do not have enough Titan blood to return home!"

"We must not destroy it," the Fulminite said softly. "If the Fury is gone, then scholars will come here. They will see what we have seen, and they will speak with the Watcher. They will learn that Na'lek is not only dead, but that he was nothing but a power-hungry tyrant."

Shera's temper flared, and she stepped up to Toyon, growling angrily. "That's barbaric, even for a Fulminite! We cannot condemn the Watcher to his life of eternal solitude. We cannot let our soldiers fight and die in an unnecessary war! We might as well be killing them ourselves. We cannot return to our homes, not only as failures but as murderers."

Toyon simply raised an eyebrow.

But Shera was all too willing to explain. "Yes, murderers! We will stand by and watch as our people die purposelessly, slaughtering monsters that had no wish to come to our world, forever knowing that we had the opportunity to stop it. How can you live with that, Toyon?"

"I will live with it because I must. We have a duty toward the greater good, Shera," Toyon said, his expression calm. "In time, our actions here will have prevented a far costlier crisis."

Tasi'a sighed wearily. "Unfortunate as it is, Shera, Toyon is right. The Tomes of Regret are the foundation of our entire society. If it collapses, there won't be any people for a god to look after."

Kaven rushed to Shera's defense. "But hundreds die because of the Fury, Tasi'a! And if what you tell me about the Watcher is true, then he is innocent. How can we leave him to rot?"

"It's as Toyon said," the Venedecian whispered, tears finally falling. She was unable to contain her sorrow any longer. "The men that suffer and die today are far less important than the generations to come.

It was cold. It was heartless. Kaven couldn't help but feel his temper rising. Toyon's attitude he could understand; he seldom seemed to care for the soldiers who died on the Wall. Fulminos did not care about the individual but focused on the whole. But Kaven never would have expected such heartlessness from Tasi'a. She was such a kind person, smart and friendly. How could she so easily condemn the Watcher and her own kinsfolk to perish before the Eternal Storm? And as the only sorceress, Tasi'a was the single person who could stop the Fury. What could Kaven do? Force her to cast magic?

Kaven opened his mouth, and at the same time Shera began to yell again. But whatever they were about to say was cut off as an earsplitting roar shook the castle, causing them to stumble as the ground rumbled beneath them. After having encountered similar sounds during his trials within the Fury, he instantly recognized the unearthly noise. It was a Titan.

# TWENTY-TWO

*"Venedecians: yours is a might of magic. Guard your secrets jealously."*

—From the Tomes of Regret, Verse 2 of Duty

SHERA WAS THE first to reach the window situated beyond the Nexus, Kaven and the others close behind. They crowded the small square window, jostling each other to see the threat encroaching upon them.

And sure enough, towering amongst the ruined buildings that lined the edges of the Fury's heart was a Titan whose body was aflame.

"Unfortunately," Shera said slowly, "the Watcher's warning was accurate. Death has tracked us down."

Tasi'a nodded. "We must halt this conversation until a later point."

Pointed nose twitching, Death raised its immense head, looking toward the castle, seeking them with steady hunger. The normally silent Titan unleashed another bone-rattling roar and began to stride toward them, immense feet making no noise as it walked toward their hiding place. Death left ash in its wake, trailing behind like dark rivers that blanketed the remains of Shilanti. Too late did Kaven realize that the city was not coated in dust, but ash. Eyes aflame with hatred, body aflame with heat, Death came forward.

Toyon grimaced, his eyes shadowed with doubt as he watched the Titan approach. "We can't beat that."

This time, it was Kaven who disagreed. "No, Toyon. We've killed a Titan before, and we can do it again. This isn't a manifestation of Na'lek's anger, only a beast."

"If I may point out," Tasi'a said softly, "the Devourer and Death are vastly different, the latter being much stronger according to our research. The chances of us defeating Death are worryingly low."

Shera drew her sword, unslinging her shield from across her back and turning toward the stairs. "Tasi'a, close the portal."

Kaven stepped after her. "You're not thinking of fighting it alone?"

"Not if you come with me," she replied, giving him a brave smile as she marched confidently toward the passage.

Any hesitation Kaven may have had at fighting a Titan evaporated at the thought of Shera standing alone against Death. Kaven ran after her as she began to descend, unshouldering his bow and readying an arrow. "I will fight by your side, no matter what happens." His own courage surprised him.

He practically leapt down the stairs, still behind Shera as they dashed through the castle with all the speed they could muster. Kaven was beginning to shake with fear, his earlier bravado melting away like ice on a midsummer day. Memories of that terrible night with Death came back to him in flashes, each one a small clip of terror. Fire dancing across the Titan, food burned and destroyed, the wind tossing him across miles of terrain, separation from his companions. It had been a marvel that they had survived that encounter with Death. Could they do it again? Before Kaven had a chance to calm his fears, if they even could be calmed, they burst through the once-sturdy doors that were the castle's main entrance.

Shera and Kaven rushed into the courtyard, only to skid to a halt upon the hard-packed earth and scattered bones. The Titan was there, standing just behind the walls, its hands placed upon them, cracking stone as it leaned inward, head stretching toward them as Shera and Kaven emerged. Death took a step forward; the wall broke into a thousand falling shards. It was as if the Destroyer itself had returned to Stormgarde, tearing down the Barrier Wall as if it were made from dust.

As the wall collapsed, a fountain of ash rose into the air. Death passed through the cloud and prowled into the courtyard, stopping to stare down at Kaven with those dark eyes. "*So.*" Death's voice was slow and grating, a sound like stone grinding against stone. It spoke softly, with great care, as if unaccustomed to speaking at all. "*Meat thought it hide here? I am not fool.*"

The Titan's broken voice thundered across the remains of the city, rattling the ground and the castle behind them. Shera's eyes were wide, but her stance was resolute. Kaven took an involuntary step back when Death spoke. The fact that the Titan was capable of speech, no matter how slow or poorly constructed, was unnerving. Kaven licked dry lips, raising his bow toward the Titan's head. He was breathing heavily, trying to think of a way to kill Death. Perhaps with lightning . . . no, the skies were clear, save for the energy funneling out of the pillar that rose from the broken castle until it touched the sky. And the city was small and completely devastated. Kaven could think of no way to stop Death. He hoped that Shera had a plan.

"*I smell you,*" Death rasped, head bent toward them, fangs bared in ghastly grin. "*I found you. Been so long, Meat. So long since I have prey.*"

"Then you'll have to wait a while longer, Death!" came a booming voice from behind them. Death looked up, eyes narrowing slightly. Kaven spun, seeing Toyon striding toward them, Tasi'a close behind. Kaven had never heard Toyon speak so loudly before, and there was a strength in his voice that demanded respect. Shera smiled at the sound, but she did not look back. Now that Kaven thought about it, it had been stupid to turn his back on Death. He turned back to the Titan quickly, eyes wide with panic. But Death had made no move; he looked up at the newcomers, eyes widening with delight.

"*More Meat,*" he cooed. "*Come closer. I will feast!*"

"We stand together," Tasi'a said loudly, the air around her crackling with power.

Shera began to whisper, voice flush with anger. "Tasi'a, you didn't stop the Fury?" In answer, Tasi'a simply shook her head, causing Shera's face to redden. "Idiot! If we die here, the portal can never be closed!"

Toyon glanced at Shera, his gaze flat. "That is how it must be."

Shera opened her mouth, but whatever she was about to say died on her lips, for Death was suddenly lunging toward them, claws outstretched. Kaven yelped, jumping to the side. Claws slammed into the ground, shaking the world. A shockwave was launched out by the force of the blow, and the wind caught Kaven, throwing him across the courtyard until he hit the ground and rolled, groaning as angry streaks of pain flared to life.

Kaven tried to sit up but could only manage it halfway. Eyes groggy, Kaven tried to see what was going on, but he beheld only chaos. Shera and Toyon had managed to roll out of the way and avoid the shockwave, but Tasi'a hadn't been so lucky. Instead of leaping to safety, she had only raised a magical shield for protection. Indeed, Kaven could see a flickering purple light, the lingering power of the shield, which swiftly faded. The force of Death's blow had broken the shield, knocking Tasi'a down. By the faint rise and fall of her chest, Kaven could tell that she still lived. Fortunately, the shield had served to prevent a death blow.

Ash fell over Toyon and Shera, blanketing them with burning cinders. Shera had dropped her shield and was wiping her eyes in a panic.

Toyon was in a better state, though he was still dusted in the dark powder. Knives glinting, the assassin was rushing toward Tasi'a, trying to get to her before the Titan did. Death's smile widened, and the Titan raised its claws once more.

Kaven groaned, grasping about himself in a futile effort to find his sword. Where was it? He had to get up! He had to save them . . . but it was finished. They had lost, and it was finally time to die.

"DEATH!" Another massive voice boomed across the courtyard, causing Death to turn toward the sound as Kaven clutched at his ears, wailing in pain. Through the fog of his vision and the agony of his protesting body, Kaven beheld a second Titan barreling through the city the way Death had come.

Kaven knew those grim red eyes far too well. The Watcher had come again. The sigh of despair that escaped Kaven's bloody lips foretold the grim conclusion that he had reached. It didn't matter what Shera said about the Watcher; the Titans would kill them all. Kaven heard his mother screaming in his head. *They're monsters! They killed my loved ones! They are monsters!*

"I shall not allow you to harm my companions, broken one!" Eyes alight with malice, the Watcher charged through Shilanti, toppling buildings and walls alike until he reached the surprised Death and slammed a massive, stone-encrusted fist into the Titan's unprotected head.

Death roared, flames flaring to mirror its pain, and the Titan fell against the wall on the other side of the courtyard, bringing a large section down as it fell. The rumble of Death's fall toppled Kaven, and his head struck the ground. Darkness took him.

Death's claws struck the ground, and Kaven was sent flying through the air. The same blow caught Tasi'a's shield, shattering it and flattening the sorceress. It was impossible to tell if they still lived through the burning, blinding rain of ash that fell upon her, but Shera was determined to save them. No matter the cost.

Shera had always wondered what it would be like to die. Death was something that all mortals had to face eventually, and for a Stormgardian, death under the Fury was the ultimate form of honor. There would be pain, certainly. Only a few were fortunate enough to leave this world in a painless manner, but the trick was to die in peace. Shera was not at peace.

The Fury still threw its chaotic energies across Lantrelia, ripping creatures from their home worlds and hurling them at the Four Kingdoms so that her kinsfolk could be slaughtered in a meaningless war. The perfect opportunity to end it was in their grasp, but Tasi'a, in her stubbornness, had thrown it away. Shera knew that she would never have peace as long as the storm remained.

And now Death loomed above her, fangs long, expression malevolent and intent murderous. The Titan was going to destroy them all, removing all hope of ending the Fury in one terrible blow. How could she defeat Death with nothing but a sword? Yes, Toyon still stood, but after the Destroyer, Death was the most infamous and terrible of the Titans. It would not be defeated by two mortals. And how could Shera die with honor and peace if her mission was a failure? And yet, there was nothing left that she could do, nothing except continue to fight until Death finally claimed her.

Toyon had dived into the ash and Shera could no longer see him. That meant Death probably couldn't see him either. Toyon was a smart man; he could keep himself alive. Unfortunately, Shera could not move through the blinding piles of ash like he could, which made that escape route unfeasible. And now that Toyon was hidden, Shera was Death's sole target.

Death turned toward Tasi'a, but Shera quickly ran between its legs, slashing at its heel with her sword. The Titan bellowed and slammed a fist into the ground. The blow shattered the hard earth around the point of impact, and the strike itself missed Shera by only a few feet. The tremors Death's blow unleashed made Shera stumble, but she managed to stay on her feet as she dodged around the Titan's claws. She had to get Tasi'a to safety; even if Shera died, the sorceress could still destroy the Fury.

Shera came up behind Death, slashing its ankle with her sword. The seemingly rocklike flesh of the Titan parted as she hacked at it, but only the rough outer layers. Only after repeated slashing did a thin trickle of golden blood appear.

Death roared, finally feeling some small measure of pain from Shera's attack. The gargantuan monster turned quickly, glaring down at her. The Titan drew itself up, arms outstretched and mouth wide, when a loud voice erupted across the ruins.

"DEATH!" The Watcher was coming, striding quickly through what was left of Shilanti and proclaiming his challenge. "I shall not allow you to harm my companions, broken one!" Swifter than should have been possible for such a gigantic being, the Watcher was upon Death, swinging a massive fist into the other Titan.

Roaring in pain, Death stumbled across the courtyard and fell into the far wall. Shera laughed joyfully, raising her sword high in salute. Somehow, the Watcher had known to come! Now they had a chance. The Watcher had felled Death before; could he do it again?

Hope rekindled, Shera charged after the Titans, following in the Watcher's wake. Death stood, grimacing in pain, dark eyes alight with fury. As soon as the Watcher had struck, Toyon had erupted from the ash piles, running swiftly until he could see the back of Death's legs. As Death advanced on the Watcher, Toyon flung a dagger with deadly precision over forty feet, burying the blade into the Titan's open wound.

Snarling, Death turned to see Toyon darting away. The Watcher struck, slamming a fist into the distracted Titan's gut. Death fell to his knees, gasping in massive gulps of air. The Watcher hit Death across the face, sending the Titan reeling. The Watcher then kicked Death in his side, rolling his opponent onto its back.

Death crawled away from the Watcher, trying to regain his footing. But the Watcher stayed on top of the other Titan, kicking and striking it relentlessly. All Death could do was wail in pain and attempt to outpace the Watcher. But the red-eyed Titan was too strong; Death could not escape.

Shera and Toyon pulled back, watching with awe as the Watcher shoved and prodded Death out of the courtyard, toward the city. Face devoid of emotion, the Watcher slammed his fists into the Titan's back, splitting Death's stony skin. Death screamed, crawling through the ruined gates, smashing ancient buildings as it went, moving steadily toward the Fury.

Seeing him like this, Shera could almost pity Death. At one point, he had been an innocent creature from some other world. What kind of life had Death had before the Fury had ripped him away and twisted him into a monster? But then again, the Watcher had retained his sanity. The Watcher hadn't turned into a monster. The Watcher hadn't come to the Wall and slaughtered men, not for food but purely for entertainment. The pity Shera had for Death vanished in an instant, and she began to cheer for the Watcher.

Fire suddenly engulfed Death, turning him into a living torch. The Watcher backed away from the intense heat. Death stood slowly, a blazing testament to the unbridled rage of the Eternal Storm. A grin spread slowly across the fiery Titan's face and it lashed out, catching the Watcher beneath his jaw.

The Watcher stumbled backward, narrowly avoiding tripping over a crumbling temple. Death advanced, chuckling softly as it came upon the Watcher, mouth wide, molten flame pouring from its mouth like boiling drool. Death attacked, claws slashing in a violent flurry. The Watcher attempted to bat Death's blows away as he retreated back toward the castle, but Death scored numerous blows and golden blood poured from long scratches across the Watcher's face.

Crying out in pain, the Watcher retreated from Death's onslaught. The attacking Titan unleashed waves of fire with each slash of its claws. Death left a blanket of ash behind him, burying buildings up to their roofs. Shera dragged Tasi'a and Kaven toward the shelter of the castle, Toyon acting as guard. What kind of fire created so much ash? It was almost as if Death's skin was burning away and regrowing so quickly that their eyes could not follow it. Great hills of ash piled around Death's feet, flooding streets and building with each step the Titan took.

Death caught the Watcher in the chest, causing the Titan to falter. Reaching down, Death took advantage of the Watcher's distraction to scoop up a fistful of ash and fling it into his face.

The Watcher cried out in pain, hands instinctively rising to wipe the stinging cinders out of his eyes. Death clenched its wicked claws into a fist and slammed it into the Watcher's face, causing the Titan to stumble to the side, blinded eyes widening in pain.

Death attacked again, slamming its left fist into the Watcher's jaw, sending him reeling in the other direction. The Watcher began to swipe blindly, but Death easily dodged the heavy blows, continuing to jab at the Watcher and push him back.

Stumbling backward through the now-ruined castle walls, the Watcher finally managed to clear his vision and avoid another blow by catching Death's fist in mid-swing. Death snarled, surprised as he tried to yank himself away from the Watcher. Death writhed, trying to tear himself free of the Watcher's grasp. But the Watcher may have been made of iron, for Death could not wrestle himself away.

Growling, Death seemed to realize that he couldn't pull out of the Watcher's grip, no matter how hard he struggled. So Death lashed out with his other fist, striking low to catch the Watcher off guard. But the other Titan was ready. Death's eyes widened as the Watcher caught the anticipated blow, wrapping his stony hands around his opponent's wrists. Death was trapped.

Shera whooped in excitement. Quickly, Toyon and Shera took Tasi'a and Kaven back up to the throne room, hiding them behind the white pillar to obscure them from Death's view. Running to the window, they saw that Death was still pinned. They watched the battle, eyes wide with awe. Shera couldn't peel her gaze away from the Titans for even an instant as they clashed. And the Watcher seemed to have the upper hand.

Death suddenly threw his full weight against the Watcher, pushing him. He continued shoving the Watcher backward. Yet still the Watcher held on. They were halfway through the courtyard and rapidly approaching the castle. Death's flames flared, his voice hoarse. "*You not beat Nagar! No one beat Nagar in home!*"

The Watcher grunted as he was forced backward, only a few colossal footsteps away from the crumbling palace. "Whether or not you could be defeated in your homeland is irrelevant to your current altercation, Death."

Death blinked in confusion, even as he slammed the Watcher into the side of the palace. Their heads rose above the structure, which creaked ominously. "*What is Death?*"

"This." The Watcher spun suddenly, spinning so that Death slammed into the side of the castle, head barreling forward. The Watcher grabbed Death by the neck and thrust his head into the pillar of light, which rose high out of the fractured roof. Death's head was engulfed by the pillar, which flared as if in protest of the foreign object.

All Shera could see was a muffled, shimmering outline of Death's face, howling in a terrible, silent agony. And then he was gone. Death's headless corpse, finally extinguished, slid down the side of the castle, leaving a wide streak of golden blood behind. *Somewhere,* Shera thought immediately, *some poor farmer on a distant world is trying to figure out how to remove a giant, severed head from his fields.*

# TWENTY-THREE

*"Kill, Fulminites; kill with stealth and craft. Become one
with the night, and unleash your terrible vengeance on the
enemies of Na'lek."*

—*From the Tomes of Regret, Verse 3 of Duty*

KAVEN HAD A broken rib; he knew this as soon as he leapt
to his feet. That was a horrible mistake, and he doubled over
to rest upon the back of what appeared to be the throne. As he
tried to ease his chest up straight, which hurt like the Fury, he
unfortunately discovered many other ugly bruises that covered
his arms and legs, each moaning in protest.

Quickly, he reached inside his pocket, delving for Animus.
He breathed a sigh of relief when he saw that his device was
unharmed. Slipping it back into the protection of his cloak,
Kaven stood.

Gritting his teeth against the pain, he eased around the
throne, using it as support as his memories returned. Death was
attacking them. Tasi'a was unconscious and vulnerable. The
Watcher had come. Kaven remembered feeling safe as he had
fallen into darkness, fainting from the pain of being launched
across the courtyard like a stone from a catapult. The sense of
security and peace had come from the Watcher's arrival, but

now Kaven was wary. Yes, both Shera and Toyon had named the Titan a friend, but the Watcher was still an unholy monster of rage, spawned by Na'lek's fury and—no . . . no he was not. The Watcher was not like the others. Those who had been driven mad by hunger or solitude. Instead the Titan had held on to his sanity through the long years. Kaven knew it; he just had a hard time believing it.

Nevertheless, his apprehension would not be easily quelled. He tripped over something, falling but catching himself with his hands to avoid facial injury. With his legs sprawled over the object, Kaven looked back to see Tasi'a lying in repose under him. Her face was smudged with dirt and her long, red hair framed her face in a knotted, sprawling mess. Tasi'a's eyes were still shut, but her chest rose and fell with each slow breath she took. She was alive—thank whatever god had created this flawed world—but still unconscious.

When had she been moved up here? For that matter, when had he been moved up here? How long had he been out? Kaven stood carefully, not wanting to wake her or touch her too much. He couldn't tell how badly she had been injured. Kaven hobbled around the throne and saw no one else in the throne room. The Nexus of the Fury still rose out of the floor, Na'lek's skeleton shimmering in place beside it. Walking slowly, Kaven made his way across the cracked marble floor. His body trembling, each step bringing him pain, he wobbled over to the window that overlooked the balcony.

He slipped on a liquid that coated the floor in front of the opening, but he caught himself on the windowsill, which was also wet. Kaven raised hands that glistened with a runny, golden substance. That could only mean one thing. He poked his head out of the opening and found the source of the blood. A Titan was lying slumped against the castle wall, head somehow torn off and coated with its own shining blood. A third Titan was dead. But was it the Watcher or Death?

Kaven could soon tell which Titan had been slain. The curved claws and mounds of gray ash surrounding the headless corpse made it obvious that the Watcher had emerged victorious. But where was he now? And where were Toyon and Shera? Images of the Watcher feasting on their bloody remains flashed into his mind, and he quickly turned toward the stairwell, only to again slip on Death's blood and fall into the puddle beneath him.

Strong hands lifted Kaven out of the blood, which was rapidly becoming stickier as it dried, and placed him on his feet. "You should be resting," Toyon said softly, holding Kaven steady, "not familiarizing yourself with the floor."

Kaven smiled despite the pain, and Toyon began to help him toward the thrones. By the Fury, Toyon could move so silently! It was good to see him alive and unharmed. "Where's Shera?" he asked.

"She and the Watcher are making a perimeter around the city," Toyon said as they crossed the room. "You know that Death sometimes hunts alongside the Ravager. We want to be sure that Death was alone."

Kaven shivered as Toyon eased him into the unbroken throne. There were still two other Titans besides the Watcher; the Gorger and the Ravager were still unaccounted for. Kaven managed to take comfort from Toyon's words; Shera was alive and well enough to go scouting. But it was unnerving to know that she was alone with the Titan, even if the Watcher had risked his life for them in confronting Death. Kaven knew that the Titan was good, but those terrible red eyes from his nightmare still haunted him.

"They will be back soon," Toyon was saying, turning and starting toward the stairs. "I am going to harvest more Titan blood for our return home. Call for me when Tasi'a awakens."

"Why do we need more blood?" Kaven asked curiously. When Tasi'a shut down the Fury, there would no longer be a need for the blood's protection.

Toyon paused, sensing his unspoken question. "We are not putting an end to the Fury."

The memories of their previous arguments came rushing back to Kaven. Both his mood and expression darkened. "We'll see."

With a nod, the Fulminite vanished down the stairs. Kaven sighed, straightening his back against the throne. Kaven was rewarded for this effort with a sharp pain in his ribs. Right-side, centermost bone. He felt at the wound softly, applying a little pressure to the rib. Pain flared up his side, but he pressed on regardless. He needed to know how bad the break was. Fortunately, his mother had forced Kaven to study the human body, especially when it came to caring for personal injuries. When it became apparent that Kaven was a failure in all things science and turned to the life of a soldier, his mother had focused her unyielding attention on making sure her son didn't get himself killed.

The bone was broken almost directly in the middle, but it was only slightly cracked, not completely fractured. It was going to hurt for a while, and it probably wouldn't be wise to hit it, but it should heal on its own. Hopefully his bruises would recuperate faster.

He sighed, settling into an almost comfortable position. Through the window, he could see the Fury churning at the edge of Shilanti, dark violet clouds swirling with incredible speed, propelled by winds strong enough to toss a house. Thunder rumbled, distant yet ominous, and it was soon followed by a faint flash of darkness. Kaven gritted his teeth, filled with bitter determination. The Fury *would* be destroyed! It must be, for the good of all Lantrelia and even the affected worlds beyond.

Tasi'a began to cough from behind the throne. Kaven twisted so that he could see around it, ignoring the minor pain the movement caused. The small Venedecian was staring back at him, lying flat on her back and covered in dirt.

She blinked and coughed again. "Ow." Tasi'a sat up, rubbing her head. "Kaven? Where am I?"

Kaven smiled, relieved to see that she was all right. "We're back in the palace."

"What happened?"

"The Watcher apparently came to our rescue," Kaven began to explain. "You and I both lost consciousness while fighting Death, and Toyon and Shera couldn't fight it on their own. But, as Shera insisted, the Watcher proved to be our ally. I haven't heard much about the fight yet"—Kaven glanced toward the window and Death's headless corpse—"but the Watcher somehow managed to rip Death's head off. Toyon is outside gathering Titan blood and Shera is on patrol with the Watcher. I don't know when they'll be back."

Tasi'a sat up, rubbing her temples with increased intensity. "Fascinating," she said softly, lacking her usual vigor. "I am glad we've all survived, Na'lek be praised." She hesitated, realizing what she had just sworn by. "Sorry," she mumbled. "That's going to be a hard habit to break."

Kaven nodded sympathetically. "It's all right." Despite his many doubts, Kaven still found it nearly impossible to believe that Na'lek truly had been nothing but a man. A vain, greedy man who had killed himself and scattered his people, yoking them with a dark storm. "Once we close the Fury, everything will be made right."

The sorceress began to shake her head but stopped, apparently not wanting to get into an argument. That was okay; Kaven didn't particularly feel like fighting right now either. Tasi'a dropped her hands, looking toward the window. "Do you really think the Watcher is an ally, Kaven? It's a Titan!"

Now this gave Kaven some thought. Like before, the terrible memories of those old nightmares materialized in his head. But why did he fear the Watcher? All he had done was stand in the distance, watching silently with those giant red eyes. In the four hundred years since his first sighting, the Watcher had never once harmed a human being or a man-made structure. But men often fear the unknown and things they don't understand, reacting with violence where none is necessary.

He knew that his fear of the Watcher was irrational, but it still frightened him. He remembered listening to his mother lecturing on the Titans at the university. She had often spoken of their horrible butcheries and the atrocities they had committed. The Destroyer, standing over the ruins of a city, leading thousands of monsters through the burning Stormgarde City. Death, walking slowly by the walls, ripping defenders from the safety of their defenses and watching them burn. The Gorger, pulling frightened people out of their homes and swallowing them whole. The Devourer, descending on whole battalions of spellcasters and draining them of magic, energy, and—finally—life. The Ravager, ripping apart large portions of the Wall and hurling the stonework into the cities beyond, smiling as he played. And the Watcher, who . . . had done nothing. He had simply stood in the distance, waiting and observing.

Kaven hadn't felt this fear when he had faced the Devourer; he hadn't even experienced this level of terror on either of his encounters with Death. Yes, he had thought he was going to die each time, but he hadn't been consumed by fear. Even now, as he sat back into the throne, he began to shiver and breathe heavier.

"Let me tend you," Tasi'a said, changing the subject. "You're favoring your side. Did you hurt your chest?"

Kaven nodded. "My ribs. I think one is broken."

Tasi'a came over and had him kneel on the ground, which sent jolts of pain shooting up and down his body. She ran her hands over his chest, below his heart, and Kaven winced. "That hurts?" she asked.

He nodded, and Tasi'a closed her eyes, beginning to glow like a candle's flame. A sharp, tingling feeling ran across Kaven's chest, like the needles a person felt after leaning on his arm too long, except this was more severe and punctuated by the unceasing throbbing of his ribs. But then, the pain began to fade away, and when Tasi'a took her hands away, any trace of pain was gone.

Kaven grinned and began to thank her, but Tasi'a waved away his gratitude and delicately peeled away the bandages on his arm. The wound from the Spinereaver was an angry red mass of fresh and drying blood, and the skin around the arm was swollen slightly. It didn't look bad, in his opinion, and barely hurt.

Tasi'a's brow furrowed as she considered the wound. "I still cannot heal that, but it doesn't look infected. How badly does it hurt?"

"Not badly at all," he replied. Ever since he had woken up that morning, the pain had been reduced to a low, minor pulse.

She pursed her lips, displeased by the sight of the injury, but Kaven suddenly shifted, eyes darting toward the window as he began to feel the tremors.

The ground shook. The Watcher was returning.

Gripping the armrests with both hands, Kaven pressed his back against the throne, wishing to sink into the stone and disappear. Where were his weapons? He looked about but couldn't see his bow or his sword.

Tasi'a was standing and leaning against the throne, one hand against the back propping her up. "It sounds like we're about to meet our new friend."

"Yeah," Kaven whispered, not daring to breathe, "friend."

A darkness suddenly blotted out the sunlight that streamed through the window. Kaven looked up, horrified, but the sun still shone brightly through the gaping hole in the roof. He turned back to the darkened window and beheld an immense eye.

Kaven was bathed in a crimson light as he met the Watcher's impressively wide gaze. The eye was the color of blood and just shy of filling the whole window. The red outer eye emitted the light, and an iris, a shade darker than the rest of the eye, reflected Kaven's terrified expression.

The Watcher's eye blinked, black stonelike eyelids blocking out the red light before opening again. "Hello!" The Titan's voice boomed into the throne room, causing Kaven to cover his ears and Tasi'a to wince.

The eye widened slightly, if that were possible. "Oh!" the Watcher exclaimed in a softer tone. "I apologize. I did not mean to harm you. You humans can be so fragile! You must be Kaven and Tasi'a. Shera has told me so much about you, you see, and I have greatly anticipated meeting you in person. As you may have been able to guess, I am the one you call the Watcher. As I said, it is a pleasure to meet you."

Tasi'a waved halfheartedly, seeming a little taken aback. "Hello, Watcher. We've, uh, heard about you as well."

Kaven just stared. It had been a shock to hear Death speak in his guttural, primitive tones, but to hear the Watcher speak, sounding as articulate as Tasi'a, was just disturbing. The Watcher sounded genuinely excited and pleased. But still, he wondered if the Watcher were tricking them with his pleasant demeanor.

There was a legend regarding the day the Destroyer came. It was more of nursery rhyme, used to scare unruly children into bed. But Kaven wondered if there was some grain of truth in it, in the nature of the Titans. The lyrics came instantly to Kaven's mind:

*The Destroyer came.*
*The Destroyer came.*
*The Titan came to play a game,*
*With armies massing in his name.*
*The Destroyer came.*
*The Destroyer came.*

*Upon the gate,*
*Upon the gate,*
*The Destroyer rapped on Stormgarde's gate.*
*No longer did he want to wait,*
*Upon the gate,*
*Upon the gate.*

*"Who is there?"*
*"Who is there?"*
*The guards did warily declare,*
*"Who's come to greet our city fair?"*
*"Who is there?"*
*"Who is there?"*

*"I am a friend."*
*"I am a friend."*
*The Titan's lies were without end.*
*"To your great king, a gift I send!"*

*"I am a friend."*
*"I am a friend."*

*"Let me in."*
*"Let me in."*
*"This gift shall be to all your kin."*
*The Titan cared not for his sin.*
*"Let me in."*
*"Let me in."*

*"Open the door!"*
*"Open the door!"*
*The guards' shouts made a mighty roar.*
*"His gift is for the rich and poor!"*
*"Open the door!"*
*"Open the door!"*

*He killed them all.*
*He killed them all.*
*The Destroyer caused the realm to fall.*
*He rained down blood on Stormgarde's wall*
*He killed them all.*
*He killed them all.*

*On your door,*
*Your heart's own door,*
*That stranger's knocking on your door.*
*Child, keep it closed forevermore.*
*On your door,*
*On your door,*
*He will torment you no more.*

Kaven didn't know if anything in that was true, or if it reflected anything about the Watcher. But it made him pause. What if the Destroyer had used flowery promises and words to trick his way into Stormgarde? What if the Watcher was doing the same thing? *Na'lek doesn't control the Titans,* a voice whispered. *The Destroyer acted on his own.* Kaven was forced to admit that the voice was right.

Kaven was pulled out of his grim imaginations by the Watcher, who was continuing to babble. "I've been here before, you see. Many times, in fact. I deduced that the pillar was the source of this portal storm. Shera tells me that you call it the Fury. Of course, your god wasn't behind it. Only one God controls the land and the sea and the plants and the—"

A feminine voice cut him off. "All right, that's enough, Watcher. This may be fascinating to Tasi'a, but you're going to kill Kaven with boredom. Besides, I think you're scaring them."

The eye looked down. "Of course, I see. You're right, Shera." The Watcher backed away from the castle, removing the red light. Shera suddenly rose in front of the window, lifted by the Titan's hand. She stepped into the throne room, followed by Toyon, who was now laden with several waterskins filled with blood. Once they were in, the Watcher's eyes returned.

Tasi'a waved happily to Shera and Toyon. "Glad to see you made it! I suppose Kaven and I aren't the only ones who've killed a Titan."

"As if the Devourer was a real challenge," Toyon mocked.

Kaven smiled. "But we didn't need the help from another Titan."

"Is the Watcher really that short?" Tasi'a asked, gesturing toward the Titan's eye. "I would think that he would be taller than that window."

Toyon smiled slightly. "He's crouching, Tasi'a."

The Watcher blinked again, sounding bashful. "Yes, unfortunately I am faced with a rather odd conundrum. I am too short to see into the hole in the roof, you see. Yet, I am too tall to be able to look through this window."

"We could move outside," Tasi'a suggested, "if you'd be more comfortable. We need to start our journey back, anyway."

Shera's face immediately darkened, but it was Kaven who spoke. "No. We aren't done here."

Tasi'a rounded on him. "Yes, we are. I told you, Kaven, we are not shutting down the Fury. The price would be too high."

"Price?" Shera stormed toward Tasi'a. "I'll speak to you of a price! You would condemn thousands of your kinsfolk to preserve a dead religion? What currency is worth more to you than the blood of your people?"

Toyon stepped forward. "Shera, there is a grand purpose. Without the Fury, without Na'lek, the Church will be dismantled and irrelevant. And without the Church, the kingdoms will fall apart. There will be riots and chaos, people will despair and lose all hope. Men will kill men to try and restore order. Do you know how long it has been since there was a war among the Four Kingdoms?"

"A long time," Shera retorted sharply. "But that doesn't matter. Yes, there will be war. But that war will end, and peace will resume. The struggle against the Fury is eternal."

"If I may?" the Watcher asked suddenly.

Tasi'a nodded, not taking her eyes off Shera. "Please do."

"This appears to be an issue of no little moral significance," the Titan said. "I consider myself an expert on such things, you see. Sometimes, it can be difficult to discern what is right and what is wrong. During events like these, you must simply trust your instincts, so to speak."

Shera opened her mouth, but whatever she had been about to say was swallowed in the sky-rending explosion that followed. The four of them fell, clutching their ears as the massive sound, like thousands of crashing stones, erupted across the city. The castle groaned as it shook, another section of the roof crashing into the floor below.

"What in the Fury was that?" Toyon demanded once it had faded.

Kaven suddenly had a feeling of dread in the pit of his stomach, one that had nothing to do with Titans. "I think that was thunder."

The Watcher spun away from the window, looking toward the Fury. Toyon rushed toward the window, scanning the sky. Kaven was at his side in an instant, searching the fields outside.

Darkness followed, dimming even the sun above as a gargantuan bolt of lightning streaked earthward. When the shadows cleared, Toyon's face had gone deathly pale. "Do it, Tasi'a," he said softly, like the proclamation of a death sentence. "Close the Fury."

# TWENTY-FOUR

*"Remember, there is nothing you can do to appease Na'lek.*
*Fight and die for his Fury; your war is eternal."*

—From the Tomes of Regret, Verse 7 of Duty

KAVEN TURNED AT Toyon's change of heart, and his own
turned to ice, sinking deep into his soul, into a place where light
and hope could not pierce. Thunder filled the sky, screaming
and thrashing, a thousand blasts all layered upon each other,
never ending.

He clutched the windowsill, his eyes wide as he stared out
beyond the ruins of Shilanti, where black rain was falling in
the form of lightning. The bolts crashed to the Fields over and
over, creating a black curtain of night that was somehow almost
too bright to look at. The Fury writhed above, the outer ring
of its clouds arching inward and outward, surging like boiling
water as endless thunder cascaded through the tormented sky.

But Kaven's eyes found the ground, where the black lightning danced across the Fields of Glory, the source of his horror.
Wherever a bolt struck, an Eye-Taker appeared, many holding
torches. There were already hundreds of them, dozens more
appeared with every passing second. They marched outward

from the grove of lightning, and Kaven was quick to recognize that they were forming battalions of infantry.

Siege weapons began to appear out of the lightning, pushed forward by more of the purple-skinned Fury-spawn. Kaven saw catapults, battering rams, and more he did not recognize, all made from a strange silvery metal that reflected the light of the moon above the clearing.

"Tasi'a!" Toyon's shout snapped Kaven out of his stupor, and he suddenly understood what was happening. This would be no minor Wall skirmish, no idle wave of Na'lek's temper. The Eye-Takers had come for war.

Toyon spun from the window, toward the sorceress. "Close the Fury, Tasi'a!"

The sorceress hurried toward them, Shera following behind, both their faces pale. "Why?" Tasi'a demanded. "What's happening?"

But Toyon stepped forward and shoved her back. "Close the portal!"

Shera had reached the window, beside Kaven. "Oh, great Na'lek above, so many Eye-Takers!"

Tasi'a didn't hesitate any further. She spun around, cloak fluttering out behind her as she scrambled toward the glowing pillar. Kaven watched as a halo of bright green energy encircled her, motes of emerald power drifting up her frame to waft upward. A spear of power erupted from her hands as she faced the Nexus, and it struck the white pillar. The Fury's heart resisted at first, but then the pillar split wide and Tasi'a's magic delved into it.

The Watcher's voice bellowed from outside of the castle, and the Titan strode into view, eyes shining in the darkness. "They are coming right for you!" He pointed with one stony figure, and Kaven watched, terrified, as a mass of dark figures rushed into Shilanti, hurrying toward them.

The lightning was still falling, summoning countless soldiers to Lantrelia.

"I can outpace the army," the Watcher roared. "Climb on me, and I will take you out of here!"

"No," Toyon commanded. "Not until the Fury is closed."

Tasi'a fought the Fury itself. Chains of emerald sprouted from her, wrapping around the Nexus. The white pillar writhed like a trapped snake, but she held firm to it, ripping into its core with whiplike tendrils of energy. Her face was white as bone, eyes bulging as a river of sweat spilled down her face. Her small body trembled.

"Can we wait?" Shera called over the thunder's screams. "Look at Tasi'a; the Fury is killing her!"

"She can do it," Kaven retorted. If anyone could do this, it was Tasi'a. It had to be. "I have faith in her."

Toyon growled. "The Eye-Takers are coming."

"Then we hold the pass," Kaven said, unsheathing his shortsword. "We protect Tasi'a." He turned to meet Toyon's gaze. "For Stormgarde, for Regelia. This is beyond debate; the Fury must fall."

Toyon nodded back, her face a twisted storm of regret, tinged with rage and, more importantly, determination. He drew his weapons, and they both stepped toward the stairwell, Shera behind them. The Stormgardian was muttering curses, but her blade was drawn, a look of strange glee on her face.

Together, they faced the Fury's final storm band.

Kaven glanced back, first through the window. The Watcher was moving to intercept the Eye-Takers, but their ranks did not falter before the advancing Titan. Many darted around him, hurrying forward unheeded.

At the pillar, Tasi'a fought on, chest heaving, body swaying in sync to the movements of the Nexus. The Fury fought on, unwilling to die. Each crash of its thunder summoned more Eye-Takers.

A rough, inhuman voice suddenly called from below, deep and dangerous. "Forward, Tana'kel! Protect the gateway!" It was followed by a different kind of thunder, as dozens of feet ascended the stairs.

Kaven swallowed, a sickness tearing at his gut. The wound in his arm burned, sending stiches of agony arcing through his hand and shoulder. His rib groaned with every breath he took, and his sword was slick with sweat, feeling as it might slip through his throbbing fingers. These weren't Fury-spawn they would face—this was not the rage of Na'lek, sent forth into the righteous Eternal War. No, this was a different intelligence, unknown and utterly foreign. These were creatures with souls, from another world, and there was no such god as Na'lek. Kaven was alone in the world, tricked by an ancient lie, faithfully striking out toward Shilanti, with the intention of saving Lantrelia.

Instead, he would die, and his soul would perish forever. It was futile, wasn't it? Kaven looked first from Shera, then to Toyon, and finally back at Tasi'a. If Lantrelia were to fall, they would all die. *Along with Gane and my parents. And Captain Mayn and all the brave soldiers of the Wall-Guard.*

*I cannot let that happen.* And he would not fight alone.

The Eye-Takers appeared at the bottom of the stairs. Kaven had never seen one so close before. They were short creatures, but they made up for that in sheer bulk, their heavy frames slamming upward, clad in steel, swords and shields drawn. Their helmetless heads revealed purple flesh, yellow eyes, and razor teeth, snarling and snapping as they rushed forward.

Then three of the Eye-Takers dropped, screeching as knives sprouted from their necks. They fell back, dragging more of their comrades down, spraying milk-white blood on the walls. Toyon drew more knives, but the Eye-Takers closed the distance.

"Keep them penned in!" Shera roared, and she lashed out with her shield, slamming into a Fury-spawn's face, as her sword went into its gut.

Kaven and Toyon moved in on either side of her, and Kaven took advantage of her wide shield, pressing close to jab with his blade, hemming in the Fury-spawn. A small voice told him that if any of them broke free from the stairwell they would all die. *Not today, Na'lek,* he snarled silently, habitually.

He put a blade through an Eye-Taker's neck, warm white blood spattering his face. He nearly dropped his sword in shock but managed to withdraw his blade with a sharp yank, watching the monster's corpse tumble backward. *I killed one,* a voice tried to whisper, but Kaven hushed it. This wasn't a place for thinking, nor for hesitation. There was only the stairway, and it needed to be held.

Toyon's knives flashed back and forth, painted white as he disemboweled his opponents, smoothly stepping out to attack before slipping back behind Shera's bulwark. The Stormgardian worked in tandem with them both, cutting into monsters whenever they tried to flank them.

The corpses were piling up below, and Kaven found himself momentarily distracted as he watched Eye-Takers at the bottom of the stairwell begin to pluck out the eyes of their fallen comrades. He shuddered, imagining their sharp claws reaching for his own, growing darker as they descended, before finally piercing and pulling.

"Kaven!"

He didn't know whose voice it was, but it jolted him back into action. Shera was falling before an Eye-Taker who was viciously hammering her shield with an oversized maul. Kaven put his blade beneath the creature's side, and it wailed as it died. *I can't be distracted.* The Fury-spawn were at a huge disadvantage, and their numbers did little to help them, but one mistake would see Kaven and the others dead. He couldn't afford anything but focus. *Just like Father.*

They maintained their stand, though for how long, Kaven couldn't have guessed. The Eye-Takers didn't stop, throwing themselves into the fray with screams of rage, heedless of any sense of self-preservation. The fury in their eyes was enough to make Kaven believe they were indeed the spawn of Na'lek, despite the truth he knew. But even so, they still died, and Kaven held firm.

Shera cursed. "Tasi'a! Titans take me, the Fury is killing her!"

Kaven dared glance back, and his heart sank again. The sorceress was bleeding, gashes arcing down her cheeks, neck, and arms, as if she were in the Shredders once more. A pulsing white light was reverberating around the Nexus, and each time it throbbed, the slashes on Tasi'a widened.

"We need to pull her out," he cried, the worries of the Fury forgotten.

Tasi'a groaned, but then she spoke. Her voice was like tempered steel. Unbreakable. "No! I can do this! Stay back, all of you!"

Kaven obeyed and cleaved the skull of an Eye-Taker as it tried to duck under Shera's shield. Toyon snarled as an axe blade nicked his chin, sending a fingernail-sized chunk of flesh spinning into the throne room, trailing the Fulminite's blood.

Shera parried the axe blow, shoving the Eye-Taker back, while Kaven prevented a flank by facing down a brute with a long spear. Toyon paid the wound no mind, stepping up beside Shera to poke out both eyes of a Fury-spawn with two thrusts of his knives.

The Eye-Takers stopped coming, leaving their dead strewn across the ancient staircase. Relief flooded Kaven's mind until he saw the archers forming up at the base of the stairs. They nocked and drew. He fell back, just as Shera vocalized the command, and they hurried away together. A volley of black-fletched shafts whistled upward to strike the roof.

"We're out of time," Toyon growled. "It's time to go."

Kaven couldn't help but agree. They couldn't fight archers. *Na'lek, why didn't I save my Firerod?* He rushed toward Tasi'a, looking to cut the cords of energy with his blade and free her from the Fury's grasp.

But then he saw a dark spot in the otherwise pure light of the pillar. The fist-sized object floated toward Tasi'a, obscured by the shimmering Nexus, like a rock half-glimpsed in a murky pool. Tasi'a screamed, pulled against the cords of her magic, and ripped the object free from the Nexus.

It actually was a rock, and it bounced across the ground, clattering away. No sooner had it been ripped free than the Nexus of the Fury winked out. The afterimage of the pillar lingered in Kaven's mind, but as he shook his head, he saw that it was really gone.

The Eye-Taker archers reached the top of the stairs, drawing their bows again. Tasi'a staggered backward, but Kaven grabbed her. Shera raised her shield, hurrying toward the window. The Watcher was already there.

"Grab the stone!" Toyon shrieked, voice loud. His next words were drowned out by a deafening crack of thunder. It knocked Kaven off his feet, and he and Tasi'a fell together. The Eye-Takers fell too, as Shilanti trembled beneath the explosion of sound.

He hurried to his feet, taking Tasi'a with him. Toyon scooped up the stone that fell from the Nexus and passed it to Tasi'a as Shera covered their rear. Kaven helped Tasi'a climb onto the Watcher's shoulder and hesitated only a moment before joining her. Toyon and Shera came behind.

"Hold on," the Watcher commanded, and they hurtled away from the castle.

Above, the Fury writhed like a wounded beast, its thunder like cries of agony. Kaven watched the Eternal Storm's death throes in awe, knowing somehow that he was witnessing the end of an age. The Fury became less a storm and more a chaotic vortex, losing all shape and substance as it fell apart. Violet and black clouds bulged, breaking apart after swelling to their bursting point. The clouds tore apart into tinier wisps, and a massive wind swept them away, scattering them. The earsplitting cracks of thunder and streaks of black lightning dimmed and then faded entirely. The Fury was gone, leaving not a trace of cloud, lightning, or wind in its wake.

They stared up into the dark, star-studded sky—human and Eye-Taker both—gazing in stunned silence at the empty sky where the Fury had once been. The ultimate manifestation of magic that had terrorized Lantrelia for thousands of years was no more. The Eternal Storm was destroyed, undone at last by the efforts of mankind.

Kaven looked back to see that the lightning was gone. The Eye-Taker reinforcements were cut off.

But the army gave chase, and Kaven hunched low against the rocky flesh of the Watcher as arrows zipped by them, whistling into the night. The Titan ran forward, heavy footfalls echoing like the now-absent thunder. His long strides swiftly outpaced the Eye-Taker army, and in a matter of moments, they were lost to sight.

"Is everyone all right?" the Watcher asked as he ran.

Kaven tried to pry himself from the Watcher's flesh but couldn't bring himself to do it. His heart and mind were racing, and he felt both elated and terrified. The Fury was gone. The

Eternal Storm, scourge of his ancestors since time immemorial, was destroyed. And with it, all the influence of Na'lek.

*Everything is going to change,* he thought. *Everything.*

Tasi'a, sitting beside him, was staring into the stone she'd taken from the Fury, her eyes wide. "I did it. I actually did it." She sounded breathless. "I didn't think . . ." Tasi'a trailed off.

Shera stood but leaned against the Watcher's chin, looking down at them with exhausted eyes. "We must bring warning to the kingdoms. There are hundreds of thousands of Eye-Takers assembling outside Shilanti now. An army of that size will sweep across Stormvault, Barrier Wall or no, if we are caught unaware. We must call all Four Kingdoms to action."

Kaven nodded his agreement as Toyon spoke. The Fulminite was holding a bandage to his chin. "Do you know the way to Stormgarde, Watcher? They have the largest army; we should warn them first."

The Titan nodded. "Oh, yes. I've made the journey many times, you see. I'm quite fast on this world; I'll have you there before dawn."

Shera nodded. "Thank you, Watcher. Lantrelia owes you a great debt."

The Watcher chuckled. "You're too kind, Heartblade. I hardly did anything, you see."

The Stormgardian ignored the remark and sat down beside Kaven and Tasi'a. "I'm going to ask something of you both," she said, her eyes alight with mingled excitement and terror. "You didn't come here to fight a war, I know. You came to escape. Like me. But . . . Stormgarde needs your help, and I'd be honored to have you fight alongside me."

Tasi'a smiled and nodded, but Kaven stared up at the young Stormgardian, finding himself again enthralled by her beauty, as he had been when he first saw her. He thought back to his home, Regelia, and to his parents. *I must fight. Not to make anyone proud. Not my father, not Shera. It's right. This is the last battle.*

"The Day of Reckoning," he murmured, thinking of Na'lek's prophesied doomsday. "The final battle will be in Stormgarde." The Eye-Takers would no doubt follow them, striking right at Stormgarde's Wall. "If you'll have me, Shera, I'd gladly fight alongside you." He smiled up at her.

Shera returned the gesture. "Thank you. Thank you, both." She turned and walked back toward Toyon, who glanced first at them and then at the stone in Tasi'a hand. They both returned to the Watcher's other shoulder.

Kaven turned to Tasi'a. "Do you understand anything that's happening right now?" He hesitated, trying to give voice to some of the confused thoughts in his head. "Do you . . . really believe that the Fury is gone? That Na'lek is dead? How can it be true?"

Tasi'a put aside the stone and then looked up at him. She smiled. "Kaven . . . some things can wait until tomorrow, can't they? Try and get some sleep. You'll feel better."

Kaven nodded, and the sorceress turned over, nestling into the Watcher's rocky clefts. He followed her advice. Some things could wait. But for tonight, there was only sleep. He realized then how exhausted he was, and he shook his head, closing his eyes.

Settling into sleep, Kaven rode a Titan across the Fields of Glory toward Stormgarde . . . and chucked at how ridiculous it all sounded.

# EPILOGUE

*"As a Zealot, there is one truth you must recognize above all other things. Na'lek is dead. You are now a god."*

—From the Tome of Zealotry, Verse 2

SAN FOUGHT FOR her life, and she loved it. The man in front of her yelled in pain, swinging his long knife for her head. San ducked under the swipe and grabbed on to her own curved dagger, which was currently embedded in the assassin's shoulder. She withdrew her blade in a single, elegant motion, and the man's blood spattered the front of her brown dress.

The assassin stumbled, but he was a big man and no small wound would stop him. San grinned, loving every moment of the fight. The assassin charged, or at least he tried, but the confines of the alleyway kept them close. He cut at her chest with wide sweeps, the blade slashing the air with sharp swoops. San danced out of his reach, letting each swipe come within inches of her flesh. Then she caught the man's arm in his next swing and slid her knife across his wrist.

The man groaned, voice quiet despite his pain. San chuckled. "Come on, then. Scream for me." She stabbed him in the thigh; he struck her in the head with his good hand.

She retaliated by cutting his arm. He was still quiet, for San knew that she was the victim. If any of the noble Stormgardian citizens in the nearby streets heard screams, they might come running. The assassin would be torn limb from limb.

He came at her again, his good hand shaking as he forced the blade down on her. She parried three times, keeping the seeking knife from her flesh. "Scream," she commanded, kicking him in the side as she spun around, running the edge of her dagger across his neck in one fluid motion. She drew a sharp breath in excitement as blood seeped from the wound.

*Finish this,* Nalain whispered from the depths of San's mind.

San ignored the woman's voice, cutting off the man's finger. He did not flee or beg for mercy. He was probably Stormgardian.

*San!* This time it was Nakan who spoke, her thought reverberating through San's skull.

*Fine,* San thought, giving both women her best mental glare. *You've both forgotten how to have fun.*

San casually stepped around the man's next swing and slammed her dagger into his throat. *I saved us all.* San sent the two a bitter thought. *You can't at least let me enjoy my work?*

*We'll be late if you don't hurry,* Nakan said, her voice angry.

San sighed but then turned to the downed assassin, and her grin returned. "I'm sorry that your death was so brief," she informed him. "But the voices in my head can be real Fury-spawn." He was beyond hearing her. San examined the assassin's corpse, feeling dissatisfied. He was a particularly handsome man, which made his death that much more enjoyable. He wore a long black beard that was tied in a cord to decrease its width. His once-bright gray eyes had gone dark as his life faded, and his dark hair hung about his shoulders like a matted shroud.

*He's dead,* Nalain said coldly. *You're finished, San.*

San tried to resist, as she always did, but Nakan and Nalain pulled her down together, ripping her away from her own body. San faded into her own subconscious, muttering dark threats as she went. San had always been the weakest of the three, but maybe one day she would be strong enough to resist. One day, she would never be stopped.


Nalain drew breath, and it was a glorious feeling. She flexed her fingers and opened her mouth wide, expelling the air from her lungs with a loud sigh. It felt so wonderful to have physical form, to have life. She hated giving it up, but sometimes it was necessary to let San out of her cage.

San was a murderous monster, and when the assassin had shown up, there had been little choice but to unleash her. But now she had been thrust back into the dark corners of Nalain's mind, reduced to little more than angry mutters.

Nakan was muttering too, but Nalain ignored her. That woman was completely useless.

Nalain retrieved the assassin's knife, but she already knew who had sent him.

*Who else could it be but Stonearm?* Nakan asked. *He is the only one who knows us.*

Nalain flipped the knife around, checking the engraving on the top of the hilt. As she expected, it depicted a fist gripping the hilt of a sword, blade pointing downward. The personal crest of Zealot Stonearm, Figurehead of Na'lek. Satisfied, she slammed the knife down into the assassin's chest.

"Stonearm should know better than to challenge me," she said aloud. Even though Nakan and San could still hear her, she preferred to talk to herself rather than either of the madwomen trapped inside her head. Nalain cleaned her own knife on the man's trousers and tucked it beneath the torn, old smock she wore.

If all went well, Stonearm wouldn't realize that his plan had failed until she arrived. She paused a moment to catch her breath—San often forgot that their body had limits—and then returned to the busy streets of Stormgarde City.

Nalain quickly ducked into the throng of people moving through the city, many of whom cast worried glances toward the Fury, which was stretching far over the Barrier Wall today. With her torn, plain clothing and greasy hair, no one looked twice at her as she rushed by, back stooped and face low. Just another urchin, trying to survive another day. It was a wonder the assassin had ever spotted her.

*Let me kill him,* San whispered suddenly. *When we get there, let me stab Stonearm. In the face.*

*We can't do that,* Nakan retorted. *We would be cut down in seconds.*

*So?* San sounded genuinely puzzled. *The more death, the better.*

*Idiot,* Nakan muttered.

Nalain ignored them both, refusing to take part in their constant arguments. They fought more than old sailors in a tavern. Besides, if she started speaking mentally, it left her thoughts open to their viewing, much as Nalain could now see every thought of either woman. When Nalain was silent, they could interpret nothing more than vague impressions of her emotions. Unfortunately, when she was thinking, it was hard to direct thoughts anywhere but toward them. It was like trying to create a battle plan while your enemy watched over your shoulder.

Nalain remained wary of any other assassins, but she navigated through Stormgarde City without further incident. Soon, she came upon a Church of Na'lek. Its black stone spire towered above the low-built Stormgardian buildings. It had little protection from the Fury's lightning, but the Church seldom had to fear Na'lek.

Nalain climbed the small set of stairs that led to the Church's only entrance. Two guards stood on either side of the black-and-gold gate, wary as they watched her approach. They wore violet tabards over silver armor breastplates. Upon the tabards was the depiction of a sword crossed with a shepherd's cane, situated beneath a wheel with sixteen spokes. This was the Crest of Na'lek. The Zealsworn wore pointed helmets and silver masks over their faces. The masks were shaped like the front of a human skull, and their eyes watched her from behind grisly sockets. They held spears in their right hands and wore swords at their waists. Small, round shields hung from their backs.

Nalain approached the Zealsworn carefully, keeping her eyes downcast and holding a hand over the spatter of blood on her shirt. "Soldiers of honor," she said pitifully, "please, I have sinned. I must seek atonement with Na'lek. Allow me to enter so that I may be forgiven."

The Zealsworn exchanged glances, and then stared at her doubtfully. It was against the law to turn anyone away from the Church, but considering what was happening today, they had a right to be apprehensive. If they had any idea who they were doubting, they might fall on their own spears in fright.

They finally nodded to each other and turned to grab hold of the handles on the immense doors. Grunting, they hauled the heavy doors open. But before the Zealsworn could open them fully, Nalain ducked through them and into the darkness of the Church.

Within the building was a large room at least fifty feet in diameter, about the same width of the Church itself. This round chamber was lit by large candelabras that sprouted from the stone walls like upturned claws, burning with a dozen flames each. Banners hung downward in between the candelabras, depicting Na'lek's Crest in the gloomy light. A simple wooden table stood in the direct center of the room. On it rested a leather-bound copy of the Tomes of Regret, and a candle stood on either side of the thick book. A single Zealsworn stood by the table, guarding the precious Tomes. Sometimes people tried to steal it, and that could never be allowed to happen.

*People are greedy,* Nakan said.

San giggled. *And you aren't?*

To San's right, a wooden staircase hugged the wall as it spiraled upward toward the distant top of the tower. At the top would be the Chamber of Regret, where the people could go to pray in peace and quiet. She ignored that path, instead turning to the stone stairs that disappeared into the ground, leading downward.

As she entered, several priests looked toward her from where they stood nearby other worshippers, here to give aid or counsel to the people. The priests of Na'lek held no true power within the church, though many believed otherwise. They served only to preach the Tomes and pray for the people. They believed in Na'lek. Nalain smiled to herself as she walked toward the stairs. One of the priests stepped toward her, ready to offer her assistance. She ignored the violet-robed man and descended the stairs before he could protest.

The meeting would start soon, and Nalain had to be prepared. The stairs led down into a long hallway, lined with dozens of rooms. Nalain chose one that had been set out for her and ducked inside.

Nalain quickly assessed that the room was empty and locked the wooden door behind her. A brazier hung from the roof, lighting the small, square washroom. An iron basin stood to one side, already filled with water, and a stand sat in the other corner of the room, complete with a mirror. Her gown was already neatly folded atop the stand, ready for her use. Her servants would be rewarded for their promptness. She stripped and piled her dirty rags in a corner, to be collected later. Nalain despised dressing as a beggar, but it was a safe way to enter a city. Nalain slipped into the iron tub, eager to be clean, but kept her two knives and dagger strapped to a belt around her waist. Yes, getting them wet might be bad for the blades, but if the servants knew she would be in this room, others might know too. Using the rose-scented soap that had been provided, she scrubbed her hair and body, removing the dirt and small traces of blood.

Once finished washing, Nalain stepped out of the basin and toweled herself dry. Her hair would be wet for the meeting, but it wouldn't really matter.

First she donned her undergarments, made from a soft but durable cotton. After that, she put on her thin leather armor. It was dark brown and tough, able to block a glancing sword blow or stop an arrow from doing irreversible damage. It only covered her thighs, stomach, and lower back. She would have preferred full armor, but she had to wear a dress, and visible armor wasn't proper. It would show that she was afraid. She made sure her daggers were securely fastened to her waist before moving on.

*We are afraid,* San whispered. *We are always afraid.*

Nalain silenced San before Nakan could. *Quiet your ceaseless ramblings. I need to concentrate.*

She then put on her dress of pale white silk. She examined herself in the mirror; the dress was simple, as she didn't want to burden herself with extravagance, yet still elegant. It was sleeveless, fastened on by thin straps, and it covered her down to her knees. It wasn't cut low either. Not too long and not too short.

It's only ornamentation was a rose formed of lace adorning her bodice. Nalain nodded in satisfaction, slipping on white enclosed shoes. Like her dress, they were soft and plain.

Nalain ignored her face, as it would be covered. Still, it was hard not to wish that her features appeared more mature. She had the figure and face of a girl no older than fifteen years, even though she had recently begun her forty-second year of life. Her skin was pale, like most Venedecians, which made her squat red lips stand out. Her nose was small and bent, the result of being broken in a fight. Her green eyes reflected the light of the brazier, making them seem like they moved of their own accord.

*My appearance is the least of Stonearm's sins,* she mused.

*The flesh rots away,* San muttered.

Using a small ivory brush, she began to comb out her hair, which was a dark red, like coals that burned with a low heat. Nalain's only came down to her shoulders, so it didn't take long to brush out all the tangles and knots that had been part of her previous disguise. She left her hair hanging in its natural, wavy state. Arrow and Xala often admonished her for that, though Nalain would rather be caught dead than with styled hair like the Fulminites and Stormgardians wore. Examining herself one final time, Nalain sighed. Her reflection stared back at her, morose and wistful. *It will all be worth it,* she told herself. *I know it will.*

*Nothing is worth this,* Nakan growled. She rarely approved of anything.

San formed an image of herself spitting on Stonearm's corpse.

Nalain forced herself to smile. The three of them rarely were united in purpose, but in this they stood together. They would kill Stonearm, no matter the cost. She bent down and took the last piece of her attire.

Her mask was made of silk, like her dress, and was the same milky white color. Aligning the eye holes with her own, she fastened the mask onto her face with a cord, which she hid in her hair. The mask completely concealed her face, from her chin to forehead, leaving only her eyes visible. She looked back to the mirror, convinced that the mask would conceal her features.

The mask smiled coyly back at her, shaped to resemble a woman much more beautiful than herself. With a steady brow, high cheek bones, and lush lips, the mask painted a picture of a strong, powerful woman. That was exactly what Nalain was, no matter how much her body said otherwise.

Nalain stepped out of the room and into her true self. She was Zealot Nalain of Venedeis, Keeper of the Peoples' Sorrow and the chosen servant of Na'lek. She was not the madwoman, and she was not the fool. She was the queen.

San and Nakan protested Nalain's comparisons, but she used her dominating will to shove the two women deep into her consciousness. They faded into soft buzzes in her mind, quiet but never silent.

Nalain continued forward through the hall until she came upon an impressive room. The immense underground chamber was plated with gold and held up by ten pillars on either side of the room, sculpted to depict images of the Fury locked in combat with ancient warriors. Gigantic crystal chandeliers hung from the curved roof, carrying enough flames to light the entire chamber. The room could hold hundreds of people and serve a variety of purposes. Other halls lined the sides of the chamber, leading underground to other churches in the city. Most often it was used by Zealots who threw balls for their supporters and allies, while it was also used for the Church tribunal for trials relating to the Fury or Na'lek. Today, it would be used solely by the Zealots.

The chamber was almost totally empty, excepting a long, marble table that stood alone in the center of the room. Sixteen identical thrones were placed around the table. The thrones were simple, carved from black stone with high-backed seats and flat armrests. The Crest of Na'lek was carved into the backs of the thrones.

The table was set with golden dinnerware and goblets, all empty like the thrones. In the back of the massive room, dozens of servants milled about as they scrambled to prepare meals for their distinguished guests. Even though the table was empty, it seemed that Nalain was the last Zealot to arrive.

Thirteen men and women looked up from their many different conversations as she approached. Nalain smiled under her mask as she approached them. Every Zealot wore a mask to conceal their true identities, each one displaying characteristics and signatures of their wearers.

Zealot Stonearm stood near his throne at the head of the table, and Nalain felt her hatred course through her as if her blood had turned to fire. San's and Nakan's mutters grew louder, a definite angry tinge to them. Stonearm was a powerful man, tall and strong. He had short blond hair and pale skin, incredibly handsome in his formal, dark purple suit. He wore a violet rose on his breast, which was fresh and full. His mask was composed from real rose petals, woven together tightly to conceal his features. The petals were the same purple color as the flower he wore.

Though Stonearm was a Regelian Zealot, his nationality was Venedecian, as was evident by his pale complexion and sharp blue eyes. He was the most powerful of the Zealots, as he was the Figurehead of Na'lek, which made him the leader of the Church. He was the most respected man in Lantrelia, and the kings, queens, and noble houses of the world clung to his every word. Any Zealot would leap at the opportunity to bring such a mighty opponent down.

Standing beside Stonearm, flanking him like loyal hounds, were Zealots Skorn and Jana. Jana was a Regelian, with dark brown hair and coppery skin. She wore a set of emerald pearls against her chest, directly above her low-cut violet dress, the bodice of which was adorned with amethysts. Her mask seemed to be made completely from the precious stones. The mimicry of Stonearm's attire was obvious, and Nalain wondered how long Stonearm would tolerate the fool.

Skorn was a tall, dark-skinned Fulminte. His long gray hair was worn back in a tight tail, which brushed against the back of his black suit. He wore a crossbow across his back, along with a quiver of iron-wrought arrows. He was never without that weapon. He was a powerful man, and Nalain knew that he held no loyalty to Stonearm. He was by far the most influential Zealot in Fulminos. His mask was made from solid wood, unpainted and carved to resemble a frowning man.

Jana and Skorn were the only two Zealots openly allied with Stonearm. The others would enjoy taking the Figurehead's life, even if they wouldn't say so out loud. However, Stonearm was far too clever to be caught unawares, and he had a powerful ally in Skorn.

However, as much as Nalain wanted Stonearm dead—not even for political reasons—he was not her current focus. She wasn't strong enough yet. Nalain scanned the room, noting the other Zealots. Sornak, a Regelian, was laughing and drinking dark wine from a crystal glass. He was a foolish man with a terrible fashion sense. Today he wore a long, narrow hat with no brim. He was conversing with Zealots Aballa and Melaya, a Regelian and a Venedecian respectively. Both women looked uncomfortable in his presence, and Aballa was actively trying to edge away from him. Relad of Venedeis, a tall, wiry man, stood just behind them, watching carefully.

At another corner, Hammer, a Stormgardian Zealot, stood alone and silent. He kept glancing at his throne, wishing to sit but not wanting to be the first to do so. Hammer was also standing near a group of three Zealots, perhaps eavesdropping.

Nalain pointedly ignored these three, who were closely allied. The Blade Alliance. All three were men, and the first was Zealot Frang of Fulminos, who had been a Zealot longer than Nalain had and throughout that time had always wielded middling power. The second was Dalath, a Regelian, who was the newest of the Zealots, elevated by Frang to be his puppet. Dalath had only been among them for a couple of months, after his predecessor was murdered. The third was Zealot Blade himself, a Stormgardian who coveted Stonearm's power above all other things.

The Zealots were the true gods and rulers of the people, though Lantrelia was not aware of this. The Church ruled in secret, from the shadows, using the words of Na'lek to influence the monarchs and noble houses of the Four Kingdoms. But the Church did not rule in unity, and they would strike each other down should their power be challenged. Rarely did the Zealots convene like they did today, unless something threatened the Church as a whole. There was only one rule that the Zealots had to abide: when it came to matters concerning the Church, the Figurehead's word was law. This was why any Zealot would want Stonearm to fall, so that they might take up his coveted title. Nalain did not care about the title or the power. Nothing else mattered except Stonearm's demise. Nothing.

"Nalain," a voice said from behind her. "I'm glad to see you could make it."

Nalain turned to see two women approach her and relaxed somewhat. Zealots Xala and Arrow were her allies, and Nalain had long ago found them trustworthy. All three of them had been hurt by Stonearm, and together they would see him burn. "You are looking well, sisters," Nalain said, having to look up at Xala since she was almost six inches shorter. They were not her biological sisters, but Nalain had come to view them as such over the long years they had spent together.

Xala smiled, full lips parting to reveal white teeth. Her mask only covered her eyes—a bold move. Xala did not have much to hide in her life outside of the Church. Most times, if your true identity was revealed to another Zealot, you'd be dead within the week. Xala wore a fine long gown, colored a pale yellow like a soft candle. She was a stunning Fulminite woman, dark of skin, with hair like a raven's wing, eyes like onyx crystals, and a figure that would turn the eyes of any man. Nalain regarded Xala's revealing outfit with irritation. Why any woman would want to flaunt herself was beyond Nalain's understanding. Xala did not notice her annoyance as she continued. "I assume that you were able to meet certain needs for us today, sister?"

Nalain nodded. "I completed a specific task." She had eradicated a troublesome noble who poked his long nose too far into their business. Nalain's mother had always enjoyed doing her own dirty work, and that was a passion that had passed on to San.

Standing beside Xala, Arrow cleared her throat. "I hope you were careful, sister." Arrow was taller than both Xala and Nalain by an inch or so and wore white as well. Her dress was decorated with dozens of tiny blue lightning bolts. They covered the sleeves, bodice—which had a modest cut—and hem of her dress. Arrow's mask was blue and like Nalain's in fashion, but it revealed her mouth. Arrow wore her shoulder-length hair down today, instead of in a normal Stormgardian fashion. It was colored a deep purple and Nalain did not know her natural color, despite having seen her without her mask many times. Many Zealots dyed their hair, and sometimes their skin, to more successfully disguise themselves. But just like the styling of hair, she found the use of dye to be unnatural.

"Be at rest, sister," Nalain said reassuringly. "I am always careful. If we wish to speak more, let us move away from Blade and his allies. I do not wish to discuss our plans within his hearing."

But before they could move, a deep, gravelly voice stopped them. "Zealots of Na'lek, it is time to begin. Take your seats." Stonearm had sat at the head of the table and gestured for them to do the same. Jana and Skorn sat down on either side of him.

Nalain sat down three seats away from Skorn, and Xala and Arrow took their places on either side of her. She stared purposefully at Stonearm, who disregarded her. He must be fuming, knowing now that his assassin had failed. She smiled beneath her mask.

The others took their seats quickly, mostly at random, though Blade and his allies sat together. Stonearm surveyed them all from behind his rose-petal mask, only his eyes betraying his arrogance. He purposefully met Nalain's eye and then Blade's immediately after. The message was clear: Stonearm would not be threatened. He also paused as his gaze swept over the two vacant seats, eyes now curious.

Nalain looked to the seats questioningly as well, and so did many others. Zealot Wella of Fulminos was obviously absent; she was on the continent of Far across the Expanse, overseeing the Church's rule halfway across Lantrelia. But the second Zealot, a Stormgardian woman who called herself Mace, had no reason to miss this mandatory meeting. That either meant she was dead or she was openly defying Stonearm's legal authority. Such a move could put the whole Church at risk. She might have just given her own execution orders.

Stonearm's survey ended and he spread his arms wide, as if to embrace them. "Welcome to Stormgarde City. I thank you all for coming on such short notice, not that you had any real choice." Stonearm paused for the polite chuckles that followed and continued. "Unfortunately, the news I bring is both urgent and dangerous. We will have to discard our animosities for the time being."

Nalain scoffed and she caught other Zealots smiling wryly. The day the Zealots formed a single alliance was the day the Fury vanished. Stonearm, however, pretended that he hadn't noticed.

"As many of you know," Stonearm continued. "The Queen of Venedeis had passed from this world and into Na'lek's embrace." Nalain glanced at Relad scathingly. The queen had been a malleable fool, and there was rumor that Relad had been the one to carry out her assassination. The new king was of a tougher breed, and at his coronation just two weeks prior, he had made his intentions of staying independent of the Church quite clear.

"A new king reigns in Venedeis, and he refuses to accept the guidance of the Zealots." Stonearm spoke dramatically, gesturing with wide sweeps of his arms and with profound voice. It was grating.

Despite her hatred of the man, Nalain saw wisdom in Stonearm's gathering. The Church could not control the kingdoms through religion alone; they needed the rulers and nobles of Lantrelia in their grip. Most times, the Zealots could influence the monarchs subtly, and the kings often came to them to seek counsel from Na'lek. However, if a ruler was particularly independent, he would have to be broken to the Church's will or else eliminated.

The only exception to this rule was the Council of Shadows, which governed Fulminos. However, given the history of the

Church and the Council, it was wise that they gave each other a wide berth. Many of the noble Fulminite houses belonged to the Church regardless.

"This new king will have to learn the error of his ways," Stonearm said. "Else we will have to arrange his demise. If it is at all possible, I would prefer to avoid assassinating him. With the queen's death so fresh in the minds of the people, the death of another monarch will only serve to dishearten them. Our grip on Venedeis is strong, and I do not want to see it loosened. We shall all go to the capital of Venedeis and visit the king in his home. We will break him together."

Zealot Blade stood. The Stormgardian was tall, as most of his people were, and had no hair to speak of. His face was shrouded behind a lavender mask and he wore robes of the same color. They were several sizes too large for him, and they hung off him like the skin of an emaciated beggar. Some might have found the look appalling or unfashionable, but robes concealed things easily and could be discarded quickly in battle. Nalain had no doubt that Blade wore at least two swords underneath those long, drooping robes. "Do you not think that the king will find the arrival of fourteen Zealots threatening, Stonearm?" Blade asked, voice gruff and annoyed. "It will be impossible to conceal our arrival from the people, especially if we meet with the king openly. If we must kill him, it will not be difficult for the people to discover who is responsible. The last thing we want is a war on our hands."

"Your concern is appreciated, Zealot Blade," Stonearm replied coolly, meeting his opponent's cold gaze. "But you need not concern yourself. I have sent my best sorcerers to the Isle of Chains, and we will have Sintari ready to assist us should the king want a fight." Stonearm chuckled, softly enough that Nalain barely heard it. "He shall bend to our will," the

Figurehead said, raising a fist high, as if challenging the king. "He will learn that Venedeis belongs to the Church!"

Nalain shivered, and other Zealots seemed just as uncomfortable. Sintari. The forgotten monsters. In the Ancient Script, their name meant *Fangs of Na'lek*, and they were the most powerful of the Fury's creatures. The Church only made use of them in the direst of circumstances. The Figurehead of Na'lek was the only one with the authority to summon these horrors to Stormvault or to Far. The Church would only need them if it were to go to war, and if that was what Stonearm wished to do, he would be threatening the secrecy of their rule. Nalain felt a renewed surge of hatred for Stonearm. *He will pay for what he's done,* she thought angrily.

*How much longer will we wait?* Nakan asked. *With every hour that passes, more die under his rule.*

*I do not care how many men or women he kills,* Nalain retorted. *We are not ready yet.*

*Let me out,* whispered San. *I can put a knife in his throat from here.*

Nalain ignored her.

"That is not what I meant," Blade snapped. "Why would you ever consider starting a war with Venedeis? You could risk exposing the Church to the people! Why not send the four Venedecian Zealots to handle their king? No other force will be necessary."

"Perhaps you don't understand how great a threat this man is," Stonearm said.

"We've dealt with rogue monarchs in the past," Blade protested.

Stonearm's eyes narrowed. "I've heard enough of your wagging tongue. I have given my decree, and it shall be followed."

"But—"

"In honor of this gathering," Stonearm said, speaking over Blade, "I have prepared a feast for our enjoyment. You will dine now." Stonearm sat, folding his arms across his chest and nodding in satisfaction.

"Fool," Xala muttered, soft enough that only Nalain and Arrow could hear her. Nalain inclined her head slightly in agreement. If Stonearm tried to control all of the Zealots, he *would* die. Nalain would be able to sit back and watch as he was torn apart by the others, like a lone wolf surrounded by snarling Spinereavers. Nalain hoped that he would be that foolish.

Across the table, Blade sat down, a hint of reluctance showing in the slowness of his movements. As soon as he was seated, the servants hurried over. They bore immense platters of all manners of food. Roasted chicken, duck, pork, and steak were presented before them. Basins of fruits—rosy apples, ripe grapes, and dark plums—were set in the center of the table, along with piles of steaming vegetables. Servants with pitchers poured expensive red wine or fine Regelia beer at the Zealots' behest.

Stonearm and his allies began eating immediately, as did Sornak, who began to stuff his face like he expected an immense famine. Nalain was sure that Sornak would be the next among them to die. He was one of the greatest fools she had ever had the displeasure of meeting.

Others began to eat at a slower rate, Hammer and Xala among them. Nalain did not eat, nor did Arrow or Blade. In fact, Nalain's mask had no opening for her mouth. *Never eat at your enemy's table; all too often it is a poisoned meal.* They were her mother's words.

Soon the Zealots began to converse with each other, Sornak loudest among them. They spoke of simple things—the prosperity of their kingdoms, the attacks from the Fury, lesser politics, and the popularity of the Church. The Zealots spoke nothing of their plans and did not mingle with their enemies. Nalain chose not to speak at all; she worried that something might be overheard.

Surprisingly, after an hour Blade stood and spoke with Stonearm privately. Nalain glanced at them suspiciously. What was he doing with Stonearm? Blade was certainly no friend of the Figurehead; he was far too ambitious and greedy to ignore him. Perhaps they were considering a temporary alliance? Truthfully, Nalain's union with Arrow and Xala, along with her popularity in both Venedeis and Storngarde, was quite possibly the greatest threat to both Stonearm and Blade. Nalain became wary of Blade from that moment on. Perhaps she would have to remove him quickly.

Nalain did not leave until Stonearm stood and declared that the feast had come to an end. "We're finished here," he said, standing. "Leave for Venedeis. Now." And with that declaration, Stonearm turned and strode out of the chamber, trailed by Jana and Skorn.

The Zealots dispersed out of the ballroom at an unhurried pace, meeting with guardsmen in the halls or else leaving with their allies. Now that the meeting was over, none of them were safe.

"That was enlightening, sisters. Wouldn't you agree?" Xala wore a coy smile as she stood up to leave. Nalain stayed close to her side, along with Arrow. "Blade is playing a dangerous game by challenging Stonearm. What does he think he can accomplish?"

Arrow stood beside her, cold, calculating eyes watching Blade carefully. "I do not believe he is making an enemy of Stonearm, but rather an ally. He is a fool to do so. Our enemy will not allow a man as prominent and powerful as Blade to exist close by. I only regret that Dalath has been swept up in Blade's schemes; he could have made a valuable ally."

Nalain smiled wryly. "Do you really think Blade will ally with Stonearm? He may be rather transparent about his intentions, but he is not an idiot. Even that imbecile Sornak can see that Stonearm is a Titan in man's clothing. To fight a Titan is to die."

"A valid point," Arrow replied. "But what is Blade planning, then?"

Xala chuckled. "I'll bet five gold marks that Blade is trying to set a trap for Stonearm."

Nalain began to walk toward the exit, sniffing in distaste. "He'll probably end up caught in his own snare. We must be careful to avoid similar traps, sisters."

Xala fell in beside Nalain, grinning. "Traps always have bait; I prefer to simply knock the bait away with a long stick."

Arrow frowned. "Your metaphors need work, sister." She glanced back at the servants who were clearing the table. "We should speak of these things in private. This place isn't safe."

"Few places are," said a voice behind them.

San rose with Nalain as she spun toward the voice, hand going for her knife. It was Blade, wearing a smile on his face and standing with hands clasped behind his back. Dalath and Frang stood on either side of him. Nalain pushed San back down; her skills would not be required here.

"Is there something you want?" Arrow asked.

"I want a great many things," Blade said with a nod. "But today I have one goal."

Nalain kept her hand close to her concealed weapons while the two women in her head growled threats. "And what is that?"

"I'm hosting a ball in Venedeis," Blade said. "To commemorate the subjugation of this new king. I'd like the three of you to attend."

"Who else will be there?" Xala asked.

"Only Dalath, Frang, and myself," Blade replied.

"What purpose would this ball serve?" Arrow asked, her eyes darting between the three Zealots.

"There is great opportunity in Venedeis," Blade said, his smile widening. "I would like to see an alliance between the six of us. We shall meet at my ball and discuss the future of the Church. Together, we will break Stonearm, and the other Zealots will bow to our strength. What do you say?"

Nalain glanced at her sisters, looking into their eyes. They were cautious but seemed interested. "We shall consider it," she finally said.

"Excellent." Blade gave her a formal, sweeping bow. "I shall see you in Venedeis. Expect a message with further details." The man turned and strode away, followed by his two allies.

Arrow watched them go with a deep frown. "What do you make of that, sisters?"

"Someone fears Stonearm," Xala said, laughing.

"Let us speak of this in private," Nalain said. "This is a startling development."

"But where?" Arrow asked. "The other Zealots may yet have spies nearby."

When they ascended back into the Church tower, Xala stopped suddenly, causing Arrow to bump into her. Nalain stopped up short, barely avoiding collision. Xala was smiling again, a slender hand pointed upward toward the Chamber of Regret. Nalain smiled back, though her sisters could not see it. She nodded once and turned toward a priest.

The Priest of Na'lek was standing before one of the tapestries, staring up at it with vacant eyes. A hand placed on his thin, bony shoulders jolted him out of his quiet contemplation. The man spun toward the three women, voluminous robes colored in different shades of violet flapping about him like the feathers of a startled bird. Brown eyes widened from behind small spectacles, which rested on a long nose, as the priest saw who had touched him. He ran a hand, wrinkled with age, through his thin, graying hair in an effort to smooth it down. "Lady Zealots!" the old priest wheezed, bowing so low that his long nose nearly touched the ground. "Please forgive my lack of courtesy. I did not see you approach!"

"The wrathful Lord Na'lek shows mercy to those who deserve it, Priest," Nalain said, a hint of sternness in her voice. "We are not offended. But be warned: Na'lek is not likely to forgive again."

The priest bobbed his head several times, stammering his appreciation. "Thank you, Lady Zealots! May Lord Na'lek be praised and his chosen ones be forever glorified! How may this humble one assist you today?"

Nalain nodded toward the winding staircase that led upward. "We require solitude and reflection. Clear the Chamber of Regret so that we may use it privately."

Wringing his hands in anxiety, the priest bowed again. "Of course, Lady Zealot. Please, allow me a moment to make preparations."

"A moment is granted to you." Nalain inclined her head slightly toward the priest. "Hurry now."

Eyes still wide, the priest scurried off and hurriedly conferred with several of his brethren. They held a hasty whispered conference, some of the priests looking surprised. The chamber was supposed to be open for all people at any time, but the Zealots could not be disobeyed. Finally, they sent three priests up to usher the people in the chamber down the stairs.

Only six people were removed from the chamber, and they muttered and glared at the priests for the intrusion. But as soon as they saw the three masked women, their eyes widened and they practically ran from the Church, lest the Zealots call Na'lek's fury down on them. Nalain began to climb the stairs, Xala and Arrow behind her. She could feel the eyes of the priests following her until they climbed up into the chamber. Fear was an important tool, though sometimes Nalain wished the people feared her, rather than the god she represented.

The Chamber of Regret was a simple room, nothing but an empty wooden floor so close to the flat roof that Arrow and Xala had to crouch. This was the very top of the Church. A single torch on the far wall lit the room, giving it only partial illumination. They climbed into the room and sat down in the middle, facing each other in a circle. The chamber had a simple trapdoor to seal the opening, which did nothing for sound so they would have to speak softly to not be overheard.

"I thought you handled that nicely, Nalain," Arrow said, crossing her legs and trying to get into a comfortable position. She ignored the awkward strain the pose put on her dress. "I know how much you hate the priests."

Xala laughed loudly, removing her mask and setting it beside her. "I expected you to kill the man right then. You had so much heat in your eyes, sister."

Arrow took off her mask and glanced toward the entrance, expression wary. "We must decide what we are to do with our enemies."

Xala sniffed, looking around at the chamber in disgust. "I wish this place had something to drink. I could go for something with a little kick to it."

"We're not in Regelia," Nalain pointed out, taking off her own mask. "If you want to see fountains of beer and rivers of wine, you should be there, rather than in a stuffy attic."

Xala laughed. "Reminds me of your home, Nalain."

"Sisters," Arrow chided, "let us focus. What do you make of Blade's invitation?"

"It could be a trap," Nalain said.

Xala nodded. "Yes, but I believe what I said before. Blade is scared of Stonearm, and he wants powerful allies to stand against him."

"What do we do?" Arrow asked. "Ignore the invitation?"

"If we do that," Nalain replied, "we will make an enemy of him."

"The only remaining option is risking the trap," Xala said.

Arrow nodded. "We could benefit from an alliance with Blade. He will eventually become our enemy, but we have a common foe in Stonearm."

Nalain was silent a moment, considering the issue. She didn't trust Blade, not by any means, but she didn't want to openly defy the man either. She couldn't fight both Blade and Stonearm at the same time. "Let us wait and decide in Venedeis," she said.

"Very well," Arrow replied. "It will do us good to think on the matter before making a decision."

"We must be careful not to let the other Zealots exploit our focus," Nalain added. "We cannot ignore them as we try to bring down Blade and Stonearm." A mistake within the Church was fatal. The Zealots were always eager to bring down one of their own to move forward in power. Nalain was highly influential now, just under Stonearm and Relad. She needed to be careful, else she'd get herself and her sisters killed. Nalain and her sisters were also feared by the others due to their strange alliance. Nalain had grown to love her sisters as if they were her own blood, and the feeling was returned. They would never turn on each other, no matter what happened. There could be no betrayal, no broken alliances, no distrust. The other Zealots feared such a powerful bond, for they knew that they could not match it. Nalain, Arrow, and Xala were currently using their combined resources to target Stonearm, but once he fell, they would be powerful enough to bring the entire Church under their command. Nalain would have the other Zealots killed one by one and replaced by malleable supplicants who would serve her and her sisters faithfully. Lantrelia would belong to them forever.

Arrow nodded in agreement. "We must be vigilant as we travel, or we could fall prey to the others. I do not think that we should travel together; I'd rather have one of us die than all three."

"Right. Someone will have to avenge us." Xala grinned at Arrow.

"I was attacked by an assassin of Stonearm before the meeting," Nalain said.

Xala's grin vanished. "Are you okay?"

"Yes." Nalain patted the knives concealed under her dress. "I killed him. But we must be careful. He may try to target us again, and next time he will send someone more skilled than the fool I slew."

Arrow shook her head. "He will only get more aggressive. Perhaps we should take a portal straight to Venedeis?"

"I do not like portals," Nalain said. She didn't like magic of any kind, but portals were especially dangerous. "I will go by carriage. But I agree that we should travel separately."

"As do I," Xala said.

Nalain stood, replacing her mask. "Then we should leave immediately. We can further discuss our plans once we see how things are in Venedeis. I'd rather not make the first move in the days to come. Instead we should see if Blade makes a mistake."

Xala straightened, pressing a hand to her back and grimacing. "This floor is sharper than a knife. I'm too delicate for such discomforts."

"Nothing about you is delicate, Xala." Arrow smiled as she pulled herself to her feet, smoothing out some of the wrinkles in her dress. "Until we meet in Venedeis, sisters." Arrow lifted the trapdoor and let herself down.

Xala watched Arrow vanish and turned to Nalain. "Safe travels, sister."

"And to you, Xala," Nalain said. With one final smile, Xala turned and followed Arrow down the stairs.

Nalain sighed softly and lingered a moment. She did not like being a part of the Church, it never seemed to suit her. But she had made a promise to herself when she had vowed to kill Stonearm. She had made the same promise to Xala and Arrow as well. Nalain lived to see Stonearm die; she knew this. There was nothing else for her, not even the prospect of dominating the other Zealots. Nalain had often considered stepping down after she secured the Church for Xala and Arrow. But one thing was certain: she would see Stonearm die.

*Perhaps he will not die,* Nakan said. *Stonearm may never make a mistake. Will we really endure long enough to see him fall?*

*I do not know,* Nalain replied. *But I will not give up. I will not cut my own wrists while he is allowed to continue living. We owe too much to our sisters. We must endure.*

San giggled, but it was a nervous, crazed sound. *But then we will die, yes? We must die when this is done.*

Nalain was silent for a long while, but then she nodded. *We will die.*


THE END

# ACKNOWLEDGEMENTS

To God, my Father, without whom I am nothing. I would also like to extend my profound appreciation to everyone who supported this book, but especially to the following people: Jonathan, Heather, Abigail, Asher and Anastasia Wood; John Robin (without your help, my campaign wouldn't have been possible); Jordan Ferrell (get used to the twists); Lisa Shumaker (my first beta reader); Joshua Negron, Shawn Wilhelm (watch for my lamborghini, my friend); Tabi Card (are we not awesome?); Ciara Wise (I hope your dictionary was in pristine condition); David Wood (your choice of character still surprises me); Ruth Gorham, Dale Lui (you made *Storm of Fury* into a much better book); Josiah Allcorn (you'll get around to it eventually, right?); Janna Bartoli, Tammi Stephens, Matthew Howard (do the voices!); Marty and Kathy Roberts, Gloria Roberts, Eddie Rodriguez and Ave Basilio, of Dreamscape Cover Designs. I would also like to thank the wonderful staff at Inkshares, who made my dream for this book come true.

Thank you.

# GRAND PATRONS

Alyce Jean Lazarus Littiken
Janna and Matt Bartoli
Billy O'Keefe
David L. Wood
Israel R. Stolze
Jason Pomerance
John Robin
Jonathan Wood
Joseph Asphahani
Marty and Kathy Roberts
Heather Wood
Joshua Negron
Ruth Gorham
Tabi Card
Tony Weist
Lisa Shumaker
Tammi Stephens